BATTLETECH:
KILL ZONE
BATTLECORPS ANTHOLOGY VOL. 7

EDITED BY PHILIP A. LEE

BATTLETECH: KILL ZONE BATTLECORPS ANTHOLOGY VOL. 7
Edited by Philip A. Lee
Cover art by Michael Komarck
Interior art by Marco Mazzoni
Design by Matt Heerdt & David Kerber

Published by Catalyst Game Labs,
an imprint of InMediaRes Productions, LLC
7108 S. Pheasant Ridge Drive • Spokane, WA 99224

Death is a feather
Overthrowing the mountain
Winter brings balance
—Haiku found among the belongings of *Chu-i* Willard Gibbs, Ryuken-*ichi*, KIA January 13, 3028

CONTENTS

FOREWORD

PHILIP A. LEE

Sometimes a plan just works out. My working title for this volume, *Kill Zone*, was initially inspired by "Those Who Stand High," by Jason Hansa, which I consider the penultimate story in this collection. A kill zone is a military term for a designated spot where a planned ambush traps and destroys an enemy force, and that's effectively what the BattleCorps stories from 2010 accomplish: they grab the reader and refuse to let go until the very last word is read.

However, as I went back through these stories to prepare them for publication, I realized that the very first story chosen, Adam Sherwood's "Tomorrow's Shine," uses the exact term in its first few pages, and that ambush kicks off the rest of the story—and effectively the rest of this anthology. At that point, the title felt like kismet, and it got promoted from "working" to "official."

For me, one of the most memorable aspects of BattleCorps's offerings in 2010 was the various themed mini-anthologies published during that year. In previous years, we had occasionally seen a few stories based on the same theme, such as the Case White stories in 2008, but 2010 was the year these themed anthologies really took off. Although the first two stories of the Operation Rat anthology were published at the tail end of 2009, the balance of this seven-story series chronicling the ravages of the Fourth Succession War was published the following year. After that came a four-story Operation Klondike series, which showcased several different facets of the Clans' conquest of the Pentagon Worlds. Lastly, a series of five stories highlighted Operation Scythe, the Allied Coalition's campaign to retake Terra from the Word of Blake; these stories served as a direct tie-in to the *BattleTech* sourcebook *Jihad Hot Spots: Terra*.

Some behind-the-scenes trivia: a fourth mini-anthology was also planned for that year but never came to fruition. BattleCorps solicited stories for an anthology about pirates, and for whatever reason— pirate mischief, perhaps?—sufficient submissions for that did not materialize. (I'm blaming pirate interference: they clearly didn't want their trade secrets for murder and mayhem made public.) However, the spirit of this intended anthology lives on in Craig A. Reed, Jr.'s "Reap What You Sow," which is included in this volume.

While assembling this collection, I realized that these themed anthologies gave BattleCorps authors something concrete to focus on and let them drill far deeper into the subject matter than might have been explored otherwise. For example, the aforementioned Operation Rat story, "Tomorrow's Shine," shows how the Fourth Succession War directly affected the Capellan people after the big battles had been fought. Jason Schmetzer's Operation Klondike story, "To Lead and Serve," focuses on the Clan auxiliaries, those warriors who were not considered good enough to be members of the vaunted Eight Hundred. And the aforementioned Operation Scythe story "Those Who Stand High" zeroes in on anti-'Mech mountaineer infantry.

Of course, none of this is to say that the only worthwhile tales in 2010 were from these themed anthologies; far from it. In fact, one of the difficulties I faced in curating this selection of stories is because there were so many good entries to choose from and a limited space I could work with. To start with, I disqualified any work that had already been made publicly available, which unfortunately culled some fantastic stories, such as Kevin Killiany's "Crucible on Campoleone," which is featured in *Chaos Formed*, and Steven Mohan, Jr.'s chilling story "A New Game," which was included in *Onslaught: Tales from the Clan Invasion*. From there I chose the best story or two from each of the mini-anthologies, and filled the remainder with other top contenders.

Among these stories are Kevin Killiany's "Bad Water," a fascinating look at a Periphery action from the view of a military watercraft rather than a 'Mech cockpit, and Blaine Pardoe's "The Loyal Son," which serves as a worthy follow-up to "Son of Blake" (featured in *Front Lines: BattleCorps Anthology, Vol. 6*). Stephan A. Frabartolo's inaugural BattleCorps offerings, "Feather versus Mountain" and "Rise and Shine," serve as companion pieces set in the war between the Draconis Combine and Wolf's Dragoons. Lance Scarinci's Operation Scythe piece, "Lyran Fire," demonstrates the resolve of an isolated House Steiner command beset by Word of Blake forces on Terra. And the new piece for this volume, "Arms of the Destroyer," comes from Travis Heerman, whose first foray into *BattleTech* fiction—"Swords of Light and Darkness," from *Legacy*—was nominated for a Scribe Award.

In 2009, BattleCorps authors set up an ambush point with *Front Lines: BattleCorps Vol. 6*, but in 2010, they got all of us in the kill zone.

OPERATION RAT: TOMORROW'S SHINE

ADAM SHERWOOD

WORKER'S COMMONS
MUNICIPAL DISTRICT 3
BUCHVAAL, NEW HESSEN
CAPELLAN CONFEDERATION
1350 HOURS TST
10 SEPTEMBER 3028

"Wait, I don't think I heard you right. You want me to do what?"

Sergeant Danny SinClair scratched the backs of his hands nervously as he quickly searched the crowded streets of suburban Buchvaal for a suitable hidey-hole. He felt very much like a child caught in the open during a game of seek-and-find. Overhead, the afternoon sun glared brightly in the late summer sky, its hot rays burning through the day's quota of industrial smog and pollution. Long, anemic shadows stretched from the tops of the dilapidated two-story tenements of the ramshackle worker's quarter. Their dark, grotesque shapes spread over the worn cobblestone-and-pitch streets below each building, partially obscuring the alleyways, street corners, and doorways from casual observation. Unfortunately, they did little to conceal his two-story-tall BattleMech.

All along the boulevard, the mixed heavy and medium 'Mechs of Bravo Company sought cover for their impromptu ambush. Normally painted in the dark blue, red, and gold of the Second New Ivaarsen Chasseurs, their BattleMechs now wore a more conservative green-and-brown camouflage pattern typical of line regiments from the Armed Forces of the Federated Suns. The unit's emblem, a golden-winged sword against a blue triangle, was displayed proudly on each

'Mech's left thigh. Everywhere Danny looked, a war machine from Third Battalion crouched in an alley or hid behind one of the city's many rent-controlled, public-assistance housing projects. Constructed of plaster, wood substitute, and low-grade ferrocrete, each apartment complex had the rundown look of a Draconis Combine prison. Made not by the lowest bidder but by the only bidder, they provided basic necessities for tens of thousands of loyal Capellan citizens. Except for some graffiti and a smattering of colorful murals painted on alley walls every block or so, each building looked virtually the same.

Workers' paradise, my ass.

"I said find a hut and park yourself inside." Leftenant Berri sounded annoyed, as usual.

Dismayed by her casual reference to what sounded like a class-two war-crime, Danny countered, "What about casualties? Chapter five of the Ares Conventions specifically prohibits the deliberate use of civilian residences to shield BattleMechs." The instructors at the academy had always stressed minimization of civilian casualties, no matter who they were. He eyed the buildings around him looking for signs of their occupants. "Shouldn't we at least send in infantry to clear the area first?"

"I wouldn't worry about that. The Capellans should have already evacuated this section of the city. Besides it's not like they're loyal subjects of the crown, right? If they're smart they'll get out of the way. If not, well..."

Her glib response did little to allay Danny's fears. "Still, I don't think we should—"

"Just pick a building, damn it! We don't have time to debate this. Work your 'Mech inside, then take up a firing position along Zhou-Li Boulevard on the north end. Captain Davis says that's where the main attack will come from."

Lance Commander Jennifer Berri, herself a fellow graduate of the NAIS College of Military Sciences, had been with the company a year longer than Danny and was considered an old hat. Although, she was good with a 'Mech, her real claim to fame was the lengths to which she would go to kiss the company commander's derriere. No doubt she had left the channel open so Captain Davis could monitor her transmissions. The fact that her father did business with the Stephensons virtually assured her continued promotion, a little tidbit she never hesitated to shove in Danny's face. Graduating in the top 15 percent of her class gave her a massive ego to boot.

Somehow she transferred that attitude to her gait as she walked her *Phoenix Hawk* past Danny's *Hunchback* and slipped into an alley between two nearby apartment buildings. On the wall to one side was a panoramic mural depicting a beautiful, provincial scene filled with trees, flowers, mountains, and young children at play. Toys littered the alleyway. To Danny, it looked like the short section of potholed road was the closest thing the kids had to a park in this section of town. Without pause Jen punched her 'Mech's left arm and shoulder into the mural then crashed farther into the building, leaving a gaping hole in the wall. A cloud of dust and debris billowed into the air, and when it settled the mural was gone. Horrified, Danny watched as the rest of the company's 'Mechs followed suit. Tim Duvalles's *Enforcer* disappeared inside a fire station farther down the block while Big Joe DuBois shrugged his *Centurion*'s shoulders before carefully pushing his way into a secondhand shop. Within moments, every single 'Mech had vanished into a different building, leaving a cloud of ferrocrete dust and broken memories in its path.

Jennifer's voice shocked him out of his stupor. "Hey SinClair! Get the lead out, idiot. Those CapCon retreads will be here any minute. We need that Kali Yama Big Bore of yours in position ASAP. Move it, mister!"

With a grimace he looked for the least livable building he could find. Spotting one that appeared vacant, he extended his 'Mech's arms, swallowed once, and pushed. Wood splintered, mortar cracked, brick crumbled, and steel buckled under the merciless assault. He felt unstoppable, regardless of his own misgivings. In mere moments he worked his way through to the far wall of the hovel and stopped behind a corner window which gave him a prime view of the streets outside. Once there he stopped to check his sensors and found that the building's walls prevented him from locating any friendly units farther than a block away. Unfortunately, his wraparound viewscreen also gave him a picturesque look at the ruinous damage he had wrought to the inside of what had recently been someone's home.

He frowned then activated his microphone. "I'm set."

"Good, let's do what we do best. Keep your reactors on low and your sensors on passive mode. We don't want the Irregulars to know we're here until it's too late." She paused. "SinClair, I want you to initiate with your Kali Yama on my mark. Got it?"

A chorus of affirmations rang out on the inter-lance net. Danny signaled in turn. "Roger, LT."

"I want complete radio silence from here on out. Berri out."

Danny wiped his sweaty palms on his thighs and watched his sector. Leftenant Berri had just placed the success or failure of the ambush—and his career—in his hands.

Seconds passed slowly as the sun blazed a path through the heavens, unaware and uncaring of the drama playing out below it. Burning brightly, it paved a way through the afternoon sky as it continued its celestial dance over the men and women of the Second New Ivaarsen Chasseurs. Protected from its dangerous rays by his 'Mech's multilayered sensors and panoptic shields, Danny looked directly at it, marveling at the sun's stark beauty even as deadly aerospace fighters streaked through the low atmosphere on their way to bombard Capellan forces on the edge of the city.

While elements of First Battalion fixed the New Hessen Irregulars in place about ten kilometers north of Buchvaal, the rest of the regiment had slipped inside and taken up defensive positions. The problem was that the Irregulars wouldn't stay there for long. Any second now they would come streaming into the city, their home turf, looking for blood. Colonel Stephenson, the regimental commander, appeared to be counting on it. Comprised of mostly lightweight chassis, the Irregulars were girded for reconnaissance and hit-and-fade actions, not the down and dirty street fights for which the more heavily armed Chasseurs were famed. But what the Chasseurs made up for in weight, the Irregulars made up with superior numbers. Luckily, warfare among the lifeless trees of the concrete jungle tended to even the odds. Regardless, city fighting was a nasty affair. Danny fervently hoped the civilians had already evacuated.

Movement on his central viewscreen brought him out of his musings. Far down the street to the west, along the stark, slate-colored buildings, a long shadow moved slowly out of an intersection, then stopped abruptly. Danny magnified the view, then nearly jumped out of his seat as a black bird jumped from the top of a rust-colored high-rise and took flight. Startled, he realized he had nearly fired on reflex alone, a mistake that could have cost them the entire ambush. His Kali Yama AC/20 was the largest-caliber autocannon made. In the right hands its hellacious firepower could destroy even a large BattleMech. The weapon's primary drawback was that it burned through ammunition at a tremendous rate. Every shot was precious. He took his finger off the trigger and took a deep breath.

Relax!

Moments later, he saw another shadow move near the same high-rise. He fought to keep his finger off the trigger.

Patience. Probably just another bird.

As he watched, the shadow grew, then split into two separate and distinct shapes. A squat, avian-looking *Locust* scout 'Mech and a humanoid *Wasp* stepped hesitantly into the intersection. Pausing briefly, both machines spread out on the street and began working their way East. Painted in dark green with yellow highlights, the regimental scouts of the New Hessen Irregulars were easy to track against the cityscape. Far behind them, Danny saw additional 'Mechs moving forward at an alarming pace, apparently anxious for their recon elements to clear the way before them. Danny clenched and unclenched his fists, then took his control yokes in his hands, preparing for the quick yet fragile light 'Mechs to enter the kill zone.

A flutter to his right caught his attention. He glanced over quickly and thought he saw a lace curtain move in the open window of the downstairs tenement immediately in front of him. The apartment's brown wooden door was drenched in pink flowers and purple polka dots. Not wanting to lose track of the rapidly closing Irregulars, he dropped his magnification square on the ramshackle apartment's window, checking it rapidly for signs of life. Finding nothing and knowing time was precious, he hurriedly brought his targeting crosshairs up on the approaching *Locust*, now less then fifty meters away, its comrades close behind. He tracked the 20-ton scout as it stalked nearer and nearer, its twin aerials swaying back and forth as it moved.

Berri signaled, "Fire!"

A tiny, brown-and-white spotted terrier jumped out of the open window across the street. It shot down the stairs and onto the cobblestone street, yapping as it ran. Dan hesitated, waiting to see the Irregulars' reaction.

The humanoid *Wasp* to the left and slightly behind the *Locust* skidded to a stop. Its bulbous head moved from side to side as it searched for a target, the right arm housing its medium laser at the ready. Behind it, a 40-ton *Cicada*, a 25-ton *Commando*, and several more *Locust*s jostled each other roughly as they moved down the boulevard, abandoning caution in their haste to locate and do battle with the Chasseurs.

Jen shrieked, "Now, SinClair! Now!"

Danny centered his crosshairs over the *Locust*'s chest and exhaled slowly, knowing his shot would be the signal to his lancemates to execute their ambush. He squeezed the trigger as the brown door with pink flowers and purple polka dots opened.

Too late to stop, his *Hunchback*'s immense autocannon vomited forth a withering hail of depleted-uranium slugs that hungrily chewed into and through the *Locust*'s flimsy chest armor to savage the tender internal structure within. Not content with their meager meal, the rounds continued through the ruined scout and into the homes directly behind it.

With the clarity of the damned, Danny SinClair watched helplessly as a wisp of a girl perhaps only eight years old, with long black hair, wearing a knee-length, lime-green dress and pink flip-flops, ran out onto the road after the dog. Instantly, a firestorm of missile, autocannon, and laser fire erupted out of the buildings around him. Armor charred, ceramic shielding cracked, shrapnel flew, and ferrocrete crumbled as the murderous fire connected with the gaggle of Capellan 'Mechs that had bumbled into Bravo Company's kill zone.

Someone screamed. The *Locust* exploded.

THE COMMONS
MUNICIPAL DISTRICT 3
BUCHVAAL, NEW HESSEN
FEDERATED SUNS OCCUPATION ZONE
0620 HOURS TST
21 OCTOBER 3028

Toma Fu Shieh stopped and shifted his package. Transferring his cane to his left hand, he pulled the tarnished brass handle on the well-used teak door. Gray primer showed where strips of green paint had peeled or worn off the wood from years of use and neglect. Intricately carved figures set into the door's archway were warped by time, weather, and a lack of attention that gave them an almost demonic appearance. Faded golden vines flowed around the edges of the molding. The words *Hsu's Teahouse* were stenciled in stylized calligraphy over the door's center panel. He could tell by the symmetry and workmanship that this portal had been a labor of love for some fine craftsman in an era long gone. Now, battered and deteriorating, it was just another reminder of the dire straits in which the Capellan Confederation, and by extension New Hessen, found itself.

Toma sighed and patted the wood like an old friend. "You look as bad as I feel."

He tightened his worn green field coat, stamped his thick, brown leather boots to clear the dust off, and stepped inside. Passing through the entryway, he paused to let his hazel eyes adjust to the dim lighting of the incense-filled tearoom. The aroma of burnt lavender mixed with the welcome scent of jasmine tea and dumplings. The smell sent his empty stomach into a churning, rumbling fit and reminded him that he had missed the last several meals. So had many other loyal Capellan citizens since the state-run supply and logistics directorate had ceased providing supplies to the citizenry. He tightened his stomach muscles to stop their tiring dance. The Fedrat lap dogs had yet to fully integrate their own logistics network into the city's supply chain. Military and governmental needs, they said, came first. Administrators, police, factory workers, and farmers ate relatively well. However, those not actively participating in the war effort, like retirees, for example, were left to scramble for whatever was left over. Distribution points rarely had much left for the Entitled. Now he waited outside the Chasseurs' encampment every day for the chance to polish a soldier's boots just to make enough money to live on. Somehow through it all, Hsu's Teahouse was able to stay in business.

Corrupt officials and bribery had their uses. So did the black market.

In fact, several customers were already there, eating heavily spiced rice meal and dumplings or sipping steaming cups of tea. Recognizing his former teacher, he nodded a greeting to an ancient, careworn man with a long, gray beard seated in a booth near the door. Wearing a traditional black vest with a high mandarin collar and matching black pants, his old *shi fu* struggled with shaky hands to bring a spoonful of hot rice to his lips. Not wanting to appear rude, Toma turned and continued into the restaurant. Hobbling past a row of low, glass-covered tables, he made his way over to the small wet bar in the back of the teahouse, away from the other clientele. He appraised the red, faux-leather cushions of the three stools there, noting that the centermost seat cover was torn, exposing the cushion inside. Selecting the most comfortable stool on the left, he sat, placing his cane against the bar and gingerly setting his wooden box on the floor below. A tall but gaunt waiter with thinning hair and bushy eyebrows, wearing a black suit with a stiff but slightly discolored white shirt and bowtie, stepped over to him, bowing curtly.

"*Ni hao.*" He proffered a small porcelain cup and filled it with hot tea placing it on the bar before him. The aroma was magnificent, making Toma's mouth water.

"*Ni hao.*"

Opening the menu, Toma saw that virtually every item had been taped over. There were now only two options, breakfast and dinner, each as expensive as any three entrees had been combined. Scrawled on a piece of tape at the bottom of the menu were the words *no trades or credit.*

With practiced impatience the waiter offered, "Breakfast consists of rice mash and dumplings." Then he added as an afterthought, "It's quite good."

Not needing to check the scant few FedSuns coins he had in his coin purse, he motioned the waiter forward and asked quietly, "Do you take *yuan?*"

The waiter backed away with a sniff. He straightened his uniform, then pretended to brush off imaginary grime from his near contact with this less-than-immaculate patron, reminding Toma as rudely as possible that he had missed a few baths as well as meals.

"I am sorry, *sir,* but we only accept C-Bills or D-Bills in this establishment. Liao *yuan* are virtually worthless now." His nasal, indignant voice resonated across the room, drawing the attention of the clientele.

Toma's face flushed with embarrassment and anger. Currently at a ten-to-one exchange rate, the *yuan* had been gutted by rising inflation and profiteering. They could still be converted under the new currency exchange program, for a modest fee of course. The little rat in front of him obviously did not want to have to wait in line to do so. *Yuan* weren't worthless. Not yet anyway. Toma stood to protest, but was startled when a gentle but firm hand settled on his shoulder.

"We say Captain Shieh's money is good here, Rory. Run along and get his breakfast."

The waiter's face turned ashen as he took in the newcomer. He bowed twice deeply, then turned and ran to the kitchen, knocking over a pile of bowls in his haste. The rest of the customers pretended not to notice as they resumed their meals in silence.

Recognizing his teacher, mentor, and friend, Toma responded, "That wasn't necessary, *shi fu*. The situation was...under control."

"Nonsense." His former master's dry, parchment-like voice brooked no argument. "The day a slimy toad like Rory denies a captain of the Home Guard a meal is the day I don a pink flamenco dress and sing Hanse Davion's praises on the palace steps."

The absurdity of the statement made Toma smile, and despite his best efforts he was soon sharing a laugh with the grizzled, old instructor. He sat back down as Master Jien Zhiang joined him at the bar. The old man placed a worn leather satchel on the bar stool between them. Moments later the waiter hurried forth with a hot bowl full of mashed rice and a plate of salted pork dumplings. Toma dug into the food, not caring if any clung to the whiskers of his scruffy beard. Master Zhiang merely filled his cherrywood pipe with tobacco and smoked. He watched in silence as Toma ate.

"How is the leg, Captain? Still troubling you?" Master Zhiang motioned for more tea and Rory quickly complied. Then, with a wave of the gray-haired master's hand, the waiter was as easily dismissed, relief plainly evident on his face.

"It's just 'citizen' now. I retired, remember?" Toma rubbed his knee absentmindedly. The cold always made his prosthetic leg ache; a complaint for which the doctors had no real explanation. Phantom pain was supposed fade with time. His just got worse.

"Once a loyal son of Capella, always a loyal son of Capella."

Toma smirked. "And that has gotten us exactly how far? Good old Max left us to fend for ourselves," he growled, referring to the illustrious Chancellor of the Capellan Confederation. It was no secret that New Hessen was low on the priority list for any counterattack. The planet's primary draw had always been training land and its closeness to the border, not industry. Truthfully, the Capellan Confederation Armed Forces could train anywhere. The likelihood that any line regiments were on their way to rescue the citizens of Buchvaal from their Davion oppressors was laughable. Toma had even heard rumors from some of his new clients, young soldiers too lazy to shine their own boots, that several regiments of the Tikonov Commonality had been wiped out or surrendered completely. Worse, the massive FedSuns invasion appeared to be just getting started. The thought of forever being subjected to the depravity of a Davionist market economy chafed at his Capellan sensibilities. Something had to be done.

Something is being done.

"Do not speak ill of the Chancellor. He would send help if it were possible." His *shi fu* ceased puffing and narrowed his eyes at Toma. "We must all do our part for a free Capella."

His mentor's conviction made it hard to disagree. After all, he was here. He was listening. He was doing his part, wasn't he? Instead, Toma changed the subject. "I can do it. I have access. They let me into the Yellow Zone a few times each day during mealtimes." He slid the box closer to the bar.

As he spoke, a young girl opened the door and scampered into the restaurant. Dressed in a thin, olive-drab overcoat and a shiny, lime-green dress, her long, black hair fell in an unruly mess about her face and shoulders. Her clothing was wrinkled and soiled. She gave everyone a timid yet endearing smile, her brown, careworn eyes reflecting an inner light. As she turned, Toma saw partially healed flash burns along the side of her face, down to her jaw and neck. The sight of her brought back a flood of memories.

Wearing pink, open-toed flip-flops that did little to protect her from the increasing autumn cold, the girl struggled to carry the large, brown box held in front of her. Carefully, she set down her load and stepped up to the counter between them. Zhiang moved his satchel to make space, and she hopped up onto the torn seat. She fished in her pockets, then triumphantly slapped down two large, shiny coins along with a FedSuns credit chit. After a few moments, the waiter brought her a plate of steaming dumplings. She promptly stuffed them into her mouth one by one, as if afraid the food would disappear before she could chew. When she'd finished wolfing down the last, tasty morsel, she searched her coat pockets and pulled out a few smaller coins counting them as a miser would count his hoard. She carefully placed them on the counter and pointed at the plate, indicating she wanted another serving.

This time Rory shook his head. "Sorry, May, that's not enough. Come back at dinner when you have more money."

Crestfallen, she sat there a moment, sniffed, then pointed at Toma's now empty rice bowl, indicating she wanted a serving.

Again, Rory shook his head. "You need more credits, May. I'll save some for you. Go get more money."

Master Zhiang tapped out his pipe, then reached down into his satchel and pulled out a package of tobacco, which he used to refill it. He signaled Rory for a light.

The girl sat there for a minute, then without a word, she pulled her coat tight around her and made to step down from the stool.

"Give the girl another plate of dumplings, Rory."

The girl froze as if she'd been caught stealing.

"It's OK, *mei mei*. I'll pay for them." Toma put his last few twenty-*yuan* notes down on the counter. He had seen the girl waiting in line to get into the Yellow Zone outside the Davion encampment each morning. While other families huddled together in the crisp morning air, she stood alone, shivering. Perhaps she was a war orphan? If she had any relatives—correction, any *living* relatives—they surely would have taken her in. It was either that or a state-run orphanage. Children were cared for in the Confederation, one way or another. It was the Capellan way. Unfortunately, it did not appear to be the Davion way.

Toma watched as Rory relit Master Zhiang's pipe, then brought the girl a fresh plate of dumplings. Giving him an inquisitive glance, she ate one, then carefully wrapped the rest in a napkin that she tucked into her coat. With a single, curt nod, she hopped off the stool, picked up the box, then sped out the door, her flip-flops clapping the ground as she ran.

"Do you know the girl?" His teacher's voice betrayed no emotion.

"No. But I have seen her before." Toma reached for his tea. "She is my daughter's age." His hand trembled at the memory.

Master Zhiang raised his teacup. "She will be missed." The lack of inflection in his voice told Toma it was a platitude.

Angered, Toma turned toward Zhiang. "Yes, she will." He set his own cup down and grabbed his cane.

"Having second thoughts? A bit late for that, would you not agree?" His calm, measured words stopped Toma before he did something he knew he might regret.

"She will be missed, as are all those who serve cause of the Confederation." Master Zhiang placed his hand on Toma's wrist. The balance of his *chi* helped sooth Toma's roiling emotions. "What we do, we do for Capella, for House Liao, for our people."

Toma sighed deeply. What had sounded so easy in the anger of the moment had become a monumental thing. What would his wife Diahnna say? What would Li Singh have thought of her valiant father were she alive to see what he had succumbed to? Fighting a battle was one thing. But this? This was something altogether different. Seeing the girl had reminded him of who he was, what he had been. Yes, he had been a soldier of the CCAF, but he had been so much more once. He had been a husband and a father. That counted for more than all his years of service. Yes, he hated the Davions for the countless thousands they had slaughtered in their battle for Buchvaal, but had the Irregulars hesitated in the slightest to bring the battle into the city? Not hardly. Yes, he wanted to see the oppressors driven from Capellan soil. Yes, he wanted to do his part for the Confederation. But this? This was not warfare. This was murder.

Reading his emotions correctly, Zhiang offered, "They said you would not do it." He referred to the growing resistance movement among the ranks of the Entitled. "I told them that you, my most prized Monitor, would come through for us as you have always done, as you were trained to do." His wide smile confused and irritated Toma.

"I have done nothing. I brought the device, but I will not deliver it. I will not dishonor the memory of my family by murdering more innocent Capellans just to kill a few worthless Fedrat soldiers." Toma shook his mentor's hand from his arm. "I want them gone just as much as any other loyal patriot, but I will not stoop to this." He stood. "It is over. We lost. I am sorry, Examiner Zhiang, but you will have to find someone else to deliver your package." He turned to leave, his heart, leaden and hollow for so long, finally felt full for the first time in weeks.

Zhiang's cold voice stopped him in his tracks. "But Captain Fu Shieh, you already have."

A pit of dread formed in his chest. Frantically, Toma grabbed the wooden box he had watched them so meticulously load with explosives that morning. He ripped off the cloth napkin that had fallen, or more likely been placed over it, then carefully lifted the lid, placing his finger under the latch as he searched for the telltale arming pin. Not finding it, he slowly lifted the top, then dropped the box in shock and horror.

Stuffed inside was a tin of black shine, a lighter, a toy dog, a few crayons, and a dirty white rag.

The girl had taken the wrong box.

SU-LOU INDUSTRIAL PARK (CANTONMENT AREA)
THIRD BATTALION, SECOND NEW IVAARSEN CHASSEURS
BUCHVAAL, NEW HESSEN
FEDERATED SUNS OCCUPATION ZONE
0705 HOURS TST
21 OCTOBER 3028

Danny shifted his basket from one hand to the other as he stood in line inside the Yellow Zone checkpoint. The morning frost burned at his ears, cheeks, and nose, but he ignored the discomfort, focusing instead on making out the nametags of the soldiers manning the heavily armed and well-fortified inspection bunker. Unfortunately, their helmets, combat gear, and face paint made it hard to differentiate between them. They all looked virtually the same and none looked pleased at being out in the cold morning, watching for intruders.

"You'd better be here, Joe," he grumbled under his breath.

As he shivered, soldiers passed through a low, sandbag- and plywood-reinforced passageway that opened into the Yellow Zone. Outside, hopeful locals lined up, eagerly awaiting the opportunity to ply their trades. The trade area, or Yellow Zone, was a 100 square-meter area separated from the base and the city with dirt berms, sandbags, and barbed wire. Anyone desiring to enter had to pass through a security checkpoint manned by a joint force of Federated Suns infantry and newly hired, loyalty-verified police. Once inside, Capellan workers, vendors, and tradesmen were allowed to perform various services for the soldiers of Third Battalion, safely away from any sensitive areas like the 'Mech pens or barracks. They provided simple services like uniform repairs and boot polishing as well as taking orders for custom leather goods and alterations. Here infantry and MechWarriors could find just about anything they needed, from shiny belt buckles made from hammered scrap armor to warm rice cakes heated by portable mini-stoves, all without ever setting foot into the city proper, an endeavor best left to armed patrols. In exchange, the soldiers provided much needed capital to the struggling economy. More importantly, exhaust vents from a nearby blast furnace kept prospective buyers and vendors warm and cozy. With so many left homeless or in shelters, the prospect of spending a day in the warm security zone turned many angry Capellan loyalists into eager trade partners, if only until the gates closed for the night.

Of the various commodities for trade, preserved combat rations were more valuable than the currency in a soldier's pockets. As such, a burgeoning black market trade had erupted between the enlisted ranks and those crafty locals who could supply the best crafts, finest leather goods, or other less tangible items. This had led to fights and even a small riot a few days ago as hungry Capellans vied for the valuable supplies. That was why Danny was nervous. Captain Davis had recently banned the trade of combat rations, supposedly to help maintain order and prevent the unit's stock of supplies from disappearing overnight. Anyone caught violating his orders would receive a reprimand and a possible court-martial. To Danny, the risk was worth the reward.

He leaned forward, trying to catch a better view of the soldiers in the booth, but saw no sign of Big Joe anywhere. He considered stepping out of line but thought better of it. Trying to leave now would look suspicious and draw unwanted attention. He swore heatedly and cursed the man under his breath.

The line moved forward, and soon Danny was standing within the checkpoint bunker under a meter of sandbags, plywood, and earth. A private motioned him forward to the inspection counter and asked for his pass, which Danny promptly supplied out of his uniform pocket. Maybe they wouldn't check his basket. He looked at its flowery lace trim and blue chiffon ribbon, a commodity that had cost him his best pocketknife. He grimaced. They would *definitely* look in the basket.

Hurriedly, a short, paunchy, blondish soldier wearing a helmet at least one size too large for his head and dark bags under his eyes slipped into the booth. A wide grin split his baby-faced mug. "Sorry I'm late, guys. *Sergeant-Major* didn't have the right duty roster." He whipped out a clipboard. "Here it is."

Big Joe DuBois had arrived.

"I'll take over here, Private Spaynck. Go ahead and sign out." Sergeant Joseph "Big Joe" DuBois handed the roster to the soldier who had been about to inspect Danny's basket. "I got ya covered. My guys'll be here in a minute." He gave Danny an exaggerated wink.

Danny pretended not to notice. It had cost him his next two passes plus a twelve-pack of black market New Hessen amber ale to convince Big Joe to take an extra duty rotation, a miracle after his previous all-nighter playing cards with the maintenance platoon had landed Joe there the day before. Joe smelled as if he had just come from another game. Danny picked up his basket and turned to leave.

"What's the rush? You got a hot date, SinClair?" Big Joe guffawed and winked lewdly. "Set me up too, will ya?"

Danny glared. *Joe, you are such a dumbass.*

"Sure thing, Joe. I'll see what I can do." Danny shrugged and walked out, breathing a sigh of relief. He could hear Big Joe laughing loudly as he walked away.

"Yeah, my buddy's gonna get me a date, you melons!"

Toma swore as he fell sprawling over a curb, smashing his good shin painfully into the unyielding concrete. His wooden box fell to the ground, spilling its contents onto the street. A wrinkled matron seated on a stoop nearby chided him in Chinese, "*Ni gan ma?*"

What the hell am I doing? Good question.

Surprised by her nasty outburst, he climbed to his feet, adjusted his prosthetic leg, then stooped to pick up the contents of the box. Hefting it under his arm, he continued onward, his cane clacking on the hard cobblestones as he moved. He had to find the girl! Of course there was only one place she would be going at this time of day if she wanted to earn more money for food: the Yellow Zone. He increased his pace.

Ahead, he saw a crowd milling about in a roped-off section to one side of the Fedrats' service gate. Nearly a hundred people, those lucky few with temporary access cards supplied by the AFFS governmental liaison, waited in line to enter the trade area. The rest stood by or huddled in groups well beyond the gates, waiting for the chance to show their wares to departing patrols or to beg for occasional scraps. Bunkers with firing ports lined the base walls. Machine-gun muzzles poked out from their dark interiors. Manning the guns, bored but alert sentries maintained a watchful vigil over the groups of potential security risks outside, training their sights on anyone who came too close to the vehicle gate. The guards would not hesitate to fire if they believed him to be a threat.

Toma slowed his hobbled gait as he approached the base. He desperately wanted to avoid attention but needed to move quickly.

If not for his false leg and cane, he might have caught up to her by now, but his injuries had slowed his progress considerably. Slipping a knit cap on his head, he began searching the crowd for her. He paced awkwardly up and down the ranks of despondent Capellans, calling her name.

"May!"

Where is she?

Danny stepped out into the trade area and was immediately accosted by a dozen or more men and women holding out various crafts and trinkets. Troops watched from guardhouses along the wall to make sure things didn't get too out of hand. Regardless, the would-be merchants made every effort to attract Danny's attention.

"You want socks?" An old man in a gray rayon racing jacket, torn coolant vest, and dirty white slacks held out a pair of AFFS-issue, summer-weight cottons.

Danny politely declined.

"You want necklace, yes?" An old, balding crone with one eye, silver hair, and wooden teeth held out a bramble of woven myomer strands and wire with teardrops of shining, melted armor dangling from it. It looked painful to wear. Danny ignored her.

"Wait, I can get you girl!" She pushed forth a plump, forty-something woman wearing a blue smock and black combat boots. "You want girl?" The doe-eyed, greasy-haired brunette smiled sheepishly, revealing a mouth devoid of front teeth. "You take inside. Just four rations! We make deal."

Danny tried not to make eye contact as he stepped around them and tried to work his way forward through the press of stale bodies. When a bloated, half-plucked chicken was thrust into his face, he started pushing people away forcefully. Eventually, the crowd gave up and went to harass the next soldier in line. There was money to be made.

Hefting his basket, Danny gingerly stepped over a mat lined with handmade pictures of BattleMechs in heroic poses, nearly tripping as the young artist seated there jumped up suddenly, paintbrush in hand, ready to negotiate. Danny muttered an apology and began searching the crowd of artisans, craftsmen, and vendors but saw no sign of the familiar face.

Where is she?

Toma was getting desperate. He had searched the crowd for nearly five minutes with no luck. Already he was attracting unwanted attention for his efforts. Several people had yelled at him for trying to cut in line or for pulling at the hoods of children he saw waiting with their families. His pretense at trying to find his lost daughter was unconvincing. Even now he felt eyes boring into him as he scanned the crowd on both sides of the fence. If he kept this up much longer, he knew he'd be taken in for questioning, if not arrested. He wracked his brain, trying to think of where she could be.

Where would I go if I were an eight-year-old child looking for a warm meal or money?

He stopped walking, took a deep breath, closed his eyes, and centered his *chi*. His leg and back wounds ached badly. Rather than succumb to the pain, he channeled it, using the energy to sharpen his thoughts, focus his mind.

Perhaps the soup kitchen?

Probably not. The kitchen on Wang Dong Street wasn't open yet. That was why they had agreed to meet at Hsu's Teahouse.

Perhaps she hasn't come here after all?

He didn't know what was worse, her bringing the device here or leaving it at some other crowded location. Either way, innocent people who had already suffered so much would be hurt or killed. He had meant to be with it when it went. As a Minder he had been trained to think of the Confederation above all else, ready even to turn in his own parents should he believe they were not of sufficient moral fiber. For thirty years he had served the state, doing their deeds with a clarity of purpose that could not be swayed. The death of his family had changed all that in one terrible moment. A stray flight of missiles had destroyed his home, his life, and everything he had worked so hard to build. Distraught, he had tried to drown himself in liquid sorrow. Only the offer from his mentor and friend to strike a blow for all those who had suffered from Hanse Davion's naked, unwarranted aggression had rekindled his will to live, if only to put his pain to rest.

But the girl...

This young, beautiful little girl was his daughter's age. Her life was just beginning. The mere thought of what Zhiang would use her to accomplish, just as he had always used impressionable young Capellan children, was intolerable. Unbearable. He could not allow it. An image of his daughter flashed through his mind.

No. I must find her.

He opened his eyes and tried not to focus on any one detail, taking in the scene as a whole instead. Details crystallized in his mind. The mother in a red scarf and maternity dungarees breastfeeding her baby as she stood pawning her jewelry. The twin brothers wearing threadbare orange sweatshirts with faded athletic letters. The grandfather sitting on a wooden crate, carefully polishing a worn brass timepiece with a cracked-glass cover. Toma took it all in, attempting to sort out the clutter and confusion. Then he heard it.

"Come on, kid, you've been standing there forever. Either let me have the box or you can't get in. Those are the rules."

The inspection booth!

Toma ran, knocking over people in his path as he struggled to make his way toward the front of the line. Stumbling and staggering, he shoved his way forward, his package in hand. He only hoped he would not be too late.

Danny saw the commotion at the outer security checkpoint and made his way toward the gate to see what was happening. A small crowd had formed around the back of the open bunker where citizens of Buchvaal had their items inspected before being allowed access to the higher-security trade area. Stepping onto an empty crate, Danny saw a district police officer and three soldiers wearing flak vests and full battle rattle inside. Two soldiers were aiming their laser rifles toward a diminutive figure the police officer was attempting to corner. The third soldier, a tall woman with bushy blond hair, was speaking into a field phone.

Seconds later a squad of infantry came pouring out into the Yellow Zone from a barracks ready room within the garrison walls. The crowd that had worked so hard moments before to delay potential customers frantically scurried away as the heavily armed detail ran toward the checkpoint.

"*Wo bu yao!*"

Her shrill voice pierced the cool air. Danny hurriedly pushed past the gawking spectators and into the bunker just as the ready reaction squad arrived and took up firing positions around the perimeter. Meanwhile, a second squad of troops pushed the crowd of merchants and vendors back to the far side of the Yellow Zone as the sentries beyond trained a heavy machine gun on the crowd. The situation was rapidly escalating.

Entering the bunker, Danny found the girl. Wearing her familiar green dress underneath a worn overcoat, she struggled to keep a large wooden box away from the policewoman who worked diligently to pry it out of her hands. The soldiers, unwilling to wait for compliance, were shouting orders at her. She jumped at each harsh word. Tears streamed down her face.

Danny stepped inside. "Stop! What's going on here?"

"Get out of here, SinClair. Everything is under control." Danny recognized the haughty voice as Leftenant Jennifer Berri. He grimaced. Of all the people in the unit to draw duty officer detail, why did it have to be her?

"No, Jen. Wait! I know this girl. Let me help." Danny spread his hands out and started slowly toward the girl. "It's all right, honey. They just want to see what's in the box. They won't keep it."

The girl whined and backed against the sandbag wall.

Jen shouted angrily. "I said get out of here, SinClair!" She pulled her sidearm. "It's bad enough you almost cost us the ambush, but I won't have you second-guessing any more of my orders!" Having had her *P-Hawk* shot out from under her by a lucky hit from a *Commando*'s SRM strike had sent her into a spiral of depression, accusation, and recrimination. Her daddy's promise to find her a new 'Mech hadn't materialized, and she was left trying to cobble together the remains of a *Cicada* that was more scrap then BattleMech. Their tension blossomed into outright hatred on her part.

Danny awkwardly held his hands up, unsure of what to do. The weight of the basket made it hard to lift his arm above chest level.

"Are you crazy? *Leftenant*, calm down!" The policewoman glared angrily at Jen. "You're making this worse."

"I am calm!" Her high-pitched scream sounded anything but. "Back off, SinClair!" She aimed her gun at the girl. "Now, you either put that box on the table, Cappie, or so help me, I'm gonna blow your head off!"

Suddenly, a man wearing a green field coat and a black knit cap toppled into the bunker from the Red Zone.

Jen fired.

Toma tripped over a line of low sandbags that served to keep rainwater out of the checkpoint interior. Struggling to regain his balance, he dropped his cane and reached for the metal table that sat lengthwise along the now-vacated inspection line. Without warning, a crushing blow smashed into his right shoulder, flipped him around backward, and sent the box smashing to the ground as his prosthetic leg collapsed. He collided with the inspection table, but instead of arresting his fall, it toppled onto its side, knocking the legs out from under one of the soldiers. The young man fired as he fell. His shot hit the police officer, who groaned in agony as she sprawled face-first onto the hard-packed floor. Toma landed heavily on his side with a perfect view of the scene.

Nearby, a MechWarrior wearing the rank and shoulder boards of sergeant swung a heavy basket at an officer holding a smoking pistol. The frilly basket broke, spilling its contents across the room. Preserved meats, cheeses, packaged paper, and color markers flew in a cascade through the air, some striking the woman, most landing on the dirty ground. The surprised leftenant ducked, then brought her weapon around to fire again, but the sergeant was faster. He dropped the basket handle and tackled her. Both of them fell in a heap onto the other side of the inspection table with a loud *crack* while the pistol flew out of her hands and clattered to the floor.

Through it all, May stood there mutely as if frozen solid. Tears streaked her dirt-smeared cheeks. Then a spark of understanding lit her face. She looked down and smiled at Toma in her angelic way. There before her, scattered amid the shattered remains of the thin wooden box he had been carrying were several crayons and a small toy dog poking out playfully from under a dirty lace curtain. She glanced at her bundle then back to the jumble of treasures now strewn about the bunker. Recognizing her shoeshine kit, she stepped forward, gratitude and joy written plainly on her face.

Toma cried, "No, May!"

She dropped the box and reached for her prize.

THE COMMONS
MUNICIPAL DISTRICT 3
BUCHVAAL, NEW HESSEN
FEDERATE SUNS OCCUPATION ZONE
1850 HOURS TST
2 JANUARY 3029

Danny parked the hovercar and carefully stepped out onto the street. It was late, but he needed to make the trip, as he had done every day for the past month. His leg still hurt, but it was healing. Fortunately, his injuries were less severe than the doctors had originally thought. With some lengthy rehabilitation, they'd said he could make a full recovery. That was the great thing about the human body: even the worst injuries could heal over time. It was the mental ones that never quite closed.

Colonel Stephenson had assigned him desk duty, since he obviously couldn't pilot a 'Mech minus one working leg. Honestly, he wasn't sure he ever wanted to get back into the cockpit again. He still couldn't shake the images of that day. Maybe he never would.

Danny set his crutches out underneath him and shuffled forward over the blackened cobblestones. He looked up at the ruined apartment complex, noting the location of each bullet hole and scorch mark in the fading light. He needn't have. He'd committed them to memory long ago. Closing his eyes, he replayed the battle in his mind as he had so many times since that day. What could he have done differently? Probably nothing. That was the stink of it. War is hell. People get hurt. People die, both soldiers and civilians. It was the soldier's responsibility to do their best to mitigate the loss, to control the chaos as best they could. But he didn't have to like it.

The unit psychologist told him he needed closure. He thought he had found it helping May. When she died, it had ripped all his wounds open again. Only now it was ten times worse. Now there was a face to the name.

They wouldn't let him resign. He'd tried. God, how he had tried. So they came up with another solution. He could stay and help administer the world, work on rebuilding. It was a job he could really get into. It helped with the nightmares, a little. He had a good budget. Prince Davion had even given him enough money for a few small memorials. He knew exactly what to do with it.

Sergeant SinClair bent down and placed the candle before the statue. It was a small affair, not too big, not too ornate. He thought he got the likeness just right. On it was a plaque. The inscription read:

Lui May Sung
Born 2 January 3020
Died 21 October 3028
May all those who sacrifice their lives
on the altar of freedom be forever remembered.
We shall never forget.

Danny whispered, "Happy birthday, May."

Dedicated to all the men and women of the armed forces who valiantly serve their countries each and every day.

BAD WATER

KEVIN KILLIANY

GREAT REEF OCEANIC RESERVE
WESTERN EQUATORIAL DISTRICT
BRISBANE
TAURIAN CONCORDAT
17 OCTOBER 3041

Terry Henderson kept one eye on the depth meter as he edged the boat closer to the reef, one hand always near the start switch for the matched pair of Royce diesels. The electric screws had barely enough power to make way against the southern current; they'd never hold if an eddy caught them this close to the coral. There was no danger of holing the hull, but repairing the hand-fitted sierra wood would be costly and time consuming. Brisbane's competition fishing season opened in less than a week, and with tens of thousands of cash-laden tourists descending on the Long Keys, the family could not afford the down time.

Terry's other eye was on the school of improbably bright blue shapes drifting just below the surface of the crystal clear water. Bonnets, warming themselves in the sun and picking off any prawn foolish enough to venture out from the reef, gathering energy before plunging into the cold deeps for serious hunting. Less than half a meter long, blue Bonnets were one of the most beautiful fish in these equatorial waters. And, armed with razor-edged fins and needle-sharp teeth, gram for gram they were one of the most successful predators on Brisbane. That combination of beauty and lethality made them highly prized among those who collected exotics.

The boy stood ready at the fantail, tanned nut brown and slender, a casting net spread in his outstretched hands. Terry was proud of how the boy stood relaxed and ready, on point but not nervous.

Judging the cast was up to him—even if Terry could see what the boy saw, calling the order to toss would give the fish enough warning to escape.

There was a world of difference between getting close to a Bonnet and catching one— which was why collectors paid top prices for a live and undamaged specimen.

Turning the screws, Terry brought the stern of the boat around toward the reef and cut power. They'd drift for a minute, sideways to their course, before the current overcame the boat's momentum and pushed them away from the Bonnets.

Terry made a point of leaning casually against the captain's perch—a butt-high rail where less serious boaters put a chair. The boy wasn't looking at him, but could probably see him out of the corner of his eye, and Terry wanted to project an air of relaxed confidence. Take as much pressure off the young fisherman as he could.

A flick of the wrists, and the net glittered briefly in the sun. Then it was in the water, and the boy was cinching the catchline at speeds Terry could no longer match.

A bright-blue shape flashed and struggled against the mesh, too stupid to pull back and search for the rapidly closing mouth of the net. Cursing the hesitation in his legs, Terry pushed off his perch and hurried back to help the boy. Two blue shapes! The boy had made a double catch. If they found a second buyer, they would live easy for a month.

Holding the net far enough from their bodies to avoid the snapping jaws and sharp fins, Terry and the boy got their catch over the rail and into the live tank. Terry made his way to the controls, and the boy secured the tank, sliding the false bottom down over their prizes. The space would be cramped, but the dark would not bother deep-sea hunters, and the steady flow of water would keep them healthy, if not happy, until they could be transferred to proper tanks at the hacienda.

A slap of the toggles, and the twin Royce diesels sprang to life, their deep-throated rumble panicking everything in underwater earshot. Terry leaned against his perch, taking as much weight as possible off his legs as the boat surged away from the reef.

When they were a kilometer beyond the limits of the restricted zone, Terry turned on his radar and transponder, making his fishing boat legitimately visible once again. His patrol alarm sounded immediately. A Brisbane Maritime Constabulary cutter was already closing on their position at speed.

Terry heeled the boat over, directly away from the oncoming authorities, and gunned the engines. Behind him, unsecured equipment and the boy fell to the deck as the fishing boat leapt forward. In less than a hundred meters they were bouncing across the gentle swells at the hull's maximum velocity.

"Mayday!" Terry shouted into the radio, set to the maritime emergency channel. "This is Big Reef Charters, Boat One, registration CB-four-six-nine-eight-one-alpha. An unidentified vessel is approaching us at high speed. Their transponder is dark; repeat, no transponder. We are attempting to evade. Location—" Terry read off their latitude and longitude, with an error in the latter that placed them another handful of kilometers away from the restricted zone.

"Cut the crap, Henderson," said a familiar voice on the radio. Boatmaster Robert Thompson, commander of the BMC Cutter *Tucumcari*. "You know damn well it's us. Heave to."

"Maritime Patrol, please respond!" Terry shouted into the radio. "Repeat, this is Big Reef Charters One being pursued by possible pirates! Location—"

Terry stopped transmitting. Hanging up the mic, he reached behind the radio and transponder receiver and pulled two unsecured wires just loose enough to break contact. The connectors would pass visual inspection, but both machines were dead.

The image of the approaching cutter was still clear on the radar, devoid of identifying data, and closing.

"What do you think?" Terry asked the boy.

Bracing himself against the jarring slap of waves against the speeding hull with one hand on the binnacle, the boy studied the radar and the map overlay.

"If we drop the Bonnets at this speed, we'll kill them," he said, pitching his voice to carry through the rushing wind.

"We could stay hull-in and heave to when the maries are right on top of us," Terry said, pleased the fish were the boy's first consideration. "Make like we just made visual, and drop them then."

"Or we could run for the hacienda."

"That's the *Tucumcari*—they've got water jets, we've got screws," Terry pointed out. "Even hull-out we can't match their speed."

It would have been more of a race if the boat was running military grade omnidiesels, but Terry had installed the Royce conventional engines long ago. They were less temperamental, more forgiving of abuse, and cheaper to feed than omnidiesels. Ninety-nine times out of a hundred he didn't miss the 10 percent of speed and power he'd lost in the trade. That one time out of a hundred, though...

"But if we go full steam the whole way, straight line, we'll still be ahead of them when we reach dock," the boy said. "Fifteen, maybe even twenty minutes."

"Think that's enough time to get the bonnets off and hidden?"

"Maybe."

"That 'maybe' holds the difference between getting off scot-free and spending the next season or two behind bars," Terry said. Bonnets were restricted, not endangered; poaching dolphins would have cost them their boat. "So do we dump or run? Your call."

The boy grinned. "Go for it, Dad."

Terry grinned back and pounded a flat button to the right of the tiller with the heel of his hand. Pounded *at*. He hit it on the second try, then stole a sideways glance to confirm the boy hadn't noticed the miss. The bounding slap of the waves against the hull disappeared as hydrofoils the tourists never saw deployed. The boat rose above the waves on jointed legs, losing its quaint seadog persona to arrow toward the Henderson hacienda at speeds no sport-fishing boat should have commanded.

Behind them the cutter dropped back, losing a kilometer or so in the time it took the boatmaster to realize what had happened. But sooner than Terry would have liked, the cutter began to accelerate. The ship would need more water than his boat to reach full speed, but with the fusion-powered *Tucumcari* running on foils it was only a matter of time before the gap between them closed; not as quickly, but inevitably.

Checking the radar readings against the chart, Terry decided his son's estimate had been optimistic, but they'd have a good ten to twelve minutes to offload the Bonnets and get them safely hidden in underwater tanks before the maries made it into the family's sheltered harbor. Particularly with the tides in. The cutter would have to slow considerably to navigate the switchback reefs leading into the cove while their boat could skate above them. If he kept a bone in her teeth right up to the docks, they'd have the time the needed.

Terry didn't bother resurrecting the radio to call ahead and warn his family. Everyone at the hacienda could read a radar and know what was happening. He was willing to bet his wife was broadcasting on the emergency channel even now, calling him seven kinds of idiot for thinking he was being chased by pirates and telling him to heave to for the maries. Her brother and their nieces would be getting the stash tank ready. The only surprise would be two Bonnets instead of one.

One big hole in the happy plan was the fact the cutter would be in sight for nearly an hour, and close enough to be identified for half that time, before they reached their cove. Terry would need a good reason not to recognize the *Tucumcari* and heave to for boarding. With the high sun sparkling off the crystal water under a cloudless sky, claiming poor visibility was not an option. No bother; he didn't doubt something would occur to him when the time came.

Terry's good mood lasted until the boat rounded the hook into Henderson Cove and he saw the VTOL squatting awkwardly on the gently sloping lawn between the hacienda and the boathouses.

He cut the throttles, and the boat settled abruptly into the water. The boy was silent beside him as he steered for the tourist dock—farthest from the boathouses—barely making way across the glass-smooth water of the family's pocket harbor.

The chopper was big—some sort of troop transport, though Terry didn't recognize the specific model—and painted coal black, with a pattern of orange-and-red flames along the side facing the water. Not the Brisbane Constabulary; the Taurian Red Chasseurs had chosen to visit his little sanctuary. Which meant whatever trouble the VTOL had brought them went way beyond two illegal exotics in the holding tank. He considered dumping his contraband, but decided to chance events distracting the maries from enforcing fish export laws.

"Help!"

The boy's shout startled Terry out of his thoughts.

"Pirates!" the boy shouted again, waving his arms and pointing back the way they had come. "Pirates chasing us!"

Terry had to admit it was a good performance, but he suspected there was little chance anyone on shore was buying it. The armed men along the dock and by the boathouse certainly didn't seem excited by the news. He was glad to see none of the soldiers were near the far boathouse, the decrepit one obviously near collapse and pasted with signs warning it was unsafe. Authorities wandering in there on top of everything else would be bad.

"Dump 'em?" the boy asked.

Terry shook his head, not bothering to explain his earlier decision.

The boy shielded his eyes from the sun as he scanned the docks and the dozen troopers, then he turned and looked back to the *Tucumcari*, just rounding the headland. After a moment he nodded, evidently reaching the same conclusion his father had.

The cutter dropped a boat, a rigid inflatable that skittered across the cove like ice on a griddle. Terry expected to be boarded, but the boat skimmed by, trying to outrun the angry-bee whine of its high-rev screw. Boatmaster Thompson stared straight ahead, ignoring Terry's friendly wave.

At the dock soldiers stood ready to catch the lines the boy tossed. Terry saw no sign of Manuel or his nieces; he hoped his brother-in-law was just keeping the girls out of sight, but suspected they were being held in the house.

The troopers weren't ground pounders, Terry realized, taking in the padded-seat jodhpurs and comm mics build into their helmets. Helping the boy tie off the boat, he got close enough to read patches.

What did the Twenty-seventh Armored Recon want with the Henderson hacienda?

Terry's legs didn't cooperate; the easy jump from deck to dock almost pitched him on his face. He faked a coughing fit to cover the stumble. It didn't fool anyone except maybe the boy, but Terry was glad to see the recon goons scanning the dock around him. They'd figured the coughs were supposed to divert their attention from something he'd ditched.

When he straightened, Boatmaster Thompson, looking as trim as Terry had been two decades ago, was striding up shoulder to shoulder with a Twenty-seventh Armored Recon officer—the guy in charge, from the look of him—followed closely by a force sergeant looking like he was the head guy's bodyguard.

Then Terry caught the red-goggle tattoo circling the officer's eyes and bobbed his head once in respect. They didn't bestow the Taurian Brand for good conduct. "Andrew," the officer's name patch read; no *s*.

"Subaltern, may I present the Terrence Hendersons, senior and junior," Thompson said as they got within easy earshot. "One of them was the best damn fast patrol-boat jockey in the Constabulary before retiring to become a poacher. The other shows potential for amounting to something if child protective services ever get him out of here."

Neither the subaltern nor the force sergeant blinked at Thompson's introduction. That told Terry Andrew and—Jerrod, the sergeant's patch read—had been in Brisbane's Long Keys region long enough to be familiar with local manners. Character, the tourists called it.

The officer ignored the father and son to run his eyes over the lines of their fishing boat. "Someone screwed the hell out of your FPB," Andrew said.

"It's a charter fishing boat," Terry countered.

"Captain Henderson, I am an officer and an armor commander," Andrew replied. "The first does not automatically mean I am an idiot nor does the second mean I have never seen a gunboat."

Turning a shoulder to Terry and the boy, he strolled the length of the boat, pointing out features as he spoke.

"Machine-gun mounts there and there are gone, cabin is stretched forward to cover the hole where the turret used to be, and from the way she sits the water, I'd say most of the armor is gone, too," he said. "That is some handsome woodwork; real craftsmanship. If I didn't know that was a veneer over aligned-crystal steel, I'd swear I was looking at a wooden boat."

The subaltern frowned at the stern. "No name?"

"Never came when I called," Terry explained.

Andrew nodded as though that were a reasonable answer and strolled back.

"Captain Henderson, Force Sergeant Jerrod and his squad are in need of specialized transportation," he said. "Which means I have a job for you and your fishing boat."

"You should have called my wife, she handles reservations," Terry said. "The first few weeks of the season are booked, but I'm sure Maria can fit you in sometime next month."

"The job is on Bromhead," Andrew said, looking as though he thought he was making sense.

Terry felt the world swirl and wasn't at all sure it was shock. He slid his right foot out a hand's breadth, taking a wider stance just in case.

"Bromhead?" he said aloud. "Thought the FedSuns stole that a few centuries back. Arid world; all deserts and mountains, right?"

Andrew indicated their surroundings, the hacienda, the hills beyond and the pocket cove.

"Any tourist guide will tell you all of Brisbane looks just like this," he said. "A water world with eighty percent of its landmass made up of islands. Say Brisbane, and people automatically think white beaches in the tropics.

"But islands—continental, coral, tectonic and volcanic—stretch from the equator to both poles, encompassing dozens of climates and hundreds of ecologies." He pointed at the cutter blocking the entrance to the cove. "Not to mention the *Tucumcari* is named for a mountain in the middle of Brisbane's Mejico Desert."

"Bromhead has oceans," Terry deduced, his eyes on Thompson.

Halfway through Andrew's speech, the boatmaster had cocked an ear toward the live tank. To someone who knew what they were listening to, the faint whine of the pump keeping the Bonnets alive hovered just on the threshold of hearing.

"More to the point, swamps and bijous along Salazaar's western coast."

"Fascinating," Terry lied, making the effort not to watch Thompson climb aboard his boat. "If they've got water, they've got boats. No need to borrow mine."

"The FedSuns have boats on Bromhead, we do not," Andrew said. "And even if we were willing to borrow one, it's doubtful anyone on Bromhead has a boat quite like this one."

"You just made a pretty speech about how big and complex a world is," Terry pointed out. "You could probably find any boat you wanted on Bromhead."

The boy muttered something beside him.

Following his son's gaze Terry ignored Andrew's explanation of silhouettes and radar imaging and relying on what is known and trusted to watch Thompson make a show of looking down into the empty live tank and then looking at the exterior housing. Anyone who knew what he was looking at understood he was telling them he'd discovered—or at least strongly suspected—the false bottom.

"Tell you what," Terry said, cutting across Andrew's assurance no enemies would be engaged. "Give me enough change to rent another boat for the season, and you can have mine."

"That is not possible," Andrew said.

"Okay, fine," Terry said. "I'll double up with Manuel. We'll lose some customers—we'll lose a lot of customers—but we'll make enough to get by. Just bring my boat back in one piece."

"You misunderstand," Andrew said. "You will be coming with the boat."

Terry's heart went cold.

"No."

"No?"

"I re-damn-tired from the maries fifteen years ago," Terry said. "Even got partial medical on my papers, from getting my head busted open on Malta in '26. Thompson was there, a shavetail on his first mission."

"I was there," Thompson confirmed. "That's why I thought of you when Subaltern Andrew asked for my best boat jockey."

Terry glared his appreciation.

"It took me my whole life to get the life I want, to finally get things right," he said to Andrew. "I've got a wife half my age who loves the hell out of me, a kid who's on course to miss half the crap I lived through, and not much time left to teach him what he needs to know."

"You're not that old, Henderson," Thompson said, jumping lightly to the dock. "You'll be giving *his* grandkids crap."

"Not taking that chance, Bobby," Terry answered. "You know tomorrow's never promised."

"And you know the only thing retiring from the Constabulary means is you're in the Reserve for the rest of your life, partial medical or no partial medical." He grinned and pulled a folded flimsy from his shirt pocket. "You're activated, Henderson."

"Like hell!"

"Like hell," Thompson agreed, extending the hardcopy of the orders.

Terry ignored it.

"The Concordat needs a boatman of your skills," Andrew said—like that made a difference.

"There's nothing to knowing a boat," Terry said. "Any joker who can read the controls can run it. Give me a couple of days and I can teach a monkey all the tricks this boat can do. What made me good—before I *left* the maries—was knowing the waters. I've never been off Brisbane and I sure as hell don't know the waters on Brombutt—"

"Bromhead."

"—Bromhead. You'll need a local pilot, not me. I'll just get in your way."

"We have a local guide," Andrew said. "What we need is a specialized boat. One that can pass causal inspection, maneuver in shallow water, and run like bloody hell when the time comes."

"You got the boat," Terry said, "I'll even throw in the trained monkey if you give me time to find one. But I'm not going anywhere."

"Constable, you have been activated," Andrew said, iron creeping into his voice for the first time. "You do not have the luxury of refusing orders."

Terry didn't bother answering. The idea of even hedging on an order was blasphemy to anyone gung-ho enough to earn the Taurian Brand. No chance of presenting compelling reasons why he should be excused from obeying this one.

No chance with Thompson, either, but he had to try.

"Can't you help me out here, Bobby?" he asked, trying not to let his plea be too naked.

Thompson looked pointedly back at the live tank before answering.

"I am helping you out, Constable Henderson."

If Terry could have trusted his arms and legs to obey, he would have punched the crap out of the smug boatmaster.

SHOLON DELTA
SALAZAAR, BROMHEAD
FEDERATED SUNS
4 DECEMBER 3041

Terry rubbed his biceps absently as he watched the water. The vaccination didn't really itch, especially a week after the injection, but the fact he'd had to have the shot irritated him. SOP when going to a new planet, the Two-seven's medico had explained. Even if the planet in question didn't have any known bugs, everyone going for the first time got a megadose of vitamins and a holiday selection of broad-spectrum antibiotics.

Not that there was anything in medical science that would make a dent in what ailed him. He was on the wrong damn planet, way too many light-years from his wife and son and the clear blue waters he should be sailing.

The water here was an ugly brown, with the black shadow of the boat stretching ahead of them as the red sun set behind them. Force Sergeant Jerrod stood in the very bow, listening intently as Sauud, the Twenty-seventh's tame local, explained something about the shore with much emphasis and gesticulation.

The sheer cliffs with turbulent hems of foam and jagged rocks they'd been keeping in sight for three days following the coast south had suddenly retreated with the morning haze, almost as if they were part of it. In their place appeared a wild forest of trees that seemed to thrive on salt water, and were unlike anything Terry had seen. A raft of them had passed close to the boat—upright trunks ten to fifteen meters tall riding a great mat of intertwined roots that stretched dozens of meters in every direction. The colony of stork-like birds nesting in the floating trees seemed unconcerned about their homes drifting out to sea—indicating they either knew something he didn't or were rock stupid.

Terry was betting the latter.

He hadn't seen anything on Bromhead that impressed him. From the wrong-colored sun to customs inspectors that would have been cashiered from the Brisbane Constabulary—if not shot—to locals who smelled funny to local food that smelled worse to, most of all, the shoddy workmanship on the commercial fishing boats he'd seen at the miserable harbor, the planet was nothing but one wrong piled on top of another.

And the biggest wrong was that he and his boat were on a world they should not be on, carrying a squad of Twenty-seventh scouts to a destination he did not want to see for reasons that made no sense to him. He was supposed to be at the hacienda, marveling at Maria's love and teaching the boy everything there was to know about living well before—

Terry cut the thought off.

He fervently hoped the trip would prove pointless. He could not imagine any chain of events involving the scouts using their weapons that ending with him safely home on Brisbane.

A few hours back, the gray ocean water had turned brown, a sediment fan announcing the presence of a river with considerable current emptying into the sea. Force Sergeant Jerrod, on the advice of Sauud, had ordered the boat to seek out the mouth of the river.

Terry pretended he couldn't feel the tremor in his left leg as he leaned easily on his perch, looking for the ripple of submerged hazards as they rode the making tide into the mouth of the shallow estuary. What rocks and non-floating trees he could see did not have dark rings above the waterline. Tide was close to full. The depth sounder on the binnacle beeped comfortably every few seconds, telling him it was watching the bottom better than he could and was satisfied with what it saw. This affected his vigilance not in the least.

Behind him the six men, no women, of Jerrod's squad lounged, conserving energy for whatever their mission turned out to be. There were bunks in the cabin, but the air below decks was stifling—Terry suspected one of the extra fuel tanks the engineers of the Twenty-seventh had added was seeping fuel. Despite being hardwood over steel, the open deck behind the cockpit was the most comfortable place to relax.

The native squatted down in the prow where he could peer at the surrounding jungle over the gunwale. He must have felt Terry's eyes, because he turned to flash a grin up at the cockpit and waved the all-clear signal. Terry nodded acknowledgment.

Jerrod worked his way back around the side of the cabin until he was standing on the other side of the binnacle.

"Sauud was telling me—"

"This is a cuspate delta screwed up by cliffs on three sides and some sort of underwater ridge," Terry said. "A big fat river has been shoving a lot of sediment into a big bowl since forever. You got rock, dry land, swamp, quicksand, soup, and water side by side by side and the only way to tell where to step is to trust a local guide like him."

Jerrod pursed his lips, studying Terry's profile.

Terry scanned the surface, one hand on the wheel, the other on the throttles.

Sauud squatted in the bow, looking tame and watching the water closer to the boat. Terry couldn't tell from his attitude if he was looking for food or danger, but either way their trusty native guide didn't seem overly concerned about impending navigational hazards.

"There's a formation like this on Brisbane?" Jerrod asked. "Marteline."

"Then you've seen this before?" Terry nodded.

"You're saying we don't need Sauud?"

"Like hell." Terry threw the soldier a hot glance. "Look around you, how the cockpit's laid out. What does that tell you?"

"That you're used to sailing with a copilot."

"What?"

"Your instrument cluster is all in this center console," Jerrod gestured. "You're all the way to the right with just the wheel and throttle and engine gauges."

"That center console is called a binnacle," Terry said. "Radar, fish finder, depth gauge, positioned so anyone in the cockpit can read them. Radio's in the middle of the dash for the same reason. Everything low. Straight ahead of me, any way I look, is water," Terry illustrated with a sweep of his arm. "Only an idiot ignores his instruments, but the only way to learn the water is to watch the water."

"That fish finder looks like a Defense Force multiphase sonar," Jerrod said. "Part of the patrol boat's original equipment?"

"You're missing the point."

"What's the point?"

"That I wouldn't get within ten klicks of Marteline without a local pilot," Terry said. "I know what kind of maze I'm looking at, but I have no clue on how to navigate through it. Bottom line, there is no damn good reason for me to be here." Terry heard his voice rising and reigned it in. "I appreciate your subaltern's estimate of my value, but he miscalculated. Anybody who can steer a boat and do what the pilot says could do what I'm doing."

As if to illustrate the point, Sauud raised an arm without looking back and waved toward the left. Terry nodded and obediently altered course toward the north side of the channel. The sunlight, hitting the water from over his shoulder, had concealed the shadow of the standing trough. A second later the depth gauge beeped a warning. The fish finder painted a jagged shape rising from the bottom.

"Low tide that'll be an island," Terry said to Jerrod. "Looks like a chunk of cliff rock."

"Our intel says the coastal cliffs stretch back about thirty klicks here, then circle back out to the ocean," Jerrod said. "The cliffs at the eastern end are almost like a dam. The Sholon Valley is on the other side. Shalon Loch, which takes up half the valley, is big enough to be an inland sea; second largest body of fresh water on Bromhead."

"And all the rivers on the west side of that mountain range feed the loch," Terry said, nodding toward the distant line of peaks dominating the horizon beyond the trees. "The lake water pours through the cliffs—probably a pretty impressive string of waterfalls—to form the delta, and there's nothing but Brombutt's famous deserts on the other side of the divide."

Jerrod studied him for a long moment.

"How did you know that?"

"Grade-school geology," Terry pointed at the towering heights of the distant mountain range. "That is a tectonic plate collision, this bowl of mud looks like and the lake valley beyond sounds like a pair of collapsed volcanoes, and with the sea behind us, anything on the other side of those mountains is in a rain shadow."

Jerrod opened his mouth, but Terry cut him off.

"Are you really an idiot, or is playing dumb some sort of interrogation technique?" he demanded. "Because if you're trying to break me down, I gotta tell you, you're *this* close to annoying me into a confession."

Jerrod met his glare with a stone face of his own. The soldier was maybe half his age and would have had no trouble snapping Terry's neck—and from his expression he was giving that option some serious thought. Terry braced himself, knowing he would be too slow for whatever happened, but after a long three count, Jerrod turned away, taking the short steps down to the deck without another glance.

Terry would have turned his head to watch him go, but his neck refused to move. That was a new one.

Eyes the water—with occasional flickered glances at Sauud and the instruments—he guided the boat through ever-narrowing channels between floating mats of trees, islands, and jagged pillars of volcanic stone. As the sun finished setting behind them, something that sounded like a giant bird filled the growing gloom with a mournful cry.

Sauud scaled the cabin and walked back to jump into the cockpit.

"Need a place to tie up for the night, mate," he said. "Don't want to buck a running tide we can't see."

Terry chuckled.

"What?"

"Your name is Sauud, and you look like an olive," Terry said. "Keep expecting you to talk soft and call folks *effendi*."

"Har, you're the first tourist to make that joke."

"Tourist board requires an IQ reduction before we're allowed on planet," Terry said solemnly.

"Air doin' a helluva job," Sauud acknowledged. "See that rock?"

Terry nodded.

The clump of boots on deck told him Jerrod had seen the conference in the cockpit and come forward to include himself.

"No moving tonight," Terry said before the force sergeant could ask. "Not chancing water we can't see."

"You've got radar, sonar, search lights," Jerrod pointed out. "You can see as well at night as you can in daylight."

"You can come back and try that with your own boat," Terry advised. "Local pilot says anchor, I'm anchoring."

"Tide's peaked," Sauud explained. "There's a lot of river water backed up behind it. This creek's gonna be a sluice in an hour."

"So we dig in every time the tide goes out?" Jerrod asked.

"Daylight we could fight it," Sauud shrugged. "Jus' don't count on making way against it. Getting out of the way makes more sense: less wear and tear. At night no question, we drop all our anchors and tie up tight to the downstream side of a rock island."

Jerrod glared at the island as Terry eased the boat close, evidently blaming it for the delay.

"Force Sergeant, I'll butt up hard on the island there," Terry said, pointing to the spot he'd selected. "Tell off a couple of your men to jump ashore and tie us off."

"Look out for rock devils," Sauud warned.

"What are rock devils?" Terry asked when Jerrod had gone back to give his men their first task of the journey.

"No idea," Sauud answered.

SHOLON DELTA
SALAZAAR, BROMHEAD
FEDERATED SUNS
6 DECEMBER 3041

Terry's prediction of spectacular waterfalls had been wrong.

A roiling brown torrent churned from the base of the cliff, indistinct in the gloom. A half dozen streams of water spewed from irregularly spaced fissures that laddered up the sheer rock wall. The highest was above the shadows of the trees, emitting a long arc that glittered golden in the sunset. Looked to Terry like a giant stream of urine.

"Is it just me, or does that look like a dam about to burst?" he asked.

Sauud laughed.

"It's looked like that since Bromhead was first surveyed," he said. "None of those jets has widened a centimeter in centuries. Another few million years, there'll be nothing but rapids here, but for now the water's punched all the holes it's going to punch."

"The surface of the loch at the top of the cliffs?"

"Gawd, no. You'd see those jets shooting from here to the ocean without touching down if it had that much pressure behind it." Sauud pointed to a spot about halfway up the wall that looked no different from any other. "A dozen or so meters above that top stream, give or take. Depends on rain and season, 'course."

"Of course," Terry agreed.

As it was, the frothy brown torrent kept the bowl at the base of the cliff clear of vegetation and floating islands. Only a few rocky spires, slick with spray and lichen, held their own against the continuous onslaught and columns of falling water. It was easy to see why the river pushed so violently against the tide.

"Low tide you can see the mouth of the tunnel, but the rocks'd keep you too far from the cliff for these billies to make the jump," Sauud was explaining. "High tide you don't see anything but the jets pouring down; all these rocks are underwater. That's when it's really dangerous. Current all kinds of crazy pushing against the tide and everything glass smooth on top. Half in or half out is the only time you can see all the dangers and have enough water under your keel to do something about them." Sauud grinned. "But you better know if it's coming or going 'cause the water's backwards depending."

Terry nodded and took his eyes off the darkling water long enough for a quick glance toward the sunlit rock towering above the shadows of the trees. He wondered if it had occurred to whoever'd concocted this whole sneak-up-from-the-side-they-won't-expect scheme that an observer on top of the cliffs would be able to track every move they made through the delta swamp.

Because, of course, the objective of the Twenty-seventh Armored Recon squad *sans* armor was on the other side of the cliffs. Intel was, Jerrod had explained in an atypically expansive mood, that a special strike force of some sort was going through specialized training on the shores of Loch Sholon. Terry had made the mistake of asking Jerrod what they'd hoped to learn eyes on that they couldn't learn from paying the guys who'd sold them the first bit of information a few bills more. Jerrod had just glared at him and shut up without telling Terry what made the special strike force so special and why FedSuns special troops getting specialized training was any of their business.

Not that Terry gave a damn.

The sonar and depth finder were useless in the debris-laden churn, leaving him with only his instincts and eyes to get the boat safely across.

"North or south?" he asked.

"Left," Sauud answered. "Whirlpool on your right will suck you down."

The pilot's tone was easy, but his grip on the trim above the dash was white-knuckled. Terry suspected this particular maneuver wasn't as routine as the native was letting on.

Eyes on the water, he angled the boat toward the cliffs north of the water's main thrust. Spray from the falling jets covered them like rain. Even on the calmer side the water was a cauldron of directionless chop as currents and eddies boiled around the base of the cliff. The steel underlying the boat's hull might be up to the buffeting—he'd already written off the sierra-wood veneer—but if they tipped enough to catch a wave, the boat would swamp. Buoyancy chambers would keep them afloat, but the twin diesels couldn't breathe underwater. He didn't fancy their chances of poling a gunwale-deep hulk out of the delta, much less getting it back to port. Keeping the boat steady while the Twenty-seventh's recon squad got from the boat to the cliff was going to require skill and reflexes. Terry knew he didn't have the moves anymore, but neither did he have a choice. He mentally rehearsed contingencies trying to loosen up his neural pathways, hoping to shave a few microseconds off his reaction time.

Like that had ever helped.

"Steady," Jerrod cautioned uselessly.

Sauud glared at the soldier on Terry's behalf, leaving him free to watch the water and rocks.

Seven pops behind him, and seven lines snaked through the air. Terry had no idea what was on the ends of the climbing ropes, but all seven found purchase on the rocks above. All seven troopers gave their lines identical test tugs while Terry fought the water, then stuck their feet in stirrups on the ends of their lines and stepped off the deck together. The lines reeled in, lifting the men—practically snapping the men—up the face of the cliff.

Terry backed the boat out into less violent water—no place was calm this close to the cliff—and managed to turn it into an open channel without hitting a rock. Plan was to find a secure location, tie up and wait for the Twenty-seventh to rappel back down the cliff three days hence.

Sauud advised there was no place safe along the main river and counseled continuing to the less tumultuous north, staying close to the cliffs. Terry obediently worked the boat in that direction, following narrow channels between floating islands close to the curving cliff until he found a rock spire Sauud pronounced suitable for a protracted stay. He idled the diesels, keeping the bow snug against the moss-covered stone while Sauud pounded pitons home and tied off lines. By the time Sauud was back aboard, he'd killed the engines and secured the controls.

"Think we'll need an anchor off the stern?" he asked as the other man hopped back into the cockpit.

The last thing he saw was the swinging piton.

It was night when Terry woke, hard deck against his cheek. He listened for a long ten count, but all he heard was water rippling and the bump and scrape of the boat's hull against something hard and gritty. Probably the rock spire Sauud'd tied it to. He tried to push himself upright, but his arms and legs wouldn't answer. Of course. He cursed their damn rebellion before the pain at his wrists and ankles registered and he realized he was bound hand and foot.

"Awake, are we?" Sauud asked out of the darkness.

Terry pushed against the deck with his bound arms but got nowhere until he convinced his knees to cooperate. Twisting his torso, he rolled over to face the general direction of his captor.

"Nope," he answered.

"Let me know, then."

A dark shape moved against the lesser darkness, giving him something to focus on. Sauud was sitting on the live tank, which meant Terry was on the main deck below the cockpit facing the stern. Armed with that information, he oriented himself to the rest of the invisible boat.

"What's with knocking the crap out of me?" Terry asked. "If you wanted me tied up, threatening to knock the crap out of me would have worked as well."

"Didn't know that, did I?" Sauud answered. "You've got a dozen kilos on me and what ain't muscle looks like it used to be. Wasn't going to chance my pretty face on you taking exception."

Terry didn't bother arguing the point.

"So I take it the Jerrod party was expected?" he said instead.

"The Jerrod party was invited."

Terry rolled on his back, bound feet flat against the deck and tried to find a comfortable position.

"Of course the brass was hoping for something a little larger," Sauud volunteered. "They didn't count on damn Taurian balls—sending a squad to do a platoon's job."

Terry made a sympathetic noise and pushed slowly with his legs. There was a gear box with various tools useful for fishing about a meter beyond his head. If he got close enough without Sauud hearing him, he could probably find something useful to do with one of the filleting knives.

"I'm wearing night goggles," Sauud said.

"Ah." Terry stopped inching toward the gear box. "So why was a Taurian recon squad invited to Bromhead?"

"We needed some fresh gear." Sauud shifted his weight like he'd been sitting too long. Terry wondered how long he'd been out. "Everything we have is a generation or two old."

"You should have asked," Terry said in his best is-that-all-it-is. "I know a great militia surplus shop over on Mandalay Cay. Get you anything you want wholesale."

"Should have asked," Sauud agreed.

"So what now?"

"So we wait until sunrise; about an hour."

"Why don't you get some shuteye?" Terry suggested. "I'll take this watch."

"I'm good."

After careful consideration of his options, Terry rolled to his side and settled in to try for fifty-five minutes of sleep. Whatever daylight brought he wanted to be fresh enough to make the most of it.

SHOLON DELTA
SALAZAAR, BROMHEAD
FEDERATED SUNS
7 DECEMBER 3041

The shadowed cliffs were lavender, clashing with the orange morning sky above them when Sauud nudged Terry awake with his foot.

Judging by his captor's haggard look, Terry figured snagging a nap had been the right choice. The formerly tame native guide was standing over him with a flat, wicked looking knife and a ration pack. He extended his arms, and Sauud sliced the rope with a flick of his wrist. Terry noted the lack of effort; there were few legitimate uses for a knife that cut like a scalpel.

"Got a climb ahead of us," Sauud said, tossing the ration pack.

"Not going to happen," Terry said.

He pushed himself upright and scooted until he could lean his back on the cabin. The ration pack was of the high protein recovery sort and tasted like packing material that may have come in contact with food once. Sauud handed him a water bottle before he asked.

"You're going to climb even if it's only because you staying alive makes my job harder," Sauud said. He turned his head, showing Terry an earphone and mic rig hooked over his ear. "I'm talking to a platoon of Second Davion Infantry up top. Their snipers have you covered."

"Right."

Sauud sighed.

"See the bumper on the rock?"

Terry followed Sauud's thumb and saw a float perched on the rock spire the boat was tied to. The little island was taller than it had been, telling Terry the tide was low. If Sauud gave any signal, Terry missed it, but he didn't miss the float exploding. A half second later the flat report of a rifle echoed down the cliff face.

"They drop some lines," Sauud explained, "I cut your legs free, and we climb."

"I don't," Terry said.

"Why the hell not?"

"Bad water."

"What?"

Terry met his gaze a long three count, trying to look immovable while he thought. He hadn't meant to answer straight, but now that it was out, he had to think what to say next.

"Sorry, Brisbane expression," he shrugged. "Means I can't keep my balance. Reflexes are screwed, too. Poacher split my head open in twenty-six and gave me what they call a TBI. Hits me like epilepsy sometimes. If the only other option is climb that cliff, go ahead and shoot me now." Terry forced himself to take another bite of the ration. "Clean bullet's a better death than falling onto these rocks."

"You get that?" Sauud asked.

It took Terry a heartbeat to realize he was speaking into his mic.

Twenty minutes later he was on top of the cliff and two of the Second Davion's finest were untangling him from the sling they'd used to haul him up.

"What's this, then?" asked another soldier.

Terry couldn't read Fed rank patches, but the guy asking the questions had two *v*'s on his sleeve, and everyone else had various combinations of straight bars, so he was probably in charge. Terry pegged him for a platoon sergeant; he didn't have officer stink.

"This is the boatman I told you about," Sauud answered. No 'sir,' which Terry guessed meant either same rank or outside the command structure. "Tucked a patrol boat right up under Hell's Spigot like he was parking a ground car."

"Thought you said that couldn't be done."

"It can't," Sauud agreed. "Plan was to let them try their dumbass suicide scheme, then steer them here when they gave up. Didn't count on this one pulling it off like he was bored with it. I signaled fast as I could."

"Not fast enough," the assumed sergeant said, but more like it was information than compliant. "We were out of position. Second Platoon's hunting them down."

He turned to Terry, who was busy trying to stand easy between two troopers and not think of the long drop one step behind him.

"I was going to ask what the Taurians were thinking letting an old man with a brain injury drive their boat, but Sauud's pretty well covered that," the soldier said. "Who are you?"

"Terrence Henderson, Brisbane Maritime Constabulary, retired," Terry said in his best name-rank-and-identification-code manner.

"Maritime Constabulary? Like boating safety and fishing laws?"

"Poachers mostly," Terry agreed. "Plus the odd smuggler and the rare band of water pirates robbing tourists, stuff like that."

"According to their sergeant, Henderson here had to be forced to come on this mission," Sauud said. "Some sort of threat against his family was involved. He's essentially a noncombatant cooperating under duress—and he gave them grief every chance he got. Didn't seem right to kill him."

"But is that any reason to keep him?"

The updraft following the cliff face sent a chill up Terry's spine. "He could be a source of useful intel on Brisbane."

"Thought you spooks were only interested in industrial centers like New Vandenberg and Laconis," the soldier with the _v_'s said, packing a lot of information he should have kept to himself in one sentence.

Terry tried not to be too obvious about pretending he'd missed it.

For his part, the soldier completely missed Sauud's glare. He jerked his head, and the pair framing Terry shoved him forward—away from the abyss.

The trip from the edge of the cliff to the Feds' compound was an hour and a half of steep trails down rocks and through dense woods. Terry impressed everyone by staggering several times and falling twice before they cut a tree branch to fit and let him use it as a staff. Handing him a perfectly serviceable quarterstaff said a lot about how much threat the Second Davions thought their prisoner was.

As Terry had expected, the Sholon Valley was a near-perfect volcanic crater, clearly the taller half of an extinct double-cone. The loch itself was beautiful, a placid expanse of indigo water that seemed a world away from the swampy delta below and gave lie to Bromhead's reputation as a desert planet.

The compound was laid out like any temporary base and nestled between the dense lower woods and the last fringe of trees before the shore of the loch. Collapsible hard-wall tents in neat rows with a pair of bigger modular structures facing each other across an open space big enough for a couple of companies to muster just inside the gate facing the water. The whole was enclosed by a fence line strung more to mark boundaries than defend anything and four turnpike gates that couldn't have stopped a determined cyclist. The Feds were either very certain of their safety or the whole setup was a trap.

Given recent events, Terry suspected the latter.

This suspicion was supported by the presence of a stockade in the very center of the camp. Metal poles and a three-meter-tall mesh of razor wire enclosed an open structure that looked maybe big enough to shield a platoon from the sun while offering no concealment. That it was empty told Terry the Second Davion's Second Platoon was having no luck finding Force Sergeant Jerrod and company.

At first Terry saw nothing unusual about the camp itself beyond a vague certainty something was off. Then what he was looking at registered. Only his escorts were kitted out in proper FedSuns gear; everyone else wore Taurian colors. There were no unit insignias in evidence, but Concordat badging and banners were everywhere. The cut of the uniforms wasn't quite right and some of the small arms were wrong—evidently FedSuns approximations—but overall the effect was unmistakably Taurian. They'd never pass for mainline troops, but in any other setting Terry would have taken them for second-string planetary constabulary without thinking twice.

He staggered sideways, barely catching himself with his staff. Sauud caught his other arm with a steadying hand.

"Sorry," Terry said.

"That crack I gave you screwed you up, didn't it?" Sauud asked.

"Friendly won't help," Terry said. "I'm no source of Brisbane info, and I've never been anywhere else."

"That was smoke for the uniforms," Sauud assured him. "You've been mis-stepping and second-guessing all the way down the hill. Your bad water acting up?"

"A bit," Terry confessed. "Unless there are two of you, my eyesight's gone double and the ground looks like I'm about to step into a trough."

"Sergeant," Sauud confirmed Terry's earlier guess about shoulder v's. "We're taking him to the infirmary."

"I'm good," Terry protested. "Just need some sleep."

"Sleep with a head injury isn't smart."

"What the hell do you care?"

From his expression the infantry sergeant wanted to ask the same question, but he marched past the stockade without a word, making for one of the larger buildings on the far side of the camp. Inside, the structure was a hollow box with partitions of heavy fabric that didn't reach the ceiling creating the illusion of rooms. Sauud, the sergeant, and two troopers led Terry past a group of desks manned by clerks who didn't look up and down a narrow hallway to a space set off by heavy curtains.

They'd taken his tree branch, so Terry kept himself oriented and on course by dragging his fingers along the partitions. His hands were dirty from his falls and sticky with sap; he hoped the stains annoyed somebody.

Behind the curtain the infirmary turned out to be a square space with four beds, each with its own free-standing privacy screen, a desk, four cabinets painted white, a refrigerator, and the first woman in uniform Terry had seen on Bromhome.

He smiled his most charming smile but spoiled whatever effect it might have had by collapsing against the refrigerator and falling into the nearest bed.

Sauud murmured quickly to the doctor as she sat Terry back up and shined lights in his eyes and pinched and poked him to see if and when he twitched. She felt his head, listened to his heart, and thumped him a few times, evidently for her own amusement, before answering.

"He said his TBI symptoms sometimes mimicked epilepsy?" she asked Sauud as though she didn't think Terry could answer. "That may be what this is, a reaction to stress and exertion. There's definitely something up with his nerves, but it's not recent trauma. Your hit on the head may have been the precipitating event, but this is not a concussion."

"So what do we do?" Sauud asked.

The doctor pulled a key down from the top of the refrigerator and opened the double door. Terry glimpsed a company's worth of new-planet vaccinations and as many vitamin boosters arranged in neat rows. She selected one of the vitamin packs and dropped it in an injection gun before answering.

"Dose him with nutrients, get him on a saline drip to keep him hydrated, and let him rest," she said, putting the key back on top of the fridge. "He's had fifteen years of dealing with this, so I'm betting when he said he needed sleep, he knew what he was talking about."

Terry took his shot and cooperated half-heartedly with getting undressed and cleaned up; leaning heavily on Sauud as necessary. He lay back obediently while the intravenous line was plugged into his arm and the medical monitors were taped to his chest. But he protested loudly when she started to attach the catheter.

Sauud caught his shoulders when he tried to sit up and pushed him back to the mattress. "Never argue with a woman holding your balls," he advised.

"I'm not—" the doctor began, then evidently recognized she was in the presence of humor.

"I don't need a damn catheter," Terry said.

"You aren't steady enough to make it to the head on your own, and by your own assessment you're going to be sleeping soundly for several hours," the doctor countered. "I don't want to have to change a urine-soaked bed with an unconscious—or worse, semiconscious and protesting—soldier in it."

"Game warden," Sauud corrected.

Terry let the misidentification pass. He also decided the doctor had a point and shut up.

"I've counted seventeen scars from evident blade injuries," she said, changing the subject. "Does being a game warden involve a lot of knife fights?"

"Knives, fishing spears, whatever's handy," Terry answered. "Poachers aren't big on firearms—they scare the fish."

The doctor pulled the sheet up to Terry's chest.

"I suppose your own physician has cautioned you about skin cancer," she said. "You've had a lot of sun."

"I've had sixty years on the water."

"Well, you might want to consider a more potent sunscreen."

Terry slid a glance at Sauud, who rolled his eyes.

"Can you put something in that to help me sleep?" Terry asked the doctor, nodding toward the bag of saline solution hanging on the mobile IV stand. "I get furious headaches."

"I can add a mild analgesic," she answered, "but without knowing more about your condition, I'm not going to risk a sedative."

Terry nodded and let his eyes drift shut as she turned away—presumably to get some sort of mild painkiller to shoot into his line. He heard Sauud hanging about, discussed his prognosis and generally trying to make small talk with the doctor. He thought about Maria, working to raise his pulse while feigning sleep.

Sure enough, the doctor noticed, helped out by the heart monitor's concerned beep. She felt his head, checked his breathing and finally picked up one of his arms experimentally and let it drop. Of course it was completely limp.

"I don't know if that's normal for his condition or not," she said to Sauud. "There's no reason why an injury that affects balance would elevate the heart rate."

Sauud eventually quit trying to chat up the doctor and left.

Terry continued to play opossum while the doctor treated someone for a minor injury, dispensed cold medication, and assessed the progress of a mending joint injury. He used the catheter once as a test. The doctor changed the urine bag herself, telling him there was no nurse to provide an extra set of hands—or eyes. He couldn't keep his heart beating fast the entire time, which was fine. Every half hour or so he focused on sex or politics or why the hell he was flat on his back in a Fed infirmary until the heart monitor beeped an alert. After the fourth or fifth false alarm, the doctor quit checking his vitals and turned the beeper off.

And eventually, after laying a hand on his forehead and listening to his heart and breathing and clucking over the monitor tape with its random spikes in his heart rate one last time, she went to lunch.

After several minutes of silence, Terry "woke" with a start and sat up. Staring around in confusion, he looked in every direction until he was sure there were no security cameras. At least none he could see. That was a risk he was going to have to take.

Climbing out of bed, he towed the medical monitor and IV rig with him as he searched the infirmary. The heart monitor dutifully recorded that his pulse was going through another one of its unexplained hurried phases. Each of the three medical supply cabinets he tried was locked, and in all three cases, the key for each was right on top. Terry didn't know about the fourth, because he found what he was looking for in the third. Taking the large syringe, he locked the cabinet and made his way back to his bed next to the refrigerator. Deciding to take a chance, he unlocked the fridge and propped the door open.

Then he sat on the edge of his bed and started looking for an inconspicuous vein.

It was full dark when Terry awoke, having fallen legitimately asleep after his exertion. "You're a lot of work, Constable," Jerrod said.

"You know this is a trap," Terry answered.

"With the big show they made of walking our one ticket out of here past the stockade and leaving him obviously unguarded in an unsecured building at the edge of camp?" Jerrod asked. "We never suspected a thing."

He grabbed Terry's arm and shoved something into his hands. Terry recognized night goggles and put them on before unhooking himself from the various machines. The urine bag was full again; the doctor had made the right call. Jerrod gave him enough time to get his pants on and shove his bare feet into his boat shoes before hustling him out of the infirmary and into the hall.

Terry counted four still forms sprawled awkwardly about the hall, their unfired weapons next to them, before they made it to the slit in the back wall. He considered asking for a knife of his own but decided he was better off unarmed. At least that way the soldiers knew he needed protection.

The moon glow filtering through the overcast was blinding after the gloom of the building. Terry squinted and made out all seven of the Chasseur scouts were present, though one was limping slightly and another was holding an arm tight against his middle. They paused long enough to move the last of the still forms out of casual sight before heading out. Terry counted twelve.

There was one prisoner. Terry was not surprised to see Sauud, gagged and with his arms bound thoroughly to his torso, being held on a short leash. Without night goggles the spy, or whatever his pay voucher called him, was also close to blind in the overcast night.

Terry took the leash and Sauud's arm and directed him after the point man as the squad made its way through the shadows.

The trail he had marked with his stumbles and falls coming down the hill was not as clear to night goggles as it would have been in daylight, but he remembered the way well enough without the markers. They were near the brow of the ridge when the camp below them suddenly erupted with light and sound.

"Assuming they know exactly where we're going, we have maybe an hour before they catch us," Terry said.

"You're assuming they don't have VTOL assets."

Terry didn't bother answering as he pushed Sauud ahead of him up the last stages of the trail. The agent was blowing through his nose, obviously struggling to breathe around the gag. Considering how out of breath he was from the forced march, Terry didn't doubt Sauud was close to passing out.

"Want to cut this one's gag?" he asked. "I don't fancy carrying his dead weight."

Without a word one of the troopers slid a knife under the gag against Sauud's cheek and sliced the narrow strip of fabric. Terry steadied his former captor as Sauud bent double to spit and cough and force the wad of cloth out of his mouth with his tongue. No way he was going to touch the soggy mass.

"I tried to help you," Sauud croaked.

"You pretended you were helping me so I'd drop my guard while you were setting me up as bait," Terry corrected. He pushed Sauud forward, covering the last few meters to the point where the Second Davion had hauled him to the top of the cliff. "But don't you worry none. I'll make sure they leave you alive right here where your boys will find you."

"You can't leave me behind," Sauud countered. "You need me to guide you out of the swamp."

"Water'll do that," Terry said. "Full moon going down means there'll be a spring tide running for the ocean about the time we make the boat. All we have to do is follow the water. A quick ride in that sluice you were talking about until we'll be clear in no time."

"You can do that?" Jerrod asked. "Whole reason we brought him along—"

"Was I told you how important a local guide was to getting through the swamp," Terry said. "Every word was true. But trusting this joker now is more dangerous than going without him."

"I'm tied up," Sauud protested. "If you go down, I'll drown."

"And dying to scuttle us would just be doing your duty," Terry pointed out. "Nobody'd expect less of you. 'Course you could do as good just by getting us lost long enough for any choppers your buddies might have to find us."

Terry turned to Jerrod. "I can get us back to the main channel easily enough, then we just ride the tide out," he explained. "It'll be a fast ride. We have to keep enough way relative to the current to navigate and avoid hazards."

"You don't have the reflexes to pull that off," Sauud accused. "Your bad water won't let you."

Every man in the squad froze. "You have bad water?"

Night goggles to night goggles, it was impossible to read the force sergeant's expression, but the tone of his voice spoke volumes.

"Yeah," Terry admitted. "I'll need help getting down the cliff. But once I'm at the wheel, I can get us out of this swamp."

Jerrod hesitated, looking to Sauud. Terry wondered what the Fed made of the scene, dark shapes conversing in the gloom.

"I can sneak us back into the port, too," Terry added.

Jerrod grunted.

"The hard part will be getting from the waterfront into the DropPort, and that's your worry," Terry pressed his point. "Now leave this joker sit, and get me down to my boat so I can do my job."

"Yes, sir," Jerrod answered.

SHOLON DELTA
SALAZAAR, BROMHEAD
FEDERATED SUNS
8 DECEMBER 3041

Knowing his boat would never leave Bromhead, Terry tried to be philosophical about the sierra-wood veneer, but he winced and cringed with every jar and bump as they raced the tide to the sea. Soon enough the scrapes were metal on stone, letting him know there was no wood below the waterline. Shooting a rapid almost holed the steel as they slammed sideways into an underwater ridge that sprang up too fast for the sonar to see coming.

The muddy water was black to the night goggles, the foam silver, and the overhanging trees surreal dream shapes that seemed to whip past as they plunged downstream. Beside him Jerrod clung to the windscreen and binnacle, glaring ahead as though trying to intimidate the flood. Terry didn't waste a glance behind, but the grim silence told him the rest of the squad was hanging on and staying out of his way to let him do his job. For that he was grateful.

They were clear of the swamp in less than a quarter of the time it had taken to work their way up to the cliffs. With the sun rising behind them, Terry could see a golden band of foam in the brown sediment stream. Tide was at its lowest ebb, and waves were breaking against the submerged outer rim of the collapsed volcano, the barrier that made the insane delta behind them possible. The way out was a clear gap directly ahead.

Throwing the wheel over, Terry turned south, skirting the edge of the swamp. Weaving among the floating islands of trees, hugging the shore for what cover he could find, Terry opened the throttles. Hydrofoils Sauud didn't know about deployed, and the boat skated away from the seaport at speeds guaranteed to defeat any search pattern. Riding the foils, they could skim over the barrier at any point once the tide started making again, and he was betting there was a good spot at the southern end of the crescent.

His lie that the recon squad was going out the same way they'd come in was Terry's final gift to Sauud. Jerrod had let the Fed live so that last bit of disinformation would get to whoever came after them, give them that much more time to get clear. Sauud had used him, but he'd been decent in the process; Terry figured they were square.

A shuttle had been hidden a day's fast sailing south of the delta before Jerrod and company had dropped by the hacienda to pick Terry up. They'd be at the extraction point while the Feds were still trying to determine if they'd died in the delta or were skulking their way north beneath the cliffs. Then it would be scuttle the boat, another bumpy ride up a cliff face in a sling, and away to the JumpShip they hoped hadn't been discovered at its pirate point.

Terry leaned against his perch, listening to the satisfied rumble of the wide-open Royce diesels and feeling the vibration of their harnessed power through the deck. Watching the water, he let his boat enjoy her last run.

LANDFALL, NORTHERN ARCHIPELAGO
BRISBANE
TAURIAN CONCORDAT
29 DECEMBER 3041

"Allah frickin' Christ, Henderson," Thompson swore.

Terry looked up to see the boatmaster standing at the other side of the bistro table glowering down at him.

"Now there's a new image to try and forget," Terry said, turning back to watch the harbor. "And it *is* good to be back, Bobby. Thanks for asking."

"I heard Jerrod's report, third hand, but I heard it," Thompson said. "You told him you have bad water?"

Terry lifted his cup of cold coffee a few fingers from the table. He let Thompson see the tremor before he set it back down.

"Damn it, Henderson. You should have said something."

"I told you I didn't have much time."

"But you didn't say *why*—" He cut himself off. "Your son doesn't know."

Terry didn't bother answering.

"Does your wife know?"

"You don't understand how marriage works, do you Bobby?" Terry shook his head. "Of course Maria knows. I cried in her arms for three nights straight after I found out."

"So," Thompson began, then paused as he evidently tried to work out how to continue the sentence. "What are you doing about it?"

"Using condoms," Terry answered. "It's only supposed to be passed by blood transfusion or open wounds, but we're not taking any chances. You have no idea how much I miss deep kissing."

"You damn ass. You know what I mean."

"I'm doing all I can do, Bobby. I'm living my life as fast as I can." Terry kept his eyes on the water. "Trying to be as much a father as I can in the thirteen or fourteen months I have left. Give the boy something to remember besides pushing me around in a wheelchair for the next twenty years."

"Y'know, there's a lot of good people working on Brisbane virus—"

"Brisbane virus is a blood-borne pathogen of unknown origin that attacks the central nervous system. Symptoms are similar to multiple sclerosis or Parkinson's disease, often leading to misdiagnosis in its early stages," Terry cut him off, quoting the standard cautionary pamphlet in falsely cheerful tones. "Colloquially known as 'bad water,' Brisbane virus requires hemoglobin to survive, making it difficult to transmit—so casual infection is all but impossible."

"Stop it," Thompson said.

"Brisbane virus is not lethal, but is aggressive; degradation of the nervous system is rapid. In all known cases victims lose mobility and fine motor control within twenty to twenty-eight months," Terry continued. "Research is ongoing, but to date Brisbane virus remains impervious to all known antiviral regimens."

Thompson stood for a long count, looking down at Terry looking out over the harbor. "What the hell you doing at the public marina, Constable?"

"Waiting for the ferry to Long Keys," Terry answered. "I figure a couple of days on someone else's boat will calm my nerves."

"Screw that," Thompson said. "C'mon. The *Tucumcari* can get you home for supper."

"Sounds suspiciously like misappropriation of a government vessel for personal purposes, Boatmaster."

Thompson snorted.

Terry picked up his kit and rose. For a moment the pier swayed and he had to shuffle to keep his balance. Thompson reached out a steadying hand, but Terry stopped him with a glare.

"Touch me and you swallow teeth."

"You know you could have told anyone at any time after we left your son," Thompson said conversationally as they made their way along the waterfront to the Constabulary docks. "In fact you should have. Brisbane virus earns you a permanent quarantine from interplanetary travel. Come to think of it, you should have a medical record. We never would have knocked on your door." He shook his head. "The doctor who didn't report that diagnosis is going to lose his license."

"He already did," Terry said. "Something about selling tourists recreational pharmaceuticals."

Thompson chuckled. "How is Illya?"

"Good," Terry said. "Got a shop on Mandalay Cay tricked out like a shaman's hut. Does steady trade selling tourists all-natural homeopathic hangover remedies, aphrodisiacs, and magical fish lures."

"I heard he was running a free clinic for locals."

"That, too."

They walked a while in silence, working their way through the crowds of tourists hunting charter fishing boats or sea taxis to whatever resort they'd booked for the season. Terry tried not to think too much about the money he would be making if he still had a boat. He said as much to Thompson.

"Jerrod says anybody else at the wheel would have left them dead in the swamp," the boatmaster answered. "He's advocating for the Twenty-seventh to buy you a new boat."

"Won't be in time for this season," Terry pointed out.

"So the way I got the story," Thompson said a few steps later. "Jerrod heard you had Brisbane virus from that Judas goat Saudi."

"Sauud," Terry corrected. "Yeah. He surprised me with a straight question and I answered without thinking. He didn't speak Brisbane, so I was able to pass 'bad water' off as a balance problem caused by you splitting my skull open with a pike."

"How many times you going to bring that up?" Thompson asked. "I said I was sorry and I made sure you got the max medical pension, didn't I?"

"I'll bet you look where you're swinging, too."

"You still haven't answered why you didn't tell anyone you had bad water before you got off Brisbane."

"I didn't give a damn about the mission," Terry said. "But once they laid it all out, I saw they were going to need a good boatman if they were going to pull it off."

"So you just went for the challenge of it?"

"Yeah."

"Yeah," Thompson repeated, stretching the word out.

The sentry at the Constabulary wharf saluted Thompson and waved Terry through. Planetary defense had been put on alert since

Jerrod's report, and only one missile cruiser was in port. From the swarming stevedores, Terry guessed it was about to join the rest of the fleet crisscrossing the open seas. A water world required special defenses.

"We're not going to stop them, y'know," Thompson said, following Terry's gaze. "The Feds lured in the Twenty-seventh so they could break our people down for current ID protocols and the like. Aside from that, they're ready to go. Someday soon—maybe even right now—they're going to drop in on New Vandy looking like they're from Laconis or show up on MacLeod's Land looking like Pinarders and talk their way through the outer defenses." He shook his head. "They'll do a hell of a lot of damage before the Planetary Constabulary knows what hit them."

"Seems like a convoluted scheme to hit one world," Terry said.

"Oh, it's a trick they can use over and over again," Thompson answered. "They just have to wait a few months for local defenders to calm down and then do it again.

"All we'll ever be able to do is hit back."

The *Tucumcari* was at the end of the last dock, dwarfed by the cruiser. Terry stopped, taking in the cutter's clean lines against the backdrop of the busy harbor.

"I already hit back."

"What?"

"I told Jerrod, but I didn't spell it out," Terry looked at Thompson. "From what you're saying, it's not in his report. But I figure he'll get it sooner or later."

"Told him what?"

"That I was alone with the Feds' medical supplies, a syringe, and my own blood for a good forty minutes."

Thompson swore.

"I didn't think I was going to make it out of that camp," Terry said. "I knew for damn sure one recon patrol wasn't going to stop whatever hurt they were going to do."

"You didn't."

"Every trooper they send at us is going to get the regulation vitamin booster and broad spectrum inoculation," Terry confirmed. "That covert company of the Davions might get in a few good raids in; might do some real damage."

He looked out over the water again. "But two years from now, they're not going to have a man standing."

THE LOYAL SON

BLAINE LEE PARDOE

GALESBURG
NORTH AMERICAN CONTINENT
TERRA
14 MARCH 3068

The visit to Galesburg had been his sister's idea, hoping it would take his mind off matters. He hadn't seen her in over a year and was not in the mood to challenge her on her choice of tourist venues. Junior Precentor Raul Tinker had not seen Dana since she had gone to Terra to continue her studies. She had wanted to go there since it was the birthplace of Jerome Blake, the visionary founder of the Word of Blake. Raul had always thought of Blake as nothing more than a man, but the Order believed he was some sort of seer, a man that had foreseen the future and had acted to preserve mankind. Raul didn't question the beliefs that the members of the Order touted about Blake. Everyone was entitled to their own belief system. If people wanted to believe that Jerome Blake was a mystic or oracle, then they should go ahead and do that.

Raul had been on Terra for a few months after postings to training facilities on two other worlds. Since had had arrived he had been going through extensive training in insurgency operations, unconventional warfare, espionage, demolition, etc., sitting through a seemingly endless series of tactical briefings and taking part in training exercises. He had come to the cradle of humanity, and so far all he had seen of it had been from the inside of the Bachelor's Office Quarters and from a conference room window. There was no such thing as free time. He had come for an assignment, a training command of some sort, but none had been provided. Instead what he found after being on Terra his first few confusing days had been pure chaos.

Now it seemed that the chaos had a name: "Jihad." Not just a war, but a holy war—waged against the Word.

The first news reports didn't seem to make sense. From throughout the Inner Sphere, stories had emerged that were startling, dark, and disturbing. But Raul's superiors in the Word of Blake did not seem surprised or shaken at all. There was, instead, a sense of dismay. The Word of Blake had wanted nothing more than to join the Star League. Suddenly it had turned into war, a war that none of the leadership seemed to want. A nuclear disaster on Tharkad was merely an accident, but ComStar media portrayed it as a surprise attack. Mistakes *had* been made by the Word of Blake, the leadership had admitted as such, but the Order was a victim, only trying to preserve the Star League and defend itself.

News reports indicated that every one of the major House governments had suddenly turned on each other. Mercenary troops, who had fed off of the rotting corpse of the Inner Sphere for centuries, were now lashing out at innocent civilians or other Houses. War seemed to be erupting everywhere at once. Some of these attacks were aimed at framing the Word of Blake for it all; that much was obvious.

The official line was that the Word of Blake was responding with the harshest possible measures to protect itself. Outreach had been reduced to a charred cinder. The Order had not started the chain of events on that accursed world, but they had certainly ended it. From Raul's perspective, it served the Wolf's Dragoons right. With them running loose, any chance at establishing order in the Inner Sphere was going to be difficult; the Dragoons had been a thorn in the Order's side for years in the Chaos March, his old home. The Order was responding swiftly and decisively, he had been assured of that by his superiors. The Dragoons' destruction gave him a feeling of confidence, as if they were in control of the situation. Mercenary scum and House lords might try to make the Order appear as some sort of dark villain in these matters, but Raul knew otherwise. The Word of Blake would bring order out of the pandemonium by restoring the Star League.

The war was all the buzz, not just in the media and between individuals on the streets. There was talk of what the Word of Blake was doing to establish stability. Rumors abounded about wonder weapons, new BattleMechs, and other devices the Order was using to bring an end to the fighting. He had heard reports of a division's worth of cyborg troops being deployed—here, on Terra. It was disturbing, but at the same time he was glad that the Word had such special troops at its disposal. There were so many enemies lashing out at them, so having the technological edge was going to be important for survival.

The more hard-line members of the Order were quoting the Master, a mysterious religious figure, saying that the war had been started by the major powers—but would be ended by the Word of Blake. There were plenty of rumors running amok about the Master, that he was a reincarnation of Jerome Blake himself or some sort of John the Baptist figure. Almost overnight there were groups of people that seemed to all but worship him (including through cyborg "elite soldiers"). Precentor Martial Cameron St. Jamais didn't deny the existence of the Master. Some rumors even suggested that St. Jamais was the Master himself.

The Master apparently was nominally in charge of the Word of Blake, or at least some part of it, though nothing official had been said. With the precentor martial not denying the Master and the loss of Precentor William Blane, for now it seemed that the Master was, at the least, maintaining order amidst the chaos. Whether he was the precentor martial, or a fantasy cooked up by what remained of the Ruling Conclave in Hilton Head, Raul did not know or particularly care; strong leadership was needed, and it was there. The hard-liners got on his nerves a little, but it was something he suppressed and kept quiet about. Most of them seemed to hold the real reins of power in the Order. They seemed obsessed with reading messages sent by the Master, attempting to interpret hidden meanings in his every word. Everyone needs something to believe in...and if they wanted to worship technology or a "shadow prophet," that was fine by him.

To Raul it didn't matter who was in charge of the Order. He didn't care if this Master was real or not, or if he was the one leading the Word of Blake. What mattered was that the Word of Blake was instituting order where chaos reigned. His loyalty was unwavering. As he had told his sister Phreda, "All I care about is that someone is in charge who knows what they are doing." Politics be damned. Only people with too much time on their hands cared about mysticism, religion, or politics. Raul didn't have that kind of free time. All that mattered to him was his obligation to the Order.

It was a debt he was eager to pay back. *When my family was lost, they gave us hope and a new life...my service is the least of my debt to them.* Since he had arrived on Terra, he had met many others who had the same feelings. The Order had reached out to many families all over the Inner Sphere and given them a chance to hope and dream again. Many sons and daughters were arriving each day to fulfill their duties, to pay back debts they owed. It was reassuring to see that he was not alone. He was part of a larger family willing to take decisive action to protect itself and innocent people.

He had applied for posting to a frontline unit, to be sent back to Chaos March or some other world to punish those who would paint his family as murderers. Instead, his superiors told him to be patient, that they had a special posting in mind for him. Raul waited, sitting in on briefings, offering what help he could, wondering when he would be assigned. *Why train me if they had no intention of using me?*

Then the news broke—a ComStar task force had entered the Terran system. He had been in class when the word came and immediately volunteered to be posted to a militia unit. His instructor disregarded the offer: "There's no way any of their ships will even reach the planet." The fight, from all indications, was taking place in the cold darkness of space. His instructor, Junior Precentor Thanes, was so confident that he had even sent him out on leave. Raul didn't want to go; he wanted to be there in case he could help—in case he could contribute. But when his sister Dana contacted him to ask about a visit, he accepted the leave his instructor had offered. After all, from what he was being told, the fight was nowhere near the planet. Besides, he had come to Terra, he should take some time to see it. Still, he found himself looking up the sky every so often.

The line of tourists and faithful seemed odd. Relative peace reigned. Here, for the moment, was an island in a sea of chaos. *The people here are so lucky they don't even comprehend it.*

The birthplace of Jerome Blake, the founder of ComStar, was impossible to see from this point in the queue. The long lines were marked with water stations along the way to help quench the thirsts of the faithful. The faithful. Raul saw them in the line, hundreds of people within his view. Most were oddly excited. To him this was equivalent to visiting a museum of some sort, but to many this was a pilgrimage. It was a side of the Word of Blake he knew existed but did not think much about. A part of him wondered if he was missing something. *Are they experiencing something that I should be?* Then he saw Dana's eyes. She too was excited. The excitement quelled her normal impatience. She told him how happy she was he could share this moment with her.

With all of this talk about the Master, he wondered if such a tourist attraction would be built in his name someday.

They shuffled along the long line leading to the home where Jerome Blake had lived. Historic markers pointed to obviously re-created buildings that were part of Blake's childhood. There was the small library where Blake had first developed his love of technology, the school where he had first attended his formal learning. People pointed, some took holophotos. With each one, Raul felt a sense of absence. These people were part of the same order he was, but they were full of energy and a euphoric excitement he was lacking. It tugged at him. He wished, if only for a few minutes, that he understood what and why they felt they way they did.

Raul's communicator buzzed in his forearm pocket. The screen pulsed red with the sword-symbol for the Word of Blake. Red meant emergency. He knew instantly something was wrong. He held his thumb down for verification and saw the image of one of the command staff speaking as the text scrolled under him. "TerraSec Command orders all ground commanders to report immediately to the nearest militia units. It was hoped that our space defenses would force the ComStar units approaching Terra to break off their assault. The surviving units are currently inbound with approach vectors all over the planet. We are at Condition One.

"All units are formally mobilized. All personnel are to report to their commands or the closest military units for immediate assignment. You are to contact TerraSec Command as soon as possible for details.

"ComStar's Jihad against the Order ends here—once and for all." Raul keyed in his authorization code. The message was sent, but there was nothing but a wheel icon spinning indicating that his message was in queue. There had to be thousands like him on Terra who were signaling in, ready to go into the fight wherever it was.

Dana stared at him. "What is it?"

"War," he said. His eyes darted up to the skies. This assault must have caught command unprepared. Now they were responding haphazardly. *Damn it all to hell.*

Then there was a stirring all along the line. People were pulling out and checking personal communicators. The relatively quiet shuffle seemed to grow to a low rumble, a murmur of tense conversations. Dana did not have time to respond as the newsflash came to her personal communicator giving the public the news. *They must have really thought they would drive them back...otherwise they never would have let me go on leave.*

Her face reddened with anger. "ComStar," she said the word as if it were bitter in her mouth. "How could it have come to this? I thought our fleet had defeated them?"

"We call it the Fog of War," he said glancing back at his noteputer, hoping for a response. None yet.

"They have to be made to pay for this," she spat.

He looked up in the air, half expecting to see DropShips whizzing overhead. "I am sure they have paid a high price already." His communicator buzzed again and he saw a junior precentor on the screen, a young redhead. "Junior Precentor Raul Tinker?"

"Yes."

"We show you in Michigan, correct?"

"Yes."

There was a pause as she checked several screens in front of her. "Most of the fighting is in the southwest of North America. There is one landing near you though, in the Indiana province, near the Ohio border. This one's odd. Either they are on some sort of raid or they are way off course from the rest of the assault landings. I am sending you the coordinates now.

"Do you have orders for me?"

"There's a TerraSec reserve militia command in Ann Arbor, that would be your closest one," she replied not even looking at him as she spoke. "Their CO has not reported in yet. I am sending you their coordinates. Report there for immediate duty."

Before he could respond the screen went blank.

"Ann Arbor," he said as if dazed. "I have to head to Ann Arbor. There are Com Guard troops on the ground not far from there, apparently."

He paused. If they came here they had to have a reason. Military troops don't just drop without a reason. "What facilities are there that the troops might be moving on?"

Dana looked at him with a cross of confusion and irritation. He understood, she was feeling violated by ComStar's incursion and he was not feeling the same way. "Look, Dana, I have to know why these troops are here if we're going to have a chance of stopping them."

His words clearly resonated with her. She stiffened as if a bolt of electricity had zapped her. "Where I work...the genetic research facility near Ann Arbor, that must be where they are heading. Their ship must have been forced to land short. There's nothing of any *real* value anywhere else nearby."

He knew his sister worked in genetics. She had always been a child prodigy of sorts, but her working in a facility that might warrant being a military target surprised him. *She's even smarter than I thought...* Raul shook his head. "It must be something else, a strategic target. Genetics research is not a high enough priority to have them send in combat troops."

His sister shook her head. Her face grew stone-like. With one hand she reached out to his shoulder and leaned into him to keep her voice from traveling. "No, Raul, you have to trust me. There is work going on in that facility that is of the highest military value to the Order. The work we do there is, well, classified. *Very* classified." The seriousness in her voice told him that she was right.

They must have overshot their target by half a continent, probably downed by fighters or ground-support fire. That, or Dana is right, maybe they need to take out that facility. He paused for a moment. *Whatever she is working on must be very important if ComStar is going after it.* He wondered just what his sister had gotten herself involved with. Raul looked around, scanning the audience. *I may not be a fanatic, but I am a Word of Blake officer.* "Attention—I need your attention. I am a junior precentor in the Order. I am in need of veterans, volunteers, anyone who can hold a weapon and is willing to fight off these invaders."

For a long moment no one in the meandering line seemed to move. Then a few people stepped forward. The first ones were older men. Then some younger people. They took long strides forward.

About thirty people in all. Raul smiled. "All right then, we're going to need some transportation and we're going to need some weapons."

His sister stepped forward as well. "I think I can help," was all she said.

Good...we're going to need it.

The armory was part of a TerraSec reserve force, a reinforced, mostly infantry Level II called the 405th Reserves, Level II B. They were based in the outskirts of Ann Arbor near an old farming complex that was now some sort of museum. The armory didn't look like anything more than a drab warehouse from the outside. On the inside it was even more drab, a reminder of how low on the pecking order reserve units were. When they arrived at the gate in the commandeered hoverbus, Raul had startled the guards on duty. Even after his identification was validated, they seemed stunned that he was there with a busload of what appeared to be tourists.

Junior Precentor Tinker had talked with them during the drive to the city. A handful were old-time members of the Word of Blake, veterans from when the Order had relieved Terra from ComStar a decade earlier. They were old, but they had combat experience— that would help. Two others were police, two were factory workers, another was a history teacher. One young woman was a marketing executive for a drug manufacturer who had served in a youth battalion as a teenager and had been trained in hand-to-hand fighting. The bus driver had volunteered when they had asked to commandeer his vehicle.

They were a motley group, but what they lacked in experience and skill they made up for in grit and determination. Loyal fighters for the cause.

Once in the base, Raul had tried to reach out to the Order's military command but found Terra in disarray with the assault that was still unfolding. Where his commanding officers had maintained a sense of calm and control when the war began, they now seemed stunned that ComStar had brought the fight right to Terra. He asked for orders, permission to move his ad hoc unit to protect the genetics facility where Dana worked. The officer he dealt with, some wet-behind-the-ears adept, seemed paralyzed with fear. He didn't want to release the troops until he spoke to his precentor, a man who simply could not be located. Like Raul, the CO must have been on leave or doing something else when the orders came through. Raul wanted to scream at the officer in frustration, but he knew that would be a wasted effort. Instead he pulled rank. Under his own authority he assumed command of the reservists.

The officers at the armory—leading barely a platoon's worth of troops—questioned his authority. He hadn't put up with that. When one adept pointed out that most of them were technicians and mechanics, Raul reminded them that they were soldiers first. His raw authority and demeanor kept them in line. The questions of his authorization to commandeer them melted away in a flood of orders and activity. The two officers, reserve MechWarriors who asked if putting the unit on a combat mission was wise, found their own loyalty questioned. *That* snapped them back in line quickly. Running on bravado and adrenaline, Raul Tinker activated the small Level II of reservists, energizing them, preparing them for the battle he hoped could be avoided.

Turning to his sister, he shut off the comm channel. "I'm going to move these troops out to protect that facility, if that is indeed their target. The absence of leadership is the same as authorization to me." She was a wizard of efficiency, pulling up maps of the genetics research facility where she worked and the surrounding terrain.

"What do we have at our disposal?" The adept in charge of the motor pool was obviously afraid of him, or scared of the prospect of going into battle, or both. He spoke with a stutter and laid it out for him.

"W-w-w-we have a P-P-*Panther*, a *Sentinel*, and a La-La-*Lancelot*," he barely managed. Raul tried to ease his tensions with a smile but it didn't help. "Th-that's it for 'Mechs."

"Ground vehicles?"

The red-faced adept stammered out the response. "A D-D-D-Demolisher, a Lightning, and two Ro-Ro-Ro-Rotundas."

Four vehicles, three 'Mechs, and maybe two platoons of volunteer infantry...better than a respectable Two—if these were line troops. There were crates of short-range missile launchers and ammunition, but from the dates he saw on the crates, most had seen their useful life a long time ago. Raul had three BattleMechs and four vehicles, the rest of his force was infantry and civilian volunteers. He had just over a Level II's worth of forces and most of that was raw recruits to hold off a Level II of probably crack ComStar troops. Not good. On paper the odds were close, but he knew the difference between trained professionals. For a moment he wondered if he should even try. He could be leading these people to certain death.

Raul pushed those thoughts aside. There was no real choice for him. The Order had saved him and his family. The least he could do was do what he could to defend their holdings. Still, there was a chance the invaders were not heading for the genetics facility at all. They may have just crash-landed, aiming for another target altogether. If they did come, he would give them a reason to hold back.

His assets were thin. The Demolisher was the heavy-hitter, along with the *Lancelot*. The Demolisher was an incredibly dangerous vehicle, but from what Raul saw, the tank's useful life had been centuries ago. Its massive autocannons were enough to make any BattleMech pause, but its speed was such that it would be a lumbering target. The Rotundas—well, those were more for stealth and scouting duty. They wouldn't last long in a real battle. That's probably why they had been relegated to the reserve unit, for use in parades or crowd control.

"Adept, assemble the drivers and the entire staff. I want to organize our defense."

"Everyone, s-s-s-sir?"

"Everyone. Pull in every clerk, driver, anyone and everyone—regardless of their leave status. In the meantime begin loading transports with every heavy-hitting weapon and SRM round we can. Prep the 'Mechs and vehicles for action. Full loadouts."

He turned to the tactical map display his sister had pulled up. Raul Tinker knew the odds were against him if ComStar did turn this way. He saw his sister in the distance. No, she would have to remain behind. He had lost too much of his family to risk losing her as well. As the adept scrambled to execute his orders, Raul approached her in the maintenance bay.

"You'll need to stay here, Dana," he said flatly.

"You're kidding, right?" Anger flared in her expression as if she had been expecting this from him.

"No. I can handle this. You're a civilian. I don't want to risk you in the crossfire if the shooting does start."

"What about them?" She pointed to some of the volunteers from Galesburg who had come on the hoverbus. "They're going to fight for the Order, and so am I."

"I can't risk losing you," he confessed.

"Do you think you're the only one that owes the Order their life? Think again. Those people are volunteering because they feel a duty, an obligation. So do I. You were not the only one who benefited from the Order getting us out of that slum on New Home. I owe my life as well. I'm going. If you try to leave me here, I'll steal a hovercar or get there on foot. That facility is important to the Order, and I intend to protect it." Her words were raw with feeling and an anger that had nothing to do with him but was going to be focused on the ComStar troopers. Raul saw that the other volunteers had paused in their loading efforts. They were watching him as well. Each had the same feeling, the same commitment, the same devotion. It went beyond family, beyond nation, beyond government.

Was this the religious zeal that people felt in the Word of Blake, given form? He couldn't answer that. He had always wondered how people in the Order had treated it like a religion; now he felt as if he were one step closer to understanding that. The look on these volunteers' faces was unanimous. They were willing to fight him to protect his sister's right to defend the Word of Blake.

What he gained from their expressions and the pure devotion of his sister was something he had not counted on—hope.

He paused for a moment. "I was wrong."

His words caught her off guard. "What?"

"You do have the right to go, and I won't stop you. I was wrong. The Word of Blake saved both of us. All I ask is that you keep your head down and keep moving."

She smiled, and Raul added one more thing. "That, and I hope to hell your aim is good. We're going to need that too."

EIGHT KILOMETERS SOUTH OF RESEARCH FACILITY GAMMA TWO
HIGHWAY 23
ANN ARBOR
NORTH AMERICAN CONTINENT
TERRA

It was not good terrain for a defense, but it was the best he could find. Highway 23 ran north and south and was the most likely route the ComStar units would use if they were after his sister's research facility. At first he had hoped to leverage the facility itself for the defense. Urban combat gave a great deal of advantage to the defenders. Dana's concern was that such a strategy would leave the facility itself in shambles. In the end, Raul had opted for a more spread-out deployment. As the afternoon sun cut through the humid air, he wondered for the last time if he had made a mistake.

An almost dilapidated barn was about one hundred meters from the road. The highway wound snakelike through two long, rolling hills topped with pine trees. The wooded area crowned the tops of the hills and ran perpendicular to the roadway, a narrow copse of old scraggly white pines that provided adequate cover. In several places, including where the road cut through the trees, the pines thinned to nothing but low brush. The twist in the road, with the appropriate hills, would have to serve as some sort of defense.

The motor pool had brought a bulldozer out and used it to throw together a few quick firing trenches on the tops of the hills, knocking down some trees to form narrow fields of fire should anyone attempt to rush the hills directly. The bulldozer and transport had been abandoned on the road to block it. For a rushing BattleMech it was not a barrier, but any ground vehicle would have to skirt the obstruction.

Barrels of fuel had been concealed along the road, rigged with detonators. A few crates of explosives had been buried in strategic spots alongside the road. If set off they would not destroy a BattleMech or a heavily armored vehicle, but he hoped they would rattle the occupants and perhaps damage some system enough to render the vehicle unusable. *If nothing else I want to shake up the Com Guards.*

Raul had ordered the volunteers into the woods at the tops of both hills, flanking the roadway, ordering them behind some hastily felled pine trees for some sense of digging in. There he had ordered the crates of short-range missile launchers be primed. Each person had about four of the launchers, loaded and ready to go. They were to hold their fire until he gave the word. Loading under fire would have been difficult for those without military experience. Picking up a loaded launcher and firing it, that was realistic. He had used a small rag on a stick to mark the maximum range along the road for them. Farther back, toward the facility, in a shallow creek bed, they had placed more of the loaded launchers. The volunteers were told to fire what they had but as soon as the incoming firing began, to drop back to the creek.

The reservists were ordered to dig concealed foxholes dispersed along the road and hillsides. He hoped their concealed positions would pose a nasty surprise for any ComStar 'Mechs or vehicles that wandered too close to them.

He knew some of them were bound to die if that happened. All of them were worried, but their fear had not overcome their devotion. His sister—he was proud of her—was acting like a squad leader, having the people dig foxholes near the felled trees. The foxholes would not help much against a BattleMech, but it might be a start.

Tinker himself opted to pilot the *Lancelot*. It was an old 'Mech, probably dating back to the original Star League era. Its medium laser was not functional and probably had been offline for a century. The *Lancelot* had a smell about it—musty, old, reeking of sweat. He hoped that it had one more battle left in it.

The *Sentinel* was poised behind one of the hills, the *Panther* behind the other hill, only partially concealed. *How do you hide a three-story 'Mech on such open ground?* Raul was at one of the crooking turns of the highway between the hills, right on the road itself. Their MechWarriors had plenty of hours in the reserves, piloting simulators, but this would be both of their first times in real combat.

He was the center of the battle line, feeling very alone.

The Rotundas were pushed out on the far flanks. Weakly armed, he hoped they would deter any immediate attempts to turn his flanks. The armored cars were not much in a fight, but their large lasers could get in some good shots. He had met with both drivers and gave them some specific orders. Neither driver liked it, but they were reservists and understood his plan. They would serve an important mission if the fight came on—as would the Lightning that he had hidden behind the shambles of the barn.

That left one piece for him to put on the game board: the massive 'Mech-busting Demolisher tank. Raul had positioned it carefully and hidden it, hopefully until the right moment. He had visited with the reservists, doing what he could to calm them. Most were technicians and paper-pushers. Some were really nothing more than cooks and motor-pool techs; now heavily armed with a handful of man-pack portable PPCs and SRM launchers and had been dispersed to individual hiding spots all over the hillsides and near the road. They were willing to fight. How long they would hang in the battle remained to be seen.

He did not delude himself; even with his preparations, there was no way his force was going to be victorious. He had contacted the Word of Blake's command, speaking with a junior precentor in Detroit who was attempting to reinforce his troops. He knew about the small force heading toward Ann Arbor and gave Raul some latitude for forming a defense. His concern was if this was an errant unit going after some secondary target, or if it was part of a larger plan. Raul didn't care and told him so. He would scramble his forces and send what he could up there, but he had said it would be many hours.

Raul toggled a discreet comm channel and coded in his sister's walkie-talkie. "Dana?"

"Raul?"

"You don't have to stay. You should fall back. We can handle this." It was more optimism than reality, but if he could convince his sister to get out of harms way, he was going to try.

"We've been over this already, Raul."

He bit his lip. "I can't stand to lose anyone else. We lost Mom in the fighting, and Dad died trying to earn money to feed and clothe us. I'm not sure I can deal with losing anyone else."

"You aren't going to lose me, Raul. I know you carried the weight of this family after Dad died. I've always studied and worked hard to make you proud. I owe the Order everything. They put me in advanced training programs and have made me successful. I am who I am today because of you and them. I owe you both this much."

He wanted to argue with her but couldn't. She was right. He toggled the comm channel off.

Watching his long-range sensors, he wondered if he had been wrong, if the Com Guards who had landed had opted to go after somewhere else. Perhaps this had all been a waste of time. Perhaps they were going after another target or had simply crash-landed far off from their objective. Then he saw it. A blip of red on his sensor display appeared, right on the highway. Then another. The battle computer tagged the approaching force, and as he saw the images appear at the top of the display, moving straight at him, he realized the uneven odds he was facing.

It was a Level II of force. Four BattleMechs and two vehicles. Raul almost moaned out loud. Even numbers on paper—but *they* were probably all seasoned veterans, while Raul had civilians and reservists.

"This is Command One. I have enemy BattleMechs and vehicles approaching from the south," he said calmly as possible. "All units hold your positions until you get orders from me." He activated the radio-control circuits for the detonators. His throat seemed to dry with his last words. For this to work, he had to stun and batter the Com Guards, hard and fast. Anything less and they would easily push through the 405th Reserves and their civilian auxiliaries. His dry mouth was the acknowledgment that his BattleMechs would be showing up on their sensors right about the same moment he was experiencing.

There was a Com Guard commander out there, with orders—which was more than Raul had—to take out that genetics research facility. He was seeing just a handful of old BattleMechs, token resistance at best. This could be over quickly from his enemies' perspective.

The ComStar advance force pushed forward on Highway 23, heading right at him. They weren't in line of sight yet. If he were them, he would be watching those shallow hills. That's where his opponent would be expecting the fight to come from.

Watching the display he toggled to a more tactical mode, feeding off his short-range sensors. Yes, the Com Guards were closing in. A *Raijin* and *Bombardier* rushed into the lead. Behind them, as if a grim reminder, was the bulk of the attackers—a *Crockett* and a *Thug*. The *Thug* looked menacing. Whoever had painted it had given the white paint streaks of gray that made the 'Mech appear to have a sinister death's-head grin on the front. The ground vehicles were there as well—a Pegasus and a heavy-hitting Burke, moving off of the highway and swinging wide to the right flank.

The image of the *Crockett* stirred Raul. As a child, before war had come to his world and had taken away his mother and his life, he remembered having a toy figure of a *Crockett*. It had always been his favorite. Now he was facing one in battle. He had not seen that toy for a long time, not since the night a BattleMech had walked through the Tinker home and destroyed his life. Not since his mother had been crushed under its stride. He felt his neck muscles tighten at the memory. Closing his eyes for a moment, he pushed back the feelings trying to surface. Now was not the time for childhood memories.

The *Raijin* was almost on top of the first trio of fuel barrels when he toggled the detonation circuit. The explosion wasn't loud but sent a plume of black smoke into the air beyond the twists in the road that obscured his field of vision. The ComStar attack force scattered off the road. He toggled the second detonator, but nothing happened—perhaps a failed circuit or a bad detonator. *Damn!* He waited as the *Raijin* moved off the flanks where the third set of barrels lay buried in a long line. He triggered them just as the lanky *Raijin* was crossing the trench. They went off, again splattering burning fuel on the quick-moving 'Mech. The damage was negligible, but it was enough to cause some concern. Suddenly the Com Guard commander had to be wondering what he was facing, how complicated was this ambush he had strolled into?

He switched his channel open. "All right, we have their attention. 'Mechs, move to your firing positions and engage. Auxiliaries, standby." He moved his *Lancelot* out, taking the two twisting curves and seeing the burning pools of fuel. The *Raijin* was closest to him, its legs blackened from the flames but otherwise ready for a fight. Looming in the distance the rest of the Com Guard attackers were like a tidal wave just before it washed over the shore.

Or broke on the shore.

The *Raijin* dodged toward the base of the hill when he hit it with his Kinslaughter particle projection cannon. The blast of the *Lancelot*'s white lightning-bolt energy weapon lashed into the already-damaged right arm of the *Raijin*, nearly ripping it off at the shoulder joint. The *Raijin* pilot reeled to the right hard, the arm hanging on by a few sparking myomer fibers and cables. The *Raijin* let loose with its particle projection cannon, hitting his right side and flash-evaporating armor on impact. He ignored it...the other 'Mechs could deal with it if they wanted to. Raul drifted to the right in pursuit of the *Raijin,* but instead locked his pair of Krupp large lasers downrange at the *Bombardier. Time to spread out the damage...share the love.*

The heat roared in his ear, and the air in the cockpit went from room temperature to a searing oven. Both shots hit the *Bombardier* at their extreme range. Armor plating splattered a glitter of white-hot globs of metal into the air, but the *Bombardier* ignored the hits and continued trudging towards him. It was a rugged fighter, and the MechWarrior inside seemed undaunted by the attack so far. A brilliant flash of a PPC discharge came off from his side—the *Raijin*, firing at him with full force and fury. The rickety old *Lancelot* lurched back as it tossed jagged armor plates all over the ground around him. The oddly shaped *Raijin* was clearly not running from the fight.

He fought the momentum of the hit, trying to avoid falling over backward. His teeth gritted as he tried to hold the ancient 'Mech upright. Slowly, almost methodically, he beat the forces of gravity and physics, and rocked forward back onto his feet. The heat around him made his body sweat at a fantastic rate. The gurgle of the cooling vest didn't seem to do much other than abate the inevitable.

He watched as the *Sentinel* from his side blasted at the ComStar *Bombardier*, autocannon rounds stitching along the front torso and cockpit of the gray-white Com Guard 'Mech. The *Bombardier* turned, and its massive torso bay doors opened, revealing the barrage of missiles it carried. Forty long-range missiles hissed out from the

Bombardier and enveloped the *Sentinel* in a ball of smoke and orange explosions. It was there, somewhere, in the middle of that impact zone, though it was barely operational. He had to admit the Reservists were hanging in tight.

"Wheels, you are a go," Raul signaled the Rotundas. From behind the hills they raced, shooting the flanks, firing their large lasers at the *Bombardier* and the *Crockett*. The shots hit, but to the massive BattleMechs it must have been more of an annoyance. They continued forward along the roadway, and Raul double-checked his long-range sensors. *Yes...now.*

He triggered the explosive charges buried down the road. The concussions rippled through the smoke of the battle. One blast tore off some armor plating off of the *Thug*. The other blast hit the *Bombardier*, sending its next wave of long-range missiles twisting mindlessly into the air.

The *Raijin* raced toward one of the hilltops where Raul's civilians were dug in. "Ground pounders, fire at will!" he barked. His own slowly recharging PPC came back online begrudgingly. He watched as a man-pack PPC fired at the *Raijin*. The Com Guard 'Mech turned to face that target just in time to be hit by half-dozen short-range missiles raining down from the hillside. In defiance it rushed across the foxhole where the infantry-held PPC had fired, trampling the trooper there under its thudding feet.

On the flank he watched the *Crockett* unleash its weapons at the *Panther*. The air between the 'Mechs was alive with the implements of death and destruction. The remains of the *Sentinel* emerged from the smoky hole where it had suffered from the *Bombardier*. It fired a long salvo into the Burke tank, hitting the turret with the ultra-autocannon. Raul juked back toward the road and targeted the *Raijin* heading back toward its own force after its rush of the trench line. The PPC hit square in the back of the Com Guard BattleMech. An arc of blue energy whipped about the head of the 'Mech, and it dropped, face-first, into the ground, plowing up the sod as it fell.

The Burke fired at the *Sentinel*, but two of the shots missed while the other found a target. The *Sentinel* was a wounded beast; its leg armor exploded from the inside out. Smoke curled up from the holes that marked multiple missile hits and the ravaging of the PPC fire. Still, it hung tough, still in the battle, still willing to fight.

But before it could strike again, the Burke mercifully put an end to the *Sentinel*. This time all three shots savaged the Word of Blake 'Mech. The stout *Sentinel* folded in on itself, cut almost completely through by the multiple hits. Raul almost cried out as it fell dead on the field.

The *Raijin* dropped at almost the same moment, victim of another wave of short-range missiles from the hilltop where his sister was. As he brought his own *Lancelot* up to a run, swinging around the hillside toward the civilians, he saw the Word of Blake *Panther* was limping now. The *Thug* and *Crockett* seemed enticed by it and moved farther to the north, near the point between the hills. Sporadic short-range missiles from the reservists peppered black marks on the *Thug* as it shifted to take out the *Panther* once and for all.

The Lightning hovercraft came down the highway, swerving wildly and firing at the ComStar Pegasus hovercraft in the distance as they broke formation and moved to the far flanks. The Rotundas were there to meet them, fast-moving clouds of dust as they drove flat-out, firing their lasers and short-range missiles at the armored vehicles.

The Com Guard *Thug*, which had been holding at the rear, picked a strange time to rush forward. It charged right through the middle of the battle at a full run, straight up Highway 23. Each footfall shook Raul in his seat. He took a snap shot with one large laser, hitting the 'Mech in the legs. Out of nowhere the troopers of the 405th Reserves poked out of their concealed foxholes. Man-pack PPCs and short-range missiles slashed and blasted at the *Thug*'s lower torso. His charge suddenly stopped. Either the surprise of the infantry attack or some other distraction held him at bay. Raul really didn't care which.

The *Panther* MechWarrior, an adept named Antonio, had other things in mind. Despite the limp, he charged as fast as he could right into the side of the *Thug*. It was as Raul had planned it; his forces could not afford to simply fall as the *Sentinel* had. The impact of the *Panther* was not devastating, but it collapsed on the *Thug*, seeming to hang on it like a drunken Marine. The MechWarrior then did what he knew he had to. Having already cut the safeguards before battle, he overloaded his fusion reactor. The *Panther* exploded, and with it the Com Guard *Thug*, enveloped in a blinding white flash.

Raul knew he would do the same...when the time came.

The loss of the *Thug* gave the ComStar force pause, if only for a moment. "Open the barn doors, now!" he barked.

The shambles of a barn seemed to move at first as the building collapsed. The Demolisher, hidden in the old building, plowed through. It fired at the *Crockett*, its closest target, and unleashed its pair of intimidating autocannons. The sound of the massive autocannons was like a rumble of thunder inside of his own cockpit—he couldn't imagine how the target felt. The explosions knocked the *Crockett* back then down to one knee, its MechWarrior demonstrating extraordinary skill in keeping their 'Mech upright.

The *Bombardier* turned and unleashed twenty long-range missiles on the hilltop behind Raul. The missiles' smoke trails raced right past his cockpit and up to the hill behind him...up where his sister and the other civilians were. He turned for a moment and saw the pine trees in flames. The earthen positions where they had been dug in along the top of one of the hills had been smashed, tossed about.

Dana...

He fired his large lasers downrange at the *Crockett*, hitting it in the left arm and side. It didn't even seem fazed by the damage. While his cockpit temperature soared, he ignored it. *Dana...damn it!* A man-pack PPC fired at the *Crockett*, only to disappear as the short-range missile pack fired back in deadly response. The Burke turned its attention to the Demolisher—it had little choice, as did the *Crockett*. Raul jogged off past the hill on the right flank and watched the Com Guards spot the new threat and move to counter it.

His 'Mech cooled according to the cockpit temperature display, but he was hard pressed to feel the difference. Raul Tinker heard the tone of his particle projection cannon recharging again. He lined up on the *Crockett*'s flank and fired. The blast tore into the side and rear of the Com Guard 'Mech as it attempted to rise to its feet. He saw the armor twist up and curl toward to the head of the 'Mech from his hit. Still, the MechWarrior shook off the attack, moving as if they were ignoring it.

Off in the distance he saw explosions marking the death of one of the Rotunda armored cars. The *Crockett* had finally gotten a good weapons lock on the armored car and sent it up at extreme range. Raul could only hope that someone had escaped the carnage. The reservists had done better than he had hoped; they hadn't run when the battle had started.

Raul's *Lancelot* jerked hard under the impact, and warning lights went off on his damage display, flashing yellow where they had been solid green before. *The Burke...it had to be.* The old Blake 'Mech managed to hold itself upright and keep together, but in Raul's mind it was an iffy proposition for a few moments.

*Time to move...*Raul throttled the *Lancelot* into a full run, juking back toward the highway again. The *Bombardier* fired a lethal salvo of long-range missiles in the air only twenty meters in front of his path of advance. They were aimed not at him, but at the Demolisher. The old 'Mech-buster tank slowly crawled out of the rubble of the barn and ignored the wave of forty missile that pockmarked the glacis armor plate. It fired off a shot at extreme range at the Pegasus hovercraft that had drifted too near. There was a massive blast as the autocannons' depleted-uranium rounds slammed into the hovertank. The Pegasus survived the blast, but its primary weapons were now a mass of twisted metal draped across the burned remains of the frontal armor.

Raul thought for a moment that the Pegasus might actually get away, but the Lightning hovercraft let loose with a barrage of crimson pulses of laser energy. The ComStar driver tried to turn wide, but their hovercraft was piloted more by Isaac Newton than driving skill. The brilliant beams of laser energy dug in deep where the armor on the hovercraft had been. Mid-turn it dipped down, and its crumpled skirt caught the ground. The Pegasus reeled, then came to a smoldering stop just at the end of the highway. He almost wanted to cheer, but the Burke then fired two of its PPCs and a wave of long-range missiles right into the Lightning. The hovercraft dipped low as it throttled forward; its skirt burst, and it hit the ground, nearly toppling over. It plowed a deep trench, ripping off armor plating as it came to its end.

He had cooled enough to take his next shot, this time at the *Bombardier*. Raul waited for perfect tone in his neurohelmet and blasted away again with his PPC. The bright white light hit the *Bombardier* in the legs just enough to cause the gray-white BattleMech to pause mid-stride.

Then it happened. A flash of charged particles danced and sparkled over his *Lancelot*, and he felt his balance disappear totally as he dropped. The Burke—it had to be that damned Burke again! Its triple PPCs were designed to cripple 'Mechs, and it had done a good job. One shot had gone wide but the others had found him dead-on. His ears rang as he saw white and blue dots in front of his eyes. It was hard to focus, to make out the details on the damage display, but he could. The armor on the front of his 'Mech was a memory. Red warning lights flashed. He had lost two heat sinks. And that wasn't the worst of it. His arms with the large lasers were still attached but were nothing but worthless scrap metal. Both weapons were there, but were gone beyond the point of repair.

As he rolled the *Lancelot* off to the left side he heard a rumble from the Demolisher—incoming, not outgoing, fire. The odds had always been against them, and now it was showing. The *Crockett* ambled forward near the fallen *Thug* and waded through the black smoke from the fallen ComStar BattleMech. Its autocannon and larger lasers stabbed out at the massive Demolisher. Nasty black scars marked the gouges of lasers across the tank turret as the autocannon devoured the remnants of the armor plate on the front of the tank.

Rising to his feet uneasily, he turned his 'Mech's waist, bringing the Burke into range. He fired his PPC, bathing his entire body in another ripple of sauna-like heat. The shot barely found its mark on the flank of the tank. Armor plating, superheated by the charged particles, exploded outward and flew into the thick sod near the highway. The Burke driver had been shaken. The tank's advance stopped, and it suddenly jarred into reverse for a dozen meters or so before stopping.

The Pegasus made a sweeping pass near him, but its shots went wide as it tried to dodge fire from a trio of man-pack PPCs that the Reservists still had hidden in foxholes alongside the road. Two of the shots hit and were enough to force the hovercraft to bank away from the front line of the fight. It left a sick black trail of smoke billowing out in its wake, a sign of more savage damage.

Raul kept his eyes on the *Bombardier* as the 'Mech paused to take careful aim. That kind of pause shook him, and he cursed that his weapons were all gone save his PPC. It lined up the Demolisher and fired away. The air filled with missile contrails as they snaked and twisted their way downrange into the tank. This time it would not be able to shrug off the damage as it had before. Explosions tore at it everywhere. It lurched forward, and a metallic grinding noise reached Raul's ears even through the cockpit.

The Demolisher had thrown a tread. It was a mere shadow of its former self, with craters covering the few pieces of paint that still clung to the old armor plates fighting to stay on. Its autocannons fired again, catching the Pegasus, the only vehicle that risked coming within its deadly range. The blast of the autocannons marked the end of both vehicles. The Pegasus erupted into a fireball as the Com Guard *Crockett* leveled another blast of autocannon shells into the Demolisher's forward armor plate. The shots found their mark. Rather than spraying the Demolisher, they dug in, one right after the other, burrowing deep into the soul of the metallic beast. The tank's twin autocannon barrels suddenly dropped down, dipping limply toward the ground. Hatches opened as crewmen scrambled from the vehicles. Smoke, white and thick, billowed out of the hatches, followed a moment later by red and orange flames that seemed as though from a furnace. Most of the crew didn't make it. One, half out of the hatch when the flames erupted, was bathed in fire. He struggled mercifully for only a heartbeat before he stopped moving. The blackened body rested half in and out of the hatch as it had died, standing proud.

Raul surveyed the field of battle around him in less than a second. The *Crockett* was still fully capable of fighting. The Burke was operational as well. The Com Guard *Bombardier* had suffered a great deal of damage, but was still a deadly threat. Six short-range missiles slithered in the air and struck the *Crockett*, proof positive that the Word of Blake Reservists were still out there, what was left of them, and willing to fight.

It was not going to be enough—not nearly enough.

The image stung at Raul. A part of him had clung to the illusion that they might somehow win, but he saw that the ComStar force was still a potent threat. It would take very little for them to push forward to the genetics research facility.

He had faced death and defeat throughout much of his life, but this, this somehow seemed wrong. This was not what he wanted. He owed the Word of Blake his life...didn't he? Dana might very well be dead already because he brought her here. She didn't fear putting her life on the line for the Order, so did he?

He eyed the *Bombardier*, which had moved past him to the base of the two hills. It was trudging forward arrogantly, proudly, continuing its mission. For Raul it gave him the answer he needed. If that invading Com Guard MechWarrior could press forward, so could Raul.

He had given the Reservists orders, final orders, they were to follow if the fight reached this stage or if they were badly damaged. Now it was his turn to fulfill those same commands.

He turned his waist mid-stride and angled his PPC on the *Bombardier*. He fired. The brilliant blast of charged particles hit the shoulder of the *Bombardier* and severed its left arm at the elbow. Even as he saw the arm hit the pavement of the highway, the MechWarrior turned slowly, calmly, methodically to face him.

Not this time. Raul broke into a run, turning to his left and to the *Crockett*. His *Lancelot* was a wreck. The *Crockett* seemed paralyzed, either from heat, damage or both perhaps injury to the MechWarrior. Another hit with a heavy weapon and it was going to be gone—he knew that. He charged as fast as he could, sweeping around to the rear of the *Crockett*. Its MechWarrior was not watching him, or didn't realize the threat that they were about to face. Raul charged right into the rear of the *Crockett*.

His cockpit looked like a spider web, and he felt something wet on his waist...those were his first thoughts as he regained consciousness. He barely remembered hitting the Com Guard 'Mech. He saw it now, filling his cockpit window. Emergency lights flickered in his cockpit, and his displays were all blank. No power. He tried to switch to his backup circuits, but nothing else came to life. He paused for a moment and listened. There was a metallic groan of strained metal but no hum from the fusion reactor. His engine was offline, his BattleMech was dead. But, he thought with a wry grin, so was the *Crockett*. Its rear armor filled his entire field of vision.

The wetness proved to be where his coolant vest had torn free and leaked all over him. He was relieved; the warm liquid could have easily been his own blood. The angle his cockpit had landed in—facedown and twisted to the side—made getting out of his command couch a little tricky. He stood on his communications console as he tossed his coolant vest and neurohelmet off. Reaching the exit hatch, he touched it to make sure there was no fire on the other side. It was warm but not hot. He popped the emergency bolts and pushed it hard.

Light greeted him as he moved the hatch halfway open. Something, some part of his own 'Mech or the one he had hit, was blocking it. He pulled and strained to squeeze himself through the hatch and outside. He looked out in front of him and saw the *Crockett* facedown, with his *Lancelot* on its back and side. It too wasn't moving. Smells greeted him—smoke, the smell of shattered heat-sink coolant, sweat, everything stung at him. Raul Tinker dropped to the ground near the highway and looked in the distance to see how the fight was going.

The white-and-gray *Bombardier* was still standing, though the fighting had turned the white into a blackened pattern. Its legs were smoldering, and he saw why. The last Rotunda armored car had followed his course of action, and it had plowed into the *Bombardier*'s legs. The tiny armored car did some damage but nowhere near what a BattleMech could do. Raul had told the Reservists that if all else failed, they should ram the enemy.

He felt proud that the militia driver had the courage to do just that. Like the *Panther* that had gone down earlier, they were fighting to the bitter end.

In the distance he saw the Burke, and it looked as if the tank had thrown a tread. It was potent, but it was not going to be moving anywhere, having been converted by battle from a tank into a pillbox. Then it dawned on him. They were not advancing. The Com Guard force had stopped.

He heard the crackle of pine sap burning in the felled trees from the nearby hilltop and from the Demolisher, punctuated occasionally by a small explosion from within the hulk of the tank. The *Crockett* popped occasionally as did his own *Lancelot*; the 'Mechs were cooling. And standing there, only a short distance away, was all that was left of the ComStar force—the battered *Bombardier*. For Raul it seemed like a moment frozen in time. Why had they paused? What was going to happen now? He braced himself, half expecting them to plow through the shattered remains of his force and onto their objective.

He wished he could see in the mind of his foe. Was he wondering if there were other forces still beyond the hills? Could he still fulfill his objective alone?

Then, as if on cue, the *Bombardier* turned around. The crew of the Burke climbed out of their tank and headed to the south on foot. The raiders marched and limped away, leaving him with nothing but smoke and death. A handful of troopers from the Reservists Level II emerged from their hiding spots behind trees or from foxholes. All were equally stunned as the Com Guard BattleMech moved off into the distance.

Raul found himself shaking. It could be the change of body temperature from the sauna-like cockpit, but he knew it for what it was: the adrenaline in his body shaking off in his system. He turned slowly and drank in the faces of the people that were there. He saw one face that caused him to run over...Dana Tinker.

The blood caught his eye; her arm and shoulder were crimson with it. Something poked out of the wound in the forearm, something covered with her thick blood. "You're hurt."

"I'm fine. It's just some splinters from the trees when those missiles hit us. How are you?" Nothing shook Dana, not even the barbs of pine stuck in her arm as she held it close. Their rough childhood had hardened her in ways that only Raul could appreciate.

He shook his head for a moment and glanced off at the disappearing Com Guard force in the distance. "I'm fine—now."

"Why did he leave?" she pressed.

He shrugged. "Their losses were too great, I guess. Maybe they were worried that we had more troops dug in along the way. Maybe they got orders to break off from their own command. Maybe they were hurt more than we knew. It's hard to say. I'm just glad they're gone." Many of the now-battle-tested Reservists were slapping each other on the back and shaking hands. In the distance, one was bent over, vomiting. A few of the civilian volunteers began to emerge as well. The jumpsuits they had borrowed from the Reservists were now dirty, blackened, and in some cases, dull red from blood. It was obvious that most wanted to pursue the Com Guard force.

Raul wanted to finish off the enemy as well but was keenly aware of just how crippled and weak his own force was. "Everyone—good job. You did it. You beat them back. Now we need to tend to our wounded. Stand down and assume defensive positions." The battle for Highway 23 may be over, but for some, the fight to survive would continue on.

REGIONAL OPS COMMAND, WORD OF BLAKE
CLEVELAND
NORTH AMERICA
TERRA
12 APRIL 3068

Raul's uniform was pressed and clean as he stood at attention in front of the semicircular table of precentors and junior precentors. They had hauled him into the room to discuss his "irregular activities" during the assault on Terra. The entire affair had been called a board of inquiry, but Raul knew an organized lynching when he saw it. This was more like an inquisition.

While some mop-up operations were still underway, the activity in his region of North America had wound down to nothing more than nuisance raids by diehard ComStar agents and operatives.

"Irregular activities"—that made him smirk. He had broken a half dozen or so formal commands, violated the command structure, and executed a military operation without authorization or consent of his superiors. It was a clear breach of regulations that he was comfortable with. Raul had endangered the lives of civilians in a military operation. He had inappropriately liberated men and materiel in an unsanctioned battle. Raul had also allowed enemy forces to escape the field of battle without detention, though he felt pursuit would have risked his force's total annihilation. Raul had endured the litany of charges rattled off at him without speaking in his defense. His time to speak had now come.

A grizzled, older Word of Blake precentor glared at him from behind his seat and the ribbons on his chest. "Does the accused have anything to say in his defense?"

Raul was not going to plea—that much he had decided the moment he heard about the board of inquiry. There was nothing to be sorry about, that much he was going to let them know. "I do."

"Proceed."

He made sure he swept the table, making eye contact slowly with each member of the board. "I am not going to waste your time or mine claiming I didn't do what I you claim I did. I did do those things. I drafted volunteers to fight with us, and I did assume command of the 405th Reserves without authorization.

"My sister let me know of the genetics facility near Ann Arbor, and I assumed that was what the ComStar troops would make a move on. I did what I was trained to do. I defended the Order and its people. I assumed command because, quite frankly, no one was giving out orders. I took action because my command structure had other priorities.

"I and my family owe our lives to the Word of Blake. If you want to toss me in prison for defending our people, then do it. If I had it to do again, I would do everything the same."

"Innocent people were killed as a result of your actions," a stern, female junior precentor said coolly. He was tempted to glare back but knew that would not make his case any stronger.

"They were volunteers. For the record, each and every one of them is a hero. They fought for the Word of Blake while a lot of officers sat behind safe desks. And, to be frank, ma'am, innocent people die in war. I didn't ask for this war, it was brought to me. I did what I was trained to do, I fought. The innocent people that died with us that day did so because they believed in the Word of Blake and wanted to protect the Order as well." He suppressed the anger in his words, making sure that he spoke calmly, evenly. *Let them see that what I did was the right thing to do.*

"You understand that we cannot have officers simply taking matters into their own hands?" another officer replied.

"I understand that. At the same time, this was war, and during war formalities often are chucked aside. You train us to fight, to think, to improvise. When the call came to action and duty, I took action and performed my duty. I did those things you've accused me of. Now you want to slap me around for doing what you want all good officers to do. Fine. Then let's do this so I can serve my time and get posted back on a frontline unit." There was no fear in his voice—if anything, there was conviction.

"Under the circumstances," the young junior precentor said, "I wish to reiterate to my brethren on this board that I think this is a damn waste of time." It was obvious that he was an officer who had been in battle as well; the medals on his chest testified to it. "I move that we dismiss this case and move on to other officers that failed us, rather than punish those that did what they were expected to do."

There were mutterings around the table. It was clear that some officers were hoping to make an example out of Raul, while others found the proceedings distasteful at best. The debating lasted for three or four minutes, and some of the words were hot, though he could not hear them too clearly. Finally the stodgy old precentor slammed his gavel down.

"Fine then. Raul Tinker, the charges against you are summarily dismissed from these proceedings. You will report to your commanding officer for assignment tomorrow morning. Your service to the Order is acknowledged, and while unorthodox, it is deeply appreciated. On a personal note—good work, son." At least two members of the board rose and stomped off. A few others gave him a knowing nod of approval. The younger one winked at him.

There was more to this inquiry than what he knew, that much was for sure. With the Com Guard landings on Terra being such a stunning surprise, a lot of people were going to have to face some blame for the events that unfolded. Raul had wondered if he had been caught up in such events. He also wondered how many other officers were having their integrity and loyalty tested and questioned in the aftermath of the strike on Terra.

As the occupants of the room shuffled away, the young junior precentor came up to him and extended his hand. "I am Junior Precentor Monos Ausdauer."

Raul shook his hand firmly. "Thank you for your support. It has been a long time since I was in any kind of trouble."

"It was worse than you probably realize," Ausdauer said flatly. "This attack by Com Guard caught many of us off guard, I'll admit that. Some are using this as an opportunity to purge some undesirables from our ranks. Some have legitimate concerns, such as punishing officers who sent other capable leaders off on leave during combat operations. There was no need to have you caught up in such a mess."

It sounded like politics to Raul, something he avoided. "I did what I had to do."

"Yes, you did at that," Ausdauer said, motioning to the far corner of the room for a moment of privacy. Tinker followed him and Ausdauer huddled close to him. "I looked over your records, Tinker. We also received several strong recommendations from those that know you well. Your military career has been relatively short, but you have shown yourself to be full of initiative and quick on your feet. It's the kind of thinking that our Order needs right now."

"Thank you, sir."

Ausdauer ran his hand through thick, immaculately trimmed black hair. "Command was planning on attaching you to your choice of a frontline unit if you got off. It was what you expressed an interest in, a unit to lead in battle. I wanted to offer you a new posting for a unit I am planning on putting together."

"What kind of assignment?"

"I refer to the work as 'counter-espionage.' This war is a means for us to accelerate what the Word of Blake can do for mankind. The old Houses and their ways are corrupt; you saw that in your youth in the Chaos March. I am putting together a unit that will take the fight to the Houses, hit them where they are soft, strike at them where they are weakest. From what I have seen, you are a loyal son of Blake. I think you can offer the kind of leadership I am looking for."

"Counter-espionage—that sounds like the work of ROM," Raul said coyly. ROM was the intelligence arm of the Word of Blake. Their name was said with caution and concern. The eyes and ears of the Order, they seemed to be everywhere. Raul didn't want anything to do with ROM. They were an aspect of life in the Word of Blake that he didn't like—but he did respect. They were a necessary evil to keep the ranks free of enemy operatives.

"No, not ROM. This is a military assignment, you have my word. It is the kind of work where an officer that is independent thinking can make a difference."

Tinker paused. It *was* appealing. What he had seen as a child was that the House governments did not care for their people. Taking the fight to them—that was exciting. "It's safe to say I'm interested."

Ausdauer grinned. "Good, I was hoping you would be. I will have the transfer orders go out to your commanding officer. You should receive word in a day or two. In the meantime, enjoy your time here on Terra. It will be a while before you are back here."

"If I may, sir, where am I going?"

Ausdauer cocked his eyebrows quickly, almost arrogantly. "That is classified. Suffice it to say, it's a secret...a place only a few people have been to in the last three hundred years."

The cryptic tone of his voice and the vague references gave Raul a hint of what was waiting for him. *I have not made the wrong choice...*

INTELLIGENCE OPS CENTER SABER-RATTLE
CAPETOWN
MARKESAN
FEDERATED SUNS
31 MAY 3068

Francis Lyman sat in the briefing room, wishing he was anywhere else. War was breaking out like a case of poison ivy everywhere in the Inner Sphere. Normally he would have gone to New Avalon, but the Word of Blake blockaded the world, which meant it was not a viable command center for the time being.

None of this had to happen. If anyone had seen the threat the Word of Blake posed. He wanted to chuckle, but the truth was dismally painful.

The ops center director came in, flipping through a hardcopy report, not even making eye contact with Lyman as he closed the door. He moved to the far end of the conference room table and slid into his seat. The man looked like any other businessman or mid-level executive on Markesan. But, in this building, during wartime, he was the most powerful person Lyman could have hoped to meet.

He still found himself bored.

"You are Lyman, Francis James?" the man said, tossing the printout to the table casually.

"Yes sir."

"I was just going over your K-17s for the last few years."

K-17s—field analysis reports. Administrative lingo for the work he had been doing. This was what it had come down to. *I spend years sneaking around the Chaos March, and it's all boiled down a handful of pieces of paper.* The director did not wait for his sarcastic response. "You are some sort of expert on the Word of Blake?"

"I wouldn't say that, sir."

"I would. At least you're one of the few people still alive who is anything close to an expert. We have been caught with our pants down. You apparently pieced together how the Word of Blake was using every brush war out there to get their officers field experience. They didn't hit us with green troops. They came in with men that had seen battle before, at least many of them. You apparently spotted something years before we did here."

"Thank you, sir. I only wish someone had read my reports *before* this bloody damned Jihad had started," Lyman said.

"Hindsight is easy. You weren't the only field operative who pointed out what they were up to. We just didn't put all of the pieces together in time. I'll cut to the chase, Agent Lyman. I'm pulling you off of field duty. You're getting promoted to our counter-espionage group. Your experiences and insight are needed to help us turn the table on the Word of Blake."

Promoted? *Damn.* He hadn't counted on that, not at all. "Sir. I'm not so sure that's a good idea. I'm a field operative. I have been dogging a list of officers in the Word of Blake—preparing profiles of them, learning their combat patterns, and gathering evidence of their actions and in some cases their crimes. It might be presumptuous to pull me off of these assignments."

The director stared at him for a full two seconds of silence. "Your file says you're arrogant; good to know it's right. Listen, I know what you have been working on. You've done good work at it. When this war is over, the information you've gathered will be put to good use, I'll see to that myself. But for now, you will best serve the Federated Suns by pursuing this assignment."

"I understand." Lyman didn't suppress the disappointment in his voice.

"This was supposed to be a compliment to what you've done. To be blunt, the woman you are replacing botched her job. That was one of the reasons we were caught so totally off guard. You picked up on the Wobbies' recruiting efforts years ago in the Chaos March. Similar efforts have been going on in the Periphery for at least as long. You saw these techno-monks for what they are—cold blooded killers. You're getting the job because you showed a spark of insight that your predecessor lacked. We don't want to get surprised again. That's your job."

Francis glanced down at the report. He could make out some of the names on it, the Word of Blake officers he had been profiling. It hurt him that he was letting them go—even on the short term. He nodded to the report. "Sir, I just don't want some of those men and women I was chasing to get off. Many were involved in war crimes, a handful of massacres, and at least one atrocity. They need to pay for what they have done."

The director offered a quick flash of a grin that melted the moment he opened his mouth to speak. "They won't get off. We'll go after them, you have my word. Right now your nation needs you. House Davion needs your expertise. When this war is over, you have my word that justice will be done."

The director rose and extended his hand. Francis stood and shook it. He glanced again at the printout report and saw one name that stirred his thoughts the most: "Raul Tinker." Memories of Bryant overcame him instantly. The smell of the rotting and charred bodies seemed to reach his nostrils again. The image of Deborah Johnston, the woman he had trained, dead in the forest at the Order's hands seemed to speak to him—demanding justice. *You may think you've gotten away, Tinker, but I will come after you at some point. When I do, you and your Wobbie associates are going to pay for what you have done.*

REAP WHAT YOU SOW

CRAIG A. REED, JR.

MACLEAN VALLEY
RENTZ
CRUCIS MARCH, FEDERATED SUNS
15 SEPTEMBER 3063

The old man looked up as he heard the sonic booms in the atmosphere. Stopping the tractor, he stuck his head out of the cab, looking for the source. A frown creased his face as he saw the glint off metal high in the sky. "Damn," he muttered.

He pulled his head back inside and picked up the radio. "Caleb to Home," he said.

"Home here," a voice replied.

Caleb frowned. He was in his mid-sixties, short white hair, tanned with wrinkles around his eyes. But there was a lean hardness about him that didn't match his age, nor did the cold gray eyes. "That you, Josiah?"

"Yes, sir," the voice replied.

"Get your father."

"Yes, sir."

Caleb stuck his head out and searched the skies again. He found the glint, and his eyes narrowed.

"Yes, Father?" another voice said.

Caleb pulled his head inside the cab. "Homer, we've got an incoming DropShip."

"Any idea where they're headed?" Homer asked.

"Looks like Southend."

"All right, I'll call Mayor Thomas and—"

"Contact Sarah Thomas," Caleb growled. "Henry will spend an hour running around in a panic. We don't have that much time."

"Yes, sir."

"Any of our people over that way?"

"Let me check." There was a few seconds of silence. "Yes, sir. Jack Megan and a picking crew are out on Orchard Forty."

"Call Megan and tell him I want him and his boys to scout the situation."

"Yes, sir. Anything else?"

"Not right now," Caleb growled. "But call your brothers and let them know."

"Yes, sir. What are you going to do?"

Caleb looked out at the field he was in the middle of plowing and sighed. "I'm coming in," he said. "Tell your mother to call Gladstone and let them know, in case they missed it."

"Yes, sir."

Caleb looked at his watch. "I'll be there in an hour," he said.

GLADSTONE
RENTZ
CRUCIS MARCH, FEDERATED SUNS
15 SEPTEMBER 3063

The militia's command center was busy. Soldiers sat staring at monitors and calling out reports while junior officers moved from one post to another, asking questions, then moving onto the next post. The atmosphere was tense but controlled.

In one corner, Captain Jeffery Morris watched silently, his bright blue eyes taking in everything. He was a tall, lean man with chiseled features and short, ash-blond hair that earned him a few appraising looks from women and a few men.

"What do you think, Captain?" the man standing next to him asked.

"Looks good so far, sir," Morris replied, his voice a soft drawl. "As soon as we know where the pirates are going to land, I'll get my boys moving."

"Good," Colonel Kenneth Pallone said. He was a short, stout man with thin white hair, a pug-like face, and bushy white eyebrows. "Ginny!" he bellowed.

A young, attractive leftenant straightened up and looked at Pallone. "Yes, sir?"

"Do we know where they're going to land?"

"Looks like MacLean's Valley."

"Poor bastards," Pallone muttered.

"Don't worry, sir," Morris said. "We'll get the pirates before they do a lot of damage."

Pallone shook his head. "I was referring to the pirates."

"Colonel Pallone!" another leftenant shouted. "Blanche MacLean's on the phone! Line three!"

"I'd better take this," Pallone muttered and walked over to an unused station, picked up the phone and pushed a button. "Blanche? Oh, I'm doing fine and so is Debbie. How about you and Caleb...? Good to hear... Dinner? When...? Sure... The entire weekend? I think we can make that... I hate to change the subject, but we've got a pr—oh... What does Caleb want us to do...? Well, we do have a 'Mech company from the March Militia here... Hold on a second." He cupped the phone and said to Morris, "Blanche wants to know if you would like to spend the weekend in MacLean Valley."

Morris stared at him. "What?"

Pallone removed his hand. "Can he get back to you on that? He's still getting his bearings... I don't know, I'll ask him." He cupped the phone again. "Captain, are you married?"

Morris stared at him in disbelief. "What?"

"The question's simple enough."

"No, but what—"

Pallone was back on the phone. "He says he isn't... Yes, I'm sure he would... Well, it'll take a couple of hours to get up there. Where should we land...? All right." He glanced at his watch. "We should be there by dinnertime... Okay, see you then... Good-bye." He hung up the phone.

"What—what was that about, sir?" Morris asked.

"I'll explain on the way, son. I'll just say that we're dealing with some *really* stupid pirates."

MACLEAN VALLEY
RENTZ
CRUCIS MARCH, FEDERATED SUNS
15 SEPTEMBER 3063

Shen Costas piloted his *Hunchback* down the ramp of the *Gorgon Gal*, a battered *Union* DropShip. As he reached the bottom of the ramp, he muttered into his radio, "Costas to *Gorgon*. Anything on radar?"

"Nope," a voice growled back.

"Keep an eye open. They may be turning out the militia right now."

Costas heard the technician snort. "Like they can stop us."

"And try to fix that air circulating system. My cabin smells like boiled cabbage!"

"I can't help your eating habits."

Before Costas could reply, a *Firestarter* strode down the ramp. "Ooh," a scratchy female voice said. "Lots of stuff to *burn*." She purred the last word.

"Focus on the mission, Pyro," Costas growled.

"But I want to burn something," she whined.

Costas tightened his hands on his 'Mech's controls until the knuckles were white. "You can burn the entire valley down after we've finished."

"Really?"

"Really. Get your lance out and make sure we don't have anyone watching us."

"Okay." Pyro's *Firestarter* started for the woods, followed by a trio of *Stinger*s. Costas watched them leave, resisting the urge to shoot Nancy "Pyro" Hoyt in the back with his 'Mech's Kali Yama Big Bore Autocannon. After a few seconds, the urge faded.

"Pyro giving you trouble?" Quinn Terme asked.

Costas glanced at his screen. A battered but still-functioning *Griffin* was coming down the ramp. "No more than usual," he replied. "She wanted to start burning everything now."

"You're going to have to let her burn something," Terme said.

"I know," Costas replied. "But only after we've taken everything we can." He looked at his watch. "We're wasting time. Let's get the *Gorgon* unloaded and show these dirt eaters why we're called Costas's Corsairs."

Five hundred meters away from the DropShip, Jack Megan watched the unloading through a pair of binoculars. "Megan to Caleb," he said into a radio.

"Caleb here. What you got?"

"It's pirates, sir. Two lances, mostly lights, with half a dozen vehicles and a couple score of thugs."

Caleb sighed. "All right, Cache Twelve is about a klick away from where you are. Arm yourselves and shadow them. Let me know where they're going."

"Yes, sir."

"Caleb out."

Carefully, Megan climbed out of the tree he'd been using as an observation post. He was in his mid-forties, lean, tanned, bald, and moved easily.

When he reached the ground, Joe Valdez, his assistant foreman, was waiting for him. "Well?" Valdez asked. He was short and stocky.

"Pirates," Megan replied. "Mister MacLean's given us the go-ahead to arm the boys. He wants us to shadow them."

Valdez shook his head. "You'd think they would've learned by now."

"There's always a few who are either too desperate or too stupid to know any better."

Everyone in the family called it "the Bunker."

The room was five meters below one of the barns on the MacLeans' main homestead, and any person who had spent time in the military would find a familiarity with the room's setup. About the size of a large bedroom, there were several communications and observation stations, chairs, a couple of tables, and a small holographic tank in one corner.

When Caleb came down the stairs, his twin sixteen-year-old grandsons, Jason and Justin, were already seated at two of the stations. "Grandpa," they said in unison.

"Boys," Caleb replied. He was still wearing work clothes. "Anything new?"

"Southend's nearly evacuated," Justin said. "Most of the town's already in the shelters."

"What about the vaults?"

"In their bunkers."

"Good. Jason, did your grandma call Kenneth Pallone?"

"Yes, sir," the other twin answered. "She said to tell you that there's a 'Mech company from the March Militia on-planet, and they're coming over with Uncle Ken."

Caleb nodded. "About time those slackers on Anjin Muerto did something right. Justin, have you tapped into the pirates' communications yet?"

"Not yet. I should have it in another fifteen minutes."

"As soon as you can, son."

The trapdoor over the stairs opened, and Caleb's son, Homer, came down the stairs. "Father," he said. He was shorter than his father, but stockier and muscular. His face was a bit rounder, but he had the same cold gray eyes.

"Well?"

"Mother's making sure that Central Valley's evacuated and the town's bank vaults are secured."

"Good. What about aerial coverage?"

"Nate's heading over to the landing strip right now."

"You told him not to get too close, didn't you?"

"I did. No lower then three hundred meters or closer than a thousand. He understands."

"Good. Jack Megan says there's two lances of 'Mechs. Some vehicles and several dozen toughs."

"Grandpa!" Justin called out. "I've cracked their comm codes!"

"Good going," Caleb said, slapping his grandson on the shoulder.

"Easier than I expected," Justin said, smiling. "Their encryption model's older than me."

"Good. Keep monitoring them."

"Yes, sir."

"Attention, pirates!"

Costas looked at his radio in surprise. "Who the hell is this?" he demanded. "Caleb MacLean," the voice replied. "This is my valley."

"I'm Shen Costas," the Corsairs' leader said. "We're here to offer you our protection."

"Don't need any," Caleb replied acidly. "I'm going to say this once. Get the hell out of my valley."

Costas smiled. "Oh? And are you going to stop me?"

"Damn right I am. If you had any sense, you'd turn around and get out of here right now."

"Why should I do that, *Caleb*?" Costas said mockingly.

"To save your lives."

Costas frowned and shifted frequencies. "Delft," he said to the man in charge of his infantry, "Check the bank."

"Already on it," Delft replied.

"Pyro," Costas continued, "I want you to check the north end of town."

"What for?" Hoyt asked in an exasperated tone.

"To make sure Farmer MacLean doesn't have any of his farm boys waiting for us with pitchforks and shotguns."

"All right. But I still want to burn something."

"Do it and I'll let you burn a few buildings here in town."

"Okay!" Hoyt replied cheerfully.

Costas switched back to the general channel. "Farmer MacLean," he said in an affable tone. "I'm sure we can come to—"

"Stuff it, Costas," Caleb snapped. "You've been warned. Caleb out."

"An arrogant bastard," Terme said over their private channel.

"Yeah," Costas replied, "but he sounded more irritated than scared."

"Maybe those rumors are true," Terme muttered.

"What rumors?" Costas asked.

"There's been stories that pirate bands have dropped onto Rentz and never returned."

"You believe that, Quinn?"

"Not a word of it, until now. I think we should tread carefully, Shen. Something isn't right."

"Costas, this is Delft. We're in the bank, but there's no vault."

Costas frowned. "What?"

"I said this bank doesn't have a vault!"

"Are you sure you're in the right building?"

"I'm not an idiot! Of course I am!"

"Check all the buildings around it!" Costas snarled. "Find that vault!"

"They can't find the vault," Justin said.

"Good," Caleb muttered, staring at the holotank. "How long until Hank team's in place?"

"Five minutes."

"Good."

The trapdoor opened, and a thin woman with gray hair, spectacles, and a lined face that still had more than a few traces of beauty came down the stairs, holding a basket. Behind her, a young boy followed, also carrying a basket.

Caleb looked up at her. "Blanche," he said.

"I brought something to eat," Blanche MacLean said cheerfully.

"Thanks," Caleb muttered, looking back at the holotank.

Blanche put the basket down on a table under the stairs. "Over here, Josiah," she said to the boy.

Josiah carefully put the basket on the table, then came over to stand next to his grandfather. "More bad men?" he asked.

"Aye," Caleb said.

"How bad?"

"I don't know yet," Caleb replied.

Costas was angry.

Delft and his men had searched both banks in town, but neither had a vault.

"Damn it!" Costas snarled as he slammed a fist on the armrest. "The vaults must be hidden!"

"We can't stay here much longer," Terme said.

"I know, Quinn," Costas grunted. He glanced over at his map screen. "We'll move northwest, toward Central Valley."

"All right."

Costas switched channels to the group channel. "All right, move out. Pyro, your lance's on point."

"Can I burn something first?" Hoyt asked.

Costas sighed. "You have five minutes to burn all the buildings you want."

"Great!"

"Everyone else, we're moving northwest."

On his rear screen, Costas watched Hoyt's *Firestarter* walk over to a three-story building. Fire leapt from the 'Mech, engulfing the building in white-hot plasma. Hoyt twisted, spreading the fire across another building. Over the radio, Costas could hear her giggling.

"Crap," Megan muttered.

From the orchard, Megan and Valdez could see smoke rise from Southend. Behind them, a dozen armed farmhands knelt or stood.

"Good thing no one was home," Valdez said.

"Yeah, but the insurance companies are going to have a fit."

"Buildings can be replaced."

"I know." Megan stared at the 'Mechs and vehicles coming out of the town.

"Looks like they're moving northwest," Valdez said.

"Yeah. Toward Central Valley." He turned to the farmhands. "All right, mount up."

"Better call Mister MacLean and let him know."

"Right."

"You didn't have to burn down the town."

Costas stared at the radio again for a few seconds before he responded. "You're watching us."

"Of course," Caleb replied. "You're on my land."

Costas chuckled. "How are you going to stop me, old man?"

"The same way I stopped those other pirates."

"And how are you going to do that?"

"You'll find out."

This time, Costas laughed. "Brave words, old man. You're sheep and we're wolves."

"You're a damn fool," Caleb growled.

"No, I'm a pirate."

"It's the same thing."

"Well, no time to talk. I have a valley to plunder."

"We'll see."

Costas smiled viciously. "That sounds like a challenge."

"You forget that among sheep, there are rams. MacLean out."

"I don't like this, Shen," Terme said.

"What? The old man's trying to scare us with words and threats. We have 'Mechs and guns! What does he have, a few farm boys with pitchforks?"

"That didn't sound like a man who's scared."

"We'll see."

Hank Foster stared down the road through a pair of binoculars. A farmhand dashed out of the grain silo and raced over to Foster. "Ready to roll, boss."

"Right," Foster said. "Get out of here. Tell Buddy to be ready."

"Okay." The farmhand dashed off, yelling for the others to load up. Foster stopped looking and walked over to where a stripped-down pickup truck with wide wheels and an overlarge engine sat. A young man with shaggy blond hair and a grin sat in the driver's seat. He was wearing overalls, and a wheat stalk stuck out of one corner of his mouth.

"Ready, Buddy?" Foster asked.

"Sure am, Mister Foster," Buddy replied in a soft drawl.

"This ain't a game, Buddy. They catch us, they'll kill us."

The smile faded from Buddy's face. "I understand, sir," he said, the drawl almost gone. "I just hope we can do some damage."

"I hope so too."

Wheat fields ran along both sides of the two-lane highway. Hoyt's lance was out in front, while half of Costas's lance brought up the rear. In the middle, two patched-up APCs bracketed half a dozen cargo trucks carrying Delft's men. Costas and Terme flanked the trucks.

"Got a grain silo coming up on the right," Hoyt said.

Costas looked where Pyro had said. A stocky, gray-colored tower rose out of the wheat. "You think they might have stashed anything valuable in it?" Hoyt asked.

"Doubt it."

Costas could hear Hoyt's indifference. "Let's destroy it, then."

The pirate leader took a few seconds to control his temper. "The silo's filled with grain dust, you idiot," he said. "One spark and there will be an explosion like—"

Shots suddenly rang out from ahead. One of the *Stinger*s, Krat's, turned toward the silo. "Some idiot's shooting at me with a rifle!"

Dust rose from the near the silo, forming into a rooster tail as something fast started moving away from the highway. Krat snarled, "You hayse—"

"Careful!" Costas roared. "Don't hit that silo!"

Snarling, Krat ran toward the silo, laser aimed at something. He fired, sending a beam that struck the ground just behind the dust cloud. He must have missed, because Krat was cursing and running after whatever it was.

Costas frowned. What was the purpose of—

The *Stinger* was within twenty meters of the silo when the structure exploded.

Krat's *Stinger* disappeared in a massive fireball, and his scream on the radio abruptly cut off. The shockwave and debris slammed into the other *Stinger*s and the *Firestarter*, knocking all three down. Costas managed to fight the shockwave, barely keeping his *Hunchback* standing. "Kali take it!" he hissed.

The fireball rose into the air on a column of thick black smoke that flattened out into a mushroom as it rose. Costas, his head ringing, couldn't do anything but stare in disbelief.

Even in the Bunker, the MacLeans could feel the explosion. "Get me camera seven," Caleb said.

Jacob touched a button on his console, and a screen above him came to life. In the distance, they could see the thick black column of smoke.

"Oh dear," Blanche said. "I hope none of our people were hurt."

"Justin," Caleb said. "Get a hold of Hank, then Jack Megan. I want to know if we hurt those pirates."

"I wish we didn't have to destroy Silo Nine," Homer muttered.

"So do I, son, but it'll be a lot worse if we let them run roughshod through the valley."

"I got Hank Foster, Grandpa," Justin said.

"Good boy," Caleb said, slapping Justin on the shoulder. "Hank, can you hear me?"

"Sure can, Mister MacLean," Hank replied.

"Are you all right?"

"Me and Buddy Holister are singed, but we're better than one of those pirate 'Mechs. It was standing right next to the silo when it exploded."

"Good. Talk to you later. Caleb out."

"You think they're going to take the Cosum River Bridge?" Homer asked.

Caleb nodded slightly. "It's his best route to Central Valley."

"Do you think the bad men will leave now?" Josiah asked.

"I don't know," Caleb said gravely. "Maybe. But I wouldn't count on it."

"Damn it!" Costas growled, looking at the damage the explosion had unleashed. Krat's *Stinger* was just a charred hunk of metal, useless to salvage. Hoyt's *Firestarter* and the two remaining *Stinger*s had been pelted with pieces of concrete and other debris, scraping armor and denting a few armor plates. The trucks and APCs suffered mostly minor damage, though the two trucks closest to the explosion had cracked windshields.

As for the silo, it had vanished, leaving only a small crater where it had stood. Around it, all the plants within a hundred meters were flattened and burned. Small fires flickered and smoldered all around them. Thick, black smoke hung the air, slowly fading in the gentle breeze.

"We should burn the entire valley!" Hoyt screeched. Her *Firestarter* looked like it had been caught in an avalanche.

"What the hell happened?" Terme barked.

"I don't know!" Hoyt snarled back.

"I warned you, Costas," a voice on the radio said. "Consider that an example."

"You bastard!" Costas screeched. "You killed one of my men!"

"So?" replied Caleb. "How many people would he have killed if I let you plunder this valley?"

Costas balled his fists. "You want war, you dirt-sucking hayseed? You've got it!"

"You can still walk away, Mister Costas," Caleb said. "Keep coming, and it will get worse."

"I am going to gut you and your entire family and leave you for the crows!"

"I've been threatened by experts, Mister Costas," Caleb said. "And you're no expert. MacLean out."

Costas slammed a fist down on his chair's armrest. "Hoyt," he said coldly. "See these fields? Burn 'em."

"I think they're pissed, Father."

Caleb looked at his son, a sandwich in his hand. "Watch your language in front of the children," he said in a soft tone. Then in a louder tone, he said, "Jason, is your uncle at the bridge?"

"Yes sir!" the teenager replied. "Uncle Elias says his boys are ready to kick pirate ass!"

"Watch your language," Caleb said in the same soft tone he'd just used.

Jason sagged in his chair. "Sorry, sir."

"Under the circumstances, I'll let it slide this time. Is he ready?"

"Yes, sir! Uncle says the smoke generators are ready and so is the lube."

"Good." Caleb walked back to the holotable, biting into his sandwich as he did so. He chewed slowly as he watched the images.

Homer walked over to him. "Do you want to deploy the Horsemen now?" His mother walked over and handed him a sandwich on a plate. Homer took the plate, but made no move to pick up the sandwich.

"Not yet," Caleb said. "I don't want to unless I have to, or the pirates reach Central Valley. Justin!"

"Yes, sir!"

"Is Nate in the air yet?"

"Yes, sir! He says the pirates have set the wheat fields around Silo Nine on fire. Says the winds are pushing the fire east."

"There goes the new harvester," Homer muttered.

"Pah!" Caleb spat. "Worry about that later." He tapped a few keys on the military-surplus holotable and the image changed to show a map. "Jason, call Chief Grable and tell him to stand by with his people and equipment, but not to move out until the pirates are on this side of the river. I don't want to give those scum-sucking deadbeats any chances to take hostages."

"Yes, sir!"

"Justin, how long does Nate think it'll take for those pirates to reach the river?"

There was a pause as the teenager murmured softly and listened to the reply. "Nate thinks they'll get to the bridge in about an hour or so."

"Good. Call Jack Megan and tell him to keep shadowing them, and harass if he can. I don't want them to get comfortable."

"Yes, sir."

"And Homer?"

"Yes?"

"Eat your sandwich."

The sight of the burning wheat fields didn't make Costas feel much better. Hoyt hadn't been stingy with the flames, and it had taken several threats from Costas to stop her. Fortunately, the winds were blowing across from their line of march. Hoyt, for all her eagerness to burn everything, wasn't stupid enough to trap her and the others in a firestorm.

"That'll teach those dirt-eaters!" Costas growled.

"I don't think MacLean's going to cave easily," Terme said.

"He will once I've razed his precious valley!"

"But let's not charge into his arms blindly. It's clear MacLean's spent time thinking about to defend his land. We don't need to play to his tune."

"He's a dirt farmer!"

"One who was willing to blow up one of his own silos to hurt us," Terme said.

Costas leaned back in his chair. Terme was right. MacLean wasn't going to be cowed by threats over the air. But in person? "All right, listen up!" he said into the radio. "We're moving out. Hoyt, you take point. Stay within a hundred meters. My lance, stay close to the trucks. And if any hayseed wannabe-hero tries shooting at you, burn them down! No prisoners!"

Jack Megan looked through his binoculars. "Harass if I can," he muttered. "How in the hell can I harass 'Mechs with ten guys armed only with rifles?"

The work-team-turned-militia was on a low rise, in a stretch of heavy woods, crouched among the tall, thick-bodied trees. Below them, three hundred meters away, the pirates were moving along the highway.

Valdez, who was watching the pirates through his own binoculars, said softly, "Take a look about two o'clock. Branch over the road."

Megan swung his opticals to where Valdez had referred to. It took him a couple of seconds to see what his assistant had seen. "That's a big nest," he said after a few seconds.

"Yep," Valdez said.

"Pity those 'Mechs don't have open cockpit windows."

"I wasn't thinking about the 'Mechs, but those trucks..."

Megan put his binoculars down, looked at Valdez, and grinned. "Holly!" he hissed.

A blond girl who looked to be all of sixteen crawled over to them. "Yes, Mister Megan?" she asked.

"There's a bewasp nest on a branch near the road, about two o'clock," Megan said. "See it?"

Holly peered through the trees in the direction Megan had shown. She grinned. "Sure can, Mister Megan. You want me to knock that nest onto one of the trucks as they pass by?"

"Yeah."

"Okay." Holly rolled away and then settled herself. She aimed the rifle at the nest, steadied herself, aimed, and slowly squeezed the trigger. The flat crack of the rifle was followed two seconds later by the bewasp nest hitting the hood of the lead truck and breaking open.

Bewasps were a native species and served the same role as Terran bees. However, bewasps were larger and more aggressive than their Terran counterparts and had a venomous sting. They were also known for aggressively defending their nests against any invader.

In this case, the invader was the pirate truck.

The swarm exploded out of the shattered nest and streamed into the cab and truck bed, crawling on and stinging the pirates. The truck wove across the road as it accelerated, ran off the road, and struck a tree head-on.

Megan grimaced at the sight. "We'd better clear out," he said, hurriedly rising.

"What the hell's happening?" Costas demanded. There had been a gunshot, then one of his trucks had veered off the road and slammed into a tree. The rest of the trucks stopped, and pirates jumped out to see to their comrades, only to grab at their clothing and start slapping themselves frantically, then running away.

"They ran into something," Terme said. "Looks like some... insects?"

Something landed on Costas's cockpit window, something as long as his ring finger, with large wings and a barbed stinger on its tail, which it tried to stab into the cockpit glass. After several seconds, it flew off in search of softer intruders.

Twenty meters ahead, Costas saw something lying near the side of the road and seemed to be moving. He adjusted the screen's magnification so he could see the object. It was about the size of his torso and covered with the hostile insects. "Looks like a nest," he said.

"Yeah," Terme said. "I think someone deliberately dropped it on us."

Costas strode forward and stepped on the nest, crushing it. "MacLean's going to pay!"

Caleb listened to Megan's report. "Good work!" he said after the supervisor finished. "I want your people to head for the bridge. Caleb out."

"How badly do you think the swarm hurt them?" Homer asked.

"The 'Mechs?" Caleb asked. "I doubt it, unless one of them was stupid enough to ride in an unsealed cockpit. On the other hand, the ground grunts probably got well stung."

"Anyone want potato salad?" Blanche asked.

"In a moment, dear," Caleb said.

Homer finished his sandwich. "You think Costas is going to back off?"

Caleb shook his head. "You heard him. He's taking it personally. Thugs like him need fear to work for them. If it gets out that a bunch of farmers drove him off, he'll be a laughingstock in the pirate community. To prevent that, he needs to find me and kill me." Caleb smiled. "And that's going to work to our advantage."

Eleven dead.

Costas stared at the bodies laid out along the side of the road, his fists clenched until the knuckles were white. One 'Mech destroyed and a dozen of his people killed, by farmers. *Farmers!* Damn dirt-eating, stupid cow-loving farmers!

He could smell the aftermath of the swarm's attack. Hoyt's flamers had burned a large part of the bug plague to ashes, while the pirate foot soldiers had dragged their comrades free of the smashed-up truck. Once most of the swarm was exterminated, Costas had climbed out of his *Hunchback* and assessed the damage on foot. What he saw didn't help his mood any.

Terme walked up to him. "Truck's a total loss," he said.

Costas glanced at the smashed-up truck. "We need to find this MacLean," he said in a low, cold voice. "And we need to kill him."

"We don't have time for vengeance," Terme said.

"It isn't vengeance," Costas replied. "We need to make MacLean and his family an example. If we don't, we might as well become farmers, because no one will take us seriously."

"Now what?" Terme asked.

Costas pulled a noteputer from the pocket of his jacket and turned it on. He then brought of a map of the valley and stared at it for a few seconds. "If we continue along this road, we'll reach the Cosum River. There's a bridge over the river." He jabbed a thick finger on the screen.

"Probably defended," Terme said.

"Maybe. But I doubt they have much in the way of defenses, not if we move fast."

"What about the bodies?"

Costas looked at the bodies. "Leave them. We'll pick them up on the way back."

"Grandpa! The pirates are heading for the bridge!"

Caleb smiled. "Jason, call your uncle at the bridge and make sure he's ready."

Blanche glanced at her watch. "I'd better make sure everyone's in the shelters," she said. "I'll also tell Tom to get the Horsemen ready."

"Blanche," Caleb began to say, "There—"

"Don't say it, Caleb MacLean," Blanche said, her motherly tone abruptly replaced by one of pure steel. "You know as well I do the Horsemen will be needed. So quit putting it off."

Caleb sighed. "All right. Tell Tom we'll need the Horsemen."

"Of course, dear."

It took Costas's band twenty minutes to reach the bridge. The Cosum River was nearly a half kilometer wide at this spot. The bridge was a two-lane steel-and-concrete construction that rose twenty meters above the dark blue, fast-moving river.

"See anything?" Costas asked.

"Nope," Terme replied. "But we'd better check and see if there's any surprises under the bridge."

"That'll take too long. How long would it take to rig a bridge like this?"

Terme blew out a breath. "A company of engineers might be able to do it an hour, maybe two."

Costas nodded. "They haven't had the time to rig it. Joff, Worms, take point."

"Us?" Joff asked with a whine.

"You see any other idiots named Joff and Worms around here?"

"All right." Joff's *Commando*, followed by Worms's *Hermes II* started onto the bridge. The rest followed.

"Joff," Costas asked, "can you see the other end?"

"Yeah," Joff said, "looks like they've got barricades and militia waiting for us. I see a couple of rifles and...pitchforks?"

Costas barked a laugh. "Let's take them!"

Elias MacLean watched the pirates through a pair of binoculars as they started running at him. Unlike his brother Homer, he was tall and lean, with a bookish face. But like his father and brothers, he had the same cool gray eyes.

"Mister MacLean?"

"What, Buddy?"

"Can we stop waving these pitchforks around? They're heavy."

"Just for another moment. I want to make sure they're all on the bridge first."

The pirates were halfway across when the trap was sprung.

First, there was a series of small explosions along the sides of the bridge, and thick white smoke billowed all along the bridge's main span, cloaking everything in a thick blanket.

"What the hell?" Hoyt yelled. "Gas?"

"No," Delft replied, coughing slightly. "It's just smoke."

"Keep moving!" Costas snarled.

"All right, Hans!" Elias yelled into his radio once the bridge was lost in the smoke. "Turn it on!"

Because of the valley's harsh winters, the bridge had been built with a de-icing system. Next to the pumping station sat a large tanker. A hose ran from it to inside the pumping station, where it was attached to a main pump. Now the system was pumping the tanker's contents through the de-icing system and onto the bridge surface.

Costas took three steps before his 'Mech's feet slid out from under him. The *Hunchback*, arms waving ineffectively, slammed into the road with enough force to rattle Costas's teeth. There were shouts of surprise and screams across the radio, followed by the ground vibrating slightly as other 'Mechs fell. There was a loud thud, followed by a splash somewhere below the bridge a few seconds later.

Costas shook his head to clear his vision and tried to push his 'Mech up, only to have the *Hunchback*'s hands slide out from under him. Cursing, Costas tried again, and again failed to gain purchase. "Costas to everyone!" he snapped. "Status!"

"There's oil on the road!" someone said.

"Figures," Costas grunted. "Everyone stand up *slowly*."

The smoke was beginning to clear, and Elias lowered his binoculars. "Time to move, people!" he shouted. "Hank, call the river patrol and see if the pilot of the *Commando* that did the header off the bridge is still alive!"

"It's twenty meters deep!" Hank Foster shouted back.

"So?"

"I'm on it."

"Wish we could use flammable oil," Buddy muttered. "One match and we could end it here."

"Yeah," Elias said. "But the last time we did that, Councilman Panosi nearly screamed his lungs out about the cost of cleaning up the mess and repaving the bridge."

"So? Panosi's a weasel, and your dad doesn't like him."

"I know, but Panosi made *us* pay for the cleanup and repaving."

It took Costas five minutes to sort things out. By then, the smoke had cleared, revealing the "militia" at the end of the bridge had vanished.

All the Corsairs 'Mechs had fallen at least once, scraping and denting armor everywhere. It took several seconds for Costas to realize that Joff's *Commando* wasn't on the bridge, but from the cracked and twisted concrete along the rail, Joff had fallen into the river below. Attempts to contact him failed, either because he was dead or his radio was damaged.

Among the vehicles, one of the trucks had spun and struck the concrete rail, caving in the truck's side and bending the rear axle. The rear APC had slid into the last truck in line, smashing up the truck's rear, flattening both sets of rear tires, and injuring several of the men riding in the truck. In return, the APC's sloping front armor was severely dented.

Costas stared into nothing, the 'Mech's controls creaking ominously under his too-tight grip as the reports came in. "Damn you, MacLean," he hissed.

As if summoned, a voice said, "Now will you leave?"

"Damn you!" Costas yelled.

"I'm not the one trying to steal other people's money and property," Caleb said in his same cool tone.

"You owe me," Costas hissed.

"You can try to collect," Caleb said. "If you're willing to pay the price. Caleb out."

The DropPort at Northend was basic and designed more for cargo than for passengers. Morris stood next to Pallone watching as the *Gressman's Triumph* unloaded its own cargo of BattleMechs. The DropPort was quiet, with only a few techs and a larger number of militia standing on guard.

"Where is everyone?" Morris asked.

"The mountains," Pallone replied, motioning to the peaks in the near background. "Mister MacLean converted a few mines to hardened shelters for cases like this. He doesn't want to risk the civilians being taken by the pirates."

"Mister MacLean sounds more like a soldier than a farmer," Morris replied.

Pallone smiled. "He wasn't always a farmer. How long before your company's unloaded?"

"Another half hour."

"Good, I'll call MacLean and find out where he wants you."

Morris frowned. "Where *he* wants me?"

"Yes," Pallone said, pulling a phone from his pocket. "As Militia CO, I learned long ago that the best way to deal with the MacLeans was to go with the flow."

The atmosphere among the pirates was grim.

It had taken twenty minutes of careful walking and driving to get off the bridge, and Costas's mood hadn't improved any in that time. Hoyt had taken her anger out on a couple of maintenance sheds and a larger building, while Delft's men shot up a couple of trucks. After letting them work out their anger for ten minutes, Costas ordered them back onto the road.

The woods were thick and close to the road, and more than a few eyes watched the branches for any more insect nests. The remaining vehicles were filled with pirates, and several more rode on top of the APCs. Hoyt's lance ranged out ahead, looking for any ambushes, while Costas's lance brought up the rear, looking for anyone trying to sneak up on them. Costas split his attention between looking at his map and piloting his 'Mech. After ten minutes, he said, "Everyone, halt."

"What?" Hoyt grumbled.

"Been looking at the map. "There's a feature about three kilometers ahead called Kalb's Notch. It's narrow and has cliffs on both sides of the road."

"Ambush?" Terme asked.

"We've already been burned twice. I'm not going to give that bastard MacLean a third chance."

"So, what are we going to do?"

"According to the map, there's a logging road about a kilometer ahead. It'll take us over this range of hills."

"Makes sense," Terme said. "Unless they have that covered."

"They can't cover everything. Let's get moving."

Caleb said nothing as Jason relayed what Costas was planning. After his grandson was finished, he said, "Justin, check with Nate to make sure they're taking the logging road. If they are, call your uncle at Kolb's Notch and tell him. Then call Jack Megan and tell him the pirates are heading his way."

The logging road was dirt and gravel, and took the route of least resistance. For a change, Hoyt's lance was at the rear, while Costas's lance, with Worms's *Hermes II* leading the way, was in front. Costas was on the right flank, Terme on the left.

The signs of logging were clear. Trees had been thinned out along the road, and a couple of places had been cleared of old-growth trees, replaced with replanted saplings. A few birds, or the local equivalent, sang while others animals watched the pirates from the safety of the deep brush.

Despite the lack of threat, Costas felt uneasy. Had he missed something?

The left side of the forest began sloping up, and the right side began sloping away to a lake below as the road continued along what was now a hill. Costas's unease grew. What was MacLean up to?

The road veered to the left, still following the hill's base. The slope was now steep, and halfway up the slope, there was a pile of logs, stacked and held in place by a wooden wall. Even as Costas's mind said *trap*, Terme yelled, "Bodies in the woods! One o'clock!"

"Now!" Megan yelled, as he reared up and fired a short burst into the first truck. A dozen others also rose up and open fired at the trucks. As the last bullet left Megan's gun, Valdez tightened his fist around the clapper attached to a small C8 charge attached to the wooden berm. The berm shattered in an explosion of splinters and fire. Like water, the logs rolled downhill, gathering speed as they jostled one other, reaching the road in seconds.

The 40-ton *Hermes II* tried to dart out of the wood avalanche's path, but the first log slammed into the 'Mech's left leg, then whipped around to smash the *Hermes*'s right knee. The force was enough to snap the log and knock the *Hermes* back into the mass of timbers. The logs and the 'Mech continued rolling down the slope, the *Hermes* bouncing and smashed by the rumbling timber and the ground. The right arm flew into the air, wires and pieces falling from it as it spun. It finally crashed into the water with the other logs, battered and broken.

Megan and the others were already gone, disappearing into the thick woods behind them before the pirates had fired more than a few shots at them.

Costas was too furious to speak.

He should have seen the ambush coming, but he hadn't. Hoyt and the rest of her lance had raced after the farmers, but they had vanished into the heavy woods. Now Hoyt was spreading flames through the woods, screaming in rage.

"We lost another four," Delft said. "Three wounded."

Costas didn't answer but just sat in the cockpit staring into space. He was being out-thought by some old farmer at every turn. Costas had 'Mechs and blooded killers, yet MacLean was making him look like an idiot. The Corsairs had lost three 'Mechs and more than a dozen men, in return for what? A few destroyed buildings and crops?

"What do we do now?" Terme asked.

"We continue," Costas said slowly.

"We've lost a lot for no profit."

"And if we run away now, we lose even more. We push on. If we kill MacLean, it'll help offset the losses."

"Assuming he lets us kill him."

"I'm sure as hell going to try. Let's get moving. I want us in Central Valley before sundown."

"They're still coming, Grandpa."

"Good," Caleb said. "Tell Nate to back off another five hundred meters. These pirates are in a sour mood and I don't want to give them a target."

"Yes, sir."

Caleb looked at his son. "Homer, call your brothers. It's time for the Horsemen to ride."

It took the Corsairs another two hours to reach Central Valley. Hoyt was on point again, while Gitner and Ringold walked along the flanks. The trucks and APCs, all loaded down with pirates, were in the center. Terme was at the rear, leaving Costas walking between Hoyt and the vehicles.

They came to the top of a hill, and at the bottom stood Central Valley. Like Southend, its streets were neatly laid out, with defined business and residential areas. There were only a few buildings taller than three stories, all of them in the center of town. Costas stopped and looked down at it. "I don't like this," he said.

"Another trap?" Terme asked.

"Right now, I wouldn't put it past MacLean to have something ready. But it's too late to back off now. We're going to go in, strip it of anything valuable, then burn it down. Hoyt, Delft, with me. Gitner, Ringold, scout east and west of town. Terme, stay here and keep an eye out for any surprises."

The trucks stayed at the edge of town, while the APC and dismounted pirates followed Costas and Hoyt into town. The town was eerily quiet.

"Where is everyone?" Hoyt hissed.

"I don't know," Costas replied.

"I should burn down a few houses, and see if anyone comes running out."

"Hold off for now and keep your eyes peeled."

They reached Central Valley's silent central square. Hoyt and Costas stayed there, while some of Delft's men broke into business and began hauling out anything remotely valuable and piling it on the sidewalk. Several pirates broke into the banks, but Costas wasn't surprised when they reported the lack of bank vaults. The mining office had a safe, but it held only papers.

With every passing minute, Costas's unease grew. In the back of his mind, he was sure this was a trap. But what kind?

"Terme to Costas. I'm picking up something on the hills on the far side of town."

"What?" Costas demanded.

"A mass of metal, but it keeps growing and fading in size and shape."

"Track it!" Costas barked. "Delft, find any trucks?"

"A couple," the ground commander replied. "We're hot-wiring them now."

"Hurry up. You have ten minutes."

"And you have five minutes to surrender," said Caleb over what was supposed to be an encrypted channel.

"You!" Costas hissed.

"Aye," Caleb replied. "And you should use a better encryption system. My grandson cracked it within twenty minutes of your landing."

"What do you want, old man?"

"I told you. You have five minutes."

"Or what?" Costas growled. "Stampede a herd of cattle at us?"

"Worse than that, you third-rate looter."

"Bring it on!"

"I've pinpointed the transmission source!" Terme yelled. "The hills north of the town!"

"At last!" Hoyt screamed. Her *Firestarter* took off down the street. "Gitner, Ringold, with me!"

"Don't move, MacLean!" Costas shouted, putting his *Hunchback* into a run after Hoyt. "It's time we end this!"

"I agree," said Caleb calmly.

The way he said it made Costas falter. And then he knew. "Pyro!" he yelled. "It's another trap!"

But Hoyt was beyond listening. Her *Firestarter* lifted into the air, landing just beyond the last buildings in town. "I'm going to incinerate him!"

"Gitner, Ringold, stop!" Costas yelled. "It a trap!"

The *Stinger*s slowed. "But Pyro—" Gitner started to say.

"Leave her!" Costas shouted. "We're bugging out! Delft, mount up and haul ass!"

"But—"

"Do it!" Costas began backing away, watching Hoyt continue her mad charge. She hit the ground running at the end of her jump, her strides taking her to the base of the hill. She took two strides before firing her jump jets again, sending the 35-ton 'Mech halfway up the slope. As she landed, she triggered her flamers. Fire leaped from her 'Mech to the trees, turning a thirty-meter swath of forest into an inferno. "Run, you damn dirt farmer!" she screamed over the loudspeakers.

"I don't think so," Caleb said in same calm tone. "Last chance, pirate."

"Die!"

"You first."

Fire erupted from the hilltop. Cannon shells, missiles, and lasers slammed into the *Firestarter*. The light 'Mech came apart in a series of explosions, scattering it across the slope.

"What the hell!" Gitner squawked.

A 'Mech emerged from the trees, and Costas's mouth went dry as his Warbook beeped unneeded identification. The *Atlas* stopped at the crest of the hill just a few meters from the *Firestarter*'s remains. Then a *Victor* strode out of the woods, followed by a *Thunderbolt*, then a *Cataphract*. All were painted in forest camo, but Costas's eyes fixed on the insignia on the *Atlas*'s chest. An *Atlas*'s head, set against the Sword and Sun of the Federated Suns.

Davion Assault Guards.

"Run!" he shouted.

"It's too late Costas," Caleb said. "Surrender or die. Your choice."

"Costas!" Terme shouted. "We've got 'Mechs moving up behind us!"

"What?"

"This is the Anjin Muerto Crucis March Militia," said a new voice on the general-use channel. "Stand down or be destroyed!"

"Captain Morris, this is Caleb MacLean. Glad you could make it."

"My pleasure, sir."

"I'm retired, son. 'Caleb' will do."

"Yes, sir."

"Thank you, Captain. Costas, it's your choice."

Costas stared at the radio, anger draining from him, replaced with resignation. He was outnumbered and outgunned. His people had been battered, abused, and humiliated. Sure, he could probably destroy the town, but for what purpose? Closing his eyes, he said the hardest words he ever had to say.

"Corsairs, stand down and surrender. It's over."

GLADSTONE
RENTZ
CRUCIS MARCH, FEDERATED SUNS
18 SEPTEMBER 3063

The cell was plain, with just a bunk and a toilet behind a waist-high wall. One heavily barred window high in the wall and a steel door were the only breaks in the gray walls. A single dim glowstrip in the ceiling was the only illumination after dark.

When Costas heard the heavy *clunk* of his cell door being unlocked, he sat up. He was dressed in an ill-fitting burnt-orange jumpsuit and thin-soled sandals. A monitoring bracelet was affixed to his wrist.

The cell door opened and a tall, lean man with chiseled features and wearing the field uniform of an AFFS soldier stepped in. He was followed in by an older man with tanned features, short white hair, and cold gray eyes. The old man wore work clothes, but Costas knew him at once. "MacLean," he said, his voice dry from lack of use.

"Costas," the old man said. He motioned to the officer. "This is Captain Morris."

"Charmed," Costas growled as he swung his feet over the side of the bunk. "Come to gloat?"

"No," Caleb replied. "Wanted to thank you for your decision to surrender."

"Not like I had much of a choice," the prisoner said. "Caught between two fresh 'Mech lances? I'm not *that* stupid."

"I gave you a chance to walk away," Caleb said. "You should have taken it."

Costas snorted and stared at the floor. "Run from farmers? I'd never be able to show my face on Tortuga Prime again." He snorted. "Once the *Gorgon Gal* makes it back there, I'll be branded an outcast, even if I escaped."

"Yes," Morris said. "About your DropShip."

Costas looked up suddenly. "What?"

"The *Gorgon Gal* surrendered as soon as we showed up," Morris said. "They couldn't leave Rentz because their air circulating system died on them."

Costas snorted. "Figured." He looked at Caleb. "I underestimated you, MacLean."

"You wouldn't be the first who's done that."

"You were the *Atlas* pilot."

"Aye. Death's been in the family for three generations."

The pirate raised an eyebrow. "Death?"

"Aye. The other three 'Mechs you saw with me are named War, Famine, and Pestilence. All of them have been in the family for generations."

Costas snorted again. "The Four Horsemen. How sublime." He looked down again. "You could have hit us at Southend."

"I like keeping them as an ace in the hole," Caleb said. "Besides, out here, it's easier to replace a silo, wheat fields, and a few logs than it is to get ammo and parts for Death and the others."

Costas leaned back so his head rested against the cool stone wall about his bunk. "Now you sound like a farmer."

Caleb shrugged. "Been a farmer longer than I was a soldier."

"I saw the insignia on your 'Mech. You were in the Davion Assault Guards?"

"Aye. So were all three of my sons. I won a few ribbons, earned a couple of medals, but this is my home." He looked at Costas, and the prisoner felt the weight of the cold gray eyes. "And I will defend my home and the people who live here from people like you. Good-bye, Mister Costas." Caleb turned and strode out of the cell.

"Tough man," Costas said.

"Yeah," Morris replied. "Consider yourself lucky."

"Oh?"

"The last two pirate bands that tried to raid this valley didn't surrender, despite General MacLean's efforts. Not many lived long enough to enjoy these cells." Morris walked to the door.

"General MacLean?" Costas called out after him.

Morris stopped and looked back at Costas. "He's retired," he said. "His last posting before retirement was head of asymmetrical warfare in the AFFS Department of Strategy and Tactics."

Costas barked a small laugh. "Beaten by a retired SpecForce general. Makes me feel a little better."

Morris shrugged. "Suit yourself. Bye."

The cell door closed and locked, leaving Costas alone with his thoughts.

ARMS OF THE DESTROYER

TRAVIS HEERMANN

CINNABAR
COREWARD PERIPHERY
22 OCTOBER 2940

"Negative contact, Skipper. The bush here is thicker than the hair on a boar's back." Arra Jackson throttled down her *Cyclops* and paused atop a hummock for a look around. All she could see around her was Cinnabar's unique brand of impenetrable bush. She couldn't exactly call it vegetation. With its pulsating sacs and pods in a hundred shades of red and ocher, it looked like masses of lungs and kidneys on gnarled, wiry stalks. Two kilometers behind her, the smoking remnants of Alpha Lance's drop pods raised dark, wispy fingers into the sky.

"It has to be there, Jackson," Kommandant Rhonda James said over the comms. "Sensors say you're right on top of it."

"Are you seeing what I'm seeing? It's like waist-deep shag carpet," Arra said. The bush did indeed reach up to her 'Mech's waist. And no higher anywhere, as near she could tell. She felt painfully exposed here on the floor of this valley. It was the perfect place for an ambush, and even though all the sensor scans had assured them Cinnabar was vacant, she couldn't turn off that feeling crawling up the back of her neck.

A teasing voice, deep and sonorous, popped in. "Quit your bellyaching, Jackson, or I'll tell these fine military folk your old nickname." The voice, one she hadn't heard in a long time, took her back to childhood again.

"Who let a civilian on this channel?" she said with mock severity.

"I pulled strings."

"Let's keep this professional, shall we, Terrence?" she said. "And bite my big toe." Hearing him calmed her, even after all these years apart. It was strange, having Terrence Larkin so close again. Duty and war could separate even the staunchest of childhood friends.

The rest of her lance of heavy and assault 'Mechs moved across the valley floor. The only break in the ocean of reds was the glimmering sheen of the mercury lake at one end of the valley. Gray-pink clouds puffed over the distant mountaintops, filling half the crimson sky.

She'd never seen anything like this bush. It was tough as steel cables dragging at the *Cyclops*'s ankles, slowing it down even at full throttle.

"How about we start burning this crap down?" Jenkins's voice came from the *Atlas* on Arra's flank, two hundred meters distant.

"Negative, Alpha Two," Kommandant James said. "Minimal surface footprint."

Jenkins's voice came to Arra's earpiece over the private comm. "You think anyone actually knows we're here? Tell me again why we're on a stupid salvage mission for something that we don't even know is there on a rock so toxic—"

"The survey team saw *something*." Arra throttled ahead again. "Now cut the chatter, Will, and keep your eyes—"

The bottom dropped out of the world. Her 90-ton 'Mech ripped through the mat of bush, falling, sliding. The gyro whined, and myomer bundles wailed as the great machine tried to right itself as it plummeted. The sky disappeared from the cockpit window. A bone-jarring *clang* slammed her teeth together as the *Cyclops* crashed against something, then a deafening metallic grating reverberated through her cockpit. Into darkness she fell, until she slammed to a stop. Shredded "vegetation" rained down on her cockpit window.

Her crash seat had softened the blows, but she tasted blood.

Her comms crackled to life; too many voices calling for her.

"No visual on Ghost One!"

"Arra, are you all right?"

"Hauptmann Jackson, report!"

Her *Cyclops* stood wedged in a crevice fifty meters deep, its back trapped against the rock wall. The glancing, dragging nature of the fall had saved her from utter destruction. The 'Mech had ripped a chimney through the overlying bush. A tiny patch of red sky hung above her. But what lay against her 'Mech's torso was what grabbed her attention.

The falling 'Mech had plowed trenches in a thick layer of scarlet, moss-like growth, revealing a gleaming metal hull. From the moss, black tendrils stretched like branching fingers, reaching for the sky, and those tendrils bloomed with the bizarre structures visible at the surface, forming a vast network that blanketed the behemoth like camouflage netting.

Arra ran a quick damage assessment while the voices from above continued to request her status. Cockpit integrity intact. Fusion bottle intact. Actuators intact. Weapons intact. She checked cockpit integrity again. Exposure to the levels of mercury in everything on Cinnabar—air, water, soil, flora—would be an agonized death sentence.

"I'm all right," she said. "Repeat, Ghost One still functional. I fell into a crevice. Anybody got a ladder?"

A flood of relief came over the comms.

Her lights swept up over the gigantic hull of the derelict ship. "And uh, I found it."

Arra sat in her cockpit, munching a protein bar while waiting for the salvage team to rig the crane that would lift her out. She would be here for a while. Real-time data from the initial scans of the crashed hulk rolled into her interface.

As the hours passed, she listened to comm chatter and catnapped. Eight years as a MechWarrior had drilled it into her: snatch whatever sleep you could. Voices dipped into her awareness.

"*Soyal*-class battleship..."

"...Holy smokes, this might be the FSS *Kali*... Lemme check the datacore..."

Military history was one of Arra's favorite pastimes, particularly about the ancient leviathans that had taken humanity's wars across the stars. A real *Soyal*-class battleship. 1.5 million tons, 1.1 kilometers long, with a complement of aerospace fighters *and* a full battalion of 'Mechs. Could the 'Mechs still be in there? Not only bristling with weaponry and untold tons of armor but also equipped with its own K-F drive *and* a hyperpulse generator. Here lay a crashed starbeast of unimaginable firepower, stuffed to the bulkheads with tech that preceded the Second Succession War. And no one today had anything like it...

What in the galaxy was it doing *here*?

That wandering thought roused her from her catnap with a sick feeling in her gut. Even as the wonders of pre–Succession War lostech fired her with excitement like a kid on her first hunt for buried treasure, an enormous sense of vulnerability settled over her. They were sitting on a treasure of immense value. The trouble with treasure: everybody else wanted it. In a galaxy ravaged by the Succession Wars, with entire worlds nuked into lifeless cinders and so much technology lost in those cinders, many societies barely clung to industrial technology, making this derelict ship the single most important object in the galaxy. The lengths the Great Houses would go to claim such a craft... Entire worlds were being destroyed, so no length was too far. Reclaiming and reverse engineering the technology within this behemoth could give the Lyran Commonwealth a significant advantage.

Through the video feeds of the other 'Mechs in Alpha Lance, she watched the 125-meter egg of the *Zephyr* descend from orbit, trailing a kilometer-long tongue of white flame. The *Excalibur*-class DropShip settled onto a solid area of the valley roughly two hundred meters from the overgrown trench the battleship had carved into Cinnabar's surface.

Terrence's voice came over the comms. "Hey, Squirty, how are you down there?"

"Call me that again and I'll jump out of this hole and kick your arse."

"Don't worry, this is a private channel. And you don't have jump jets."

"Note my previous statement."

"So is it fun driving a building around?"

"Loads. It assuages my destructive tendencies."

He laughed. "Have I told you how great it is to hear your voice, Squirty?"

A flush washed up her neck, but she growled, "I was going to say 'Same here.'"

"Sorry, I've been waiting eight years to call you that. It really is great to be working with you. What are the odds?" The sincerity in his voice rang true. The resentment about how they'd parted seemed like a well-forgotten dream. "I wanted to meet you during the voyage..."

"It's not like either of us had time with the frantic way they put all this together. Ghost Company had to service our 'Mechs en route. I think I managed about six hours total bunk time."

"They must have had some inkling about what we were going to find."

"If they'd known what this was, they'd have sent a whole regiment, with air support to boot." That feeling of vulnerability surged again, not for herself—she was a soldier—but for Terrence. The thought of him in harm's way... If the any of the Great Houses got word of what they'd found, her paltry 'Mech company wouldn't stand a snowflake's chance in a blast furnace against what they would send. And who knew what petty kingdoms and mercenary gangs lurked out here, salivating at the chance to get their hands on pre-Star League lostech. Cinnabar lay close to the Draconian Drift, but way out here on the Periphery, anything could happen.

She steeled herself to ask the question that had gnawed at her in those quiet spaces between training and battle. "Why didn't you ever write?" After four unreturned messages over the HPG network during the first months after she left for the Military Academy of Somerset, she had given up.

He took a deep breath and let it out. "Because I'm an arse."

"Duly noted." But he was still the smartest man she'd ever known. "How about we just leave it at that?"

"No dice, buddy. I've been chewing on that question too long."

"Then you shouldn't have left for the academy without telling me." His tone was friendly, but old resentment lurked in the undertones. "I never got to say goodbye."

"Yeah. That was a pretty crappy thing to do, wasn't it?" She'd never been any good at farewells. Her nineteen-year-old self's plan to spare herself some pain had ended up backfiring hard.

This voice from her past, the boy she had gone to school with; the boy she had run through the parks and backwoods of Taunton with on Somerset; the boy who used to put beetles down her back, who called her Squirty; the young man who had been there for her when her parents died, who convinced her she could be something besides an orphan; this voice dredged up clouds of memory, light and dark.

Or maybe this story she'd been telling herself was all a lie, and she had left without saying goodbye because on the night of their graduation from secondary school, there had been a single, brief kiss. The memory of it was still confusing. Too much like kissing her brother, if she'd had one. They'd laughed it off. *Well, that wasn't a good idea, was it?* She couldn't remember for certain who'd said that. Or if it was even true.

Even the sharpest memories of youth could be dulled by the terror and rage of battle, driving a gigantic machine whose sole purpose was to broil you in its belly.

"You still there?" he asked.

She cleared her throat. "Sorry. Fell asleep."

"I guess I'll have to work on my conversation skills."

"Yeah, you'd better. Here we thought this was going to be some stupid salvage mission. But you're going to be famous, the man who gets to reverse engineer all this lostech. They'll name an institute after you."

"I shall name it the Terrence and Squirty Institute for Amazing Stuff."

"And then you shall be a dead man."

Six hours later, the salvage team had cleared the area over her and erected a mobile crane capable of lifting her *Cyclops* out of its hole.

As her line of sight cleared the mass of organisms covering the surface of the area, she could see a tremendous amount of work was already done, creating a flat compound around *Zephyr*'s landing site, as well as paths for haulers and dozers to prepare access to the downed WarShip.

Moments later, Will Jenkins's voice sounded over the lance channel: "Have a nice rest, Hauptmann?"

"Beautiful, plus a nice soak in the hot tub," she said as the crane swung her *Cyclops* away from the crevice and set it down. She powered up all systems, initiated another round of diagnostics, and flexed the machine's great arms and legs, checking for damage. Some scuffing on the armor but nothing significant, thanks to the cushioning of the "vegetation."

The other three 'Mechs in Alpha Lance stood sentinel on a nearby hill that could well have been the hull of the WarShip.

Kommandant James's voice came over the company channel. "Hauptmann Jackson, report to 'Mech bay for repair. Environment suits are mandatory everywhere except quarters."

"You got it, Skipper," she said, then sighed.

Cinnabar's toxic environment was going to exacerbate the danger and complication of this mission by an order of magnitude. Decontaminating her 'Mech of all the accumulated mercury would be a pain in the *Arsch* the size of this worthless planet. Mercury was in *everything*—the native organisms, the underlying rock, the surface water, the air itself. As such, it made perfect sense that no record of survey or colony existed of this place beyond a name in the star charts. A potential benefit of all this liquid and vaporous metal was that it disrupted sensor sweeps, which was how this downed ship had lain hidden for a century. From an orbital survey, sensors had to be focused on its location to see it at all, especially after the native growth had covered it. It had taken a low-altitude survey craft using high-definition lidar to spot the gigantic, buried shape. Mercury also reduced the range of their transmissions, but it also dampened them such that passing in-system ships might not notice them. Then again, the chance of any ship simply passing through this system was slim to none. The only people out this far were pirates and wildcat settlers. A potentially serious downside was that the mercury would also reduce the range of the 'Mechs' targeting and fire-control systems. Hopefully, however, that drawback would not come into play.

How and why a WarShip had found its way out here, she could not fathom, except that mercury was a valuable manufacturing resource. But why send a WarShip of this magnitude?

Dozens of environment-suited civilians buzzed around her 'Mech's feet, deploying equipment, standing at the ragged edges of the WarShip's trench, driving earthmovers. Which of them was Terrence? He, as leader of the science team, would be at the forefront of explorations into the downed leviathan.

There. Perhaps seventy meters away, an environment suit that didn't quite reach her *Cyclops*'s knee waved at her. She returned the wave with her 'Mech's massive right arm.

Arra walked her *Cyclops* across Cinnabar's stony crimson soil toward the open hatch of *Zephyr*'s 'Mech bay, wondering how long they had before hell rained down on them.

"I feel it in my gut, Skipper," Arra said. "Something's not right here."

Twelve MechWarriors sat around the table in Kommandant James's ready room. Only twelve. One company. Ghost Company. The *Zephyr* carried bays for up to ninety combat vehicles, but most of those had been filled with salvage and construction equipment, the rest left empty to carry home whatever they found. Aside from the *Zephyr*'s inconsequential armament, twelve 'Mechs were this expedition's only firepower.

Kommandant James said, "As soon as we identified the nature of the derelict, I sent an encrypted message to *Pony Express*. As of now, the JumpShip is preparing to jump to the closest system with an HPG to forward my message directly to High Command."

Invader-class JumpShips like *Pony Express* had to recharge their K-F drive from the local star's energy after every jump. It was still parked at the star's zenith jump point with its solar sail unfurled, as it had been since *Zephyr* decoupled and burned across space for planetfall on Cinnabar.

"How long before they can go?" asked First Leutnant Jenkins, Arra's second-in-command in Alpha Lance.

"Four days," said Kommandant James.

First Leutnant Nate Justil, commander of Bravo Lance, put his elbows on the table. "So if an overwhelming force of hostiles shows up, we don't even have evac."

Arra knew Justil well enough to be sure he had meant his statement to express the direness of their situation, but to some it might hint at cowardice. She cleared her throat and said, "How soon can we expect reinforcements?" The closest LCAF base was Somerset, Arra and Terrence's home planet, four jumps away. The trip here had taken three weeks.

"This far out, there are few to be had. But *if* the message gets through, and *if* High Command is on the ball, we're looking at maybe a month. That is, unless there's a significant force that I'm unaware of. Lowly kommandants are seldom graced with the intricacies of LCAF wisdom."

First Leutnant Stacy Carina, commander of Charlie Lance, spoke up. "The good news is that the cold breeze whistling over our collective buttocks from hanging in the wind applies to everyone. The only other systems within one or two jumps of here are Periphery colonies and petty kingdoms. The most likely enemies we have to worry about are Dracs, but unless they're out there hiding behind an asteroid, they have just as far to come."

"So," Kommandant James said, "let's settle in, people. Give the civilian teams every courtesy. The sooner they finish their jobs, the sooner we can get off this toxic rock. Dismissed."

"It's not gourmet fare," Terrence said, setting down his tray, "but it beats food bars by a couple parsecs at least."

The crew mess deck's proximity to *Zephyr*'s command decks meant the food was indeed better than what was served in the troops' mess down in the greasy bowels of 'Mech bays and ammo racks.

"What do you mean? This isn't the Belle Ritz hotel?" Arra said. She couldn't tell what all the food was, but he had to be right in its comparison to food bars.

"It's weird finally seeing you in person," he said, his eyes lingering on her from every angle. "What's with the gray hairs?" His smile was like an elbow in the ribs.

"I call those 'markers of confirmed kills.'"

He looked away, smile fading.

"Sorry, did I say something wrong on our first day?" she said.

Mustering a refreshed grin, he raised his aluminum cup of vegetable juice. "To old friends."

She *tink*ed with him and dug in.

For her, it was as if they had only been apart for eight days rather than eight years. For him, though, there seemed to be a tightness in his shoulders. He laughed less easily than she remembered, and the old sparkle didn't always reach his eyes. She had her handful of gray hairs among the black foam of one temple; he had more lines in his face, on his hands, deeper furrows across a brow that had once been smooth and carefree. He was not the young man she'd left behind, nor was she any longer the person who'd done it.

They spent most of the meal catching up, talking about their families, news from home, updates of ongoing wars and rumors of impending ones.

When the food was gone, she refilled her water cup. "So tell me about our prize. I spent the day at the bottom of a hole."

"We've only barely stepped inside, but this is what we know. It's a command and control ship named FSS *Kali*. As near as we can tell, it's been here about a hundred years. It disappeared in 2838."

"Have you found the ship's logs?"

"Not yet. There's a crew working on getting some portable generators inside to see if we might power up a few subsystems. Things will go faster once the ramp is built and we don't have to rappel inside..." Even as he said that, his voice lit up with the challenge of it. "Can you imagine? A lostech WarShip! That thing has to be crammed to the bulkheads with technical specs and data. We just need to get it out."

The way he blossomed when he spoke of it warmed her inside. "I sense a 'however' coming," she said.

"The interfaces and hardware are...let's just say we don't have anything that plugs into it. It's going to be slow going."

"Well, that's good, because it's not like we have anywhere to go or any way to get there." The mess hall had emptied except for a couple of cooks banging pots and pans in the kitchen. The lights dimmed. A video screen offered a view of the spectacular sunset over a distant mountain, an explosion of more reds than language had names for.

She crossed her arms and put her elbows on the table. "So I've had enough dancing around. Something is eating you, and it's not the food. Spill it."

He looked at her for several long moments. "You've changed, Arra."

Bittersweet melancholy surged up in her breast. "Of course I have. So have you."

"You're still Squirty, but—"

"I have one request before you continue. No one would ever believe that 'Squirty' does not relate to something biological, instead of my collection of water pistols I had when I was ten. I have to maintain military discipline."

He took a deep breath and nodded. "Fair enough. You're still Arra, but..."

"But what?"

"You're a warrior now. I wasn't expecting that, I guess. I was, and I wasn't. I didn't know what it meant. I should have, but..." He shrugged.

Eight years of training and battle lay behind her, strewn with smoking hulks, dead civilians, and slain comrades. The horrors of it lapped at her memory like a tide that would come in waves, surging and subsiding but never ceasing. The worst was the stench of cooked flesh boiling out of a ravaged 'Mech. She doubted she'd ever eat barbecue again.

"You're harder now," he said.

A tear formed in her eye, and then she bristled. "I certainly hope so! You don't do what I've done—"

He raised a hand. "Sorry! Sorry, I started in the wrong place. I didn't mean to upset you. What I mean is...that hardness is part of this whole amazing package. You are a hauptmann! You're in command of your own company. I always thought you were strong, but now there's this *presence* about you. You could be a general someday."

She wiped her cheek. "Thanks." Then she twisted up her face. "But I'd have to marry a Steiner to get that far, and who'd want to spoil a family tree that's a flag pole?"

They both laughed.

He reached across the table and squeezed her hand, light skin over dark. "This life you've chosen. It suits you."

She smiled again leaned back, taking away her hand, warmth flooding her. "Well. Haven't you just turned into all kinds of sweet talker."

Arra lay in her bunk later—alone—wondering what the hell had just happened.

She was no stranger to sex. Like a lot of soldiers, she took it where she could find it, no strings attached, because tomorrow she could be dead. A MechWarrior's life in the thirtieth century didn't exactly allow for extended entanglements. She had made that choice the day she walked into Somerset Academy. But tonight, in the lift that took her back down to the near-empty bays where the grunts grunted and the grease monkeys monkeyed, she had been 100 percent full-throttle turned *on*.

But it was Terrence, which made it—weird.

Dammit...

She could not afford complications. Those kinds of feelings would dull her edge, stifle the killer instinct. When there was no one to go home to, you didn't worry as much about going home.

Cinnabar's density gave it a stronger gravity, about 1.2G, which was tolerable, but by the end of the day, she felt like she'd been trampled by walruses. Nevertheless, she heaved herself out of her bunk and headed for the simulator. By now the techs would have the simulators loaded with accurate terrain maps. If she wasn't going to sleep, she might as well do something useful.

No complications.

CINNABAR
COREWARD PERIPHERY
26 OCTOBER 2940

Four days later, their JumpShip's drive had been recharged. *Pony Express*'s jump officer's voice came relayed through *Zephyr*'s comms, "Calculations locked. See you on the flip side, *Zephyr*. Jumping in ten...nine...eight..."

No "zero" came, but a voice from *Zephyr*'s command crew said, "JumpShip away, Kommandant."

Due the light-speed transmission delay, by the time they received this communication, however, *Pony Express* had been gone for several minutes.

"Very well, Leutnant," Kommandant James replied. A moment later, her voice came over the command channel. "MechWarriors, this is *Zephyr* actual. You know what this means. Keep your people sharp."

"Ghost One," Arra said. "Copy that, Skipper." Alpha Lance was mapping the ridgeline of the mountain range five kilometers northwest of the crash site.

"Charlie One, copy," Leutnant Carina said, scouting the mouth of the valley where the crash site lay.

"Bravo One, copy, Kommandant," Leutnant Justil said.

Ghost Company was getting the lay of the land so they could complete their defense planning, familiarizing themselves with sight lines, the high ground, vantage points, and pitfalls. Any incoming hostiles would face defenders who knew where the best cover lay, where to set the most advantageous firing positions, and where to set an ambush. Given the fact that *Kali* was over a kilometer long, that was a lot of ground to cover, impossible to defend with only twelve 'Mechs.

A slashing rainstorm heaved over the mountains, covering the scarlet landscape with diaphanous gray veils, and that feeling of tense vulnerability washed through Arra again. She chided herself for foolishness. No one knew they were on this planet. (Did they?) They were too far out on the Periphery for anyone to reach them before reinforcements arrived. (Weren't they?) Such thoughts wouldn't leave her alone. It was worse now that Terrence was here, along with three hundred-odd civilians, all running around out there where one little puncture in their environment suits could dose them with enough toxic atmosphere to grant a long, lingering death. Cinnabar's atmosphere of carbon dioxide, argon, and nitrogen wouldn't have been immediately deadly except for the high percentage of mercury vapor. She had to protect them—protect him—which was a whole different scenario than slogging through sleeting autocannon fire with a thundering wall of stomping badassery at your back.

Her lance continued its patrol, sending loads of high-definition survey telemetry back to *Zephyr* with every step. In another few days, they would know every pebble and lung-bush within a ten-kilometer radius.

It was nearing another sunset when the kommandant's voice crackled again over the comms. "MechWarriors, back in the shed. Now."

"What's up, Skipper?" Arra said.

"Back to the shed, Jackson. *Zephyr* actual, out."

Jenkins's *Atlas* stopped a hundred meters away, its torso rotating toward her. "What the hell just happened?" he asked over the lance channel.

"Can't be good," said Fitzmeyer from his *Zeus*, two hundred meters distant.

"Cut the chatter, folks," Arra said. But Fitzmeyer was right. Whatever it was, the Skipper didn't want to put it on the airwaves.

The kommandant's ready room was full of not only MechWarriors but also the leaders of the civilian salvage and science teams. Terrence stood along the wall behind the kommandant, knuckle pressed to his lips.

"Dr. Larkin, if you please," Kommandant James said.

Terrence stepped forward. "As many of you know, we've been patching power back into some of *Kali*'s subsystems so that we can begin retrieval from its databanks. *Soyal*-class WarShips are equipped with mobile hyperpulse generators. When we patched power into that system..." He cast a worried look at Kommandant James. "The moment we applied power, it came online, but then it began transmitting. We don't know what it sent, only that it sent several encrypted bursts."

"Messages stored in the buffer?" Hauptmann Carina said. "Waiting for over a century?"

Rupert Adams, a short, stocky man with the hairy, no-nonsense look of a stereotypical salvager, put his knuckles on the table. "Or an intruder alert. A distress call."

"Now?" Arra said.

"We think the messages were queued, but the ship lost power before they could be sent," Kommandant James said. "Who knows what they went through actually landing this thing more or less in one piece?"

"So where are the crew?" Arra said.

Adams replied, "We don't have a count yet, but it looks like they're all still in there. We're still working on clearing the corpses. Ship's log says there was a complement of six hundred and nineteen crew, plus forty-eight MechWarriors. The ones the crash didn't kill probably starved to death or succumbed to mercury toxicity. Some parts of the ship still have air seal."

"But now," Kommandant James said, "someone might know *we're* here. We all know how valuable this find is. The last war put us almost back to the Stone Age."

Terrence said, "We don't have the equipment to try to hack the transmissions, and the encryption is beyond our capabilities."

Kommandant James said, "In short, we don't know what was sent, or to whom. So, I want to hear *useful* speculation. I want to hear contingencies. I want to hear every damn thing you can think of to prepare for possible company coming."

When the meeting ended two hours later, Arra tried to catch Terrence's eye, but he ignored her and hurried out with the rest of the scientists. The furrows on his brow ran deeper, and his fists clenched. She had a load of preparation to do anyway, and the weight of uncertainty looming over her had just redoubled.

This weight seemed to turn every effort over the next three days into slag. Mercury condensation had seeped into her missile-targeting system, fouling it, forcing her to spend a full day in the 'Mech bay for repairs.

Arra kept reading snatches of conversation over the local intranet.

>*No one's used that kind of power coupling in a hundred years!*

>*I'm going to be all day rigging up a thousand-signal databus. Get off my back.*

>*We need a medical team now! Miller just broke his leg! Repeat, medical team now!*

>*If they crash-landed this thing from orbit, it's a miracle it's not just a debris field. That helmsman had to be a genius.*

The salvage team had dug a ramp down into the WarShip's launch bay and created an airlock system into various areas of the ship. Enough hull integrity remained that the airlock would keep out the poisonous atmosphere so crews could work without the cumbersome environment suits.

The pressure, the frenzy, the sense that a bigger dog could come along and steal their bone at any moment led to squabbling and malaise. The worst of it was when two salvagers were killed when a crane malfunctioned and dropped forty tons of hundred-year-old aerospace fighter onto them. High Command would be jumping up and down and crapping in their diapers if they could salvage even half of what was on this ship, the fighters, the 'Mechs.

While her own 'Mech was being repaired, Arra donned an environment suit and ventured through the downed *Kali* until she found the 'Mech bay. There they were. A full battalion of 'Mechs. Many of them had busted loose of their moorings in the crash, cast about the 'Mech bay like gargantuan, discarded mannequins, but they were 'Mechs just the same, every one of them infused with its own history of battle scars, triumphs, and defeats. The sad part was that she had no one to pilot them. Ghost Company consisted of twelve MechWarriors. And even if they had enough MechWarriors, they wouldn't be able to pilot them without some serious training. They could be repaired, reverse engineered, brought into service to bolster an LCAF desperately in need of firepower, but not by Arra's little band. Somebody else would get to drive these bad boys.

The ship's logs also revealed the reason for *Kali*'s presence here—a mis-jump. They were aiming for somewhere else and somehow ended up here. Mis-jumps were rare, with the centuries-long refinement of K-F drive technology, but not unheard of.

During all of this, Arra tried to find time to see Terrence, but their schedules wouldn't allow it. She had to content herself with a few text messages now and then. As the days passed, no matter how much she fought it, a yearning to see him face-to-face grew to the point she had to act.

There was something she had to know, something she had to test.

It was the dead of sleep cycle, and she wasn't sleeping anyway when she went to his quarters and knocked on the door. As head of the science team, he had been granted private quarters. The rest of the scientists shared rotating berths.

There was no answer.

She pounded on the door, and then waited with her arms crossed. There was no way he was not in his bunk. He had been going hard lately, but he had to sleep sometime.

From the other side came a bleary, muffled, "What is it?"

"It's me."

The door opened and Terrence stood there in his underwear, rubbing sleep from his eyes. He gave her a slight but confused smile. "Hey, what's up?"

She stood there, arms crossed, and eyed him for a long moment.

"What?" he said. "I just hit my bunk about an hour—"

She stepped into the doorway, slid her hand around the back of his neck, and pulled him down to kiss her. His eyes bulged and their lips met. But they didn't just meet. They melded into a perfectly executed docking seal.

Through those two points of contact—hand and lips—she felt his body surge to wakefulness.

The awkwardness of that long-ago kiss on Graduation Day was nowhere to be found. She pulled him down, and he leaned into her. Her heartbeat surged and the heat level of her face hit the caution line. His hands circled her waist and drew her close, pressing his body against hers.

Then she drew back and put a palm on his chest, opening the distance. More confusion bloomed on his face.

She smirked at that.

His mouth fell open. "Uh, you want to come in?"

She turned away, paused, and winked at him. "Maybe next time."

Then she walked away, smiling, feeling his befuddled, tantalized gaze on her back. That ten meters to the lift was one of the longest walks of her life.

Test passed.

The next day, Terrence was much less distracted by science and salvage. They exchanged long strings of increasingly flirtatious text comms. As she occupied her day with continuing preparations for defense of the *Kali,* remembrance of that kiss was fresh on her lips, eclipsing any doubts about its truth or reality.

One moment during that day she found disconcerting. The random comm chatter from the salvage teams flowed endlessly, and she would monitor it occasionally to amuse herself in down moments. But then it stopped. Maybe an hour passed before she noticed it, but it was simply gone.

And there was nothing on the emergency feeds, so those workers were fine.

Scrolling back she found the last message on the civilian salvage channel: *Oh my god! No one is going to believe this!*

Her first thought was that they must have found something momentous. But what was it? Shutting down the channel likely meant they had been ordered to comm silence, to keep something secret.

So of course her curiosity would not sit still. Terrence would not be able to escape this interrogation. She chewed on possibilities for a while until her duties reabsorbed her attention.

Then something came over her private channel from Terrence.

>*This planet is red.*

>*Lasers are blue.*

>*Kisses are sweet.*

>*And I got something for you.*

>*My first poem since I was ten.*

>*Dinner?*

Suddenly she couldn't keep from grinning at the goofiness of it.

>*Bring it on*, she replied.

Over a dinner of mystery meat and gravy, he reached across the table, took her hand, and stroked it with his thumb. She squeezed his hand in return. And it felt natural, as if it should have been happening all along.

She took a moment to enjoy this feeling she had never experienced before. A fair share of lovers had crossed her path, but no crush had ever come together for her, always hampered by school, by duty, by circumstance. The moment took her by the heart and led her toward a path she had never trod. But there was also something she wanted to know.

"So what happened today?" she said.

He drew back and released her hand. "What do you mean?"

"Something happened. This really excited message came over the salvage-team comms, and then nothing for the rest of the day."

"Oh. You saw that, did you?"

She nodded. "So spill it."

"You have top-secret clearance?"

"Comes with the rank."

He leaned closer, glancing about for potential eavesdroppers, of which there were none. "We powered up *Kali*'s central databanks..."

"And?"

He took a deep breath and whispered, "It's all there. Undamaged."

"The data?"

"We have full access to an incredible trove of information. Technical readouts. Ship designs. 'Mech designs. Fighter designs. Targeting and sensor technology. Star maps. Lostech like this is worth more than I can even imagine. We could erase decades of technological Dark Age."

"And we have to get this back to High Command."

"And guard it with our lives until we do. This stuff could tip the galactic balance of power." Then he took a deep breath. "And there's something else." The trepidation on his face made her lean forward expectantly. "You would not believe the firepower this thing would have if it was operational."

"Refresh me on naval armament."

"*Soyal*-class battleships were one of the few that came fitted with a *mass driver cannon*."

Her eyes bulged. "You're kidding." Mass drivers could fire a 'Mech-sized slug at near relativistic velocities. Due to the structural and power requirements, they required enormous ships to mount them.

He nodded soberly. "And nukes. It has nukes."

A sick feeling filled her gut. With a mass driver *and* nukes, this ship was practically a genocide machine.

"It has six Killer Whale–class missile batteries. We're still checking, but at least two of them are loaded with Peacemaker warheads. According to the datacore, those are five hundred kiloton tactical nukes. Radioactivity scans confirm they're still there."

The implications grew in her imagination like mushroom clouds. They were sitting on at least two tactical nuclear warheads, the guidance and control systems of which consisted of century-old parts.

Terrence was still talking. "...preparing to transfer the databanks into the *Zephyr*. We have to move them physically. There's too much data there for ours to hold. It's going to be a tricky process." As he moved on from talking about the weapons of mass destruction, the excitement in his voice returned. He was a kid who'd just found real buried treasure. "Oh! I almost forgot." He reached into a cargo pocket. "I found this." On the table between them, he placed a sapphire the size of a child's fist. "I found a whole rack of these."

It vaguely resembled the emitter jewel for a large laser, and it was one of the most beautiful things she had ever seen. It caught the light and glimmered in strangely iridescent patterns.

She hesitated to touch it. "Are you allowed souvenirs?"

"This is a *salvage* operation, after all, and I'm the head of the science team. There are dozens of these. When we get back to civilization, though, it'll be worth a small fortune all by itself."

Its surface was impossibly smooth and polished. Her reflection was one of goggling eyes.

"Maybe you could retire and use it to, I don't know, start something else." His eyes held hers for a long moment.

She recoiled from the thought of giving up her life to be with him. That was a roaring train showing up ahead of schedule. She wasn't ready. But he knew as well as she did that last night could be the start of something. After that kiss, she sure as hell wasn't ready to let him go without finding out. This whole thing could go nuclear.

He looked flustered at her reaction. "Are you going to take it?"

Closing her hand over it, she looked him in the eye again. "Yes. But I'm going to have to think about the rest."

"I get it. Too soon."

She pocketed the massive jewel, then reached across the table, seized him by his collar, and pulled him halfway across the table to her. Her gaze met his with a growing heat. "Some things, though, don't need any more thinking about."

CINNABAR
COREWARD PERIPHERY
30 OCTOBER 2940

Arra and Terrence slept little over the next few days. If anyone in command noticed the fraternization, they kept it to themselves.

At one point, however, Jenkins said to her, "Your *Cyclops* practically has a spring in its step today."

"Does it?" she said.

"See, that's what I'm talking about. My CO has been swapped out with a *döppelganger*."

"I'm just excited by all this. Aren't you?"

"I'm tired of using a hundred-ton engine of destruction to schlep shipping crates."

Jenkins was right about that, at least. With defense prep mostly squared away, the 'Mechs with hand actuators had been enlisted to serve as freight haulers. The salvage team was stripping as much as it could from the interior of the *Kali*.

The datacore proved more challenging. Its design fully integrated it into the WarShip's structure. It would have to be cut out with surgical precision or else risk damaging its priceless data.

While the salvage team focused on extracting the datacore, the science team's attention turned to the WarShip's HPG, but they hadn't been able to crack the access codes. Direct communication with High Command, the slimmest knowledge that reinforcements were coming to help them guard this incredible prize, would have felt like emerging from weeks of blackness into the light of day.

Zephyr had stationed a sensor buoy in orbit to warn them of any arrivals, planned or otherwise. When *Pony Express* missed its return jump the following day, however, the expedition's general mood took a dark turn. When the announcement came that *Pony Express*'s scheduled return had come and gone, everyone stopped their work for a moment. The fate and commerce of the entire galaxy rested on the reliability of JumpShips. They ran like clockwork. As hours passed with no emergence signature, rumors buzzed back and forth like bees—Malfunction? Foul play?—as poisonous to morale as Cinnabar itself.

Nevertheless, crews busted their humps around the clock, and occasionally Arra would hear a bleat of triumph over the comms.

"Hey, we got one of the dorsal laser batteries working!"

Sounds of applause followed. A functional naval laser battery had just added a major punch to their defensive capabilities. Its firing arc would be limited, but when they pulled the trigger it would give any incoming enemies something serious to think about.

In celebration, someone called out, "Fire in the sky!" And a sizzling blue column of coherent light speared into the clouds, blindingly bright.

For a moment, the tenseness of her lance faded, as if a deadly specter from the past was now watching over them like a guardian, a guardian with a great big stick. *Kali* boasted a dozen such lasers, plus heavy Gauss cannons and autocannons, but unfortunately the majority of them were buried or destroyed in the crash. The mass driver would also be unusable, as it fired only in a narrow forward arc.

The next few days saw the successful connection of the WarShip's laser battery to *Zephyr*'s fire-control system. Meanwhile, the DropShip's bays were filling up with tons of salvage, including disabled 'Mechs.

It was a day of toxic downpour and poisonous, crimson slurry when the shout came over the command comms.

"Attention! Attention! Multiple emergence signatures."

CINNABAR
COREWARD PERIPHERY
3 NOVEMBER 2940

"Ghost Company, this is *Zephyr* actual. We have three emergence signatures. Telemetry indicates one *Star Lord*-class JumpShip and one more, configuration unknown. I'll be the pessimist and presume it's a WarShip."

A *Star Lord* could carry six DropShips.

"Sounds like an entire regiment," Arra said over the command channel, a ball of cold lead forming in her belly. "Are they ours?"

"Negative."

"DCMS?"

"Unknown."

The channel fell silent. An entire regiment. A WarShip's worth of aerospace support. And *Zephyr* had nowhere to run. Its JumpShip was gone. If they tried to flee into space, they'd be brought down like a sheep by a pack of wolves. If they bugged out, they'd have to leave their treasure behind, handing it over to their enemies. There were still 'Mechs to be brought out, and aerospace fighters as well. The datacore extraction was still in process.

"When do they hit orbit?" Arra said.

"Best estimate is forty-eight hours," Kommandant James said.

"Have they hailed us?"

"No. And we're not going to hail them on the off chance they're just passing through. Effective immediately, we're shutting down everything except passive sensors, life support, and low-power point-to-point communications. Radio silence."

"Aye aye, Skipper," Arra said.

Terrence's voice cut in. "Kommandant, if I may?"

"Keep it short, Doctor."

"With forty-eight hours, my people might be able to get more of *Kali*'s weapons systems online."

"Make it happen, Doctor. And I'm evacuating all civilians into *Kali*." It was a much more durable target than a lone, exposed DropShip. "Hauptmann Jackson, initiate defense plan Alpha."

CINNABAR
COREWARD PERIPHERY
4 NOVEMBER 2940

The utter silence was deafening. No more comm chatter. No more background updates. Only the sound of the wind and rain in a cold, dark 'Mech.

Arra sat in her powered-down *Cyclops* about six kilometers from the *Zephyr* on a high escarpment overlooking the easiest land route into the valley. She and rest of her lance stood like dark, humanoid sentinels, with clear lines of fire and excellent cover. They'd been in position for almost twenty-four hours, covered in sensor-dampening netting and freshly painted in red-and-ocher camouflage to match the landscape's natural colors.

At night, when Cinnabar's face had turned from its small, red star, the planet occluded any incoming telemetry, any indication of what the bogies were doing. Were they coming? Were they merely pausing to recharge their drives and jump away again?

Life support aboard the *Zephyr* had been reduced to air scrubbers and water reclamation. All to impersonate a lifeless rock on an uninhabited world.

In the bowels of *Kali*, the science and salvage crews worked feverishly to bring the WarShip's munitions and energy weapons online, but a hundred years of corrosion, dust, and leaching mercury had wreaked hell on everything.

During the night, the cloud cover dissipated, and a sliver of scarlet sun reared over the jagged horizon.

Kommandant James's voice came over the low-power laser comm. "We've been scanned. Hostiles inbound. We have visual confirmation. Still too far out to read any markings, but we have five *Union*-class DropShips and one *Vigilant*-class WarShip inbound."

Five 'Mech companies, plus aerospace-fighter support and naval weapons from the WarShip. It was a full battalion, and then some. And there was nowhere to run.

"ETA?" Arra said.

"Twelve hours."

"Have they hailed us?" Arra said.

"No."

"Your orders, Kommandant?"

"Defend the crash site. We will use *Kali* against incoming DropShips as best we can."

"Aye aye, Skipper."

"Godspeed, Hauptmann."

As their fusion drives brought the incoming ships nearer, Arra expected updates of hails or some indication of who it was. It had to be Draconis forces. But the minutes ticked into agonized hours with no news.

In these interminable hours, she could stand it no longer. She tried repeatedly to raise Terrence over the network. Finally his grime-smeared face appeared on her screen. He smiled crookedly. "Hey, Squirty."

"Yeah. Look, I just want to say, we're going to get through this, all right? We're going to come out the other side, and we're going to get off this rock, and we're going to—"

A shower of sparks lit him from behind, making him flinch. "You got it. We've almost got a Gauss battery operational..." He glanced over his shoulder. "Well, maybe not. Where's maintenance when you need 'em, right?"

She smiled. "I just...wanted to say—"

A voice called from behind him. "Terry! We need a hand calibrating this targeting feed!"

"Gotta go, Squirty. Watch your arse until I get to."

"Ditto," she said.

Then his face disappeared.

She had wanted to say that their nights together had been some of the greatest in her entire life, that she didn't want them to end, and that surely they could find a way to be together, even in a galaxy as complicated as this one.

Would she ever get the chance?

CINNABAR
COREWARD PERIPHERY
5 NOVEMBER 2940

Teams were still working around the clock, down to the last minute. MechWarriors remained on station, quiescent, waiting.

Eleven hours later, the incoming ships fell into orbit around Cinnabar. The sky above was the color of congealed blood. The potato-like shapes of Cinnabar's two small moons shone gold on the horizon, bathed in falling sunlight. Alpha Lance still held position six kilometers from the crash site.

Kommandant James came over the comms. "Still no attempt to hail us. And as yet, they have not made any deorbiting maneuvers."

"Any visuals on markings?" Arra said.

"Not yet. But they must know we're here. They're assuming geosynchronous orbit above the crash site. Without cloud cover, they can see us with a good pair of binoculars." An exaggeration to be sure, but no less true. "It's time to warn them."

"Warn *them*?" Arra said.

"Unknown vessels," the kommandant said, "this is the LCS *Zephyr*. We are engaged in a lawful salvage operation for the Lyran Commonwealth. Please state your intentions, or we will assume hostile intent."

Moments later, an unfamiliar voice crackled over the comms, "This is *Tai-sa* Aaron Tanaka of the DCS *Kuromaru*. Cinnabar is under the protection of the Draconis Combine. You will cease all salvage operations and vacate the surface of this planet immediately."

"You have no claim to this planet, *Tai-sa*. We are well outside the boundaries of Combine space. We will not warn you again."

"That's where you're wrong, Kommandant. We laid claim to this system some years ago. In fact, three of our deep-space mining colonies are on asteroids in the outer system. We have found this system to be quite valuable in its abundance of heavy metals. Cinnabar possesses a unique set of...challenges, but we lay claim to it nevertheless. Now, I will not warn *you* again—"

"Cut the feed," Kommandant James said.

From near the kommandant, the executive officer, Hauptmann Van Hughes, spoke up. "They must have picked up that HPG burst. But if they had known about *Kali*, they'd have taken it for themselves a long time ago. They probably can't see it with their scanners and the environmental interference."

"XO, pull up anything you can find on this *Tai-sa* Aaron Tanaka."

"Aye aye, sir," Hughes said.

"Fire control," the kommandant said. "Target all of *Kali*'s available batteries on their lead DropShip. If they make a single deorbiting maneuver, open fire."

Reading the ship's records, Hughes said, "*Tai-sa* Aaron Tanaka. Remarkably undecorated for an officer of command rank. Assumed command of the *Kuromaru* three standard years ago, assignment unknown. His early career was marked by unspecified 'improprieties.' My assessment, Kommandant, is that he sounds like someone of marginal capability relegated to a guard post in the middle of nowhere. That could mean he's going to try to show his superiors some ambition for reassignment back to civilization. He might feel he's been out in the cold too long. That could make him more aggressive. Especially if he's certain he has us outgunned."

"How badly *are* we outgunned?" Kommandant James said.

"A *Vigilant*-class is a corvette, less than ten percent of *Kali*'s tonnage. Five naval autocannons, plus four lasers, three cannons, four PPCs, and three White Shark missile batteries. They can pound us to pieces if they feel like it."

Arra felt helpless as she listened to the audio signal from *Zephyr*'s bridge. There was nothing she could do until enemy forces hit the ground. But she could see the kommandant's strategy. A full naval salvo from *Kali* might take out one or more DropShips, each carrying a company of 'Mechs, which would make them retreat out of range, deorbit below the horizon, fly in low, and force their 'Mechs to march overland. The enemy would hesitate to return fire until they assessed the ground forces. The hundred-meter-high *Zephyr* had no capital ship weapons—it was not designed for space combat—but it could defend itself from a 'Mech ground assault with PPCs, lasers, missile racks, and an autocannon. On the other hand, it was a sitting target, slow to get moving.

"Firing solution entered, Kommandant."

"Wait for any deorbiting maneuvers," the kommandant said. "Then concentrate fire."

Silence crawled past.

Arra tied one of her screens into *Zephyr*'s tactical display, which showed the enemy ships in orbit.

"Any response?" the kommandant said.

"Negative... Wait! *Kuromaru* is opening its launch bay."

"Fire!"

The landscape blazed with deadly light. Two naval laser batteries, then the single naval Gauss cannon, an order of magnitude more powerful than anything a 'Mech or DropShip carried, blasted spaceward. Arra's eyes flicked between her tactical screen and the clear, crimson firmament, combing the sky for debris falling into the atmosphere.

"Fire for effect," came the kommandant's voice over the eerie hush of the quiet wind.

Kali unleashed another blinding barrage from the only batteries it could bring to bear, punching crackling holes in the sky.

"Target is venting atmosphere. It has lost attitude control."

"Firing solution on number two DropShip," the kommandant said. "Fire when ready."

Then the sky lit up from on high, like a rain of meteors from orbit.

"Warheads inbound from *Kuromaru*! White Shark missiles."

"Warhead targets?" the kommandant said.

"*Zephyr*, Kommandant."

Then a tremendous crashing, crackling noise over the comms made Arra flinch. From her six-kilometer distance, she caught the vertical, slashing glint of incoming autocannon rounds onto *Zephyr*'s position. A DropShip, even one as a large as *Zephyr,* could not take a pounding from a WarShip for long.

"Thirty seconds." The stunned surprise and resignation in the comm officer's voice turned Arra's stomach into molten lead.

The White Sharks came down on tongues of brilliance, waves of them streaking toward *Zephyr*'s position, converging onto a single point. Enough of them would turn *Zephyr* into shrapnel.

"Ghost Company," Kommandant James said, "your orders are to defend *Kali* at all cost. We *cannot* allow the Dracs to take home our prize."

Another autocannon round tore through *Zephyr* with the sound of metallic thunder.

Arra said, "Understood, Kommandant."

"Twenty seconds."

"*Zephyr* gunners, target incoming missiles," Kommandant James said. "Godspeed, Ghost Company."

"Ten seconds."

"Concentrate all fire from *Kali* on those DropShips."

The missiles erupted in a fusillade of fury. The detonations vibrated up through the legs of Arra's 'Mech, even at this distance. Destruction continued to blast skyward from *Kali*. White Shark missiles would barely scratch the WarShip's paint.

The tactical feed from *Zephyr* went blank on Arra's screen.

"*Zephyr*, this is Ghost One, come in," she said.

No response.

She made several more attempts but received no response.

The fire from *Kali* fell silent, eliciting a moment of rising panic in Arra's throat. Then she remembered that *Kali*'s fire control had been shunted to *Zephyr*'s gunners and targeting systems.

She keyed the civilian comm channel. "Terrence, come in, this is Arra."

"We're okay in here," Terrence said.

She hoped no one else heard her choked sound of relief. "It's good to hear your voice. Ghost Company is intact."

"I think *Zephyr* is gone. Our data and video feeds are down."

And just like that, Arra became the senior officer. She was now in command. And she did her best to tamp down the thought of how many hundreds of people had just died.

Terrence continued, "We're working on transferring fire control back here, but it'll be a few minutes."

"We may not have a few minutes. If you don't bring down those DropShips, we're going to be neck deep in enemy 'Mechs."

"I know that." Desperation tinged his voice.

She didn't need to tell him that the future of the Inner Sphere was at stake here. If the Draconis Combine acquired the information in *Kali*'s datacore, they would become unstoppable. "We're going to get through this." She didn't know how, but she needed to tell him.

"I'm the one supposed to say that to you. I'm the one with bigger guns."

"Just get them pointed the right direction. Out."

A minute later, *Kali*'s Gauss cannon blazed back to life, pouring destruction toward targets too distant for sight.

"Ghost Company," Arra said to her fellow MechWarriors, "maintain positions and hold to defense plan Alpha. And keep your eyes open for fighters. The WarShip up there can carry a full complement."

Acknowledgments pattered back over the comms.

Defense plan Alpha had been developed over several weeks of topographic study and strategic examination. *Kali* lay in a valley approximately twenty kilometers long and seven across at its widest point, at one end of which was a lake of mercury. A jagged mountain range dominated the northern side of the valley, with a rugged scree plain on the south. The floor of the valley was mostly level but with a number of prominent rock outcroppings scattered across it. Close scans of the valley walls revealed four entrances to the valley floor from the south, crevices navigable by 'Mechs. Two of those entrances had been blasted shut with explosives, but with enough pounding or orbital bombardment, they could be opened again. Two were too wide to be closed without a significant construction effort, but they had been too short of workers for such a task.

With the *Kali*'s guns still operational, incoming DropShips would deorbit out of range, deploy their 'Mechs, and send them in on foot. The enemy would have to pass through those two choke points. The choke points were eight kilometers apart, too far from each other for three measly lances to guard both effectively. Could Ghost Company—twelve 'Mechs—hold against an entire battalion?

Where the hell were the reinforcements?

Minutes passed. Fire poured skyward from the distant *Kali*. Had they managed to take out any more DropShips? Each one destroyed took with it a company of 'Mechs plus other ground forces. The WarShip continued to rain destruction from orbit onto *Zephyr*'s position.

From his *Atlas* a few hundred meters distant, Jenkins said, "Good grief. The bastards are trying to turn *Zephyr* into gravel."

The enemy knew how lost the Lyran force would be without the support of *Zephyr*'s sensor package and resupply base. They would have much less information about what was happening in orbit or where any surviving DropShips landed. And then there was the morale blow of losing their only ride off-planet. Moreover, they had zero air assets, either for reconnaissance or close-support. They were effectively blind, stranded, and without support of any kind. They were screwed unless the cavalry arrived.

"Terrence, this is Arra," she called. "I need a status report on those DropShips."

"We took out one more, but lost track of the other three," Terrence said.

"Have they deorbited?"

"We don't know. But it looks like you're going to have company."

"Boss, we have incoming," said Jenkins. "I count twelve bandits, deorbiting to the north-northwest. *Hellcat* fighters by the look of them."

That would make defending those choke points even more difficult. Air support negated Ghost Company's terrain advantage.

Alpha Lance, comprised of assault 'Mechs, now guarded the eastern valley entrance. Bravo Lance's heavy 'Mechs watched the western entrance. Charlie Lance's light 'Mechs held a reconnaissance position on the plain above. With their agility, jump jets, and high speed, they could retreat into the valley once the enemy committed their forces.

Where the hell was *Pony Express?*

The incandescent tails of atmospheric entry turned into contrails as the *Hellcat*s streaked lower, arcing straight toward the crash site. *Kali* took a few shots at them, but the fighters were too agile, too fast, the civilian gunners too inexperienced.

"Ghost Company, hold your fire," Arra said. "Don't give away our positions."

Terrence said over the comms, "Arra, those fighters are mighty difficult targets."

"Focus on the big target. That WarShip is those fighters' home base. It hasn't shown any inclination to shoot at you. Maybe they're unwilling to cause any damage to the prize. Try to drive them off station, or else it could start bombarding my people like it did *Zephyr.* Fighters get mighty uncomfortable without a barn to fly back to." Like 'Mechs without a DropShip.

"Understood." Then his voice came over a private channel. "Be safe, Arra. You mean the world to me."

Her eyes blurred for a moment. "Right back at you. In your spare time, start thinking about nice places to live on Somerset."

She could hear his smile. "I'll put that on my list. Out."

Silvery points appeared at the head of the incoming contrails, then hurtled in for a supersonic pass directly over the columns of smoke where *Zephyr* had rested.

Twelve *Hellcat* fighters could cut a single 'Mech lance to pieces. Furthermore, each of them boasted a shocking amount of armor. The only way to punch through that armor would be to use long-range missiles to ablate the armor and try to punch through with lasers and PPCs. Such a tactic would leave her 'Mechs' ammunition depleted for when the ground forces showed up, and there would be no chance of resupply. But if Ghost Company didn't take out those fighters as quickly as possible, there wouldn't be any Ghost Company left to face the incoming 'Mechs.

One of the most useless things in a MechWarrior's life was ammunition left in the magazine of a dead, smoking 'Mech.

The fighters banked toward Bravo Lance's position.

"Uh-oh, they've made us," Leutnant Justil said.

"Bravo Lance, lock onto my targeting signal," Arra said. "I will concentrate your fire from here."

"Roger that, Ghost One," Leutnant Justil said. "Range, three klicks and closing. Two. One. Fire!"

Arra piggybacked her *Cyclops*'s command-and-control suite onto Bravo One's scanners and optics, putting her virtually into targeting command of Bravo Lance. Relying on her help, they could effectively concentrate their fire to maximize damage to fast-moving targets.

The four heavy 'Mechs defending the western entrance unleashed everything they had. Large lasers, PPCs, and missile racks spewed destruction at the incoming fighters. Far out of range, Alpha Lance laid low. Charlie Lance remained hidden.

A conflagration of sapphire needles from the *Hellcats* raked Bravo's positions. As the combatants surged into closer range, the emerald lances of medium lasers stabbed back and forth like a knife fight. Rock exploded and vaporized in fire and smoke, obscuring visual contact. Arra's telemetry feed flickered with explosions. Two *Hellcats* fragmented into smoking fireballs that scattered over the terrain, the rest streaking past and peeling away for another run.

Arra's eyes were glued to her command readouts. Bravo Lance's damage report rolled across her command screen, telling her they wouldn't withstand another strafing run. Justil's *Marauder* had lost one of its two PPCs, its most powerful weapons, which meant the armor on its right torso was also compromised. "Take cover, Leutnant. You can't go toe-to-toe with them again."

Ten 60-ton *Hellcats* remained, and as they carried only energy weapons, which required no ammunition, they could rain death onto Ghost Company's heads until they ran out of fuel.

"Alpha Lance," Arra said, "when they come around again, open fire with energy weapons even if they're out of range. Let's try to draw them off Bravo Lance. Lock into my targeting control to concentrate our fire."

"Copy that, Boss," Jenkins said.

The *Hellcats* wheeled high, high overhead and came down on a course splitting the center of the valley, soon to pass within a kilometer of Alpha Lance's position.

Arra locked onto the lead fighter. "Coming into missile range." Her sensors would set off the fighters' threat warnings and reveal Alpha's presence. "Fire."

The combined long-range missiles of Alpha Lance's four assault 'Mechs—eighty-five missiles per salvo—blasted skyward and streaked toward the fighters. Alpha would get two, maybe three salvos before the fighters passed out of range. As heavy fighters, *Hellcats* had enough armor to withstand one, perhaps two, such salvos.

"Pound it!" Jenkins said.

Arra held her finger to the fire button, counting the milliseconds as her missile rack reloaded itself then launched another salvo. More missiles boiled into the crimson sky. The fighters jinked and flipped, but the missiles' guidance systems held sure. Showers of sparks and smoke burst from the *Hellcats'* engines as two of them went barreling into crimson ground cover.

Her moment of elation was quashed by the knowledge that eight fighters remained, along with unknown companies of enemy 'Mechs. Ghost Company's missile racks, impressive as they were, had no means of reloading. Soon, Shetty's 85-ton *Stalker* on Arra's flank would be reduced to spitting at the incoming enemy, as it carried only long-range missile racks.

The remaining fighters peeled off, but they made the mistake of gaining a shade too much altitude, bringing themselves into the firing arcs of *Kali*'s laser batteries. In what must have been incredibly lucky shots, the naval lasers blasted two of them into spinning chunks of debris.

The *Hellcat*s executed an incredibly high-G maneuver and streaked up toward the stratosphere. PPC bursts tracked them upward but without any further hits.

Clapping and an exuberant whoop sounded over the comms.

"Back where you came from, cowards!" someone shouted.

"Don't get cocky, Ghost Company," Arra said. "We're going to have 'Mechs inbound. Stay frosty. Leutnant Carina, does Charlie have eyes on any DropShips?"

"Negative, Hauptmann," Carina said. "Passive sensor suites are up."

Arra keyed the civilian channel. "*Kali*, come in."

"*Kali* here," Terrence replied.

"Good shooting. That last salvo took those fighters off our backs."

"We're quick learners around here," he said, but then his voice darkened. "Look, Arra, there's something you need to know."

"What?" A tone in his voice struck a chord of worry in her chest.

"We *cannot* let *Kali*'s datacore fall into Combine hands. We've got it wired with enough thermite and high explosive to slag an asteroid."

"Understood. We'll do our best to keep them off your doorstep. What about the WarShip?"

"It's holding station above us on brute thrust. It hasn't fired back, like it doesn't know what we are or where to target. We've been trying to hit it, but we haven't done much more than scorch the paint, thanks to these decrepit sensors."

"Keep punching."

"Will do."

Her tactical display beeped at her again. Six blips were once again coming down from the fringe of space but toward an area far to the north of the valley, using the mountain range to shield themselves from *Kali*'s batteries.

Minutes again ticked by with *Kali* pouring fire into space at the distant hulk of *Kuromaru*, just barely visible as a shiny, ovoid smudge with Arra's optics on full magnification.

"Hauptmann!" Carina cried. "Multiple contacts! Grids Sierra Twelve and Echo Fourteen."

Arra checked her map overlay. Contacts in those two zones meant that at least two DropShips had landed, at least two companies incoming. And they were approaching both entrances. "Mark your bandits and hold position, Charlie One."

There were few places for a ten-meter-tall 'Mech to hide on that plain, and the native organisms grew to only waist high. Charlie Lance was positioned in natural rock formations enhanced to camouflage them from both eyes and sensor sweeps.

Six deadly shapes wove out of the northern mountain peaks, slashing low across the valley toward Bravo Lance.

"Bravo, you have incoming!" Arra called, feeding them another target.

"Copy that."

Lasers and electric-blue PPC bursts pierced the sky. In another high-G maneuver, only five fighters rocketed spaceward again.

Then the bombs exploded in a crackling, thundering, rock-splintering barrage around Bravo's position.

Arra's tactical display beeped warnings at her as damage reports from Bravo Lance filtered in. Bravo Three, Elenor Marris's *Warhammer,* turned deep scarlet with a slash through her icon. If her cockpit was compromised, the mercury vapor in the air would render her a slow, agonizing death.

They were trading blows but couldn't withstand this continued punishment with at least two companies of unscratched 'Mechs bearing down. The enemy was winning the battle of attrition.

That was when dusk fell. Cinnabar's thin atmosphere and *Kali*'s near-equatorial location meant that night descended almost like flicking a switch. Arra had been too preoccupied to notice the time of day.

This was both good and bad, more difficult for MechWarriors to use their naked eyes, but in cooler air a 'Mech's heat bloom shone like fireworks, even from orbit. That WarShip could easily target them. And there was no cover from such a devastating attack.

Even as the thought crossed her mind, fresh explosions rocked Bravo Lance's location. Rock exploded in molten gobbets from the energy transfer of naval autocannons. From Arra's distance, they looked like sparks but were likely the size of boulders.

The pummeling hail continued.

"Bravo One, this is Ghost One. Displace immediately. I repeat, displace. Fall back to Grid Foxtrot Three." An arroyo there would provide some cover.

Justil's voice sounded shaky, overwhelmed by the thunderous concussions. "Copy, Ghost One."

Bravo Lance barreled out of their positions at full speed.

The crimson sky faded to starry black. The WarShip overhead was a small sliver of silver visible to the naked eye and standing atop wandering auroras kicked up from its drives pummeling the atmosphere. *Kali*'s batteries illuminated the valley like lightning flashes, casting stark, shifting shadows.

"Bravo Lance has reached Foxtrot Three," Leutnant Justil said. "We no longer have enfilade on the west entrance, though. If they rush it, they'll be all over us before we can react."

"Hold there, Bravo One," Arra said. "We'll—"

Then an ephemeral voice crackled over the command channel, distorted by distance and cosmic radiation. "*—phyr*, do you read? This is the LCS *Wagner*, inbound on the planet Cinnabar. Please respond. Orbital insertion in forty-six hours and fifteen minutes. *Zephyr,* please respond. This message will repeat—"

Arra clamped a hand over her mouth, tears welling. A bigger dog had just claimed the junkyard. A *Commonwealth*-class WarShip, *Wagner* significantly outgunned the *Kuromaru* and also carried eighteen fighters, three times as many fighters as *Kuromaru* had remaining. Orbit above Cinnabar was going to get interesting. But Arra had no way of contacting *Wagner*. A 'Mech's communication system was not powerful enough to reach beyond orbit.

Could Arra, her MechWarriors, and the civilians on *Kali* survive another forty-six hours? It all depended on what the Dracs did with that same allotment of time.

The answer came less than a minute later. *Kuromaru* turned the full fury of its batteries on *Kali*. Autocannon rounds hailed down. The upper atmosphere crackled with sonic booms from their hypersonic entry.

"Terrence, come in," Arra called.

Terrence's face appeared on her screen, shuddering with the concussions of bombardment. His face looked haggard, his eyes bloodshot. "Good to see you, Squirty. We can't see much of what's going on out there with only targeting sensors. Most of our data came from *Zephyr*."

She gave him the best shaky smile she could manage. "The cavalry has arrived, but they're forty-six hours away."

The shuddering in the video ceased.

A voice hailed them. "Lyran forces on the planet below, this is *Taisa* Aaron Tanaka of the DCS *Kuromaru*. I offer you and your remaining forces quarter. Surrender your 'Mechs and the hulk you're scavenging, and you will not be harmed. You have five minutes to respond."

Terrence had heard the message. "We can't let them have *Kali*. The damage they could do with this technology...millions of lives, billions. A *mass driver*!"

"And I'll be damned if I just hand over my 'Mech."

"Can you hold out for forty-six hours?"

"I have to," she said. *For you. For both of us.*

Kali's armor would withstand orbital bombardment for a short time, but once the hull was penetrated, *Kuromaru*'s guns would rip through the interior structure like paper and expose the civilians to toxic atmosphere.

Arra needed to buy them time. With the *Wagner*'s arrival, Tanaka was no doubt aware that his ship was now outgunned, so he was trying to rush a resolution that would allow them to get away before the *Wagner* reached fighter range, which would be a handful of hours ahead of orbital insertion.

In battle, when lives were on the line, every minute counted.

She hit the hailing channel. "*Tai-sa* Tanaka of DCS *Kuromaru*, this is Hauptmann Arra Jackson. Perhaps I should tell you what you're about to destroy."

Tanaka replied immediately, his voice flat with annoyance. "You should have taken my offer of quarter, Hauptmann."

"Do you wish to know or don't you?"

"Yes, yes, fine. Tell me."

"What would you say if I told you you're blasting holes in century-old lostech?"

"I would say you should turn it over to me immediately, and we shall have an officers' agreement for your safe passage."

Her mind spun its treads. The bigger the lie, the more plausible it might be. Mix it with enough truth... "This hulk is the *Kali,* a *Soyal*-class battleship. These century-old naval batteries still work pretty well, wouldn't you agree?"

"No more mincing words, Hauptmann. Cut to the bone."

She didn't need to tell him about the mass driver. His records would have that information easily at hand. "This WarShip carries six Killer Whale batteries. Two of them are pointed at you."

Killer Whales were ship-killers, enough to give him pause.

Arra went on, "These two in particular are loaded with five hundred kiloton tactical nukes. See, while we've been talking, the folks onboard *Kali* have been prepping those for launch."

"You have no such weapons!"

"Now, don't you bet your life on it. I'm sure the plutonium still works just fine. You're going to withdraw your vessel, right goddamn now, or we're going to turn your ship into a beautiful meteorite shower. We don't even have to hit you. We just have to get *close*. It'll be an awfully pretty show from here."

Tai-sa Tanaka's profile, its lack of decoration for a command officer, his placement out in the Deep Periphery, seemed to indicate an unwillingness to put himself squarely into harm's way, or at the very least, a reluctance to take chances. Tanaka already had at least two companies of 'Mechs groundside, perhaps three. He might choose to move out of range of any threat and let his 'Mechs move in to do the dirty work.

"We're not going to fire a warning shot," Arra said.

Arra silenced the channel to *Kuromaru* and opened the civilian channel. "Terrence, this is Arra."

"Terrence here."

"Can you open one of the Killer Whale launch tubes?"

"Um, maybe? We don't have the power to launch anything, though."

"You can't launch at all?"

"We'd have to reroute the power from the gun batteries, and I doubt we'd be able to put it back in time if this doesn't work."

"Understood. Get one of those launch tubes open. Let them see it."

"I'll see what I can do."

Arra clicked off and waited.

A minute later, Terrence came on. "One launch tube open, as requested. Remind me never to play poker with you."

"A wise man you are," Arra said.

Moments ticked by.

Terrence came over the comms again. "Arra, you're not going to believe this, but we're seeing main engine blooms on the WarShip. They're moving away." She could hear cheering around him.

She smiled grimly.

"That's the good news," Terrence said, his voice turning dark.

"And the bad?"

"Their last salvo collapsed a section of the hull. We're trapped in here. It'll take us days to cut free."

"Do you have hard seal?" Death by mercury vapor wasn't something she would wish on anyone, especially Terrence.

"Negative. We've gone to suits." They would be fine for a few hours, but the air supplies in environment suits would not last until *Wagner* arrived. The civilians would have to find airtight chambers to reestablish life support. All while still manning the guns and keeping enemy fighters off their backs.

"Then hold tight. We'll take care of the incoming 'Mechs."

"'Mechs?"

"At least two companies inbound. Time to go to work."

"Give 'em hell, sweetheart."

Warmth flushed through her. No one had ever called her that before.

"Hauptmann," Leutnant Carina said, "inbound 'Mechs approaching both entrances. Two full companies."

"Copy that," Arra said. "Displace to grid Echo Three and provide support for Bravo Lance. Bravo One, come in."

"Bravo One," Leutnant Justil said.

"You're clear from above. Reestablish enfilade and hold that entrance. Charlie is coming to back you up. Terrence, come in."

"*Kali* here," Terrence said.

"Do you have a firing solution on Grid Echo Three?"

"Negative. Terrain interference because um...we're buried in the ground."

"Damn it." She had been hoping the naval guns could support the valley entrances. *Kali* would be useless in the ground fight. "Keep your eyes peeled for incoming fighters. We need you to watch our backs."

"Understood," Terrence said. "The fighters have withdrawn to orbit, but we'll keep an eye on them."

"How are your people?"

"Don't you worry about my people. You just do your job and kick some ass."

Her eye caught the flickering blue of a PPC burst eight kilometers distant, like a tiny shooting star streaking over the lip of the valley.

Carina said, "Ghost One, this is Charlie One. They've seen us, changing course to follow."

Forty-five hours until the *Wagner* arrived. The battle would be over in two. Arra's mind flashed with wishes. Air support. Explosives. Ammunition. Everything she didn't have and desperately needed.

"Bandits in the trench," Leutnant Justil said. "Two kilometers and closing. Looks like assault and heavy lances." Even with Charlie Lance backing them up, the battered Bravo Lance was ridiculously outgunned. The trench's enfilade gave the defenders an advantage, but how much? If they could give the attackers a black eye, would they retreat? The Combine MechWarriors had to know the *Wagner* was going to be breathing down their necks.

"No lights?" Arra said. Yellow blips appeared on her tactical display, relayed telemetry representing the unknown enemy 'Mechs.

"Not yet."

Then more yellow blips appeared on her display. More bandits, these coming down Alpha Lance's entrance. As the seconds passed, her targeting computer would make best guesses of class and weaponry. "Alpha Lance, heads-up." Her lance leaned into the rock formations they would use as cover.

Jenkins said, "I see them, Hauptmann."

This was it. Time to protect *Kali*...and the people inside it.

In a minute or so, the incoming assault 'Mechs would be within LRM range. The telemetry started to come back. A *Victor*, an *Awesome,* two *Atlas*es. Some long-range capability, but a force that would punch like a sledgehammer at close range. Much like her Alpha Lance. She'd call that an even fight, except for the four blips right behind the incoming assaults, no doubt a heavy lance. Again, no sign of any light 'Mechs.

"Bravo Lance," Justil said, so far away at the western trench. "Weapons free." Lights flickered in the distance. Glowing threads of missile fire arced and fell.

The lead enemy *Atlas* crossed into Alpha Lance's missile range. Arra's targeting system seized it and locked, feeding to her comrades. "Light it up!" she said.

Eighty-five missiles streaked high and pummeled down onto the *Atlas*. It responded with its own missile salvo, peppering Shetty's *Stalker*, then still more missiles blasted from the other *Atlas*.

Amid the hail of punishment, the lead *Atlas* hit the brakes and started to reverse. The second *Atlas* charged forward, hoping to make Alpha Lance change targets. Their only hope was to concentrate fire, but they didn't dare leave cover or they'd be shot to pieces when the heavy lance came in range.

Missiles spewed back and forth. Shetty's *Stalker* jerked and stumbled at the continuing punishment.

"Shetty, keep your head down!" she called.

The *Stalker* ducked behind the rocks, and an incoming missile salvo sprayed ineffectually against the opposite face.

The enemy assault lance halted their advance and took cover in the crevices of the arroyo.

But the heavy lance charged through them, two *Orions* launching their LRM racks and two *JagerMechs* blasting their autocannons.

Arra had no choice but to try to take out the nearest targets, so she shifted targeting to one of the *Orions*.

Ghost Company's seething volley of LRMs pummeled the *Orion*, staggering it, and then Fitzmeyer stepped out and delivered a lucky laser strike that speared into the *Orion*'s cockpit, doubtless turning the MechWarrior inside to ash and mist.

Another rock outcropping would provide cover, if Arra could reach it. Her path would take her within short range of the nearest *JagerMech*. She would be able to bring all her weapons to bear and deliver an alpha strike while minimizing her exposure to fire. A direct hit from her autocannon could punch through a *JagerMech*'s armor.

With the quickness of instinct, Arra punched the throttle to full, steering toward the outcropping and turning her torso toward the target. Threat alarms blared, but she focused her concentration on a spot on the closest *JagerMech*'s torso. The distance closed...*wait for autocannon range...hold the spot...*

Her thumb triggered the alpha strike. Armor exploded in molten gobbets as combined laser fire, a rack of short-range missiles, and that colossal autocannon barrage slammed into the enemy 'Mech. A twin burst of sparks and smoke erupted from the far side. A secondary ammo explosion blew the autocannons off its arm and ripped through the fusion bottle. The *JagerMech* ground to a halt, spewing white-hot flame.

In recompense for the alpha strike, heat boiled into Arra's her cockpit like an out-of-control sauna.

Arra hauled back on the throttle the moment before her 90-ton behemoth slammed into the face of the rock cropping she would use for cover, a perfect moment to let the near-lethal heat spike dissipate.

Two enemies down.

"Ghost One, they're all over us! Please advise!" Justil called.

She checked her display. The enemy 'Mechs had charged through Bravo and Charlie's fire, losing a 'Mech in the process, but now the skirmish there was pure chaos. Light 'Mechs on both sides ran in swirling circles, trying to land shots to the thinner armor in the rear of their enemies. Assault 'Mechs stood their ground and protected their flanks as best they could, relying on thick armor to hold while they lashed out with staggering firepower. The enemy combatants had the weight advantage, but Charlie Lance were all experienced light drivers. A veteran MechWarrior in the right light 'Mech could run circles around an assault 'Mech and cut it to pieces—at least for a little while.

Damage displays flashed red in Arra's HUD. Thunder and fury blazed in the distance, stark flashes like distant firecrackers.

"Bravo One, this is Ghost One. Feeding you target data now. Harness the chickens and concentrate your fire," Arra said. "Chickens" were what happened when the frenzy of battle obliterated the training of even the most veteran MechWarriors, turning an ordered skirmish into a manic free-for-all, with targets of opportunity coming and going. She keyed her system to target one of the *JagerMech*s facing Bravo and Charlie. They packed almost as much medium-range firepower as an assault 'Mech but with far less armor.

"Bravo! You heard the lady!" Justil roared. "On me!"

The rest of Alpha Lance drove forward, combined their fire, and blew one of legs off the last *Orion*, leaving it open for a coup de grâce from Arra's autocannon.

But the assault 'Mechs, seeing their cover lance diminished, surged from cover and thundered down the arroyo at Alpha Lance. The *JagerMech* wheeled and rushed for the safety of the assault 'Mech screen.

Then Jenkins cried, "Contact! Contact! Contact! Light 'Mechs rushing from behind!"

Four, then six, then eight blips zipped into existence on her tactical map, closing at over a hundred kilometers per hour.

Arra's breath left her.

Jenkins's *Atlas*, closest to the oncoming threat, turned to face them, unleashed an alpha strike on a fast-moving *Jenner*, sending it tumbling as thirty-five tons of smoking wreckage. However, he soon found himself bathed in laser beams and short-range missiles from the rest of the enemy light 'Mechs. Even an *Atlas*'s armor couldn't last long against the combined fire of seven light 'Mechs, especially *Jenner*s that packed four medium lasers each.

The light 'Mechs swarmed the *Atlas* like a pack of wolves around a grizzly bear, their lasers and SRM volleys peeling the armor from the *Atlas*'s torso and legs. Cinnabar's strange vegetation, however, dragged at the light 'Mechs' legs, slowing them down sufficiently for Jenkins to deliver several solid shots that sent the lights scrambling away.

The enemy assault lance bore down on Arra's lance like a hammer descending inexorably toward the light 'Mechs' anvil.

Jenkins cursed through the concussions of missile impacts. His *Atlas*'s autocannon roared, punching into the fusion core of a jump-jetting *Javelin* as it tried to leap away, but the targets were too fast-moving to land another.

The rest were too close for his LRMs to lock on. They continued pouring weapons fire into the 100-ton behemoth, until finally, as it must, something found its way through a breach in the armor. A massive explosion, probably the autocannon ammo, threw Jenkins's 'Mech onto its back, where it lay motionless.

"Dammit!" Arra said, her voice thick.

Arra's cover erupted into gobbets of molten rock. PPC bursts flashed, lasers speared all around her. She set her lance's targeting to acquire the nearest enemy, then threw her BattleMech from cover and delivered an alpha strike that severed the arm of the nearest *Atlas,* depriving it of its massive autocannon. Shetty and Fitzmeyer followed her lead and surged to the attack. Their target proved to be the one damaged in the initial contact, and the combined fire of three assault 'Mechs made short work of the remainder of its torso. It fell forward onto its face with a concussion that Arra felt at over 150 meters.

The smaller swarm of light 'Mechs barreled past Jenkins's fallen behemoth—straight for Arra's *Cyclops.*

Her autocannon took a *Spider* square in the chest and sent it skidding facedown into the cinnamon-colored dirt before the rest of them were on her. An explosion rocked her cockpit. She caught a glimpse of her 'Mech's right arm and one of her lasers spinning away. She felt a leg buckle. Blazing heat surged through her cockpit like she'd just opened an oven door. Smoke burst from her control panel. Lights and displays flickered and went out. The buckling leg gave way with a screeching *snap.* Servos and myomer bundles screamed with the effort of keeping the *Cyclops* upright on one leg.

Another explosion, and her world turned sideways.

Arra's teeth snapped together hard as her *Cyclops* slammed onto the ground. The impact sent supernovas through her vision.

She heard the hissing of atmosphere. The air smelled strange, metallic.

The mercury. *The mercury!*

Massive legs thundered past her cockpit window.

A cacophony of destruction crackled over the comms. She still had comms? The expletives and outcries bursting over the comms made no sense to her.

Her hand reached for a supply locker above her. She hit the latch and stuff tumbled out around her, including what she sought. A breath mask. Her hands wouldn't work properly. She fought to get the mask over her face. It was like sparring in the dark with arms made of rubber.

She reached for the comms button but couldn't find it. "Terrence..."

"Arra! Squirty! Are you there? Over! Arra, do you read? Over!"

The voice was there, crackling and terrified, but she didn't know what to do with it.

"Arra! Tell me you're still with us!"

Her eyes watered with smoke and ozone. Her cockpit was dark. The landscape flickered with the light of weapons fire.

"Ghost One, this is Charlie One. Bravo is out. Repeat, Bravo Lance is out."

Arra tried to say "Protect the *Kali*." But she couldn't muster the breath.

A black shroud fell over her.

When it lifted again, the world around her was quiet.

A sliver of red sun nosed over the distant mercury lake.

"Arra! They're here! They're cutting their way in. Are you there? Tell me you're out there!"

Somebody was in trouble, but she couldn't remember who.

"I have to do it! I'm sorry! If you can hear me—"

A distant voice screamed, "Do it, Doc! We're ready!"

"I'm sorry, Arra...I love you."

The channel fell silent. A distant explosion boomed through the landscape, rattling pebbles and grit around her.

Darkness came again.

Rain pattered on the cracked, blackened cockpit window. Arra's *Cyclops* was dark, dead, still. Only the emergency life support in her cockpit still functioned, as far as she could tell. Her vision was blurry, with blotches of blindness in it that would not go away. The air felt strange on her skin. At least she had managed to don the breather mask before she blacked out.

She still lay sideways, strapped into her seat. Her eye caught a profusion of personal effects scattered on the instrument panels beside her, strewn from the open locker above her head. Photographs, protein bars, a bracelet her mother gave her with a miniature blue-green globe of Somerset.

The command channel crackled again. "To all Lyran forces, this is the LCS *Wagner*. Do you read?"

A voice from somewhere answered, "LCS *Wagner,* this is Leutnant Stacy Carina, acting commander of Ghost Company."

"What is your status, Leutnant?"

"Three of Ghost Company remain, as near as I can tell, ma'am. *Zephyr* is gone. So are the civilian salvage and scientific teams. If only you'd come a day sooner... Boy, did we have a prize."

"And the *Kali*?"

"Blown up, ma'am. At least the important stuff."

Arra reached for the emergency beacon. Her hands trembled so badly she missed the button five times.

"Wait!" Carina said. "Ghost One is back online! Hauptmann, are you there?"

It was more work than it should have been to speak. "...I'm here."

"Hauptmann Jackson, are you there? Over!"

"I'm here!"

"Are you there?"

Maybe her transmitter was out.

"We'll get a rescue team down there as soon as possible, Leutnant. Hang tight. The bad guys have bugged out."

Nestled in a corner of the instrument panel was an orange plastic water pistol.

She recognized it instantly. But it couldn't be here. It wasn't possible.

With nerveless fingers she groped for it.

One of her eyes wasn't working right.

She dragged the old toy into her field of vision, unable to turn her head. It weighed a thousand kilos. There was a note tied to it. She blinked and squinted and tried to focus her eye.

Dearest Arra,

I stole this from your collection when we were ten. I don't know why I never gave it back. I forgot about it for a long time, and then my mother found it in some old things after you left.

I wish I had been a better friend. I wish we'd have had more time. I'm sorry.

Love always,
Terrence

She had loved this one, with the grip that looked like jewels and sparkled in the sunlight. When it disappeared, she had torn the house apart and cried for two days in bewilderment.

It felt small in her hand, yet as familiar as if she had just held it yesterday. While she waited for the rescue team, she thought about running through the parks and gardens of Somerset with her best friend.

OPERATION KLONDIKE: TO LEAD AND SERVE

JASON SCHMETZER

22 KILOMETERS SOUTHEAST OF FIREBASE DELTA
MCMILLAN COLLECTIVE
DAGDA
THE PENTAGON WORLDS
2 AUGUST 2821

Lightning flash-burning afterimages across her vision didn't scare Kami Sword, but her hand shook nonetheless. She regarded it, safely inside her thin polymer tent where none of the auxiliaries could see. Her fingers trembled when she held them out in front of her. The shadow, cast by the thin light of Dagda's sun through the film of the tent, trembled in time. She frowned. *It's okay to be afraid–but this–it's not like*—and then her fingers clenched into a fist.

The ground cracked open, red and hot, and the heat alarms screamed to life and her radio screamed too and then she was slamming her feet down, crushing the jump-jet pedals even as a bit of vertigo told her the Phoenix Hawk *was already falling and then it wasn't and she climbed out of the trap but her Star didn't the screams oh gods the screams–*

"Star Captain?"

Kami blinked and opened her eyes. Her hands—both of them—were clenched into fists and pressed against the bare skin of her thighs. Crushed-white skin flooded with red when she lifted her fists free, shaking out the cramps in her fingers. She blinked hard and leaned forward, unzipping the tent. A close-coupled man of near forty leaned toward the entrance, blue eyes intent. The tangs of diesel exhaust and gun oil whispered in the open flap. Kami raised an eyebrow.

"Signal from the pickets, ma'am," Sergeant Leo said. "They're coming."

Kami lurched forward onto her knees and shoved her body out of the tent flap. The sergeant retreated, giving her room to exit and then falling into step beside her. His right hand played with the butt of a matte-black pistol on his thigh while he talked.

With the fall of Firebase Delta, the McMillan Collective's military—most of a regiment strong, in the old way of organizing things—had scattered into the badlands south of the compound. The leader, Collector James McMillan, had led his mobile forces out so they could reorganize, rather than engage the invaders piecemeal. It was not a decision any of Clan Goliath Scorpion's planners had expected the man to make, and it'd thrown a wrench in their plans to quickly consolidate the positions. Much of the Goliath Scorpion *touman* had been spread around the badlands in penny-packets, hoping to locate and destroy the Collective units before they could draw together. Both Khans were in the field, searching for the Collector and his 'Mechs. Smaller groups, such as the ad hoc group under Kami's command, were stalking other formations.

"Still ten kilometers out, but toward the firebase. Kendall says he thinks they're coming this way."

Lightning crashed against across the low-hung clouds. Kami eyed the direction they were traveling while she walked. *I hope someone grounded my 'Mech.* Around her the bivouac was trundling to life as infantrymen clambered out of tents and vehicles rumbled to life. Above them all rose the lithe horror of her modified *Phoenix Hawk Special.* Kami kept her fingers half-clenched as she walked.

"IDs?"

"Kendall says two 'Mechs and a passel of tanks, ma'am."

Kami stopped. "That's it?"

"Might be some of the tanks are infantry carriers," Leo allowed.

"No, I mean he doesn't have models? Numbers?"

"Not that I heard him report, ma'am," Leo said.

Kami exhaled slowly. *And we find why Corporal Kendall is an auxiliary and not a full Goliath Scorpion.* Any true warrior—any *soldier!*—would know to report precise numbers and classes. Especially with the Khan so desperate to get this rabble cleared up. The saKhan had taken the firebase quickly, but the soldiers of the McMillan Collective had scattered, making it difficult for the Goliath Scorpions to declare the area secure and move on. There was still much of Dagda to pacify. Being trapped on the nowhere edges of Riva appealed to no one.

"Get your men and women up," Kami ordered. She started walking toward her 'Mech again. Leo followed. "I want your hovertanks on the flanks and the APCs loaded and ready in case the tanks make a break for Castleton or Beasley." The two small towns, both about three kilometers east and west of her bivouac, were little more than a collection of building and mining outstations. They were big enough to shelter a goodly group of men, though, if they took a mind to hide in the mines.

"Ma'am—"

Kami stopped again. "Yes, Sergeant?"

Leo chewed his lip for a half-instant. "We can fight with you, ma'am," he said, gesturing with his hand behind him. "We may not be warriors, not like you and the ilKhan think, but we can still fight."

There were any of a dozen warriors Kami knew who'd have struck the man for daring to assume that he could fight aside one of the Eight Hundred. Nine of them had died just a few days ago, when the McMillan trap had burst the lava field's cap and sucked nine Goliath Scorpion warriors to their deaths. Kami felt her fingers begin to tremble again at the thought. Sulfurous smoke—days old, and immaterial everywhere except her memory—filled her nose.

Kami reached out and touched the sergeant—former sergeant, really, but even auxiliary units had to have some semblance of hierarchy—on the shoulder. "I know you can, Sergeant," she said. "I'm sure you'll get your wish. But for now the Khan set me to stopping these bastards from getting away." Leo's face was inscrutable but his eyes were not. They burned with both pride and dismay at the same time.

"Yes, Star Captain," he finally said. "If you'll excuse me..."

"On your way."

Kami watched the stocky man trot toward his tank while she walked toward her own 'Mech. The Eight Hundred were the warriors of the Clans. So decreed Nicholas Kerensky and so decreed the intense rounds of testing on Strana Mechty. Kami had earned her place among the Goliath Scorpion *touman*, earned it with blood and sweat and horror. The auxiliaries like Leo, the men and women, veterans all, who'd fought and tested and been bested by the Eight Hundred but still volunteered to man the tanks, the WarShips, the infantry platoons of the Clans, had no less devotion.

Just less skill.

The *Phoenix Hawk*'s imposing bulk resolved into detail as Kami reached its foot. A noteputer hung from the ladder in a weatherproof pouch: her technician's notes. All of the damage from the earlier battle had been repaired. He'd had to strip out the large laser, though, and replaced it with two more medium lasers, two more machine guns, and another double heat sink. Kami considered as she climbed and was satisfied by the time she reached the cockpit; that would give her better close-in and antipersonnel firepower, which was what she needed against the 'Mech-light forces of the Pentagon Worlds.

And when the 'Mechs did show up...Kami admired the heat-scorched barrel of the *Hawk*'s ER PPC. She could deal with 'Mechs, too. As she slid into the cockpit and settled into the command couch, though, her nostrils flared as her mind went from heat-scorched to heat to scorching heat to—

Stop it.

The *Phoenix Hawk*'s cockpit hatch closed, sealing her inside with the scent of sulfur that no one else could smell.

Storm-Captain Aldous Raine reached up to undog the tank commander's hatch in the Burke's turret and cringed as his shoulder seized. The pinched nerve pushed a spasm into most of the muscles around his shoulder. He hissed in pain and leaned back, using his other arm to raise the hatch. A kick engaged the seat's lift, raising him out of the cupola so he could see. He massaged his seized shoulder and looked around.

Barclay and Diggs's 'Mechs were trailing the column, both of them laboring along at far less than their optimal speed. Both Raine's Burke and its sister, under Sergeant-Commander Hasegawa, were running full-out—barely more than thirty kilometers per hour. *At this rate we'll die of old age before we get to Castleton, much less complete the patrol circuit to Beasley.* Letting go of his shoulder, Raine touched his throat mike.

"Simms," he said to his radio operator, "anything?"

"Nothing, Storm-Captain."

Raine slammed his palm against the unyielding diamond-weave armor of the Burke's turret. Which hurt, and he wasted an instant staring stupidly at his hand in betrayal. *The shoulder's not enough, you idiot?* He keyed his mike again. "Keep an ear out, Simms. The Collector is out here somewhere."

"Roger that, sir," Simms said.

"Storm-Captain?" Lieutenant Barclay asked. "We have units out this way?"

Raine half closed his eyes. "Most of the Collective military is out here, Lieutenant," he said. *Also, this stuff you're walking on? It's called ground. Up there? Stars. That thing on the end of your arm? A finger. Try not to shove it too far up your as—*

"I'm reading at least one 'Mech," Barclay said.

"How far?"

"Two or three klicks," the MechWarrior said. "Moving, I think."

"Toward Castleton or Beasley?"

"Toward us, sir."

Raine frowned and looked at the horizon, broken by a line of low hills. He glanced down at the repeaters for the main display beneath him, in the turret. Nothing showed. *But it wouldn't—that* Crab *has better sensors than this old girl.* "IFF?"

"Not yet," Barclay said.

Raine twisted around to glare at the *Crab*, then glanced at the *Champion* pacing it. "Diggs?"

"A flicker on my MAD, Storm-Captain," the other MechWarrior reported.

"It could be the Collector," Raine mumbled.

"By himself, sir?" Diggs asked.

"No," Raine said, blinking. "He'd be screaming for help. It's those other people. The insects."

"Goliath Scorpions, sir?" Barclay asked.

Raine pinched the bridge of his nose. *How did that moron ever make MechWarrior...* "Yes, Barclay."

"He's all alone."

"Contact!" Simms yelled, interrupting.

"Report!" Raine ordered.

"RF contact, encrypted zip-squeal," the radio tech said. "I think it was behind us, sir."

"Anyone else?" Raine asked, keying the company frequency. "Maybe we can DF the bastard before his 'Mech gets here." The other vehicles signaled negative. Raine watched the ridgeline for a moment, then kicked the seat lift gear. His fingers rubbed unconsciously at his sore shoulder as his thick tanker's helmet fell beneath the rim of the turret.

"Scouts out," he ordered as the hatch clanged shut above him.

"Sir?" Sergeant-Commander Platt asked. His two-vehicle section of Beagle tanks were no match for a BattleMech.

"Go lure that big bastard back here," Raine said. "We'll set up for ambush. Bring him straight back. Don't get dead."

"Do my best, Storm-Captain," Platt said.

"We're the best troops on this continent," Raine said, still on the company frequency. "They may have *temporarily* taken the firebase away from us—" not that he'd admit how not temporary that was going to be "—but we can take some pansy bunch of people who've named themselves after an insect." He paused, watching his gunnery repeaters. Gunner Thomas pre-heated the PPCs.

"For the Collective, people."

"Star Captain, two hovertanks are headed this way," Sergeant Leo reported.

Kami dialed down her heads-up display and settled her hands on the *Phoenix Hawk*'s controls. "Hovertanks?"

"Beagles, ma'am. Sorry."

"And behind them?"

"We're not yet to the crest, ma'am."

"I need IDs, Sergeant," she said.

"One minute, ma'am."

One minute. Dolt. Those tanks will be here in one minute. Kami drew in a deep breath and checked the *Phoenix Hawk*'s displays. All was in readiness, and she forced herself to calm down, breathe deeply again, and find her center.

You are a Goliath Scorpion, warrior of the Eight Hundred. These are the scum that destroyed our new Star League. They deserve your scorn. They deserve your justice. She pushed the throttle forward a touch, feeling the computer bend the *Phoenix Hawk* into a run. "Moving forward," she said.

"We're almost there," Leo protested.

"As am I, Sergeant," she whispered. The ridgeline rose in her HUD. The rangefinder painted the crest as almost 120 meters—and damn near sheer. "Is there a lip at the top?"

"I think so—"

"Cover, Sergeant." Kami kicked her boots down on the pedals. The massive jump jets on the *Phoenix Hawk*'s back burped blue fire and flared, tearing the *Phoenix Hawk* free of Dagda's gravity and hurling it upward and forward. Kami watched the ground carefully— *no lava, there's* no *lava, no* lava—and brought her 'Mech down on a scrap of rocky clearing just behind the lip of the ridge.

Alarms screamed to life as active sensors painted across the *Phoenix Hawk*'s sensors, but her Tek electronics were already sorting. IDs and schematics flickered through a wireframe box in the lower right corner of her HUD as the computer identified her enemy. Two 'Mechs—she noted the models—and six tanks. Two heavy, ground-hugging, 'Mech-killing Burkes. A pair of Beagles already skating backward, trying to dump thrust and edge away from her. And, worst of all, two long-barreled Fury main battle tanks. A scattering of APCs belching diesel smoke behind them all as they fled.

"Father-of-All," she whispered. The scout blowers aside, she was the lightest 'Mech on the field. Hell, the *tanks* outmassed her by a factor of almost two each.

"Star Captain!" Sergeant Leo yelled, his voice hoarse with exertion.

"Get back to the tracks," Kami ordered.

"But—"

"That's an order, *auxiliary*!" The alarms filling her cockpit changed tone as the search beams playing over her 'Mech were replaced by smaller-wavelength targeting beams. Smoke bellowed from the exhaust tubes of one of the Burkes as missiles came toward her.

Calmly, Kami sidestepped the missiles, letting them vent their fury on the rocks where she had been standing. A Gauss round from one of the Furies turned a boulder to crystalline shrapnel six meters from her *Phoenix Hawk*'s left foot. Kami ignored it, drawing a bead on one of the fleeing Beagles. The PPC coils hummed readiness, and she caressed the triggers. Her cockpit snap-flashed blue-white-purple as if lightning had struck.

The Beagle exploded too fast for Kami's eyes to follow, but her recorders saw it all. The burst of accelerated ions smashed the light hovertank's rear skirts down and tore them out, then its fans, before the rebounding body flipped ass-over-eyebrows and tore itself apart.

Kami grunted with satisfaction and hit her jump jets again, returning the way she'd come. The ridgeline claimed her line of sight to the enemy, but her sensors had enough of a look to track them from their passive emissions. It wasn't enough to target, but it'd tell her roughly what was coming around or over the ridge.

Sergeant Leo and his squad were sprinting toward the waiting infantry hatch on the rear of the Fury tank. She'd asked the saKhan for Demon tanks, but the Furies were just as fast and well armed, and had better armor to boot. As the last infantryman clambered aboard and the hatch irised closed, Kami started the *Phoenix Hawk* walking backward.

"Make for Beasley," she ordered the trio of tanks with her. The three Furies were too heavy to act as flankers or scouts. They were her slowest element but also her most powerful. Three Furies working in concert could threaten both of the Burkes in the McMillan force. "Signal the flankers to move that way and get the infantry into the village now. I want to know if there's an ambush waiting before we lay our own."

"Roger that, ma'am," Leo said. His voice was hoarse with exertion but the tanks moved in concert. "You think they'll follow us?"

"One 'Mech and three tanks? They've got twice that. Unless their CO is a total idiot, they'll push me like nits on a corpse."

Kami watched the shaded carets on her HUD. If her computer was reading thing right, both the 'Mechs were coming around the edge of the ridge, through a low pass, opposite the direction she'd sent the tanks. She shifted the *Phoenix Hawk*'s course to open the range, waiting for them to appear.

"Star Cap—" Leo's shout was washed out by interference as the Fury's turret snapped left and fired. The other McMillan Beagle had whipped around the other end of the ridgeline, closest to the tanks. The auxiliary's fire missed, blasting a divot out of the ground behind the hovertank. Kami ratcheted the *Phoenix Hawk*'s torso around, dragging her crosshairs toward the blower—

One of the other Furies smashed a round into the Beagle's side, possibly even straight through it. One moment it was a well-built amalgamation of metal and weaponry, and the next it was a rapidly spreading swath of broken tank.

"Never mind," Leo sent.

Kami smiled. The tankers had been itching to get into the fight— all the auxiliaries were, and from the Khan down, each of the Goliath

Scorpions admired them for it. They weren't warriors, not in the same class that the Eight Hundred were. They'd never be. But they were soldiers still—and even a dull knife can cut. Kami had taken the Beagle on the other side of the hill, fresh from a 180-meter jump, with the target moving well over a hundred kilometers per hour. And she'd tagged it in one shot. The Furies had needed three. Wasteful.

I am not—warriors *are not*—*wasteful. Not in combat.*

A large laser beam flash-heated a small rock to explosion forty meters to her side. The *Crab* had fired too early, giving away its position. Kami adjusted her aim; she'd already known they were coming. Now she knew they were green.

Her lips pulled back from her teeth in a manner a shark would have recognized.

Raine heard the hiss-snap of the laser firing through the thick turret armor and shook his head. A sidelong glance told him the Burke's gunner was doing the same thing. An instant later the comm light burned to life.

"Wasn't him," Barclay reported.

"Wait for a target, Lieutenant," Raine said tightly. Then he checked to make sure his microphone was off, cursed the profane deities that conspired to make his predecessor, Storm-Captain Jonathan Barclay's, son such a shitheel. When that *Crab* had been Johnny's, no one, not even the Collector himself, much cared to challenge him. *Now I wonder if he can keep triumphing over gravity.*

The 'Mechs were a couple hundred meters in front of the Burkes, and the Furies half the distance between them. He'd already heard Platt's screaming as his Beagle was destroyed as easily as the first, but now he knew. Three Furies and a *Phoenix Hawk*. Even for this "Clan" that was little enough force, but a nice morsel to pick off if he could catch them.

Barclay—the idiot—made it around the hillock first. Raine watched his displays, wishing he could raise his chair and watch with his own eyes, but he knew better. You could chance putting your head out when you were riding through town, or putting down insurgents with rifles and the odd grenade. Sticking your head out when their were 'Mechs on the field, or even just another tank with big PPCs like his Burke, was suicide. Even a miss would kill you when it was charged particles floating by at a sizable fraction of *c*. The *Crab* strutted around, straightened and took two steps toward what Raine's repeaters told him was the insect *Phoenix Hawk*.

The *Crab*'s armor exploded, backlit with blue-white fury. Barclay's return laser fire streamed ruby-red lances into the thin clouds overhead. Diggs's *Champion* broke into a run, trying to get around the hillock. Raine urged the Burke faster, slapping the console with the palm of his hand.

"The tanks're bugging out," Diggs called. His big autocannon coughed a cloud of projectiles. "Miss. God, he's fast."

"Surrender," a woman's voice said. Raine looked down—the signal was on the open frequency. "I'll let you live."

"Okay, *she's* fast," Diggs said.

"You don't get a second warning."

Raine keyed his microphone back on. "I'll make you the same offer," he said. "We value good soldiers in the Collective. You might even join us, someday."

Musical laughter trilled across the radio. "Not a chance. I'll kill you all if you don't surrender, right now."

Raine grinned. "Your tanks are running away. My tanks are running toward you."

"I'm faster than your tanks."

She has a point. "This is my land, lady. You can't run that far."

Static hashed the carrier as her PPC ignited again. The bolt took Barclay's *Crab* low in the shin, staggering it. Despite himself Raine watched—*he's going to fall!*—but the kid recovered and fired back.

"Who said anything about running?"

Kami closed the radio circuit and cut her *Phoenix Hawk* to the left. Another pad began blinking on her console, but she ignored it. It would be Sergeant Leo, wanting this or that or just whining. She didn't have time. Right now she had two 'Mechs in front of her, both of them heavier than she was, with heavy tanks coming up in a minute or less.

The *Crab* was wobbly—being hit twice with a PPC in the span of fifteen seconds does that. Kami watched the rangefinder—she was in range with the PPC, but too far for the *Crab's* lasers or the *Champion's* cannon. *Hi there.* Kami cut back the way she'd come, staggering the *Phoenix Hawk* a little. *Let them think I'm scared...* She was scared.

But not of them.

The trials the Khan had put the warriors of the Eight Hundred through had taught her that she could take on two Pentagon 'Mechs at once, perhaps even three of them. The MechWarriors of the McMillan Collective were knowledgeable, and the Collector himself was reputed to be a fearsome pilot. But they weren't Clansmen. They didn't eat, live, and breathe excellence in combat.

They would have all died in the ambush that sank the rest of her Binary into the lava. Kami forced her emotions down. She couldn't afford a scene now.

The tanks coming were a problem. The Gauss rifles on the Furies would give them the range and power to hurt her *Phoenix Hawk*, and the PPCs on the Burke were more than triple her own particle cannon's throw-weight. Her only advantage was speed. Skill, of course, but that was almost a given. Khan Elam had trained the Goliath Scorpions not to underestimate their enemies, but she'd faced these Collective soldiers in battle. She knew.

Another burst of canister fire from the *Champion* skittered into the ground near her *Phoenix Hawk*. One diamond-hard sliver nicked the armor over the *Phoenix Hawk*'s right thigh. She ignored it. Her PPC indicator glowed the hungry green of ready, and she brought her crosshairs over the *Crab*, trying to get near enough to hit her. She breathed in, thinking back on her training, and let her mind level out.

The PPC took the *Crab* high in the shoulder, shattering the last bit of armor over its upper chest and coring into the foamed-bone skeleton. The pilot jerked his 'Mech to the side, trying to hide his wounded flank. Kami chuckled. *As if I could miss a twelve-meter 'Mech at half a kilometer.*

Part of her training on Strana Mechty had been long-range gunnery at speed—she could hit a one-meter target traveling on a jagged track from six hundred meters while her own 'Mech was moving at more than sixty kph. She could do it seven times out of ten. She'd spent so much time on the range that that sort of accuracy had become almost second nature, but she suppressed the urge to close, to bring her augmented close-in weaponry to bear. She could take the *Crab* easily, but that would give the Furies and the Burkes time to close.

Sergeant Leo's tanks had made the first of the switchbacks that made up the badlands between here and Beasley. In the lowlands the air was thick enough to breathe, but when she looked up she saw the spine of the Dangmars and knew that up there the air was thin enough to need a respirator. The saKhan was already outlining plans to move that direction once the Collective was dealt with. Kami wasn't looking forward to it.

Beasley was only a little more than three kilometers away. Her APCs and hovertanks should be there already, and Leo would only need at most ten to get through the badlands and into the village proper. Not that she relished the idea of fighting in among the buildings, but if the Collective thought that she'd threaten their serfs, then perhaps they'd keep pressing at her. The harder they pressed, the more they'd get strung out.

"Leo—what's in the town?"

"Marston reports it's deserted, ma'am. A few holdouts, but they say the rest of them fled south to the coastal cities when we took the SDS." The rumble of the Fury tank's treads was audible beneath his words. "The blowers are on the far side, ready to respond, and he's got the infantry dug in along the approaches."

"Kendall?"

"He's hanging back, ma'am." Tightness filled his voice. "I told him too. One man on a skimmer won't make a difference."

Kami suppressed a chuckle. *He doesn't trust him either.* "I'll try to draw them toward you. If they get past me, use the Furies to hold them out of the town and send the blowers for saKhan Scott. She's supposed to be out here somewhere."

"Yes, ma'am," Leo said. "Star Captain? What if they don't follow you?"

"You ever lead a pig, Sergeant?"

"No ma'am."

"Been taunted by a girl?"

"Once or twice," Leo allowed.

"It's the same thing," Kami told him. She ducked the *Phoenix Hawk* almost to its knees behind a boulder of ash-covered obsidian. Her heat sinks labored to bleed the waste heat from the *Hawk*'s body, and even with the extra heat sink replacing the large laser, it was an arduous task. Between the high-heat ER PPC and the jump jets, her *Phoenix Hawk* ran hotter than most 'Mechs. "You tap them on the nose, they'll follow you anywhere."

Raine rubbed his shoulder and looked at the icons representing Barclay and Diggs on his display. He let off the kneading long enough to key his radio. "Damn it, wait for the rest of us to get up there."

"She's getting away!" Barclay protested.

"Don't be stupid," Raine snapped. "She's faster than all of us put together. If she wanted to disengage she would have. She's luring us into the badlands, where she'll probably have those three Furies and Lord knows what else hiding behind every turn and escarpment. She *wants* you to follow her, dumbass."

"But—"

"But nothing!"

"He's right, kid," Diggs said. The *Champion* slowed up, barely moving forward a little more than ten kilometers per hour. The distance between his 'Mech and the slow-moving Burkes began to fall. "Hold up."

"She's right *there!*"

Raine cut off the channel. The *Crab* slowed a moment later, unwilling to advance without the *Champion*'s cover. His fingers felt like claws when he pinched the bridge of his nose, and he kept squeezing until someone cleared his throat. "What?"

"Shouldn't we pull back, Storm-Captain?" Simms asked.

"We should not."

"But you just said she's luring us in. That means she has the initiative. The Collector always says, 'Never fight where the enemy wants you.'"

Raine opened his eyes. An image of Simms's helmeted face rested in the lower-right quadrant of his display. He opened his mouth to retort but held off at the innocent uncertainty in the young RTO's face.

"Any other day you'd be right, Simms," he said. "But we're already on the defensive. We can't let this one escape to rejoin the hordes that took Firebase Delta away from us and drove the Collector into the badlands."

"So—"

"So we're going to chase this bitch and her curs down and gut them," Raine said. "Even if we have to crawl after her in these bloody damn *earthworms* the whole way." As a defensive vehicle the Burke was nearly unmatched, but they weren't built for a pursuit.

"The Collector—"

"Isn't here," Raine snapped.

"Sir," Simms said, backing down. His image disappeared, leaving the red-and-green hash marks of his units pursuing the insects. Raine eyed the image, trying to see her plan. She wasn't running away—she'd already be gone, with her speed advantage and her jump jets. He'd never get his Furies, much less his Burkes, through the badlands in time to catch her. The fact that she was here meant that she meant to hurt him.

And if I'm in range of her, she's in range of me.

"Hasegawa," he said, tapping a different channel.

"Storm-Captain," the other Burke's commander said.

"We're going in after them," he said. "I want the Burkes in front, with the Furies in support. Keep them close—I know we're at a disadvantage at knife-range with the PPCs, but we've got three barrels where the Furies have one."

"Understood, Storm-Captain," Hasegawa said. "Moving to the lead." The other Burke cut across Raine's path, blocking him. Raine repeated his orders for the gunner and driver of his own tank and the sergeants-commander of the Furies. By that time his tanks had reached the two McMillan 'Mechs, which fell in behind the tanks.

"Watch your backs, people," he said. "We're in her playground here, but we're going to remind her what happens when you catch a puma in a groundhog's cage."

"There's nothing to send," saKhan Jenna Scott's voice decreed, cut by static but still understandable in the *Phoenix Hawk*'s cockpit. "I'm sorry, Star Captain, but there it is. What's left of the Collective military is out here with us, and I've got everyone not busy with the Khan out looking for them. My Star is chasing a lance of 'Mechs—maybe even the damn Collector, for all I know. I can't break any fast forces loose to help you run down two 'Mechs and some tanks."

"I understand, my Khan," Kami said. Her *Phoenix Hawk* was atop an outcropping, using its long-range comms to bounce a signal to the saKhan's field force. The signal was wide-band by necessity, but no one really suspected the Collective would be able to break the Goliath Scorpions' encryption before they were all brought down. If one of the Pentagon bands used the signal to locate on the Clan forces, well...so much the better—it being much easier to lure vermin out and slaughter them than to go into their den.

"If you need to disengage to preserve your forces, Kami, you may do so." The frustration in Scott's voice was palpable even across ionization tracks. "We cannot afford the losses we've already taken. Every 'Mech, every warrior—even every auxiliary—is precious right now."

"I can take them, my Khan," Kami said. Her fingers were trembling, but her voice was not. "It will cost me if they corner me, but I am faster."

"Do your duty, Star Captain," saKhan Scott said, and cut the signal.

Kami kicked the *Phoenix Hawk* off the ledge and let it fall back into the badlands, using its jump jets to soften the landing. She hadn't expected the Scorpions to really have anything available to send, but she had to try. It would cost her to defeat this force on her own, and she knew as well as the saKhan—*better, since they were* my *Binary-mates*—how much the decimation had cost the *touman*.

Her computer pinged as it completed the survey she'd set it while she spoke with Scott. A full mapping survey would have taken days, but the computer had managed to collate the last hours' radar returns to give her a decent picture of the terrain. A kilometer or so behind her, the ground leveled out into the depression within which Beasley sat, and in that depression the bulk of her auxiliaries were ready to strike any of the Pentagon forces that emerged. She needed to whittle the odds down a little, though—the 'Mechs at least.

"Leo," she said.

"Here, Star Captain," came the instant response. The sergeant's tank was barely a kilometer away—his voice was much clearer than Scott's had been.

"Shoot anything that comes out of the badlands that isn't my 'Mech."

"Of course, ma'am."

"I'm going for the 'Mechs."

"Bring 'em out for us, ma'am. We'll make you proud."

Kami toggled the channel closed and examined her HUD. The *Phoenix Hawk*'s computer was doing its best to keep track of the Pentagon force as it entered the badlands, but the maps were incomplete, and without a line of sight it couldn't be sure. She knew they were somewhere over *there*—a patch of canyons and arroyos covering most of a square kilometer—but not exactly which one.

Well...let's go find the bad guys.

Raine watched the head and shoulders of Barclay's *Crab* disappear beneath the rim of the canyon while his Burke waited its turn. The two 'Mechs were leading, since they had the better sensors. Not even their powerful beams could see around corners, though, and only the 'Mechs had a chance of getting clear before an ambush consumed them.

"Gunner," Raine said, "you see a target, you hit it. Don't wait for me to call them."

"Roger that, Storm-Captain."

The Burke shuffled like a nose-down retriever as it started down, but all Raine could do was watch the blackened, ash-covered walls of the canyon rise up around him. Dagda's thin sky didn't lend itself to too many instances of beauty, but he didn't like seeing only the small ribbon above his head.

I should have another dozen panzers. This is tank work, not 'Mech.

Part of him wanted to back off, to go back to the compound and rally another team of heavy tanks. It was the smart play, and if they'd still held Firebase Delta and the Collector was still in command, he might have. McMillan wouldn't thank him for using the wrong tools for the job. *But McMillan might be dead.*

The view on Raine's displays changed as the gunner traversed the turret, angling it so it would be pointed directly down the next defile as the driver made the turn. Why he expected someone to ignore the two BattleMechs and wait to shoot at a tank was not logic Raine could follow, but he didn't fault the man being prepared.

And it's only a Phoenix Hawk. *Its speed will be useless in here.*

Kami halted the *Phoenix Hawk* as an alarm sounded—the 'Mech's sensors painted the half-ghosted caret of a possible contact in front of her. The switchback in the canyon was about ninety meters in front of her. She twisted the 'Mech closer to the wall and advanced, weapons at the ready. If the McMillans' sensors were any good at all, they'd have picked her up at the same time.

Thirty meters from the edge, the half-caret solidified around the bullet-shape of the McMillan *Champion* as it crab-walked quickly to the side. Its weapons boomed immediately. Autocannon submunitions rang the *Phoenix Hawk*'s armor like a tocsin but did little real damage. Five of the six short-range missiles the enemy 'Mech burped at her destroyed themselves in the canyon wall; the sixth plowed into the soft ground between the *Phoenix Hawk*'s feet. Lasers cut at the armor over her *Phoenix Hawk*'s right chest and arm. Kami let the 'Mech absorb the damage while she held her aim true.

The *Phoenix Hawk*'s PPC blew a divot the size of a large man's chest from of the *Champion*'s torso armor. The four machine guns chattered, spitting bullets to pock and scar the *Champion*'s armor across its front side. The two medium lasers that shared the *Phoenix Hawk*'s right arm with the PPC burned parallel scars down the *Champion*'s chest, while the two in the left arm stabbed into the 'Mech's right arm and leg. The wash of firepower was enough to overbalance and surprise the *Champion*'s MechWarrior, and the 'Mech collapsed on its side, crushing more armor from its right arm.

Kari hissed as the temperature in her cockpit went from comfortable to nova-hot in two heartbeats. Seals on her neurohelmet snapped shut, and cooler air blew against her face even as the cooling suit fought to protect the rest of her body. She took two short breaths and then bit her lip—*this is going to hurt*—and kicked down on the jump-jet pedals. The massive thrusters on the *Phoenix Hawk*'s back ignited, throwing it upward. The canyon lip was only a little more than 120 meters high—a good burn, to be sure, but doable—but the added heat from the jets nearly broiled Kami alive in her cockpit. The 45-ton BattleMech settled heavily onto the ash-ridden ground and half bent over. Kami didn't even try to move immediately; none of the McMillans could follow, and her heat sinks were laboring to bring the waste heat under control. She'd known it was going to be hot when she fired, but she hadn't realized *how* hot, not with the two new lasers and a good long jump thrown in.

And I'm going to have to do it again. And again. Mobility was her only advantage—and the only mobility she had in these canyons was vertical.

"No excuse, sir," Diggs said. He didn't sound particularly penitent, but Raine forced himself to calm down. Diggs's 'Mech couldn't climb the walls after the *Phoenix Hawk*, and he had managed to tag the bitch with several weapons. Not nearly so well as she'd returned the favor, of course, and neither had she fallen over her own two damn feet.

"Keep moving," he ordered. According to his map display, the ledge she'd landed on ran along their direction of travel for three hundred meters and then turned away. *Assuming she doesn't just jump to the next one.* The storm-captain chewed on his lower lip for a moment, then toggled the intercom.

"Gunner, I want a barrage of missiles on the ground two hundred meters in front of us." He eyed the walls—too great a chance—and spoke again. "Be ready to repeat as necessary, keeping the aiming point at the same distance."

"Sir?"

"I need cover," Raine said. "All units. We're going to lay down an obscurement barrage and move under it. I want us out the other end of this thing and moving on Beasley. If she's meeting us in here, there's something there she doesn't want us to get."

The ten-tube long-range missile launcher on the Burke's bow rippled with smoke and flame, and the explosions in the soft, ash-covered earth threw up a good cloud of dust and debris. It wasn't as good as a dedicated smoke round—they'd still shine on thermal with waste heat—but it was something.

Jump into that, Raine dared the Goliath Scorpion, as he checked to make sure his hatch was dogged tight.

The heat sinks finally dragged the *Phoenix Hawk*'s heat back down to manageable levels as explosions sounded from the canyon floor below. Kami walked her 'Mech closer to the edge so the sensors could see directly down, but all her eyes showed her were clouds of smoke and dust roiling up at her. Her fingertip toggled the HUD through various scanning modes: visual light was useless; magnetic anomaly detection just showed her a mass of magnetic metal in the walls and floor of the canyon; and thermal was somewhat confused but showed a cluster of shapes moving beneath her, toward Beasley.

She brought the *Phoenix Hawk*'s right arm up, but the thermal targets weren't well-enough defined to take a shot at. She triggered one anyway, flickering blue-white actinic light through the dust cloud.

Damn it.

Raine grinned as the dust cloud fluoresced with light. A whip-crack explosion hammered the side of the Burke with sound but did not damage. *You're not sniping at* me.

No return fire came out of the canyon at her shot. Kami started the *Phoenix Hawk* walking at half pace, parallel to the canyon's trail. She saw the squat shape of the *Crab* emerge from the leading edge of the dust cloud, but a flight of missiles from behind it threw up a fresh cloud before she could target it. Even so, she saw it take the turn toward Beasley.

She had two options, and Kami couldn't decide between them. She could try to keep dipping into the canyon, hoping that her gunnery would be more accurate than the McMillans' and that she'd be able to escape up the walls before they could bring the big guns on the tank to bear. That idea appealed to her immensely, because it gave her something to do besides run and take shelter beneath Leo's guns.

Her other option was to do just that: to run to Beasley and let the Pentagon forces run into Leo's ambush. Her *Phoenix Hawk* was more than powerful enough to hold the back door against them if they recoiled from the Goliath Scorpion auxiliary ambush. They'd eventually overwhelm her, but while they turned to fight her, Leo and his Furies would be backstabbing them with 125-kilo Gauss rounds. The auxiliaries weren't up to the skill level of the Eight Hundred, but they were still head and shoulders above the drivel driving the McMillan tanks.

Kami dodged the *Phoenix Hawk* around a break in the ledge and kept moving. The canyon ceiling closed to nearly a cave roof, cutting off her view of the McMillan units moving beneath her. Briefly she considered trying to bring the canyon walls down on top of them but quickly discarded the idea. She didn't know where they were—and the ghosts of her dead Binary-mates wouldn't be satisfied with her merely crushing them beneath stone.

The loss of direct observation made up her mind for her. She toggled her radio. "Leo, they're coming toward you."

The reply was immediate. "We're ready, ma'am."

"I'm going to shadow them as close as I can—they're in the canyons, and if my map is right they'll be there in a few minutes. Once you hit them I'm going to come in behind them. We'll have them between us. I want you to concentrate on the armor—the Burkes first, then the Furies."

"I'll see to it, Star Captain," Leo said.

"You have the infantry where they'll do some good?"

"I was a sergeant for a long time, Star Captain," Sergeant Leo said. "I know what I'm doing." Kami grinned inside her neurohelmet. Not too many of the auxiliaries would have taken that tone. Leo wasn't Eight Hundred, but he was good.

"You wanted your chance, Sergeant," Kami said. She pushed the *Phoenix Hawk* onto a course toward Beasley, and a bit away from the McMillans. "It's headed for you."

"That was the last salvo, Storm-Captain," the gunner reported. Raine grunted and watched through his viewer. Thermal imaging wasn't any more precise from inside the cloud than it was from outside, but the McMillans had better maps than anything the Clans might have brought with them.

"We're close enough," Raine decided. "Hasegawa."

"Here, Storm-Captain."

"Let the 'Mechs flush the ambush when we get into the open. I want an orderly advance on the town. If we don't take fire during the approach, we'll let the infantry do a sweep of the buildings. If the insects have left, we'll return to the compound."

"Understood, sir."

"And if we take fire, sir?" the gunner asked.

Raine closed his eyes. "Then I guess we'll just shoot back, won't we?"

Kami crouched the *Phoenix Hawk* behind the lip of a canyon rim, with barely the sensor intakes built into the BattleMech's head showing so she could see the approach to Beasley directly. The *Champion* led the way out of the last arroyo, rising from between the jagged black rocks to sweep first left then right. The *Crab* followed a few dozen meters back, doing the same. They advanced slowly, waiting for the squat shapes of the Burkes and the more angular Furies to follow. Adjusting her view, Kami searched for any sign of the hidden Goliath Scorpion auxiliaries. Nothing was easily visible on vislight, but her HUD painted green carets over their positions.

Any moment...

"Nothing so far," Barclay said.

Raine resisted the urge to snap at him. *You think?* Instead he watched the tactical map for red flashes. He knew the 'Mechs' sensors would detect any hidden enemy vehicles before the tanks did, but the data links between them would report it instantly. Oftentimes in ambush situations the computers weren't sure, and the icons would fluctuate between enemy and nothing. To a computer, that wasn't enough to report.

To Raine, with three ammunition-independent particle projection cannons in his turret, it was enough to fire a location up. In the old days he'd have used artillery, but the insects had taken the Collective's few cannons in the first wave of attacks.

A flicker. "Gunner, target two o'clock."

"I don't see anything, sir."

Raine read off the coordinates. "Fire anyway. One tube."

The centerline PPC flickered and snarled to a brief-instant's life. The ground in front of a pile of boulders exploded into a cloud that flew ten meters into the air. A breeze quickly blew the smoke away. *More rocks.* Raine started to look away, toward a second red-nothing flash—

—a glint—

The Burke's hull rang like a bell, and the display console tried to smack Raine in the forehead. He slammed his arms down against his seat hard, holding himself in place. His eyes snapped back to the steaming rock pile. The questing snout of a Fury tank's main gun appeared between two rocks. Steam rose from the barrel, too— moisture superheated by the magnets' capacitors in the Gauss rifle.

"Contact front!" Hasegawa screamed. Static filled the comm lines as more Gauss rifles fired, each an electromagnetic snarl in Raine's headphones. He *heard*—through his own hull, not over the radio—the hammer-*bong* of another Gauss round striking Hasegawa's tank. Raine swore and dialed his tactical display back to show a full kilometer's view.

Three tanks were dug-in between the McMillan force and Beasley. Raine searched the rest of the display desperately, trying to locate the rest of the Goliath Scorpion forces. He knew there were more tanks—*she has to have some blowers out here, somewhere*—and at least the one *Phoenix Hawk*. He had more tanks, and heavier—and two 'Mechs, besides— but she'd chosen to hold her ground here. *Why*?

It wasn't the village. Beasley didn't have anything to offer the insects that they hadn't already captured in Delta. He wasn't attacking the village, so there was no chance they were there on some misguided defensive mission. The only target out here was his tanks and 'Mechs. If she was standing here—and the tanks were dug-in and hull-down, so she wasn't feinting—then she wanted to fight here. Raine dialed out to two kilometers. *Why* here? That was the first thing you learned in tactics classes: never fight where the enemy wants to fight if you can avoid it.

"Damn it," he muttered.

"Moving forward," Diggs said. Raine heard the whoosh of missiles firing through the signal as the *Champion* unloaded its short-range missiles. "I get three Furies, Storm-Captain."

"Same here," Barclay reported.

Raine chewed his lower lip. "Hit 'em hard, troopers." He dialed his display back down. "Clear them out quick, and let's move into town. I want to be done with them before the 'Mech shows up."

The Burke surged as the driver lurched it forward, trying to close the range. All three PPCs showed green readiness indicators, but the gunner triggered all three before Raine could do more than glance. From the dust and smoke, at least one of the shots missed the Fury he was aiming at, but the eardrum-threatening clamor in the turret a moment later told him the Fury had not missed with its return shot.

I should have gone back for more tanks—

An impact slammed Raine's seatback against his shoulders before he could finish the thought—

—alarms—

—a new red caret on his display—

"Contact rear!" Simms yelled.

Kami grinned as her PPC splashed hypervelocity ions against the thinner rear armor of the rightmost Burke heavy tank. Her *Phoenix Hawk* ate up the distance in meters-long strides, moving obliquely behind the McMillan tanks. She wanted to get closer but not too close that the Burkes' old-style PPCs could range on her. The two Furies in the Pentagon force were already swinging their turrets around. Kami grinned—*go ahead, waste your ammunition shooting at me. All-Father knows you're not going to hit a 'Mech moving almost a hundred kph when you can't even hit a stationary tank hidden behind some rocks*. She adjusted her course to put a boulder on the edge of a depression between her and one of the tanks.

Leo had done a good job. The three Furies were in defilade and able to shoot at the McMillans with reasonable security. The rocks around them absorbed a number of shots intended for the Furies, which helped negate their lack of numbers. She didn't see the infantry—*ah*.

The two McMillan 'Mechs were charging forward, trying to get inside the Furies' range where the Gauss rifles would have trouble targeting. As they approached the breaks, the Scorpion tanks were sheltered behind a swarm of light rockets swept out to pepper the *Champion* with explosions. There were barely three squads of troopers—and if Leo gave them more than one LAW apiece, Kami'd be amazed—but the McMillans couldn't know how many infantrymen the Goliath Scorpions had brought.

"Leo," Kami said. "Send in the blowers."

"Already, ma'am?"

"While they're confused."

"Signaling now, Star Captain," Leo said.

Kami nodded, alone in her cockpit, and dragged her crosshairs over the Burke she'd hit again. It fired at the Furies, all three PPCs, an instant before she fired. At least one of its barrels missed again, throwing up a cloud of dust and debris.

Her PPC did not.

Raine ran his tongue along the inside of his mouth and leaned forward to spit blood into the patterned floor of the tank. The damned *Phoenix Hawk and* one of the Furies were concentrating on him. Who ever heard of blasting tanks when there were 'Mechs on the field? And now there was infantry in the defenses in front of the tanks?

"Let's get out of here," Raine muttered. "Diggs, Barclay: start pulling back. We're leaving."

"We're going to get hammered if we run," Diggs put in.

"We're getting hammered now."

"Track damage!" Raine's Burke's driver yelled. "I'm down to half speed, Storm-Captain. That last PPC from the 'Mech put some armor over the tracks." Raine listened to the sound of the track motors grinding against melted metal. Too much more and they'd throw the track completely.

"Damn it!"

"We still leaving?"

"Best speed back into the badlands," Raine ordered. "Hammer the *Phoenix Hawk*."

"That leaves—"

"God damn it, I know what that leaves!" Raine screamed. "If we can make it into the canyon, we can concentrate our firepower." He thumped the armrest of his chair with a fist. "Enough to put down a Fury, that's for sure."

"If we make the canyon..." the driver muttered, loud enough for the intercom to pick up.

Raine ignored him. "Gunner, put that *Phoenix Hawk down*."

Kami ducked the *Phoenix Hawk* as both Furies put Gauss rounds into the ash-ridden soil around her. The snap-*crack* of the projectiles' passage shook the 'Mech, but she straightened up just as quickly and raised the 'Mech's right arm. The PPC snarled a burst of ions into the Burke's turret armor. She smiled, leading the 'Mech across the direction of the McMillans' retreat, judging their course.

"Leo," she said, "when they turn, I want you to switch to the 'Mechs."

"That's a lot of armor for you to burn through, Star Captain," the sergeant replied. "Concentrate on the *Champion* first."

Kami watched the 'Mechs back away, keeping their thicker frontal armor toward the Goliath Scorpion auxiliaries. Neither 'Mech could afford to take more than one or two hits from the Furies' Gauss rifles, but their own weapons were spitting fire, keeping the tanks behind cover. The infantry was impotent, their rockets shot out. The tanks had already spun about and were charging toward her.

New icons appeared on her HUD as eight Zephyr hovertanks literally streaked out of Beasley and across the field. They closed the range with the McMillan units in seconds, zipping past the 'Mechs to concentrate their fire on the McMillan tanks. Each Zephyr mounted a trio of lasers and a six-tube short-range missile launcher, and they concentrated their fire on the Pentagon Furies as they passed.

A dozen medium lasers painted each Fury tank with coherent light, slicing at the thick armor plates and turret assemblies. The barrel of one actually dipped as the laser breached its structural integrity before both tanks were obscured in smoke and flame as *two dozen* short-range missiles washed across them like sere wind. The Goliath Scorpion blowers angled around the *Phoenix Hawk* and reformed into two platoon elements. Kami laughed as the smoke cleared—one Fury, the one with the bent Gauss barrel, was on fire. She watched the tank's driver climb out of his hatch and start running toward the badlands. The other tank had exploded—its turret lay more than a dozen meters away.

Cheers erupted on the Goliath Scorpion channels.

Kami almost joined them, but two PPCs from one of the Burke tanks slammed into her 'Mech's chest, jostling her and nearly throwing the 45-ton 'Mech to the ground. She clutched at her controls while the 'Mech's gyro whined, keeping it upright. The second Burke fired, this time striking her left leg with one PPC.

I think they're pissed.

Two steps out of the stagger she'd fallen into, Kami stabbed another PPC into the thick glacis of the leading Burke. It was faster—the other must have a bad track—but the dense armor just absorbed the damage without slowing. Behind it, the two 'Mechs finally spun around and broke into runs.

"No," Kami whispered. She charged.

The two remaining Scorpion Furies surged forward, barrels questing. Both fired at the same time, but only one connected, smashing the thin rear armor over the *Champion*'s back and destroying its delicate gyro. The 'Mech thrashed to the ground, legs still kicking as the pilot tried to drive the 'Mech onto its feet by sheer force of will. The *Crab* twisted its torso enough to aim one claw-fist back and stab a large laser beam into the Fury's turret armor.

Kami closed in the Burke. As soon as she was in range she triggered all four of medium lasers. Three of them struck, two of them increasing the scar her PPC had burned previously. The third melted a rivulet of armor into the turret traverse mechanism. Nine more steps and she was close enough to chew at its armor with her machine guns, covering the armor with pockmarks but doing little additional damage. The Burke's treads chewed at the soft soil, trying to aim the frozen turret toward her as she passed.

The second, trailing Burke fired again, hitting her 'Mech in the left arm and again in the chest. Alarms blared to life as the last of her armor fell away over the *Phoenix Hawk*'s left breast, but the PPC spent itself on structure rather than the delicate engine shielding. Kami let the 'Mech stagger, shifting her damaged side away from the tank.

Ash howled into a maelstrom as one section of Zephyrs buzzed past her at flank speed. All four blowers converged on the fallen *Champion* and blasted it with short-range missiles and lasers. The 'Mech lay still once the smoke cleared.

The second section of Zephyrs charged toward the *Crab*, but that MechWarrior was ready for them and blasted the leading hovertank with both its arm-mounted weapons. The two large lasers ripped through the steel skirts holding the hovertank off the ground, dropping it and the delicate lift fans they protected into contact with the hard, wind-blasted earth. The Zephyr came apart as it rolled across the terrain, and the rest of the section was so distracted by their leader's destruction that they didn't manage to land a single laser or missile on the *Crab*.

Heat raged against Kami's skin even as the heat sinks struggled to vent it. She brought all her weapons to bear on the hobbled Burke, searching and holding and praying for a good lock. Her crosshairs warbled between green and gold—

Raine watched the insect hovertank explode and looked at the *Crab* with new eyes. He hadn't expected Barclay to be able to hit the ground if he fell. He opened his mouth to congratulate the MechWarrior, but a muttered curse from the gunner made him look the forward display. The *Phoenix Hawk* was bearing down on them.

"Can you hit her?" Raine asked calmly.

"Recharging."

"How long—" The *Phoenix Hawk*'s arms came up.

"Too long," the gunner said.

The storm-captain, second-in-command of the armies of the McMillan Collective, closed his mouth and sat back, watching the Goliath Scorpion BattleMech come. *God damn it—*

The heat sinks hadn't had enough time yet, but Kami ignored the heat alarms and fired everything again. Her PPC ripped a massive hole in the scarred armor over the Burke's turret. One of the two hatches was torn entirely away. Her lasers played across the frontal armor, melting and singeing, before one of them played across the damaged track and sliced it free. The tank lurched to the side as its road wheels drove right off the broken track. Heat shimmered between her eyes and the HUD, distorting her view. The display itself flickered. Her skin felt like it was cracking...

Her ring finger closed on its own, firing all four machine guns.

Heat and air smashed to an instant's compression assaulted Raine in his seat. Clean light glared at him from where the tank commander's hatch had been torn away. He stared upward dumbly, amazed to see the wisps of Dagda clouds with his own eyes. Sound from the battle raging assault his helmeted ears, no longer muffled by the massive, deadening lump of the Burke's armor.

He heard the chatter of a machine gun, several machine guns. Impacts struck sparks from the ruined armor above his head. He had time to think *ricochets*—

The *Phoenix Hawk* shut down. Kami tried to override its heat systems, but the automatic safeties dropped into place and hurled the fusion reactor to standby while the heat sinks vomited waste heat into the thin air. Kami gasped as the heat began to penetrate even her neurohelmet's seals, scorching her throat. The impact when the 'Mech fell slammed her restraints into her shoulders. She screamed as her left shoulder wrenched beneath a twisted belt. The *Phoenix Hawk* fell with its port facing away from the dead Burke—and toward the other.

Blinking to keep her dry eyes working, Kami watched the triple-barreled turret of the other Burke rotate toward her. The tank's treads chewed ground as it moved to bring the frozen turret to bear. She saw the static discharges cascading around the barrels, characteristics of hot weapons nearly ready to fire. Her hands, on their own, jerked at the controls—but the 'Mech was still quiescent, still immune to her rages. The three barrels lowered, flame-scorched maws starting directly at her cockpit.

A shape hurtled across her field of vision. There, backlit by the hellish blue-white glare of three PPCs, one of the auxiliary Zephyrs drank in the energies from all three bolts and exploded. The shockwave rocked the *Phoenix Hawk*. Kami screamed mindlessly, ready to die and yet denied.

A rumbling, shaking hum announced the *Phoenix Hawk*'s engine starting back up. Kami jerked the controls again, feeling the *Phoenix Hawk* thrash. She managed to get it to its knees, still watching the enemy Burke. The tank shuddered around, PPC barrels still following her. Pain screaming from her shoulder didn't stop her from raising the *Phoenix Hawk*'s left arm and triggering both medium lasers and both machine guns. The Burke's armor absorbed the fire with little effort.

Get up, you stupid bitch! she raged at herself. The Burke shifted again, following.

Not moving fast enough—

An impact, so hard and heavy that the 75-ton tank rocked, slammed into it. It took Kami's heat-addled mind a moment to identify it. Gauss round. A second followed, striking low on the Burke's rear quarter. Two heartbeats later a wash of black smoke erupted from the hole, and blue-purple arcs of electricity played across the tank as the capacitors discharged into the interior of the tank. Kami worked the *Phoenix Hawk* to its feet and looked toward Beasley. Both the remaining Goliath Scorpion Furies were trundling forward, Gauss turrets aimed at the smoking wreck of the second Burke tank. A surge of pride suddenly washed over her. *He was right*—damn *his bones, Leo was right. They're not Eight Hundred, but they're still damn fine soldiers.*

"Thought you could use a little help, Star Captain," Sergeant Leo said. His tank was near-shredded, covered with laser burns and missile scars, but the gun was still up and the tracks still rolled.

Kami laughed. "I could, Sergeant," she said. She looked at the smoldering wreckage of the second Burke.

"I told you we were—*traverse right!*"

Kami looked back in time to see the McMillan *Crab*—*shit, I forgot about that one*—sprinting toward the two Furies. It closed before Leo's turret had time to swing around and raised a foot. With fifty tons of BattleMech behind it, the *Crab* brought its foot down and crushed the Fury's turret. Electricity arced and flashed as the Gauss rifle's capacitors exploded. The second Fury fired, but the range was too short and the shot hurried, and the solid shot gouged a twelve-meter divot in the ground behind the *Crab*.

On its feet with its heat burden nearly gone, the *Phoenix Hawk* had its customary nimbleness back, and Kami used it for all it was worth. In barely nine seconds she closed the range to the *Crab* to less than a hundred meters. Its claw-fists came up and its lasers flashed, but Kami was too fast. Both shots missed.

Unwilling to shut down again, Kami withheld her PPC, but all four lasers and machine guns spat fire. The *Crab* shook as the pilot tried—and failed—to dodge, but Kami didn't slow down. The *Crab* backpedaled, arms leveled, while it waited for its lasers to recharge. The *Phoenix Hawk* leaned over, lowering it right shoulder. The *Crab*'s lasers finally fired, burning uselessly at the armor over one arm and leg.

Forty-five tons of *Phoenix Hawk* met fifty tons of *Crab* at better than ninety kilometers per hour. The *Phoenix Hawk* lurched as if it had hit a wall but stayed on its feet as Kami clutched in her controls. The *Crab* did not, going over onto its back in a pile of broken armor plates and exposed myomers.

At the edges of her 360-degree vision strip, Kami saw the remaining six Zephyrs circling around, hoping to strafe in the way they had against the *Champion*. She ignored them, twisting the *Phoenix Hawk* around and slamming its heel into the *Crab*'s chest. Battered armor and structure collapsed. The medium laser mounted there snapped in half, and the 'Mech's right arm flopped to the ground useless as her foot cut its controls. Then she ground her heel in, collapsing the shielding enough around its fusion engine to drive it into automatic shutdown.

Kami looked down at the *Crab*'s cockpit. Her hand twitched, almost bringing the PPC in line. Out of the corner of her eye she saw the smoke billowing from the litter of Leo's Fury. She pulled the *Phoenix Hawk*'s foot free and toggled the infantry channel.

"Someone pry this piece of shit out of his cockpit."

Two days later Kami stood beside saKhan Scott in Beasley, looking out to where the Goliath Scorpion technicians were stripping the hulks of any useful equipment. The saKhan had arrived an hour or so earlier, fresh from her victory over Collector James McMillan and his scratch lance.

"You did well here, Kami," Scott said quietly.

"Thank you, my Khan."

Scott looked at her. "I saw your request for advancement into the Forty for two of your auxiliaries. The Khan hasn't decided how we're going to make good our losses."

"They are worthy," Kami said.

"They failed the trials on Strana Mechty."

Kami sucked her lips in. "No, my Khan."

"Oh?"

"We *defeated* them in the trials. That doesn't mean they failed them." Kami watched the saKhan's face, to see if the woman would see the difference in her words. "Every contest has a victor. Every battle a winner. But defeat doesn't always mean failure. It simply means that we were better than they were."

"I'm not sure..."

Kami pointed to the untouched hulk of Leo's Fury. "That man, my Khan, was a warrior. He was not one of the Eight Hundred, but he was a soldier. All of them—all of my auxiliaries— fought in the best traditions of the Goliath Scorpions. That they didn't earn one of the forty slots doesn't mean they aren't soldiers still."

"The ilKhan taught us that warriors lead, Star Captain Sword," Jenna Scott said. "We earned our place in the Forty."

Kami remembered a Zephyr exploding. "That they cannot lead, my Khan, doesn't mean they cannot *serve*."

FEATHER VERSUS MOUNTAIN / RISE AND SHINE

STEPHAN A. FRABARTOLO

PART 1: FEATHER VERSUS MOUNTAIN

CERANT, AN TING
GALEDON MILITARY DISTRICT, DRACONIS COMBINE
7 JANUARY 3028

An eerie, unnatural silence hung over the normally bustling city, accentuated by distant sounds of battle. The rubble-strewn streets were deserted save for a lone man marching down the broad avenue towards Central Square.

In a way, the man's rundown appearance mirrored his surroundings. Willard Gibbs was lean, of average height, and dressed in plain, slightly worn clothes. His haggard face looked unhealthy but for the sharp, perceptive eyes, and his haircut had the telltale marks of neurohelmet use.

A charcoal-gray *Rifleman* bearing the insignia of the Ryuken-*ichi* stood guard on the square's edge, its double-barreled arms trained at the sky. Silent, motionless except for its rotating radar dish, it did not seem to take notice of the puny figure walking past.

Gibbs had deliberately avoided coming to Central Square in his SecurityMech to spare himself the scorn of the MechWarriors patrolling here, and he had not worn his Civilian Guidance Corps uniform either. It would have stressed that he was not one of them, and he could not stomach that. He had been a true MechWarrior once, a scout pilot in an elite unit. It seemed a lifetime ago. He tried to ignore the looming *Rifleman* as much as it ignored him.

Although he was no scout pilot anymore, Gibbs still routinely accumulated and digested information from his surroundings. Everything he saw and heard suggested that the situation was far worse than Jerry Akuma, the Ryuken commander, would admit.

Wolf's Dragoons had been revealed as murderous criminals. They had brutally quelled civilian protests in the city, even killed demonstrators. Then the ComStar compound had been attacked. Four days ago loyal House troops, the Ryuken-*ichi*, had finally moved against the renegade mercenary garrison in earnest and turned Cerant into a battlefield.

Gibbs's civilian contacts throughout the city had confirmed his suspicions: the battle was not going well. Wolf's Dragoons outmaneuvered the Kurita forces on An Ting at every corner, targeting supplies and maintenance facilities in masterfully executed hit-and-run strikes. It was no surprise, considering how skillful these same mercenaries, then working for the enemy, had defeated House Kurita before. In that fateful battle back on Dromini VI, Akuma and Gibbs had been lancemates. Akuma had shamelessly framed and bad-mouthed others to evade the purges in the officer corps following that costly debacle. Now, six years later, Wolf's Dragoons were in the employ of the Draconis Combine and Jerry Akuma was their liaison officer.

Of course, the military situation was none of Gibbs's concern anymore, but the welfare of the city and its population was. And as well as Gibbs knew Akuma, it would be the reverse for him.

In the lobby of Government House, the great skyscraper overlooking Central Square, the security guards conducted a very thorough, humiliating search on Gibbs that was obviously not rooted in any serious security concerns. Akuma, who seemed to consider him beneath his notice otherwise, must be in dire need if he tried to intimidate Gibbs so openly.

Dispossessed after losing his *Ostscout* on Dromini, Gibbs had accepted the honorless position of SecurityMech pilot for the Civilian Guidance Corps. His GS-54 *Guard* was an awkward quadruped monstrosity of questionable Capellan workmanship, a far cry from a BattleMech's proud elegance. He was in command of An Ting's sixteen PoliceMechs, tiny 15-tonners toting machine guns for riot control. The weakly armed and armored 'Mechs of Guardian Company and Sentry Lance, his command lance, were deathtraps when set against real BattleMechs, but that did not mean they couldn't be useful for Jerry Akuma. He would not have summoned Gibbs otherwise.

Gibbs was ushered into Akuma's tower office a few minutes later. Akuma wore his dress uniform, the image of a career officer and a stark contrast to Gibbs's nondescript civilian attire. He did not bother to offer Gibbs a seat.

"I thought I would never see you again, Gibbs. It is a strange twist of fate indeed that we must once more stand together against Wolf's Dragoons."

"I know what you want, Jerry, and you're not getting it."

That raised an eyebrow, but Akuma remained calm, almost indifferent. "You cannot always run away, Gibbs. Remember, it did you no good back on Dromini VI. If you had been closer to the rest of the company we could have protected you. As it was, you couldn't run away from that LAM when it broke through and caught up with you."

Akuma paused to let it sink in, then continued in a milder tone. "I believe I never told you, but I think the blame for your becoming Dispossessed really lies with Tetsuhara. He placed a disproportionally high value on your *Ostscout*'s sensors, all but forgetting its true nature as a BattleMech. His orders to keep you in the rear and leave the fighting to the rest of the company were unbecoming of a MechWarrior. He deprived you of real combat experience, when you really needed it. Even an *Ostscout* should have been able to handle a *Wasp* LAM in combat. Especially one from the Swords."

Gibbs flinched inwardly at the implied accusations of cowardice and incompetence, but he managed not to show it.

"Keep the old man out of this, Jerry. He's a fine samurai, one like you will never be. He had a deep understanding of things, where you only ever wanted to rush headlong into a battle and blast everything with your PPC."

"Oh, yes, the superiority of the samurai. Tell me, Gibbs, how come staunch samurai like you or your revered Tetsuhara remained Dispossessed and dishonored after Dromini while I am now in command of a BattleMech regiment? I will tell you: *because you fools lost the battle for all of us*! It was *your* fault we were defeated! If you had just knocked off your stupid *bushido* we would have prevailed, but you refused to grab victory when it was offered on a silver plate. We could have killed Colonel Wolf right then and there. Now he and his rabid mercenaries have turned against House Kurita and are ravaging this very city. And for the fine samurai you fancy yourself, you are telling me you cannot even bring yourself to stand up and defend House Kurita here in Cerant?"

"So you admit you've lost control of the situation?" Gibbs hissed, approaching the desk. "That the mercenaries to whom *you* have been assigned as liaison officer have turned renegade under your leadership and are crushing your precious elite regiment that was supposed to sheepdog them? That you have a war at your hands, in *my* city?"

Akuma stood and met Gibbs at eye level, leaning over the desk's marble surface. His voice lowered to a threatening growl. "I seem to recall that the Civilian Guidance Corps is responsible for maintaining civil order in the city. A task at which you have miserably failed over the past weeks. Where were your vaunted SecurityMechs when the ComStar compound was attacked? It took one of my *Vulcans* to root out the attackers. I'm offering you this one chance at redemption, Gibbs. You better take it, or you and your incompetent RiotMech pilots will face a firing squad when this is over!"

Gibbs stiffened. "Wolf's Dragoons have been declared rogue. That marks them as a military threat. They clearly fall into your responsibility, not mine."

"Clearly, you say? Certainly not. It is a most difficult legal question, yet I am certain Warlord Samsonov shares my conclusion that the CGC 'Mechs must be deployed here so that the mercenary menace can be overcome. We both know that if you go, your men will go as well."

Gibbs replied slowly, as if thinking every word through. "*Chu-sa* Akuma, I serve the Civilian Guidance Corps. I am not a soldier anymore. And I believe you have no command authority over the Corps. The PoliceMechs under my command are obviously not required to restore order among the Combine population. I don't see any heavily armed mobs of rioting citizens that must be gunned down by 'Mech-scale firepower."

"Very well, *Corpsman* Gibbs." Akuma took a sheet of paper from a drawer and placed his trump card on the desk. "I hereby inform you in the name of the Dragon that you, as a reservist from the Second Sword of Light, have been reactivated by and for the Draconis Combine Mustered Soldiery. As of this moment, you are to integrate yourself into the local DCMS command structure. And as it so happens, I am your superior officer."

"You're assigning me a BattleMech?" a befuddled Gibbs asked.

Akuma smiled cruelly. "No. That will not be necessary. I do not intend to make you a MechWarrior again. I just want to see those ultralight machines of yours put to some good use. And I need you and your CGC pilots in them because no MechWarrior would put up with a SecurityMech. Since I need an officer commanding them, you were reactivated with your former rank of *chu-i*. Now be a good little samurai and get those 'Mechs into the fight. Quinn is waiting for you in the office next door with your orders and the tactical details. You are dismissed, *Chu-i* Gibbs."

Stunned, Gibbs took the document, read it briefly, then slowly turned around and walked out to receive his orders. There was no doubt that he would carry them out. He was a samurai, after all.

CERANT, AN TING
GALEDON MILITARY DISTRICT, DRACONIS COMBINE
12 JANUARY 3028

Five days after being drafted into the Ryuken, Gibbs had a much clearer picture of what was going on. It was Dromini VI all over again. Akuma was too full of himself to see the disaster unfolding.

Although considered an elite formation, the Ryuken-*ichi* were outclassed and outmatched by the Dragoons. The real elite pilots from the original training cadre had mostly transferred off-world to join the Ryuken-*ni* regiment on Misery. Akuma's Ryuken-*ichi* was an overblown melting pot of MechWarriors from all over the Draconis Combine who had been assigned to this unit only recently. They were not yet accustomed to working together, much less the new fighting style for which the Ryuken regiments supposedly stood. The death of *Sho-sa* Chou in an ambush yesterday had robbed the Ryuken-*ichi* of their only competent officer, and they had really begun to fall apart since. Gibbs could not care less for Akuma and his Ryuken-*ichi*, who had brought this on themselves, but he felt responsible for his CGC pilots. Although the entire group had been drafted into the Ryuken, he still thought of them as policemen, not as soldiers. Many of them he had recruited himself.

The Ryuken MechWarriors, for their part, shunned the lowly SecurityMech pilots and refused to socialize with them. That had at least kept the SecurityMechs away from the frontlines. They were used for rearguard duties, freeing up what Akuma called "real BattleMechs."

On this late night what remained of Guardian Company was escorting a supply convoy through Cerant while Gibbs and his command lance were guarding the makeshift Ryuken field base on Central Square. His radio crackled. "Four, this is Seven. We're encountering light resistance from infantry, some with inferno SRMs. The 'Mechs can handle it, but if one of the ammo trucks cooks off, then we're done for. I think we need to stretch out more, to keep the J-27s at a safe distance from each other."

Gibbs groaned inwardly. Such a simple trick, and Takeo was falling for it. It was no surprise, given that he had no military training. As a CGC pilot, Takeo considered the situation from a security viewpoint, and putting more distance between the trucks for safety was a logical conclusion from that angle. Gibbs wondered just what chances Guardian Company really had if it wound up in any serious fighting. They had already lost two 'Mechs and their pilots yesterday, along with the entire field command camp of the Ryuken's First Battalion. Another had been damaged by infantry and was out of commission since the techs at Central Square had extricated its gyroscope to use it as a replacement on a cored-out *UrbanMech* instead.

"Seven, this is Four. Stay together. I say again, stay together. If they had enough forces to attack the convoy proper, then they would have done so. They're just harassing you, trying to goad you into stretching out so that they can pick you off one after another. Don't allow that to happen."

Because the SecurityMechs were normally deployed alone or in pairs, they were numbered from One to Sixteen. Within the Ryuken they were left to themselves and had retained their radio callsigns. Gibbs's command lance claimed the first four numbers, and he had selected Four for himself. He was sure Jerry Akuma would not understand the hint.

That the Dragoons tried to intercept the vehicle convoy was disturbing news. The Ryuken had declared the route safe, and once again they were wrong. It would be amusing, except for the good people who paid for the Ryuken's ineptitude with their lives. *His* people.

After a brief argument over the battalion frequency, the Ryuken commander claimed he had no BattleMechs to spare for the convoy's rescue, and ordered Gibbs's command lance to move out instead. Against infantry, SecurityMechs would suffice. Gibbs could tell he regarded them all as expendable, but arguing was not going to save his men now. His lancemates followed him out into the dark maze of the nightly city to help their comrades.

"Movement to the east! In the building just opposite of that garbage container. I'll check it out." Although Corpsman Miura was too excited to maintain proper radio procedures, Gibbs recognized the young hotshot's voice. "Three, Four. Caution, Miura! Stay back. It might be a trap." Gibbs moved his crosshairs over the container and triggered his machine guns. Tracer bullets drew bright lines through the darkness between his *Guard* and the container. The result was a fierce detonation that peppered the SecurityMechs with shrapnel. A trap.

"This is Four. One and Two, go check that alley to the left. Three, circle that building right. Shoot anything that moves." Gibbs frowned. For all the fireworks, the blast had caused surprisingly little damage to the building. Something was wrong. Perhaps they had arrived early, before the trap was properly set.

"Four, Three. Engaging target." Gibbs could not see what Miura was firing at on the other side of the building, but his machine guns raked the four-story building where the unknown attackers had retreated. Suddenly he heard another detonation a short distance away, from the alley where the two others had gone. A panicked voice came over the radio.

"Uh, Four, One. Two's down. Must've hit a mine or something. I... whoa! No! I'm on fire! Infernos!"

The voice cut out, but the staccato of machine-gun fire mixed with the sounds of missiles and small-arms fire from the alley. Black smoke billowed up behind the next line of buildings, highlighted by bright flames from underneath. The container bomb, Gibbs realized, was just a ruse to split them up. "This is Four. Get back to my position. Stay together!" Gibbs scanned the area. With one 'Mech already down, he needed to keep his troops together.

"Four, Three. I've found a couple of APCs. Engaging." More staccato fire, this time from the right side. Both engagements took place out of Gibbs's line of sight. He heard frantic exchanges of fire. "Negative, Three. Get back here!" Explosions, more powerful than the previous ones, shook the ground. The building Miura had been firing into collapsed in a heap of rubble, revealing his 'Mech in a losing battle with several hovercraft. Miura ejected just before a devastating volley of short-range missiles from a Harasser hovertank literally ripped his small 'Mech apart. Two Bandit APCs were already speeding off into the darkness between the buildings. The Harasser, however, had sustained crippling damage to its skirt and could not disengage. It was a dangerous wounded animal: it could not flee, but as long as its ammunition lasted, it had superior firepower and a definite advantage in range. Unfortunately, it sat right in the middle of Gibbs's scattered forces and its turret turned towards Gibbs.

In the knife-fighting ranges of city combat the tank's superior range did not count for much. Instead of retreating, Gibbs moved across the rubble toward the stranded hovertank and fired with all he had. Despite its ungainly looks, the *Guard* was fairly nimble on its four legs, which seemed to surprise the tank crew. Even as the Harasser fired another salvo of SRMs at this new assailant, all of which went wide, hundreds of bullets from the *Guard*'s twin machine guns bit into its armor. One penetrated a live missile in the ammo feeding mechanism. A spectacular series of explosions ripped through the vehicle and sent the turret flying.

The shooting stopped as abruptly as it had begun. Swirls of smoke and small fires danced across the field of rubble that had been an office tower a few moments before. It was then that Gibbs realized he had not heard anything back from One and Two. Two telltale columns of black smoke rose from the alley. On the other side the dust and smoke had cleared to reveal the broken and barely recognizable wreck of SecurityMech Three lying on the pavement. The devastation looked particularly grim in the gloomy, flickering light of the fires.

Over the radio, Corpsman Takeo reported the convoy under heavy attack from at least a company of BattleMechs before the radio channel fell silent. It was just before midnight, and Guardian Company was no more. They had lasted for less than six days.

Gibbs was alone.

CERANT, AN TING
GALEDON MILITARY DISTRICT, DRACONIS COMBINE
13 JANUARY 3028

A minute past midnight, the battalion frequency erupted with hectic chatter. Several pickets reported advancing enemy forces all at once. The Ryuken's overtaxed command, control, and communication capacities, weakened from the recent losses of men and materiel, could not cope with the flood of reports, and pandemonium ensued. Battalion command was too busy to take Gibbs's report regarding Guardian Company and finally simply ordered him to "shut up" while they frantically tried to get a picture of what was going on.

Always the scout, Gibbs was quick to analyze the situation from the reports he overheard. Quicker than battalion command, in fact, since he had been the local CGC PoliceMech commander for several years and was intimately familiar with the city's layout. The situation was serious. It had to be the Dragoons' final push to dislodge the entrenched Ryuken from their positions. The convoy, and Guardian Company with it, had apparently become a target of opportunity for an enemy force that had somehow flanked or penetrated the picket line ahead of the main assault. That only made sense if...

Gibbs blinked, then looked at the map display. His *Guard* was the only unit standing between that enemy force and the weakly defended Ryuken HQ in Central Square.

Jerry Akuma could keep a grudge forever. He'd wanted the CGC 'Mechs badly enough to draft them into his unit. But he had carefully avoided reinstating Gibbs as a MechWarrior out of sheer spite, by restricting him to his 15-ton SecurityMech. The Procurement Department's definition of a proper BattleMech called for at least twenty tons of mass.

However, Akuma had overlooked a small but crucial detail: the Procurement Department's restrictive definition did not apply to commissioned officers. The exemption was meant to ensure they retained command authority even if their vehicle was disabled, no matter what replacement vehicle they received. In this case, it had an unintended side effect. Gibbs had uncovered an ancient law from the early days of BattleMechs. Conceived centuries ago to prevent the proliferation of BattleMech technology through IndustrialMech exports, it defined a BattleMech as essentially any armed 'Mech. Although forgotten, it was still technically valid and effectual. The catch was that Gibbs's SecurityMech met all criteria for a BattleMech as laid out in that law. Since he had been reactivated with his DCMS officer rank, no mass limit applied. With a scratch of a pen, Akuma had legally transformed the SecurityMech into a BattleMech and made Gibbs a MechWarrior again.

Fate had a way of balancing things, Gibbs realized. The pieces of the puzzle fell into place. He now had the rematch at his hands that could remove that stain on his honor and restore the balance that had been upset. Not by winning the battle against Wolf's Dragoons, of course; it was evident that the Dragoons outmatched the Ryuken on An Ting like they had on Dromini. There was no hope of victory here for House Kurita. But there was hope for Gibbs to set things right. Akuma believed that Gibbs, a loyal samurai of House Kurita, would be compelled fight to the best of his abilities. That he would fight Akuma's battle for him and then disappear back into the ranks of the Dispossessed, humbled and forgotten. In truth, Willard Gibbs did not want to win or even survive the fight. He only wanted a glorious death in battle as a MechWarrior.

According to standing orders with his command destroyed and his last mission objective now impossible, he was to report back to Central Square, resume guard duty, and await further orders. Since battalion command refused to hear his report, nobody else was aware of the danger to Central Square HQ and to Jerry Akuma personally. Without a warning from Gibbs, they would never know the attack was coming.

Now all he had to do was to earn his death before he had to report this to somebody.

Following his orders to the letter like the good samurai he was, Gibbs turned his *Guard* around and raced back to Central Square for the final stand, keeping strict radio silence all the way.

Death is a feather
Overthrowing the mountain
Winter brings balance
—Haiku found among the belongings of *Chu-i* Willard Gibbs, Ryuken-*ichi*, KIA January 13, 3028

PART 2: RISE AND SHINE

CERANT, AN TING
GALEDON MILITARY DISTRICT, DRACONIS COMBINE
13 JANUARY 3028

Wolf's Dragoons Lieutenant Thomas West was not afraid of urban combat, but he certainly did not like it. It was brutal and hateful, as the clashes between Wolf's Dragoons and the Ryuken in Cerant demonstrated, with no quarter asked or given. After more than a week of fighting off Kuritan attacks, the Dragoons had finally turned the tables and forced the Ryuken-*ichi* regiment on the defensive. Unfortunately, city fighting favored the defender. Entrenched in their defensive perimeter encompassing Government House and the starport area, the Kuritans fought tooth and nail to slow down the nightly Dragoons advance. It was the grunts who were buying time—with their lives—for their despicable officers, especially that bastard Jerry Akuma, to retreat to the DropShips and escape.

Captain Fraser's ad hoc Dragoon unit of fast 'Mechs and tanks had hoped to prevent that when they had set off around midnight. Bypassing many enemy units instead of neutralizing them, they had penetrated deeply, but by dawn the defenders had them surrounded and outnumbered at the edge of Harmony Park.

Harmony Park was a stretch of pleasant green in the middle of Cerant, wide gardens with a smattering of trees scattered. It was deceivingly peaceful in the twilight of this early morning, just before sunrise. The open area was perfect for long-range weapons such as his *Griffin*'s particle projection cannon and missiles. Unfortunately, the defenders had figured that out as well. Enemy forces were entrenched on the far side to pick off trespassers in the open. Fraser's unit was threatened with being crushed between this anvil and the hammer formed by the bypassed defenders, who were catching up.

A *Quickdraw*, one of a group of pursuers that had been shadowing them for some time already, appeared down the street West was guarding. Its charcoal-gray camo pattern made it nearly invisible, except to the *Griffin*'s sensors. Exhaust fumes blurred its image as it fired its missiles. Before West could react, the *Griffin* took hits to the left torso, but the warheads could not penetrate the thick armor. West immediately fired both his weapons. His missiles went wide, blasting chunks out of a building behind the *Quickdraw*, but the PPC snapped the enemy's already-damaged leg clean off.

"Good shot, West!" Gatlin announced over the radio. He was one of the Dragoons scouts, monitoring the battle for Captain Fraser with his *Ostscout*'s sensor suite. "But watch out, there's something big coming your way down that street. Looks like they're throwing their reserves at us."

The crippled *Quickdraw* was still potentially dangerous. While West was still considering whether he had time to deliver a coup de grâce, another more massive Ryuken 'Mech appeared from a side street. It had to be an assault 'Mech, although it moved impossibly fast for one. And gracefully, West noted. This was a dangerous foe. The targeting system identified it as a CGR-1A1 *Charger*, an ultra-heavy scout 'Mech often ridiculed for its weak and ineffective armament, especially the short range of its lasers. The confines of the city negated that drawback, of course. The sheer mass of the *Charger*, combined with its above-average speed, made it an exceptionally dangerous opponent here. West moved the targeting reticule up from the fallen *Quickdraw* and fired his weapons at this new threat even as it ran toward him. *Time to get out of here.* He didn't take the time to see if his shots hit before he kicked the jump pedals. Pressed into his command couch by the sudden burst of thrust, West maneuvered across two apartment blocks, out of harm's way.

He paused to cool off his *Griffin's* excess heat and checked the tactical map. His jump had put him farther away from friendly forces, with that dreadful *Charger* between him and them. Gatlin's *Ostscout* had linked up with the other Dragoons who were pulling together to make a stand. The nearest Dragoons 'Mech was Walden's *Wasp* four blocks north of West's position, moving in to finish off the fallen *Quickdraw*. Even together, they were hardly a match for a *Charger*.

"West here. I'm cut off to the far south by a *Charger* on the main road."

"Understood. Stay put, help is on the way. We're linking up with you and then we take on that *Charger* together." That was Captain Fraser. On the tactical map display West saw his *Shadow Hawk* approach with a *Wolverine*. The *Charger* moved to intercept them, its attention drawn away from West's *Griffin* and the *Wasp*. Time to attack. West engaged his jump jets again.

The *Charger* met the *Shadow Hawk* and *Wolverine* head-on, concentrating on the *Wolverine*. Its lasers melted some armor away before it literally charged the *Wolverine*, toppling it. Autocannons, lasers, and short-range missiles ate away at the monster's armor in return. West's PPC and missiles cut into the *Charger's* thin rear armor from afar as he approached, but it continued to shoot and kick at the downed *Wolverine* like a berserker, ignoring the other Dragoon 'Mechs. That was when the *Wasp* joined the fray. It jumped in right behind the *Charger* and fired six small lasers into its thinly protected rear, melting away any armor that remained. Then it punched the *Charger* with both arms. When the *Wasp* withdrew its arms from the *Charger's* chest cavity they held on to cables, myomer bundles, coolant tubes, and reactor shielding, quite literally ripping the 'Mech's heart out. The fusion reactor went into emergency shutdown, and the *Charger* immediately went limp, crashing to the ground like a puppet that had its strings cut.

The *Wolverine* slowly got back up. Its armor was shredded, revealing broken internal structure, and its awkward movements indicated gyroscope damage. Just as they turned back north to rejoin their lines, Gatlin's voice cut in again. "Captain, we're under heavy attack from their reserves. The 'Mechs from the park are now moving in to attack us, too. Better get back here quickly, or you'll be cut off."

Captain Fraser uncharacteristically hesitated for several seconds before he replied. "Gatlin, did you say they're committing all their reserves from both the park and Central Square? Are you sure of that?"

"As sure as I can be under the circumstances, Captain. My sensors show Central Square empty. They're all here and tearing us apart. You're welcome to bet your life on it."

After another brief pause, Fraser issued his orders. "This is our chance. Dominguez, get back to the others and make a stand until the main force arrives. West, Walden, you're with me. We break through." They moved to the edge of Harmony Park between two office buildings and engaged their jump jets.

When West's *Griffin* hit the ground again halfway through the park amidst some trees, it was thrown off-balance by a fierce explosion. West barely managed to keep the machine upright.

"Mines!" he warned. "I've got armor damage. Nothing serious, though."

The other two 'Mechs had been luckier, but the mere existence of the minefield urged caution and slowed them down. The park was not devoid of enemies, either. The Armstrong autocannon on Fraser's *Shadow Hawk* fell into firing position over its shoulder and spat out a salvo of slugs, followed by a flight of long-range missiles. The target, a *Warhammer* standing waist-deep in a small lake some four hundred meters to the south, responded with its dual PPCs. One of the bright particle beams incinerated a tree next to the *Shadow Hawk*; the other hit the dark blue *Hawk* squarely in the chest, scorching away a good share of its armor. West fired at the *Warhammer* in turn. Only a few missiles hit, spreading small pockmarks across its impressive armor. The shrugged off the slight damage and held its position.

"Move it! Get past and go for Central Square!"

West needed no encouragement. Another jump brought his 'Mech to the far side of the park, out of the *Warhammer*'s reach. Walden's *Wasp* was hit by the twin PPCs in mid-jump. Trailing black smoke and with one arm ripped off, the small 'Mech plunged out of sight somewhere between the luxurious condos on the park's edge. Fraser's *Shadow Hawk* had a shorter jump range than either the *Griffin* or the *Wasp* and did not reach the other side as quickly. He ran the last meters, but just as he was about to slip between two tall apartment buildings on the other side, out of the *Warhammer*'s line of sight, another enemy 'Mech stepped into his way, guns blazing, and blocked the path to safety.

The new 'Mech was a peculiar little machine, a machine-gun toting quad painted in the white-and-red color scheme of the Civilian Guidance Corps. It had to be an IndustrialMech of some sort, probably a light SecurityMech, but West was unfamiliar with the type. The tiny 'Mech was no match for a *Shadow Hawk*, but he had—by chance or by design—appeared in an exceptionally bad spot because he barred Captain Fraser's escape. West watched in horror as two more PPC blasts from the *Warhammer* lashed into the *Hawk*. One smashed into the head. The *Shadow Hawk* staggered and fell to the ground.

Enraged, West jumped on the SecurityMech's position, fully prepared to execute a death-from-above maneuver. He needed to get that thing away from his commander. When he touched down again, however, hidden from the *Warhammer*'s sight, the SecurityMech had already retreated deeper into the city.

"Thanks for the help, Thomas." Immensely relieved, West saw the *Shadow Hawk* rise to its feet again and move to take cover among the buildings. The head-mounted SRM launcher was gone and the canopy was cracked, but Fraser was alive.

Determined to finish off the pesky little machine that had almost killed Captain Fraser, West pursued it around a corner and down a side street. Behind him, the *Shadow Hawk* and the *Warhammer* exchanged parting shots as the faster *Hawk* disengaged and marched on toward Central Square.

The SecurityMech was surprisingly swift on its four legs, making good use of lateral movement as it maneuvered through the maze of buildings. Although West managed to keep up, it somehow always managed to disappear around the next corner just before West could acquire a target lock. Just when West began to suspect that it might deliberately lead him in a circle and back to the *Warhammer*, another explosion rocked his 'Mech.

Something was wrong, terribly wrong. He felt it through his neurohelmet, but it took a second or two before West understood that the blast had amputated his *Griffin*'s already-damaged right leg. Then he hit the ground hard.

The clever bastard had lured him into a hidden vibrabomb that was completely harmless to the lighter 'Mech, set to detonate only when a heavier 'Mech such as his *Griffin* passed along.

"Captain Fraser, this is Lieutenant West. I've hit a vibrabomb and my right leg's gone. You're on your own, sir. Sorry I can't come with you. Godspeed!"

If he could get up on one leg he might at least provide covering fire. There was still a *Warhammer* out there, and that darn SecurityMech... West began to move his prone 'Mech about in order to get up again.

The small 'Mech returned. It dashed out of an alley, machine guns firing, obviously intent on finishing him off. West's mind raced. His missile rack was useless at this range, as was the PPC. Punching the enemy 'Mech was impossible from his prone position. Machine-gun bullets crackled across the downed *Griffin*, shattering armor plates here and there. Immobilized, there was no way for West to evade the weak but steady rain of slugs that took his helpless 'Mech apart bit by bit.

West refused to give up. When he had left his home to join Wolf's Dragoons more than a quarter of a century ago, he had proudly named his *Griffin* the Nova Cat as a reminder to who he was and where he came from. West was an old man now, approaching sixty years, and he felt that his time would soon come. He had always known that he and the Nova Cat would die together. But not today. Even while his 'Mech withered away under the relentless machine gun fire, he dialed the battalion frequency.

"Calvin, this is Thomas. I bid for your help. Do you copy?"

No response. The damage control display was now yellow across the board, with some red spots. Right leg gone. Right arm armor breached. With a thundering sound, the other 'Mech kicked at the prone *Griffin*. Right torso breached. LRM launcher gone.

Finally, he made out a voice through the deafening impacts. "Wakeman here. What seems to be the problem, Thomas?"

Hastily, West issued orders and keyed commands into his onboard computer. Another kick from the unrelenting enemy 'Mech penetrated the cockpit's ferroglass and sent shards flying everywhere. The damage control board was more red than yellow now. With a blood-smeared finger, West transmitted the targeting data.

In unison, the entrenched Dragoons BattleMechs and tanks near Harmony Park turned their long-range missile launchers and fired at an unseen target indicated by their forward spotter. Over a hundred missiles rose into the morning sky. Glittering in the rays of the new day's sunrise like a veil of polished steel, they arced across Harmony Park and descended somewhere on the far side, converging on a single point hidden between the buildings. Most of them missed their target, peppering the general area around West's prone *Griffin*, but enough hit the SecurityMech to savage the thin armor that protected its ammunition bins. Amidst the deadly rain, the small quadruped vehicle disintegrated in a cataclysmic explosion.

When the dust cleared, West saw Captain Fraser's *Shadow Hawk* sparkling in the sun some distance to the northwest, free of its pursuers and closing in on Government House. The breakthrough had been successful. He only hoped it was worth the cost.

OPERATION SCYTHE:
THOSE WHO STAND HIGH

JASON HANSA

EAST OF GUNNISON, COLORADO
NORTH AMERICA
TERRA
9 OCTOBER 3078

The Cobra transport VTOL screamed over a sea of grain, less than a hundred meters separating the plane's belly and the waving fields. Leftenant Samantha Webb swept her eyes across the plains, forgoing her night-vision devices to bask in the milky-white glow reflected off the crops. The pilot wore a pair of goggles that leaked a greenish glow around his cheekbones, but his copilot went without, splitting his attention between the black horizon and his instruments.

She looked around the darkened cockpit. "It's probably a little late to ask now, but I thought the Word mostly used Cobras? "

The pilot grunted. "It's a good plane."

The copilot nodded while shrugging. "I know MechWarriors don't want to use salvaged Blakist equipment, but there's not as much stigma attached to vehicles. Besides," he added with a laugh, "this really *is* a good plane."

"Thanks for inviting me up. This is amazing," she said, dim instrument lights playing off her face in a kaleidoscope of colors. The pilot smiled, but didn't take his eyes off the horizon.

"You never get used to it," the copilot agreed. "I flew aerospace fighters for a while, but it bothered me. Too empty, too alone out there. Flying like this, the ground racing along underneath you—this is *flying*."

"It's so flat here," she said after a moment. "That makes it easy, right?"

Both men chuckled.

"More dangerous," the pilot said, his voice low.

The copilot nodded, half turning toward her. "Land this flat can make you complacent: there's lots of nothing, and then suddenly you're plowing into some farm you didn't see, or a rise that comes out of nowhere and catches you off guard." He waved toward the rapidly approaching mountains on the horizon. "There are a lot of hazards flying in a mountain range, but out there you remember them. It keeps you on your toes. Here, just us, the wheat and the cows? Dangerous."

The pilot grunted in agreement. Silence fell in the cockpit for several minutes as Webb let the pilots return to their work.

"First flight is popping up," the copilot said, and flipped a switch. Turning, Webb saw two red lamps light up alongside the rear cargo ramp. "The second flight hovers in fifteen minutes, and we're on schedule for wheels down ten minutes behind them. Make sure you and your boys off-load quick—the engineers will be touching down ten minutes behind us. If you plug your headphones in back in the bay, you'll be able to listen."

"I will," she said. "Thanks for the lift," she added cheerfully to the copilot, patting him on the shoulder.

"Thanks for flying Rattlesnake Air," the copilot replied good-naturedly, flashing a bright smile at her before returning to his instruments.

Grabbing each handrail of the steep ladder leading from the cockpit to the bay, she jumped off and slid down, feet planting firmly on the metal bay floor. Sergeant Major Dennis Meyer looked over at her.

"Twenty-five minutes out," he mouthed, waving at the red lights from his seat. She nodded, the roar of the jet engines too loud to yell over. She looked over at her troops, a smile on her face.

Her whole company was in the one aircraft, two long lines sitting on the outside facing in, with two shorter lines in the middle and facing out. Their AFFS issued eggshell white light armor over green shrapnel "resistant" cold weather jumpsuits contrasted against the gun-metal grey of the aircraft's interior. All of them wore issued foliage caps, warm headgear that covered the entire head and neck, with a long brim to block sunlight. At the feet of each infantryman was a large, bulging rucksack, with many soldiers holding spare bags, radios, and other important equipment on their knees. There was just enough room for the cargo master, a dark man in a purple jumpsuit, to squeeze through as he double-checked the palletized cargo behind the inboard seats.

He turned toward her and gave her a thumbs-up, and then pointed to his air-crewman helmet and the spaghetti-cord connecting him to the intercom. She nodded and picked up the spare helmet on her seat before buckling in. She put it on, and the noise of the aircraft was replaced with the noise of combat.

In front of the cargo aircraft was a double-flight of Draconis fighters, pilots borrowed from the Seventeenth Benjamin Regulars flying close-air patrol over the airfield that she'd be landing on soon—the mission was vital enough that support aircraft and troops were pulled from three separate task forces, the forces of four Great Houses working together to take Gunnison. She listened as they talked in clipped, tight conversations, describing the anti-aircraft fire they were receiving and their attack maneuvers. Every so often she heard a Japanese expression, a pilot reverting to their native language in the heat of the moment.

"This is Phantom-lead, droppers are away. We are RTB, out." She sucked in a breath, and then locked eyes with the sergeant major, plugged into the wall on his own set. He nodded.

It's beginning, she thought, then flipped her channel to the ground command frequency. She now heard the reports being called in by various company commanders to their battalion leadership, mostly quiet updates of defensive installations they could see from their vantage points a thousand meters in the air.

Those Lyran paratroopers are nuts, she thought. *There's easier ways to die than jumping out of perfectly good aircraft.* She looked back at the loaded pallet, containing the heaviest of her unit's winter and mobility gear, and smiled slightly. *Of course, they probably think we're the crazy ones, scaling up cliffs to jog down the other side in snowshoes.*

Samantha hadn't planned on joining the infantry, much less joining a regiment that specialized in mountain operations. All her life, she'd been an athlete—she was generally the best at any sport she applied herself at, excelling at gymnastics and cross-country running. Growing up, her mother had pushed her in the way only the child of a wealthy baroness could experience; with the best trainers and coaches available, anything other than excellence was unacceptable.

She'd won planetary gymnastic competitions since she'd been eight, moving on from the rural world of Manassas to winning matches across the Crucis March. She'd held the singular record of having won back-to-back gold medals in three events while in the junior competitions. But it hadn't been enough for her mother.

It had come to a head when she'd left for the tiny capital university. She'd met "a boy," and her mother hadn't approved of him or of Samantha dating without her permission. She'd taken up parkour, sometimes known as free-running, a particularly liberating and difficult sport that combined her love of running and gymnastics. She'd also started rebelling, acting foolish, and having a few scrapes with the law. Nothing the family lawyer couldn't get her out of, but embarrassing to her mother.

After a particularly loud and vicious argument, she found herself wandering late at night, drifting from bar to bar, with an occasional stop into a coffee shop for a caffeine fix to keep her moving. With most of the street dark, the glaring fluorescent lights of an AFFS recruiting station seemed out of place, yet welcoming. Paying for a coffee, she sipped it as she wandered over— they had been open all hours, every day since the Jihad began, and she stared through the large windows at the holo images of AFFS troops running through obstacles and jumping over forests in Cavalier battle armor.

"Need a refill?" a smiling sergeant had asked, holding a coffee pot. She had smiled back and walked in.

Due to the shortage of junior officers, her basic training and officer course had been abbreviated, and she was quickly sent to a combined infantry-mountaineering school that consumed nearly a year of her life. She'd excelled at all aspects of the course, her competiveness serving her well in a unit made up of individuals as motivated and fit as she was. She never did learn to enjoy the cold, but even while soaking wet and freezing, she'd been known as unshakably optimistic.

What she'd never told anyone was the reason she was so cheerful on the outside was because she lived with a constant, berating voice inside her mind.

The paratroopers will get all the glory, the voice told her now, her mother's nasal whine filling the silence between radio updates. *Or worse, you'll make a fool of yourself in front of the sergeant major: he knows how young you are, he's expecting you to screw up.*

Shut up, Mother! she thought viciously, closing her eyes and concentrating. A paratrooper hauptmann called up a contact report, and she focused on that, trying to visualize the battle in her head to chase out the self-doubt.

The first ones on the ground would be the Lyran paratroopers, a battalion of light infantry that would secure Gunnison Airport's two runways. Twin strips of reinforced ferrocrete on the south side of town, they could handle any size cargo aircraft required to support the Star League-era Castle Brian just to the west of town. One of the massive fortresses scattered around Terra, the Gunnison Castle Brian had been quickly identified as the probable destination of several shattered bands of Word survivors scattered across the North American Great Plains. Stone had decided on a bold airlift to get light forces to Gunnison and either secure the facility or deny it to the enemy.

The 199th Lyran Jump Regiment had barely survived the Battle of New Avalon, the tough Lyran Alliance Armed Forces paratroopers reduced to a few companies fighting alongside the First Davion

Guards. Her regiment, the Forty-fifth Cerulean Mountain, had been attached to the Second Davion Guards once their parent BattleMech regiment, the Third Davion, had been destroyed. Before the jump to Terra, however, some reassignments had occurred: the rebuilt 199th had been attached to an LAAF unit, the Fifteenth Arcturan Guards; in exchange, the AFFS had assigned her regiment to support the First Davion.

She listened to the battle as it progressed. There was less than a company of local defenders, but they were in well-placed positions. The Lyrans were getting chewed up even before they landed, but as units were forming, they were attacking.

The red light in the bay blinked off, then turned back on. *Second flight is heading in*, she thought. After the casualties the Guards had taken inbound to Terra and in Dallas, the Forty-fifth had been consolidated into two battalions. First Battalion was in the next group of planes, but, unlike her battalion, which had to land to off-load, they would be using their VTOL capability to hover over designated areas.

During the mission briefing, the purple-clad squadron commander of the Third Free World Legionnaires had objected to his lightly armored Karnovs remaining motionless near a runway that might or might not be secured, but he'd been flatly overruled. First Battalion had to assist the paratroopers in securing the runway for both Second Battalion and the engineers in the third flight. Having First Battalion rappel out of the Karnovs was faster than landing them, a concession to the danger; but the runways had to be secured for the engineers and their heavy equipment no matter the cost. The men and women with the rattlesnake patches sewn on the right upper-chest of their flight suits had accepted the decision in cold silence.

"We've got 'Mechs in the woodline, coming from the college!" a voice called over the channel. "*Mein Gott*, that's a *Rifleman*!"

Her blood ran cold. The *Rifleman* was one of the most efficient anti-aircraft BattleMechs ever created. The slow-moving Karnovs hauling First Battalion would be easy and lucrative targets for a defending MechWarrior. The reports came quick.

"Incoming! A Karnov is hit!"

"Alpha Company, fire at that 'Mech! Pour it on!"

"She's veering—oh, Christ!"

"It exploded! The *Rifleman*'s turning!"

"Alpha, fire LAWs *now*!"

"Another Karnov is hit; it's heading toward the runway—"

"It's breaking up—"

"Hit him again, Alpha, right torso!"

"The Karnov is down; it's broken and burning on the runway! I say again, the Karnov is burning on the runway, the runway is *closed*!" Webb looked over at her sergeant major, worry in her eyes.

In less than a minute, a single BattleMech had killed nearly half an infantry battalion.

EAST OF GUNNISON, COLORADO
NORTH AMERICA
TERRA
9 OCTOBER 3078

As Webb watched, the cargo master practically scrambled over her troops to get to the sergeant major. She looked around—many of her troops, especially the experienced ones, had been asleep, knowing they didn't need to wake up until the lights started flashing. They now looked up with concern, the inexperienced ones with alarm. The cargo master said something to the sergeant major, who then looked at her, and motioning to the frequency knob on the side of the helmet, mouthed "air." She nodded and flipped channels.

"This is Rattlesnake Air Two actual to all Two Flight, the runway is hot. Runway two-four is closed, shift approach vectors to runway three-five. Touch-and-goes at ninety-second intervals; pilots, inform your pax. Two actual out." She didn't know what "touch-and-go" meant, but the cargo master's dark face went pale.

He mouthed "intercom," and she flipped channels again as the aircraft made a steep bank to the left. "LT, Sergeant Major, this is Lieutenant Boyd," the copilot said, and Webb could hear the stress in his voice. "Here's what's going to happen—we're going to go in at near full speed, and come to a crash-halt at approximately halfway down the new runway. The cargo master will shove the pallet off the ramp; your unit needs to disembark in ten seconds or less, because we have to get the hell off the runway. Your company will have to manhandle that pallet off the tarmac before the next plane lands—you'll have about thirty seconds. Maybe less. Any questions?"

The sergeant major shook his head.

"Fly fast and safe, Lieutenant," she said over the intercom.

"Kick theirs; cover yours," he replied. She took off the aircrew helmet and put on her foliage cap, fastening it at her neck and adjusting the fit of the earpiece. She listened as the sergeant major bellowed over the noise of the aircraft to relay Lieutenant Boyd's instructions, although with significantly more profanity and passion. She nodded at his instructions—one platoon set up security to each side, in this case, the east and west, while Third Platoon shoved the pallet off the runway. He asked if she had anything to add.

She looked over her troops, still sitting, staring at her. Normally, a full-strength mountain company was forty-two soldiers, but only thirty-eight faces looked at her. Casualties from taking Dallas had whittled them down to thirty-three, and had left her in command. However, when the regimental commander had assigned the Third Battalion sergeant major to her—to help balance out her inexperience—he'd also brought over the remains of a Third Battalion weapons platoon, five soldiers and a semi-portable autocannon that had brought them almost back up to strength. Instead of yelling, she clicked her radio over to the company frequency.

"Remember to check your fire, there's friendlies in the area. There's a pair of BattleMechs down there, make sure you can reach your LAWs." She paused and then forced herself to put optimism back in her voice. "Let's get this done!" Her more experienced troops smiled back as the red light began to blink—the rest simply looked somewhat less scared.

The cargo master ran to the rear and unhooked the pallet as the sergeant major bellowed, "Outboard *stand up*! Inboard *stand up*!" The company stood as they were called, putting on their rucksacks, and faced the rear of the craft as the engine's tone shifted to a banshee howl. The Cobra bounced once as rubber screeched against the runway, sending soldiers slamming into each other, then the plane landed with a solid thump, engines and brakes screaming as it slowed.

The rear ramp was lowering, and as it went horizontal, the cargo master began to push the pallet, assisted by a couple of infantrymen. The pallet flew out and landed flat, sending sparks as it slid along the runway, and the red light turned green as the plane shuddered to a halt.

"Go!" yelled Samantha, the cargo master, and the sergeant major simultaneously. The soldiers ran out in files, each of the outboard units cutting east and west while the soldiers in the middle sprinted toward the pallet sitting almost one hundred meters behind them. Samantha ran down the ramp and leapt off the Cobra. It began accelerating to full speed, the cargo master giving her a half wave as he raised the ramp. She ran toward the eastern edge of the runway and then took a knee in the damp grass next to the platoon sergeant.

"All Alpine elements, this is Blue-Six, we're down, over," she called over the battalion net, as she looked around. At the far western end of runway two-four to the north, she spotted a small firefight as the paratroopers cleared out the remnants of the defenders, tracers and lasers visible against the dark sky. The eastern side, however, was a scene of chaos and destruction.

On the northern side of the runway was a burning pyre from the first Karnov the *Rifleman* had shot down; the shattered remains of the second one formed a flaming wall on the runway itself. The sky above the fires glowed red, and the *Rifleman*, backlit from the flames, was a darkened outline running south between the wrecks toward her unit while torso-twisting toward the west. Without warning, twin laser streams strafed the BattleMech, one from each side.

The MechWarrior returned fire toward his western opponent, hitting the fighter, but the lasers of the eastern wingman punched deep into the heavy 'Mech's rear. With a shudder, the 'Mech came to a halt and then exploded from within; the damaged fighter, Samantha could see, was burning out of the sky, heading toward town. Several seconds later, there was an explosion as the Benjamin fighter crashed into Gunnison proper.

She almost sighed in relief before she caught sight of the second BattleMech approaching from the north alongside runway three-five. In a red-and-white paint scheme that matched the *Rifleman*'s, with the words "Physics Department" written on it, the ancient *Thug* BattleMech ran through waves of shoulder-fired missiles.

"*Sergeant Major!*" Samantha screamed as she reached for her LAW.

"I see him!" he shouted back from across the runway. "Third Platoon, get that autocannon up!" Before the massive assault 'Mech was in range of her company, though, it stopped, and raised both of its arms at a target in the sky.

"Oh no," she whispered, turning to look south. As she feared, the last aircraft of Two Flight was on its final approach. Flaps extended and wheels down, the Planetlifter was seconds from landing when she heard the engines increase thrust, the massive cargo aircraft desperately clawing for altitude.

"Climb, please, *climb*," she whispered at the aircraft containing not only one of her sister rifle companies, but the battalion headquarters platoon, and both the regimental headquarters and support companies. Almost 150 infantrymen were aboard the twin-engine craft as it overflew her company, both engines pushed to maximum.

The *Thug* methodically took aim; still ignoring everything First Battalion threw at it, it fired, an azure bolt of man-made lightning unleashed from each arm. One PPC missed, but the other hit the right-hand engine, blowing it into a cloud of fire and shrapnel, and then scored across the wing to blast a pair of ailerons apart. The Planetlifter tilted to the right and fell.

"Down!" Samantha and the sergeant major both screamed, the young woman pressing herself as flat as she could against the cool Colorado grass and willing herself to merge with the soil itself. The right-hand wingtip touched the ground, and the wing sheared off, spinning toward the east as the rest of the Planetlifter tumbled forward, incidentally absorbing the *Thug* into its wreckage as it turned one whole flip and then exploded. Samantha felt the air blast over her head in a superheated rush, and then the earth shook in the concussive shockwave as the tons of aviation fuel on board ignited into a fireball that rose into the night sky. She kept her head down as flames and shrapnel fell from the sky, then, as it seemed to clear, slowly got to a knee.

"I need a casualty report," she said over the radio to the sergeant major, and he nodded in acknowledgment across the runway to her. She looked to the north, the three burning aircraft clearly illuminating the two runways and surrounding fields in flickering shades of yellow and orange. Firing had tapered off with the destruction of the *Thug*—the Gunnison airfield was theirs.

NORTH OF COALDALE, COLORADO
NORTH AMERICA
TERRA
11 OCTOBER 3078

Captain Schultz popped the triangular viewport of his neurohelmet up and rubbed his eyes with his right hand. Grabbing an electrolyte drink from a small side pocket on his command chair, he gulped greedily, relishing the sugary fluid despite its warmth. Putting it back and slapping his viewport closed again, he quickly scanned his monitors to see if anything had changed.

Still nothing. They'd been getting intermittent contact with a light tracked vehicle, but it'd disappeared shortly before midnight, and they hadn't found it again. Schultz knew it had gone to ground, whether to hide or to ambush his lance, he wasn't sure. He also knew they couldn't bypass it, but every minute spent looking for it equaled more distance that they'd have to make up to regain contact with the main body of Word forces they'd chased across Kansas and most of Colorado.

They'd already destroyed a battered *Raijin II*, and killed a reduced squad of Purifier battle armor that had cleverly tried to hide among the warm heat signatures of a buffalo herd. Ironically, the animals themselves gave away the Word troops, leaving large holes in their herd as it moved, avoiding the strange creatures they couldn't see but could smell.

But this one was giving them problems, and Schultz suspected it was probably TerraSec. Defensive units raised and assigned regionally, TerraSec troops were often intimately familiar with their home terrain. Schultz frowned—somewhere nearby was a tank, hiding in a fishing hole or make-out spot that only a local would know about, and without either a stroke of luck or genius, they probably wouldn't find it for hours.

"Contact! I'm taking fire from my eleven!" Leftenant Becker, Schultz's executive officer, yelled in her *Men Shen*. Spinning his *Uziel* 2S in place, Schultz accelerated northwest toward his lancemate.

Unless they come out of hiding, he corrected, somewhat satisfied by the result. Becker's *Men Shen* would probably be more than enough to take care of a lone light vehicle, plus any troops that also might be lying in ambush. But while he was heading over to ensure it ended quickly enough not to delay their mission, Schultz was also being driven by something he hadn't felt in a long while—the need to not disappoint someone counting on him.

The briefing by the intelligence officer had been deceptively simple. He'd delivered a staggering amount of information concisely and efficiently: only minutes in, Schultz could see why he'd been pulled up from the Marlette Crucis March Militia to work with the Guards, a move that had probably saved the officer's life.

The main body of Word of Blake forces had split into three thrusts, one heading east, one heading north, and one heading west toward Albuquerque. Devlin Stone and Galen Cox had managed to catch the western group between their units and smashed them outside Dodge City. The remnants of the Albuquerque thrust had squeezed through a gap between the Fifteenth Arcturan and the Twelfth Vegan Rangers and immediately scattered.

Breaking into groups of three and four, most of the surviving Word forces had run hard and fast in nearly every direction. The exception, however, was a pair of ragged Level IIs that had headed straight west.

The officer had immediately guessed their intentions, since they were heading toward Gunnison on almost as direct a bearing as possible. Unfortunately, though, the Marlette officer had been unable to determine the status of the Gunnison Castle Brian. Most Castles Brian on Terra had been reported as locked, but a few had been found open by Coalition forces. Devlin Stone and the various regimental commanders of the two task forces had agreed that they couldn't take the risk of having the shattered Word forces get inside to resupply and rebuild.

When the operations officer had explained the airlift portion of the operation, the room had gotten very, very quiet. Any infantry force light enough to be lifted into place at Gunnison would be too light to hold the Word Level IIs for long, and casualties would be high. A fast BattleMech force was needed to follow the Word and perform a traditional cavalry mission: pursue the Word relentlessly, hunt them down, and whittle them away to nothing.

The operations officer had looked around the room, and Schultz had surprised himself by quietly raising a finger when his gaze fell on him. The major had nodded—Schultz's friendship with Samantha was well known across the unit.

"Schultz. Yeah, you and your 'recon-o'-hammer' would be perfect to lead this. We'll build you a lance, and you'll leave at dawn."

"Targeting computer has an ID, it's a Galleon one-oh-three," the third member of his lance reported, racing his *Legionnaire* BattleMech ahead. "Looks like it's inside that series of ridges to the northwest." Schultz noted the quiet fourth member of the lance, also in a *Legionnaire*, shadowing the first. He hadn't worked with the two MechWarriors everyone called "the brothers," but he could see why they were known as that. The pair worked as one, the two BattleMechs moving in a fluid, bounding overwatch without signaling or communicating to one another.

He hadn't been pleased when they'd told him he couldn't use his normal lancemates, though he'd understood. Sergeants Thomason and Kim, in their *Rakshasa* and *Thanatos*, were simply too slow to maintain pursuit. Across his company, only Leftenant Becker, in her captured Capellan *Men Shen*, had the proper blend of firepower and speed required for this mission.

The two *Legionnaire*s were assigned to round out the lance, and to give him a pair of MechWarriors used to working together. Since it was an ad hoc lance, it was hoped that assigning it in pairs would help with cohesion as they raced across the Great Plains.

It would also, hopefully, simplify logistics, keeping Schultz's "tail" as small as possible. With the two identical BattleMechs in the lance, and with the *Men Shen* in the D configuration, the unit's makeup minimized the varieties of ballistic ammunition required. Following his lance approximately ten kilometers behind was a small support element. Consisting of not much more than a couple of trucks containing spare parts and ammunition, a squad of technicians, and a double-squad of Cavalier battle armor assigned for security, the support element bounded from town to town as they followed Schultz and his 'Mechs.

"I've got eyes on the Galleon," Leftenant Becker said. "They're trying to hide—whoops, they spotted me; they're moving. I'm engaging."

"Edwards, you and Khoshaba hang back," Schultz called to the lead *Legionnaire* and his partner. "We'll handle this with energy weapons. You guys watch our backs."

"Understood," Edwards replied, a note of disappointment in his voice. He turned his 'Mech back toward the north-south highway and started accelerating to top speed. "We'll swing north, make sure he's by himself."

Schultz acknowledged, leaning his *Uziel* forward slightly to compensate for the steep gradient. On his viewscreen, he saw the two *Legionnaire*s running along the road in step, the two 'Mechs less than fifty meters apart. As standard *Legionnaire* variants, they didn't have Beagle Probes; but the two pilots had repeatedly demonstrated that the design had enough speed and firepower to keep them out of trouble if another ambush was sprung.

Schultz quickly scanned the terrain as he crested the ridge. The series of tightly packed ridges looked like ripples on an algae-covered pond in the green-hues of his light-enhanced viewscreen. They were uniformly spaced, green waves of curving, grassy ridges separated by deep canyons that seemed to swallow the half-mooned sky. His viewscreen flared briefly, and Schultz angled toward the flash of PPC fire.

The *Men Shen* was running along the ridge, away from him, torso twisted to the left and firing down the steep slope at the fleeing light tank. The Galleon was speeding downhill, skidding out of control for a moment as the driver lost traction. This inadvertently slipped the tank out of the way of Becker's twin pulse lasers, buying the tank another few seconds as her weapons recharged.

Schultz twisted his 'Mech slightly, lined up the crosshairs on the tank, and waited for them to pulse. The pip blinked once, twice, and he squeezed the main interlock trigger. Both blue beams ripped apart the night and struck the Galleon's left side. The vehicle flipped over on its right, then flipped again, end over end, a burning wreck that tumbled the rest of the way down the slope.

"How bad you get clipped, Becker?" he asked.

"Armor damage only," she replied, fatigue in her voice. "A couple of hits—the gunner had a bit of skill."

"Right. Edwards, where are you?"

"North of the ridges, looking over a great valley of nothing. Want us to come back?"

Schultz yawned. "No. We'll come to you, walk the Beagles over these ravines and see if they sniff anything else out."

An hour later, Schultz and Becker slowly approached the *Legionnaire*s. The two MechWarriors had taken up covered positions in small swells of trees while waiting.

"Nothing?" Edwards asked.

"Nothing we could find," Schultz said wearily. He could almost see Becker's chicken-legged 'Mech sagging from fatigue. "Hell, we're so tired, unless they jumped out and yelled 'Boo!' at us, we would have walked right by them." He paused. "There's something about that Galleon that's been bothering me, and I can't put my finger on it. Something I would know if I wasn't so damn tired," he finished, frustration creeping in his voice.

"There wasn't a Galleon in the group we've been pursuing," Khoshaba said quietly.

As one, the three BattleMechs slowly turned toward the taciturn MechWarrior. Schultz had quickly learned that Khoshaba rarely spoke, but when he did, it was important. "I believe that the Galleon, the Purifiers, and the *Raijin II* were a separate group of stragglers. We may have lost contact with original force we had been chasing."

Schultz was quiet for a moment, thinking, and then slammed his hand against his command chair. "Dammit!" he yelled, and then collected himself. "I should have seen that."

He sighed, looking over his secondary monitors while the radio was quiet. "Becker, you got anything on your Beagle?" he asked.

"Nothing but us, Captain."

"Okay, let's pack it in. We'll head back to Coaldale, let Chief Black put some fresh armor on the *Men Shen*, and get some rest. Maybe in the morning the intel weenies will know where they disappeared to."

EAST OF GUNNISON, COLORADO
NORTH AMERICA
TERRA
11 OCTOBER 3078

Samantha spun on her left heel, walking backwards for a few moments, and looked down the column of marching troops. Spread out with at least five meters between each trooper, her company stretched down both sides of Highway 50's eastbound lanes, marching in the cool mountain air.

It'd taken the better part of a day to reorganize the Forty-fifth Mountain's survivors. Two full line companies, plus nearly all of their supporting elements, had been shot down, with only a handful of badly burned survivors to evacuate to the small Gunnison hospital. The two battalions had been reduced to four companies, with only the ammo on their backs to fight with.

The regimental operations officer had flown in with First Battalion, and had assumed command, absorbing the Lyrans and forming a combined rump regiment. He'd reestablished communications with Stone's headquarters and passed along word of their situation. Late on the tenth, he'd held a commanders conference to bring all the company commanders up to speed. Samantha had arrived with the sergeant major to find that she was now not the only leftenant commanding a full company.

For resupply purposes, they were now going to be drawing off of Connor Sortek's Seventeenth Benjamin Regulars; the first Planetlifter's worth of supplies and a Benjamin field-gun battery were due to arrive around noon of the twelfth. Since the engineers had landed safely after the destruction of the *Thug*, they were going to continue their mission—they would be heading west toward the Gunnison Castle Brian at first light on the eleventh. Along with a company of paratroopers for security, the engineers would attempt to open the Castle Brian if it was locked—or breach it if it was occupied.

At the same time, Samantha's company was to head east on their own. Originally, the whole regiment was to emplace in a pre-designated location on Highway 50: an S curve, it was the textbook definition of an *l*-shaped ambush site. However, Samantha's company was the only one to have not received any casualties the previous day, and the numbers of troops available to ambush the Word had been cut by over a third. She had now been told to head east until she ran into the Word, slow them down, and buy as much time as possible. The longer she could hold the Word, the more wounded troops could hopefully be returned to active duty—and they might possibly even receive reinforcements from Sortek.

The operations officer had ended his mission brief to her with a falsely optimistic, "When you can't hold them any longer, fall back and lead them to us." At that, she'd just glanced over at the sergeant major. His hooded eyes wordlessly told her his estimation of the odds of them living that long.

Before answering, she looked at her fellow commanders sitting or standing around in the small tent serving as the Gunnison temporary headquarters. A collection of dirty and sweaty officers stared back, some with unreadable expressions, some with a semi-shocked, weary look. Many were wounded themselves, with bandages taped under their uniforms and stained rust red from their own dried blood. She'd looked back at the major, who, like her, had suddenly had command thrust unexpectedly on him when everyone above him was killed.

"We'll hold, sir. We'll buy you as much time as you need. You can rely on us."

He looked her and gave her a thin, stressed smile. "I will."

Samantha waved down the line at the sergeant major at the rear of the company and then spun back toward the front with a semi-smile on her face. She couldn't help it; though she was tense, she felt better now that they were finally on the move: marching with the sun low on the horizon of a beautiful autumn morning, in the mountains, on Terra *itself*. They had a mission—a dangerous one, to be sure—but she led highly trained and motivated troops and would be fighting on their preferred terrain. In her eyes, though things could be better, they could also be a lot worse.

"Vehicle to the front!" The unit quickly took up prone positions at the shout, the southern troops to the side and in the grass, dusted with a light layer of snow; the inside squads taking up positions in the wide, deep gulley in the median. It had been a calculated gamble, moving in column, but she had agreed with the sergeant major that getting east as fast as possible and into their ambush site outweighed the risk of someone counter-ambushing them. The last reports they'd received hadn't shown any organized resistance in this part of Colorado—of course, they hadn't shown that Western State College had possessed a pair of BattleMechs in their College of Science, either.

The white pickup, with the battered look typical of a farm vehicle, sped toward them in the westbound lanes. A hundred meters away, it slowed and then came to a screeching halt. The driver got out, hands out in front, and slowly approached the first squad leader.

At a hand signal, Samantha came jogging forward. A rugged older man, approximately fifty years old, appraised her before saluting.

"Good morning, Leftenant. Adept Lewis Smith, Two-oh-first ComStar Division. That's my son," he said, waving his hand toward the teenage boy sitting in the truck with a pale expression and hands firmly on the dashboard.

She quirked an eyebrow. "They're dead. Have been for almost twenty years."

"All but," he replied, with a sad smile. "A few of us escaped—I had a sister-in-law up in Vail that I made my way up to. My ID's in my jacket." He slowly reached inside, aware of the rifles pointed at him, and started to tear at the liner. Once it was halfway ripped out, he reached deep inside, and pulled out a thin sheaf of older-styled ComStar IDs. Samantha looked them over, and passed them over to the sergeant major who'd jogged up.

She walked over to the pickup, looking over the interior, and then the teen before smiling at him. *Kinda cute*, she noticed, absently tucking a loose strand of hair back behind her right ear. He smiled back and began to relax as she turned back to his father.

"I was heading to Gunnison," Smith went on. "I'd heard friendly forces were in Kansas, and I thought I'd sneak into the college, try to steal myself a BattleMech. There's a *Thug* there I'm qualified to pilot—or I was, a long time ago." She frowned as the sergeant major passed the documents back to the former Com Guard.

"It was destroyed."

"Oh." Smith paused. "You do know there's a Castle Brian to the west of Gunnison, right?" At her nod, he asked, "Then why are you way out here?"

Samantha clenched her jaw for a second as her mother's voice told her that trusting him would doom the company. She decided to trust him. "We're a blocking force. The Word is sending BattleMechs to the Castle, and we need to hold them until reinforcements arrive."

He looked at her for a second. "They won't come through here! They'll take one-fourteen, cut across on Route Forty-two to Highway One-forty-nine; it'll lead them straight to it." Her jaw had dropped and then closed, a questioning look on her face. "You didn't know that?"

"No! Why would you think that?" she demanded.

He shrugged. "Because that's the route *we* took."

COALDALE, COLORADO
NORTH AMERICA
TERRA
11 OCTOBER 3078

Schultz was sitting in a family-run diner, eating an omelet and drinking a large cup of coffee when Leftenant Becker walked in. Wearing her long, red hair in a single braid that ran down her back of her green AFFS-issued jumpsuit, she smiled and came over. He saw dark circles under her eyes, but they weren't as bad as they had been for the past couple of days.

"Good morning, Gretchen," he said, reaching over to the far side of the booth to flip the second coffee cup upright. Before Becker even sat down, a waitress swept in to fill it.

Gretchen wrapped her hands around the cup with her eyes closed, inhaling for a second. "If I'd known how good Terran coffee is, I would have pushed to invade Terra *first*, and *then* polished off the rest of the Protectorate," she said before taking a sip.

He chuckled in amused agreement. He'd had Terran coffee before but had paid handsomely for it, as anything exported from "the cradle of mankind" drew top price across the Inner Sphere. Having excellent coffee cheaply available in every town they'd stopped in had been a wonderful discovery.

She looked at him. "How long have you been up? I thought I'd overslept, but I ran into Chief, and he said you'd given orders to let us sleep in." They'd gotten back from the ridgelines about 0200 local, and he'd immediately ordered his MechWarriors to their rooms at the motel they were using. He'd left orders for Chief to wake him at seven, or if anything happened, but to let the lance sleep in.

"A couple of hours." He shrugged. "Intel has nothing for us, and they're going to send a recon flight just before noon. Things might get a little hectic after that, so I wanted you guys rested."

"What about you?" she asked, concern in her eyes.

His eyes grew hard. "I'm fine." Much of the unit had the misperception that Schultz was sleeping with Samantha, but Becker knew the truth—Schultz needed her friendship. He'd been commissioned straight out of the Sanglamore into the Fifth Donegal Guards and joined the Federated Commonwealth Civil War. His unit had been on New Avalon, accused of war crimes when the Jihad started, and had all but been destroyed; he was one of the few survivors, proudly displaying the unit insignia "*Nondi*," the cigar-smoking bulldog, under the Davion Guards on his *Uziel.*

Schultz had buried countless friends and gained two ex-wives over long, nearly continuous years of war. His need for Samantha's friendship was far deeper than any physical desire: her enthusiasm for life helped him stave off the depression and battle fatigue constantly threatening to overtake him.

There was silence for a moment as the waitress returned. They'd found that while the Terran populace wasn't rising up to help Stone's coalition overthrow the Word of Blake, most weren't hindering them either. They'd been positively hostile when they'd first landed, and they still ran into bastions of hostility, particularly in towns that believed the Coalition was behind the nuking of Dallas. But as Stone's forces began holding the majority of North America, public affairs officers had started fighting the Word's propaganda campaign with one of their own.

Schultz had found that, for the most part, the citizens of Kansas and Colorado had become decidedly neutral, appearing to take a "wait and see" attitude about the invasion. A few incidents of rock throwing as they'd passed through some towns, and an obscene graffiti about Stone and an improbable relation to his mother were about the worst they'd recently seen. As long as the MechWarriors watched where they stepped and paid for anything they needed in C-Bills, the townsfolk left them alone and held their own counsel.

As Becker ordered, a local came in, shrugging out of his long coat. "Good morning, Father," the waitress said as she passed by him. The older man smiled, nodding at her, then approached Schultz, the white collar of his dark suit clearly visible.

"Are you Captain Schultz?" Schultz nodded, and introduced Becker. "Excellent. Your mechanic told me I could find you here—may I join you?"

"Please," Schultz said. Gretchen slid out of her booth, then walked over to Schultz's side and slid in next to him, unlocking the clasp of her thigh-mounted pistol holster in a smooth motion that he doubted the local noticed. "Coffee?"

"No, thank you." The local leaned forward. "As you may have noticed, Coaldale is a small town. Therefore, much of my flock lives outside city limits—ranchers, farmers. Truly, 'the salt of the Earth,' as the expression goes."

Schultz nodded, unsure where he was going.

"This morning, I received a call from one of them. He lives far outside town, to the west. I've known him for years, a solid man in the church. He saw something last night and wasn't sure what to do with the information. He called me and asked my opinion of its importance."

"What did he see?" Gretchen asked as she curled her left hand around the cup of coffee. Schultz almost smiled—though her curiosity was clearly aroused, she still had her shooting hand on her thigh. Old habits, especially those formed from pain, died hard.

The older man looked each way, and then leaned in a bit farther. "BattleMechs."

Five hours later, Schultz led the lance at a run up a tight, mountainous road. They had raced out of Coaldale quickly after talking in the diner, leaving the foothills behind and entering the Rocky Mountains. Barely two lanes wide and covered in a thin layer of water from ice and snow melting in the morning sun, the road was mostly buffered on both sides by high cliff walls. Occasionally, a wall would disappear and turn into a cliff, sloping dozens, sometimes hundreds of meters to the valleys below.

They were fighting a classic pursuit battle through some of the most expansive vistas Schultz had ever seen, with snow-topped, forested mountains ranging in every direction. It was beautiful, but as he looked at them, Schultz worried that the Word would be able to get more forces into the mountain range. If that happened, they could have the ability to fight a guerrilla war almost indefinitely. They had the Word on the run and were pushing them hard. They stayed constant blips on his monitors now, though Becker, three hundred meters back, couldn't detect them. In between were the *Legionnaire*s, their rotary autocannons pointed to the left and right to protect against any ambushes.

They'd already found a damaged, broken-down Puma earlier that morning, the ancient machine simply unable to maintain the rushed pace of the Word force. Chief Black and his technicians had stopped there, about ten kilometers back, to see if they could resurrect it.

Schultz slowed down, seeing an odd blip on his secondary monitors approximately four hundred meters away, on the far side of a hairpin turn. Turning the corner, his now-unobstructed Beagle-enhanced computer shrieked in warning as a Burke assault tank, sitting on the straight road, fired all three PPCs at him. His *Uziel* shook as it was hit by two; he fought for balance as he lost more than a ton of armor in seconds, and then quickly fired his twin PPCs in a snap-shot that missed before ducking back behind the corner.

Edwards and Khoshaba began taking turns poking around the corner, firing at the tank backing up the mountain, the eighteen-degree slope slowing the massive vehicle to a near crawl. There was a cliff between the lance and the tank, the hairpin turn almost a switchback, and the far side was a sheer drop. Schultz jumped his *Uziel* up the cliff in two bounds and swept around the rear as his lance continued to distract the Burke, then jumped behind the tank.

The road was narrow and straight, the PPCs having a clear shot at his lance when they peeked out, however, the Burke filled nearly the entire road. Barely two meters of ground were on either side of the assault tank, and when Schultz landed, the tank simultaneously tried to pivot-spin in place to face him and rotate its turret counterclockwise, PPCs spinning over the empty valley to his left and front armor rotating to the right, toward the wall.

Schultz waited for a second and then fired directly at the left rear of the Burke, his PPCs blasting deep into the roadway and starting a rockslide. The tank's left tread slid into the gap, quickly followed by the rear of the vehicle, and the rotating turret froze, the tank teetering with the front of the tank two meters off the ground. Schultz walked his *Uziel* up and gently stepped one leg onto the front of the Burke. As he put more weight onto the tank, the front glacis returned to the ground as he called his lancemates forward.

Hatches popped open, and Word crewmen clambered out and stood off to one side, hands over their heads and relief evident on their faces. "Edwards, you get on this side, and you two pull this forward a bit." The two *Legionnaire* BattleMechs, once in position, grabbed the tank and dragged it forward a few meters, with Becker's *Men Shen* pushing the rear with her 'Mech's beak-like nose as best as possible.

"That'll do," he said, as the Burke settled back onto the roadway. "Gretchen, did you call Chief, tell him to come pick up this tank?"

"Yes, Captain."

"Thanks," he replied calmly as he turned his *Uziel* toward the crewmen. Placing the aiming pip on the senior man, he squeezed the thumb-nub and activated his twin machine guns. Pulling from right to left, and then back once for good measure, he gunned the five men down before they could do anything but scream.

"If they were TerraSec, I might have trusted them to disable their tank and walk down to meet up with Chief," he said quietly. "But I'll be dammed if I leave them with a fully operational Burke between us and our support."

There was silence for a second as a large stream of blood formed and started to run off the road, staining the storm gutter dark red. Becker finally spoke. "They were Blakists, Captain. Did you hear us objecting?" She turned her *Men Shen* west. "I'm starting to lose their signal. You want point, or should I lead?"

It was already cold and dark in the mountains when Samantha had finally called a halt. After almost sixteen continuous hours of marching up and down trails, logging roads, and firebreaks, they'd gone about twelve kilometers in a straight line—but double that including elevation changes.

There had been a little griping—she had highly trained soldiers, not robots, and a certain amount of complaining had been expected. But she'd encouraged them, kept up their spirits, and the sergeant major verbally lashed anyone who threatened to fall out. None had, though everyone was tired and a few were limping from blisters by the time they'd stopped for the night.

Once Adept Smith had quickly summarized his unit's flight twenty years earlier, Samantha had immediately decided to change direction and locate a new blocking position. Adept Smith had immediately volunteered to assist them and sent his son, Martin, home with instructions for his wife. He marched with them until Martin had returned a little over an hour later in the original white truck, with the adept's wife driving an even larger pickup behind it.

The sergeant major had quickly ordered the company to split their rucksacks in half, placing their larger, heavier packs in the trucks, along with the autocannon, leaving the soldiers carrying nothing but their assault packs and weapons. Lewis and Martin had taken turns marching alongside her in her unit's formation as the two pickups followed the company, carrying the bulk of their heavy equipment. The elder Smith had asked her endless questions about the state of the Inner Sphere, in particular the Jihad; the younger had asked about her upbringing, briefly and awkwardly inquiring about her relationship status.

With the majority of their heavy equipment in the trucks, the company had been able to move quickly over the mountains—and without the usual series of sprains and twists that would usually accompany such a lengthy forced march. About twenty minutes after Samantha and the sergeant major had held a quick conference and decided they'd moved far enough for one day, they came across a small mountain glen.

The sergeant major quickly set the perimeter while she had the RTO establish communications with Gunnison. While squad leaders checked on their soldier's feet and their fighting positions, Samantha, the sergeant major, and Adept Smith decided on their route for the next day. She felt glad to have the adept along—even though it had been twenty years, he'd been trained at a ComStar military academy, survived both Tukayyid and the Blakist invasion, and had extensive knowledge of the local area.

The temperature began to drop severely, and Smith went to check on his wife. An experienced outdoorswoman originally from Denver, she had brought camping gear for the family and set up a small tent near the two trucks. She'd also brought a few boxes of hard candy, a thoughtful gesture that had been well-received by the soldiers.

"Can't help but notice Martin Smith set his sleeping bag pretty close to yours, LT," the sergeant major said quietly as they walked the perimeter. She couldn't see the smile on his face in the starlight but could hear it.

"I think the boy has a small crush on me," she said. "But he's only eighteen."

"'Living with the immediacy of death helps you sort out your priorities in life,'" he said, reciting something she'd once read in university. "'It helps you to live a less trivial life.'" He paused for a moment, silent, reflective. "The odds are against us on this one, LT. Why spend what might be your last night alone?"

She didn't reply as they checked the position of a pair of troops, waiting until they got out of earshot. "Are you married, Sergeant Major?"

"I am, ma'am. When we're done here, I'm going to try to find New Avalon in the night sky, I'm going to think about her, and then pray to the Lord to give me courage and resolve," he replied, almost too quietly for her to hear in a night full of animal noises unknown, yet somehow familiar. "If you don't want to spend time with the lad, I understand. But you're wound too tight, and it'll affect your judgment tomorrow. I don't know what it is that haunts you—and yes, you hide it well—but try to find some peace tonight."

Ten minutes later, having walked the line, they checked in with the private monitoring the long-distance radio-transmitter. She passed over a message from Gunnison to Samantha, who quickly skimmed it and handed it to the sergeant major: regiment had a separate confirmation that the Word had changed direction.

She suspected it was Hans, still in pursuit, and relaying that the better part of two Word Level IIs were estimated to be heading toward her. They discussed the message briefly, and decided not to change their current timeline. Bidding the sergeant major goodnight, she headed toward the small depression she'd tucked herself into, and noticed Martin's sleeping bag about two meters away.

"You warm enough in there?" she quietly asked, walking around him and between a pair of saplings.

"Yeah. It's, uh, warm and big enough to share—if you want."

She paused, thinking about the sergeant major's words. She heard her mother call her *hussy* in her head, and the corner of her mouth quirking up into a smile, she turned back toward him.

NORTH OF HIGHWAY 42, COLORADO
NORTH AMERICA
TERRA
12 OCTOBER 3078

Samantha slipped out of Martin's sleeping bag just after three, stepping barefoot into a thin layer of fresh snow. She shivered while she quickly threw on her uniform, the cold seeping deep into her as she tightened up her boots and ice-cold armor. The sergeant major had been right, and a quick roll had relaxed her nerves and buoyed her confidence. She warmed as she quickly walked the perimeter, the waning moon low on the horizon reflecting blue against the snow. Every soldier on guard duty was awake and alert, and Samantha spoke a few quiet words of encouragement to each before moving to the next position. She knew she'd be tired later, but she chuckled as she told herself, "I'll sleep when I'm dead."

She then realized she might not survive past lunch.

Schultz's lance was moving just before dawn, the mountains behind them starting to tint pink on their edges with the rising sun. Fueled on cold field rations and the double-caffeinated dehydrated coffee that came with them, Becker took the lead again, her *Men Shen* setting a quick pace up the mountainous road toward the enemy. Though her Beagle Probe and his were functionally the same piece of equipment, MechWarriors held a certain superstition that Capellan built-BattleMechs were better at both ECM and detection, and were simply "sneakier" overall. Whether it was true or not had never been proven, but even he preferred to have Becker's *Men Shen* out front than to rely on his Lyran-built Beagle.

They'd lost contact with the Word the night before, while they'd waited for Chief to arrive, watching the enemy slowly disappear off their monitors; by leaving before dawn, he hoped to make up for lost time before the enemy woke up and started moving.

They'd been moving for two hours, the sun rising behind them and splitting the valleys they charged past into deep shadows and brilliant displays of green on snowy white, when Becker finally spoke up. "Captain, I've got three BattleMechs—they're distant, but solid. I've also got something fuzzy, and a lot closer."

With a frown, Schultz checked his own screen and saw what she was talking about: three fuzzy contacts halfway between them and the BattleMechs. Could be powered-down enemies in deep woods, or could be sensor ghosts of the 'Mechs, caused by the irregular terrain.

"Slow us down, Gretchen, and let's tighten up." They turned a corner that led to a straight, narrow road about a kilometer in length, with a cliff on their left side and a fall-off on the right. Where the road curved to the right, nine hundred meters up a slight incline, there were stands of trees.

"Boss, this is damn near identical to where the Burke ambushed us, and the Word isn't smart enough to come up with new tricks in two days," Edwards warned.

"Well, the Burke was left behind to delay us because it was too slow to keep up," he said, "but you're right, I don't like this either. Gretchen, speed up—let's take this one at a run."

They had been marching since dawn, and had finally hit Highway 42. Setting up a perimeter north of the road, she sent out a squad in each direction to find an ambush position while the rest prepared for battle. Cold weather gear was shifted from assault pack to rucksack, canteens topped off and extra ammo stuffed into pockets, weapons were checked and double-checked.

She was standing next to Adept Smith and strapping a pair of shaped charges to her leg when the sergeant major walked over. Cylindrical canisters the size of softballs, three of them could be latched onto the left-thigh armor with quick-disconnect brackets. While wearing all three, however, the leg became off-balanced and too heavy to march comfortably for any significant distance—most mountain troops wore one while on the move, and only attached the second two when combat against 'Mechs was imminent.

"Ma'am, Corporal Bowden just got back, found a spot about three hundred meters to the west that should suit our needs perfectly," the sergeant major reported.

She nodded, and turned toward Smith. "Lewis, you and your family need to leave." He began to shake his head and respond, but she cut him off. "You need to backtrack a couple of klicks. We'll come get you after the fight, or by dinner if nothing happens. If you don't see us by nightfall, get the hell out of here." He grimaced in distaste at the order, but then nodded.

He pointed at a dark shape lazing on the breeze. "That's a bald eagle, Leftenant. It's good luck around these parts." He turned to her, shook her hand and then the sergeant major's, and then headed through the pines back toward the trucks.

They watched him go for a moment, and then Samantha asked, "Let's get into place, Sergeant Major. I hope we haven't missed them." Before he could reply, in the distance they heard faint but unmistakable *snap-boom*s echoing down the valley from the east.

"Gauss rifles, ma'am," the sergeant major said. "Only thing that makes that cracking sound. About three klicks away, but hard to tell with the echoes."

She nodded. "Let's get moving."

The four 'Mechs had been about halfway down the straight road when a pair of wheeled Demons opened fire on them. Schultz swore. Heavily armed and armored, each 60-ton Demon outweighed any one 'Mech in the lance, and the pair of them were over half the lance's combined weight.

The fact they were trapped on a straight line made a dangerous situation potentially lethal. Gretchen caught the first round, the Gauss slug catching her *Men Shen* in the right leg mid-stride, sending her crashing to the asphalt in a heap.

"Edwards, Khoshaba, go!" Schultz yelled. The two *Legionnaire* BattleMechs were capable of running 118 kilometers per hour, faster than his *Uziel* or Gretchen's downed *Men Shen*, and the best tactic—the only tactic, in this situation—was to close the distance as fast as possible. The twin 50-ton 'Mechs began sprinting, carving great divots into the lightly snow-covered highway, opening up the distance between them and his *Uziel* as Schultz tried to keep up. They fired again, and Edwards, in the lead, staggered as both Demons hit his *Legionnaire*. The medium 'Mech stutter-stepped as it lost nearly two tons of armor in a moment, but kept charging forward, closely followed by Khoshaba.

The moment they were in range, they both fired their rotary autocannons at double rate, a rain of brass streaming out behind them as they ran. The twin streams of tracer fire converged on the front glacis of the left-hand Demon, scarring armor but inflicting no further damage. Schultz finally entered range with his PPCs, and fired at the right-hand tank. One missed and incinerated a pair of thick trees, while the other blasted armor off the tank. Waste heat rushed into his cockpit from the PPCs discharge, immediately raising the temperature from moderate to sauna.

Becker's *Men Shen* rose to its feet, and he heard her say, "Holy crap. Hans, the third tank is coming in behind you," she said, incredulousness in her voice.

"Where?" he rasped, scanning the 360-degree band at the top of his monitor. On his secondary monitor, he could see an enemy contact nearly on top of him, but he couldn't find it.

"I've got it." Tilting her birdlike 'Mech backwards slightly, Becker fired everything she had into the sky, an alpha strike with both missile racks and lasers, then her ER PPC. As he ran, he saw a mass of white paint, fire, and smoke crash into the road behind him, bouncing hard once before rolling off the road to tumble down the cliff.

"What the hell was that?" he bellowed, firing both PPCs at the same Demon again, and once again, only missing with his right one.

"I think I just killed the last Kanga in the universe," she replied, using her *Men Shen*'s MASC system to accelerate. The sudden burst of speed threw off the aim of the right-hand Demon, a silver blur passing behind her 'Mech, but the other Demon slammed Edwards again, and his BattleMech seemed to crack in half. His 'Mech stumbled, and his left arm was severed at the shoulder and flew in a boomerang-arc toward the cliff. He slowed, barely keeping his 'Mech upright.

Khoshaba passed him and, pulling ahead, tore into the Demon with his weapon's maximum rate of fire.

"Good God," Schultz said, never failing to be impressed by the volume of shell casings a RAC could produce. The stream of brass fell like rain, bouncing up from the road in a bright clatter, catching the sunlight and gleaming. The autocannon dug deep at the intersection of the Demon's Gauss rifle and turret, sending smoke billowing out of the tank.

The right hand tank fired again, and on his rear monitor, Schultz saw Gretchen's *Men Shen* tumble as its right leg snapped off at the knee. Her 'Mech slammed into the cliff and then fell onto its right side, crumpling armor and remaining motionless.

"Gretchen!" He fired at the same time Edwards and Khoshaba did; this time, both blue bolts of lightning struck the Demon, closely followed by twin streams of autocannon fire. The tank sagged inwards and then exploded, setting the surrounding woods ablaze.

"I'm fine," he heard Becker reply in a groggy voice. Her *Men Shen* began a scrabbling motion as it tried to get upright, armor screeching as it dragged against the asphalt. Bracing the nose of her 'Mech against the cliff, she pushed forward with her good leg. Her 'Mech took further damage as armor lost the fight against the Colorado mountain and was crushed inwards, but her *Men Shen* shakily stood, leaning drunkenly against the cliff.

"Khoshaba, check on the second Demon. Edwards, status?" Before Edwards could answer, a six-pack of short-range missiles erupted from the Demon, quickly followed by twin laser beams. The missiles scattered, half rocking the wounded 'Mech, but the lasers lanced deep into a gaping breach on the right side of Edwards's *Legionnaire*. Before anyone could say a word, his ammunition cooked off, and with a scream of tortured metal, the 'Mech exploded. Shrapnel rained as a dark smoke cloud arose from the pair of legs still upright on the road.

All three remaining 'Mechs lashed into the Demon, the three PPCs evaporating the remaining frontal armor and digging deep into the internal structure of the tank, setting it ablaze, and Khoshaba's RAC finishing it off in an ammo explosion matching the first Demon's destruction.

"Damn it," Schultz whispered, first turning toward the remains of Edwards's 'Mech, then toward Becker.

"Hans, look at your display. The enemy 'Mechs are almost on top of Leftenant Webb," she said, stress in her voice. He paused, unsure. "Just go, dammit! I'll be fine here!" He spun his *Uziel* and began running up the road, passing the burning Demons at full speed. The remaining *Legionnaire* fell in behind him.

"I've got your six," Khoshaba said.

Samantha watched the small open-topped jeep approach, surprised that the Word was leading their retreat with an infantry squad. Light and unarmored, it was a small four-wheeled transport common to motorized units around the Inner Sphere, and it was just entering her company's kill zone.

Both sides of Highway 42 were bordered by gently sloping saddled ridgelines that suddenly rose into high peaks. The effect was a bowl-shaped valley, which the Word was entering through the eastern side. The sergeant major was with First Platoon on the north side, and she was with Second on the south, both platoons hiding behind thick trees and the boulder-sized rubble that made up the slopes. Third Platoon was on the western end, with their semi-portable autocannon anchoring the position.

The plan was simple. Third Platoon would initiate the ambush, First Platoon would attack whatever went toward the north, and she would do the same on the south. Each soldier had two single-shot LAW rockets to fire, and the three shaped charges to conduct anti-'Mech attacks with. They had also been issued, as the regiment's main effort, an expendable Dragonsbane pulse laser weapon. Also a fire-and-throw-away weapon, it was more powerful than the LAWs, and she had doubled the Dragonsbanes for Third Platoon, distributing the rest equally.

Behind the infantry trundled a single Fury, a dangerous Gauss-rifle-armed tank common in the AFFS and respected for its rugged durability.

Three large shadows entered the valley, spaced about fifty meters apart, and Samantha felt a shiver of fear. Three BattleMechs! The first was a *Champion*, an odd-looking, winged 'Mech. Behind it was a *Sentinel*, a dangerous opponent for infantry due to its Ultra-class autocannon. She sucked in her breath. The final 'Mech was a *Black Knight*, a heavy 'Mech known for its resilience and firepower. That one 'Mech by *itself* could weather everything her company could throw at it and still exit the western end of the valley.

Two more jeeps were interspersed among the 'Mechs, and she saw one jeep in the trail position, watching the rear. The Fury and every 'Mech showed various amounts of damage, including a gaping hole on the *Champion* where its autocannon should have been. Most of the enemies were in the kill zone, with only the *Black Knight* and final jeep outside, but she couldn't wait on them, or the leading elements would be able to flank Third Platoon.

She keyed her helmet radio once. With a roar that echoed in the small valley, Third Platoon's autocannon tore into the lead jeep. The battery-powered vehicle immediately exploded, sending shrapnel and fleshy shreds of TerraSec infantry in every direction. The

Word's response was quick: the monstrous barrel of the Fury swung toward the autocannon crew and fired, the thunderous boom of the magnetically powered cannon echoing, while the *Champion* pulled off the road toward First Platoon.

From behind rocks and trees, First Platoon fired their Dragonsbanes into the right side of the 60-ton 'Mech, and the surprised *Champion* spun toward this new threat. The Fury pulled off to the right and dropped its troop hatch; six troops poured out and took up positions alongside the assault vehicle.

"Wait for it, Second Platoon," she said over the radio. The *Sentinel* swung off the road toward her position, accelerating into a run, and headed toward Third Platoon, which hadn't fired again since their initial strike. The second jeep had pulled off the side of the road, and took up position on the south side, facing north.

Half of the Fury's infantry fired at Second Platoon, with three men setting up a mortar position. "You've got to be kidding me," she muttered, watching the position of the *Sentinel*.

"Third, the Fury is yours, and kill that mortar. Second, stand by," she said into her headset. Instantly, waves of red-tinged pulse lasers washed over the Fury as Third Platoon, her smallest, hit the tank with their Dragonsbanes. The infantry, both by the Fury and on the south side, turned to face this new threat as the autocannon lashed the mortar position. One TerraSec mortarman was blasted in half by the heavy weapon, and then the mortar ammunition cooked off in a sympathetic explosion.

First Platoon had switched to LAWs, hitting the *Champion* with a wave of light rockets. The damaged BattleMech fell forward, and First Platoon charged the 'Mech as it rose. The *Sentinel* fired its Ultra autocannon at Third's position, joined by the boom of the Fury's Gauss rifle; the *Champion* unleashed a wave of short-range missiles at First Platoon as they approached.

The *Sentinel* came within range of Second Platoon, and Samantha yelled into her radio, "Second, now!" She didn't have a Dragonsbane, so she sighted down her rifle and fired at a Word infantryman aiming at First Platoon. She saw him fall the same time the *Sentinel* reeled from Second Platoon's attack.

"Switch to LAWs," she ordered, watching First Platoon charge the *Champion*. Normally, the mountain troops would conduct kneecapping attacks, placing their small charges in the knees or hips of BattleMechs to cripple them. With the damaged *Champion* prone and struggling to rise, however, First Platoon was able to swarm the 'Mech with their grapple rods, placing their charges in much more vulnerable areas.

With every other infantryman firing rifles at the 'Mech, the rest of First Platoon fired grapple lines for an anti-'Mech attack. Mountain infantry used a grapple system that was equally adept at taking them up mountains or on the attack, a small bar with a piton on one end and a foot strap on the other. The piton would be propelled at a velocity capable of punching into twenty centimeters of rock or into BattleMech armor, and then, foot in stirrup, the cylinder's internal winch would yank the trooper upwards. The piton could be released with an embedded explosive charge, and then the system could be reloaded and used again.

She saw First Platoon scaling the *Champion*, the handless, damaged 'Mech at a disadvantage in repelling the boarders. The Word infantry had spun around and began firing at her platoon, and she saw one of her soldiers get hit and crumple behind a boulder to her front left.

With a whoosh, Second Platoon's LAWs struck the turning *Sentinel*, its autocannon searching for targets. Her company medic ran over to the wounded man, red crosses visible on her white chest armor, and she saw the Fury track the running figure.

"Get down!" she screamed, and then ducked back behind her boulder. There was a thunderous explosion, and she saw the Gauss-slug remnants ricochet into the clear blue sky as gravel rained down on her. She peeked back around, and her two mountaineers—and the boulder they'd been hiding behind—were gone.

"Third Platoon, take the Fury *out*! Second, rope the *Sentinel*!" she yelled into her radio, grabbing her grapple bar from her back. As she charged, she saw the *Sentinel* firing at members of the platoon, and a quick head count gave her a tally of only eight attacking the BattleMech.

"The Fury is down! They left the troop hatch unlocked!" she heard in her ear, but ignored it, ignored the sergeant major barking orders to the other platoons, focusing on the attack. The 'Mech towered above her, and she yanked the stirrup out to its full length. Aiming the bar roughly like a rifle, she pointed it toward the BattleMech's right side, intent on placing her charge into its hip. As she fired, however, the 'Mech's right arm moved in the way, and the piton sunk in deep as she put her foot in the stirrup.

She was yanked off the ground by a combination of the winch and the 'Mech's movement, spun through an arc underneath the arm and up in front of the *Sentinel*'s body, where she was flung off the line. Tumbling through the air toward the 'Mech's left, she could see the autocannon beneath her. Her eyes narrowed, a crazy idea formed, and she shifted her weight in midair to decrease her spin.

It'll never work, her self-doubt/mother intoned. *You're terrible at the beam.*

She landed on the autocannon in a three-point crouch, grabbing for a shaped charge on her leg with her left hand and smiling a wide grin—because she finally realized the voice was wrong, it had *always* been wrong.

She'd medaled on the beam.

The *Sentinel* had frozen, probably in surprise, as she charged up the weapon, her AFFS-issued mountain boots easily finding purchase on the metallic surface. The MechWarrior began to raise the 'Mech's arm, but by then it was too late. She skipped-jumped to the top of the shoulder, slapping her charge into the shoulder gap for good measure, and from there, it was a simple two-meter jump across to the arched roof of the *Sentinel*. The MechWarrior reared his 'Mech back, like a bucking horse, but again, her boots caught and gripped, and she hung onto a handhold used by technicians with her right hand and freed another charge.

She heard the first charge go off as she slapped the second shaped charge against the ejection hatch, directly over the head of the Word MechWarrior, and as the 'Mech reared forward, used the momentum to slide down the right side of the cockpit. She heard a second explosion, and the 'Mech staggered as she ran down the right shoulder; as the 'Mech fell forward, she ran down the right arm. The *Sentinel*'s knees hit the ground, the right arm flung forward, and she jumped down the almost three meters to the rocky soil, landing hard and stumbling forward, catching herself before she fell on her face.

Crouching, she reached for her pistol—she had no idea when she'd lost her rifle—and looked around, trying to assess where she was and the situation. And froze. The *Black Knight* stood less than two hundred meters away, raising the massive bore of its right-arm-mounted PPC toward her.

Rifle fire sparked as it impacted the 'Mech, and a few scattered LAWs streaked up, one burrowing into a hole on its left-hand side and exploding deep within, but the 'Mech ignored all of it to focus on her. Her adrenaline-fueled brain searched for options, but realizing there were none, she waited for her self-doubt to chime in.

When it didn't, a sense of peace washed through her as the PPC's muzzle began to glow blue. She almost smiled at the irony of finally becoming comfortable with her life seconds before she lost it.

She heard a PPC discharge, and then another; the *Black Knight* stumbled forward twice before falling with the distinctive lack of grace indicative of a destroyed gyro. Charging down from the eastern entrance was a Davion *Uziel* with a distinctive cigar-chomping bulldog insignia, followed closely by a *Legionnaire*.

"Davion 'Mechs, check your fire, the Fury is friendly. We've captured the Fury," she heard the sergeant major say over the radio. The firing around her tapered off as the remaining Word infantry threw their weapons down. She tried to holster her pistol and realized she couldn't; her hand was shaking violently as a wave of cold rushed through her, adrenaline leaving her bloodstream and relief entering it.

"You okay, Sam?" she heard, concern evident in Schultz's voice, and the *Uziel* slowly approached her. She focused, slid the pistol home, and reached up to her headset with a still-trembling hand.

"Yeah, I think so," she managed to say.

"I saw what you did—that was amazing. Never seen anything like it before." She nodded, still too overwhelmed to respond coherently. "It was a terrible dismount, though."

She looked at the *Uziel*; overcome with the thrill of surviving and the absurdity of her friend's statement, she couldn't help herself.

She began to laugh.

OPERATION SCYTHE: LYRAN FIRE

LANCE SCARINCI

DROPSHIP *BRIGADA*, HIGH ORBIT
NORTH AMERICA
TERRA, BLAKE PROTECTORATE
19 AUGUST 3078

"Brace for impact!"

Even behind his fear, some detached portion of Conner's mind marveled at how those three little words tore his reality away. He swayed as the blood retreated from his head, and his perception drowned in surrealism. The *Brigada*'s bridge faded to a vivid, fanciful blur, while all sounds were reduced to a single, deep rush. The only sense that seemed to work anymore was taste, telling him he had something metal on the roof of his mouth.

A strong hand shook his shoulder. "Stay with me, Hauptmann," growled a voice in heavily accented English. It was Grumman, the ship's captain. "Strap in, now! I don't need you decorating my bridge."

Conner nodded and sank into his jump seat. He scrabbled for the harness, which danced away from his grasp under the shaking ship. He fumbled with it for a moment, then just watched dumbly as the shiny buckle vibrated. A pair of gnarled hands shoved him back into the seat, grabbed the balky belt, and fastened it roughly over his chest.

"*Dummkopf!*" Grumman muttered, and cuffed him lightly on the head before turning back to the rumbling chaos.

Conner blinked a few times and willed himself to get a grip. Strapped into the seat next to him, Barnes stared ahead unblinking, his face ashen. "This isn't going well," Conner said, the words sliding out in flat neutrality. Barnes did not respond. A drop of sweat rolled down his twisted nose.

It certainly wasn't going well. This wasn't supposed to be a combat drop; otherwise he'd have been in his 'Mech, not on the bridge of the *Brigada*. They were just making a standard landing. The Fifteenth Arcturan's LZ was secured, their approach clear of Blakist ships. The Word must have skipped the briefing.

When two fighters had rocked the *Brigada*'s hull in a sudden pass, even the hearty Grumman had yelled in shock. When their second attack blew out one of the *Fortress*-class DropShip's massive engines, the entire bridge had erupted in frenzied yells. The ship listed crazily, the horizon shifting on the view screen, until the helmsman corrected it with a complicated maneuver that required shutting down the drive opposite the damaged one. Though the tactic leveled the ship out, the remaining engines lacked the power to bring the ship down safely, and the *Brigada* had already sunk too far into Mother Terra's gravity to escape. Instead of reaching their LZ, they were going to land right now, and much harder than planned.

Grumman's crew, steadfast in their training, kept to their posts amid the shaking. "Altitude two thousand meters," someone shouted. "Fifteen hundred. One thousand." Land was approaching fast, resolving into a verdant mountain range. "Five hundred!"

"Prepare to kiss your mother, children!" Grumman shouted in German.

When the impact came, it wasn't accompanied with the fiery explosion Conner expected. Nevertheless, his subconscious mind paralyzed him with the conviction that those flames would kick down the door and devour him and the bridge crew with greedy delight at any moment. He yelled as the impact flung him about, his harness digging into his chest. The terrific screech of tearing metal reverberated in his ears, and they plunged down again as at least one landing leg tore free. The ship's rump hit with a jarring boom, rocked once or twice, and finally settled at a slight angle.

Sparks and the tang of ozone swam in the air. The only sounds were the ragged breathing of the crew, and the occasional pop of a circuit failing. The deep rumble of the DropShip's engines had ceased. A backup generator whined, and hazy screens flickered into life again.

Grumman recovered first, with a captain's vigilance. "You're not dead yet, children. Damage reports! Tell me where we stand. Mister Marsters, where are those Blakist fighters? Are they coming back around?"

From the tactical station, Marsters said, "Negative, Captain. They're moving off."

"Of course." Grumman actually sounded offended. "There is more glory for them above. They will let the gropos deal with us. The Word has bagged one dropper today, but not her crew. We must establish a perimeter. That is your duty, Hauptmann."

Conner didn't reply. He knew Grumman's words were meant for him, but there wasn't enough of him present to respond.

"Hauptmann DeVries!" Concern etched Grumman's wizened brow. "You can let go of your seat now." A few snickers crossed the bridge.

Aboard his ship Grumman took orders only from God, but now that they were grounded, tradition made Conner the senior captain, as he was commander of the unit's BattleMech contingent. Command now belonged to him.

Fumbling with his harness, he cast a glance at Barnes, who still sat rigid, staring straight ahead. "You still with us, Adam?"

Barnes gave a weak groan.

Conner stood carefully, bracing himself against the bulkhead. The realization that the worst had passed sank in, and he felt much better, even a little euphoric. He fought this, knowing it was only the adrenaline teasing him as it departed, and giving in to it could be deadly.

"Come on," he said to Barnes. "We've got to check on our people."

"I'll be along in a minute," Barnes said, color just beginning to creep back into his face. "I've got to change my uniform."

Despite the hard landing, there were blessedly few casualties; only two serious injuries were reported. The cargo hold looked like the result of a colossal child's temper tantrum, and several 'Mechs had toppled over in their cubicles. These were quickly righted and found to have only superficial damage. Only one combat vehicle had suffered heavy damage, a Warrior VTOL that had its rotor bent beyond repair. Barnes was glad it was not his favorite toy, the Pinto VTOL he'd captured from the Word on Demeter.

"Small blessings," Conner said three hours later as he sat in conference with Grumman, Barnes, and Giovanni Kobol, captain of the armor contingent. Though the circumstances brevetted Conner to kommandant, he'd refused the title when Grumman tried to force it on him, preferring to remain a hauptmann, though senior among the four.

They had set up a temporary command tent, complete with an old Arcturan Guards banner, in the lee of the *Brigada*. The DropShip, now a fortress in fact as well as in name, provided them with a base of operations, but its immobility also left them vulnerable. The main power plant had suffered severe damage on impact, and many subsystems had been shut down to conserve power. They ran nothing but sensors at the moment; the techs in the repair bay were operating their equipment by plugging it into one of Kobol's Alacorn tanks. Six BattleMechs stood watch while the remainder had their scuffed armor repaired, and Barnes had sent scouting parties to the cardinal points and a spotter to set up a post on the mountaintop to the northeast.

"No sign of the Word," Barnes said. "We're safe for now, unless they show."

"They'll show," Kobol grumbled. He was a dismal, pessimistic man, an attitude he defended by saying he was just a realist, and that by expecting the worst he was never disappointed. The flaws in this logic could not be pointed out to him.

"When they do, we'll deal with them." Conner said. "We've got a mixed battalion at near full strength, and the terrain favors us."

He flipped on a portable holomap. The *Brigada* filled the display, as seen from a satellite Grumman's comm officer had hacked into. A great white ball amid the green, it lay settled in a bowl formed by a rough semicircle of ridges. A great, forbidding mountain rose out of the northwest, covered in thick, green forest. Beyond it lay a broken land of wooded peaks and valleys, impossible to traverse. The opposite slope ran down into an area of rolling hills, where many small farms and a single larger settlement were visible in the distance. The only approach was from the south, and an attacker would have to scale the ridge in full view. It was also their only way out.

Conner gestured at the image. "We got very lucky with our landing. Just a small deviance in any direction, and the *Brigada* would have been rolling down one of these ridges."

"Luck, bah!" Grumman spat. He puffed with pride. "Leutnant Valis is an excellent pilot. It is to her we owe our safe landing, not some trick of fate, mark me."

"Of course," Conner conceded, knowing the old man would defend his crew until Armageddon. "This is an excellent defensible position. We can hold here for a long time if we need to. I'd feel safer moving out ASAP, but we need scouting reports. I don't want to run into a Blakist regiment as soon as we leave."

"We don't have the assets to carry all of our support personnel." Kobol said. "We'll need to commandeer something from the locals."

"That always goes well," Barnes said, rolling his eyes.

"Unless you want to leave them behind? It's one or the other."

"I'm not comfortable leaving anyone behind," Conner said. "The Word's not known for treating prisoners well. It's everyone or no one. We'll need to work on transport. and unfortunately, we'll need to scuttle the ship."

"Curse the gods for their ill humor!" Grumman slapped the table hard enough to rattle it. "We defeat an entire SDS network at Hean, but here we fall to two *schweinehund* fighters! Two fighters! My beautiful *Brigada* has crashed, but she is not ruined, and I will not scuttle her. Stone will win this world, mark me. We will take Mother Terra from the Word, and after we win I will salvage my ship."

"Aw, Christ, will you stop with the 'Mother Terra' already!" Barnes groaned.

Grumman fired back in German, and instantly the two men were bickering and gesticulating wildly at each other. It was a celebrated pastime, and Conner let them go on for almost a minute before shouting them both down.

"Let's focus, gentlemen," he growled, toggling the map to a different location. "This is Texas, where we're supposed to be." He zoomed out and scrolled over a great deal. "And this is North Carolina, where we are. We've missed our mark by over a thousand kilometers. Not that I blame Leutnant Valis," he added with a glance at Grumman. "Between us and the rest of the Fifteenth lie these mountains, some forestland, a very wide river, and a whole lot of open ground. That open ground is most likely filled with the Word."

Kobol leaned forward, resting his bearded chin in one hand. "What about Stone's task force? Their objective was Hilton Head, in South Carolina. It might make more sense to link up with them than trying to cross all that."

Barnes nodded. "We could roll in with the Twenty-fifth easily enough."

"I've thought of that," Conner said. Their fellow Arcturan Guards, part of Stone's task force, would accept them without question. "But we should make every effort to return to our own first. We'll see once we know what we're facing."

"Can we use our satellite to scout?" Barnes asked.

"*Nein,*" said Grumman with a shake of his head. "It is a weather monitor. Resolution is *Scheiße,* no good for scouting. We'd need a spy satellite for that, and those are much harder to hack. On top of that, between the mountains and the Word's jamming, we are having trouble with long-range comms, which means no intel from our allies."

"We'll have to rely on your people, Adam," Conner said.

They spent another hour discussing options, making plans and discarding them just as quickly. Outside, the Guards prepared fortifications. Emplacements were dug for the larger tanks, and Sergeant Almont's *Griffin* tore a path up the east ridge for their Sturmfeur to ascend and dig in, providing it with a superb field of fire. Grumman ordered the *Brigada*'s unpowered weapon bays stripped of ammo and spare parts for the ground forces.

Their ideas had nearly run dry when the first scouts returned. A sweaty, dirty man came into the tent and saluted. Barnes saluted back and handed him a bottle of water. "Sit down, sergeant. What can you tell us?"

The infantry soldier took a seat next to Kobol before the holomap. He took a long pull on his water and launched into his report.

"This is a rural region, but still more populated than you'd expect. Lots of civilians. We found a kind of roadside way station and got some intel from the owners. There are a lot of smaller burgs around here, but only one major city—Hickory. It's big enough to warrant an airport and a small Blakist garrison."

Barnes nodded. "We'll need to get some transport assets from the locals, as well as basic supplies."

The scout shook his head. "I don't think we can, sir. The civvies we met in that roadside were hostile. One of them even fired on us."

"You were fired on by civilians?" Kobol asked, incredulous.

"Yes, sir. They were not happy to see us. Called us 'invaders.'"

"Well, that's distressing," Conner said.

"I didn't think the Word would let the populace have any weapons," Kobol said.

"Rural people always have guns," said Barnes. "Nothing will ever change that. If Cameron St. Jamais himself went door to door demanding these people give up their guns, all he'd get would be the ammo."

The other scouting parties trickled in with similar stories. The locals, though not flashing Word of Blake regalia, were uniformly unwilling to help them. More than one scout had taken light fire from angry farmers or shop owners.

Deciding they had to try to get some kind of transport for the noncombatants, Conner ordered their Packrat scout car disguised with a Word insignia and guided down a tricky path to a mountain road. Barnes wished the crew luck before sending them off. He returned to the tent with rations for everyone, and they ate a cold meal while debating whether to hold their ground or strike out blindly into enemy territory.

Grumman's personal comm squawked, and he excused himself, muttering into it for a moment. His face darkened. "We have a problem. We need to go to the ship."

The four made an exhausting climb via service ladders up to the *Brigada*'s observation deck. Without life support systems, the ship was a stuffy heat box in the summer sun. Operations had been moved from the bridge to a console on the windowed observation deck, providing both light and fresh air. Grumman immediately went to one of the tiny monitors, where Marsters, the tactical officer, leaned close to the screen. They conferred briefly in German, then Grumman beckoned the others over.

Conner squinted at the display, which showed an open sky streaked with wispy tendrils of white. Far above floated a regular, oval shape as white as the clouds it cowered behind. "What am I looking at?"

"Airship," Grumman said.

"Civilian?" Barnes asked. He didn't sound hopeful.

"*Nein*. She's been circling for twenty minutes. It's a spy ship, mark me."

"Great." Kobol hung his head. "If they didn't know where we crashed before, they certainly do now."

Barnes waved a dismissive hand. "What can they see from that high up?"

"They see everything we do, *dummkopf.*" Grumman's wiry brows knitted together. "Spy ships like that have strong cameras. They can see every pore on that wrecked hull you call a nose."

Barnes stroked the side of his bent nose with a middle finger.

Conner watched the ship circling like a shark in the skies high above and imagined a giant eyeball on its belly, peering down at his men as they worked. "Everything we do," he muttered. "How high is it?"

"Ten thousand meters," said Marsters. "Far outside our ECM bubble."

"Can the Long Tom reach that far?" The great cannon in the *Brigada*'s nose ran off its own backup power source and could still fire.

"Horizontal, easily," Grumman said. "Vertical, I wouldn't like to try. The angle is too steep."

Barnes stuck his head out a hole cut in the plastisteel window for ventilation.

"You can't see them, Adam," Conner said.

"No, but they can see me." The infantryman made a rude gesture toward the sky. The tension broke, and Conner found himself laughing. Even Kobol cracked a smile.

Two hours later, the Word arrived. A mixed force of BattleMechs, tanks, and infantry roughly analogous to their own materialized in the rolling hills to the south. They bore the logo of TerraSec, the planetary security force. It was a blessing inside a curse. TerraSec would not be as staunch a foe as regular Word troops, but they had placed themselves solidly between the Guards and freedom. They had waited too long. For good or ill, the Lyrans would have to hold.

TerraSec did not attack that day, but they sent a scout VTOL for a look at the encampment. Stacy Meadows, Conner's XO, deterred it with a burst of flak from her *Defiance*'s autocannon. After that, the Blakists were content to set up a watch on the Arcturans. The next morning, the Blakists gathered near the base of the southeast ridge. 'Mechs formed their front rank, followed by tanks interspersed with platoons of jump infantry. Though they stood prepared, the Word did not advance.

"Why are they holding back?" Conner muttered, watching them from the cockpit of his *Rifleman* halfway down the slope.

"The *Brigada*?" Stacy suggested. "They can't know its guns are out."

"Because they have something planned," Kobol said from his Alacorn high above.

Conner knew he was right because the Word's MechWarriors confirmed it. A 'Mech was a machine, but the neurohelmet necessary to pilot one provided a link to its pilot that ran in two directions. The helmet read data necessary for balance, but the MechWarrior's brain sent other things as well: subtle twitches and shifts of balance that could be read by anyone experienced with body language. The Word 'Mechs stood tense, expecting.

"Eyes on the skies, people," Conner said. "An air strike is most likely, but—"

The ground erupted in a violent spray of dirt, sending gravel and a small tree cascading over him.

"Artillery!" Stacy yelled, as a second round tore up the earth. Conner swore. "Spread out!"

The Arcturans retreated, spreading themselves wide. The Blakists had a legion of spotters to correct the artillery's aim, and their next barrage landed closer, following the Guards up the ridge. Fortunately, the *Brigada* could answer, if it knew where to look.

"Adam, we need a counter-battery spotter!" Conner called.

"I'm already in the air," Barnes replied. High overhead, his captured Pinto sped southward. "Grumman's people gave us triangulation. They're ready with the big gun. The Robes want arty, we'll give them arty! Just sit tight."

"Easy for him to say," Kobol grunted. His slow-moving tanks, though much farther from the incoming fire, were most susceptible to it.

They endured three more barrages, each one climbing farther up the ridge, while the Blakists 'Mechs began a steady advance. Conner guessed their plan was to drive his forces right up to the *Brigada* and pound it to scrap with artillery before sending in the 'Mechs and infantry to clean up any survivors.

Glancing up, he could just see the barrel of the *Brigada*'s Long Tom cannon peeking out of its bay. Grumman had informed him— with a few "*dummkopfs*" and a "mark me" or two—that the ship's list would be a problem for the big gun. It was unbalanced and might not fire straight. Conner prayed it would.

The first Word 'Mechs reached the extreme range of his weapons, accompanied by infantry hopping along on bursts from their jump packs. Kreutzfeldt's *Zeus* sent missiles and PPC fire into them, scarring a battered old *Lancelot*. Most of the TerraSec machines looked older and careworn, a sign that boded well for the Arcturans.

Stacy's *Defiance* joined Conner's *Rifleman* in savaging an *Orion*. The combined PPC and autocannon fire ravaged the Blakist's heavy armor, but it steadfastly returned fire with its LRMs, peppering both of them, until Stacy fused its knee joint with a lucky PPC bolt, and the *Orion* executed a hobbling retreat.

The Blakists fought cautiously, sniping from long range at the retreating Guards. They did no significant damage but were unwilling to close the gap and risk being hit by their own artillery shells. The Arcturans returned fire as best they could, missing more often than not.

"Conserve ammo, people," Conner said. "Don't waste it on suppression fire." His *Rifleman*'s ammo bins were deep, but they would bleed out quickly in a protracted fight. Only when his targeting reticule glowed gold did he pull the trigger.

He had just disengaged from a gangly *Crab* when another artillery shell crashed down close by, blasting MechWarrior Stokes's *Wolfhound* off its feet. The light 'Mech lay where it fell, unmoving.

"Darryl, get up!" Conner yelled. He got no response. Seconds later, another shell landed almost on top of the *Wolfhound*, tearing through its armor like paper. The fusion engine lost its containment with a flash, violently obliterating what remained of the 'Mech. Shocked voices filled the comm. Stokes had been a rookie, only a year off of Arcturus.

Conner gritted his teeth. "Hurry up, Adam."

"We've got 'em!" Barnes yelled, voice tinny over the comm. "A pair of Thumpers about three klicks due south."

"Distract them! Don't let them get off another shot."

A burst of gunfire came through the comm. "Consider them distracted! Fire control, receive coordinates." Barnes spat out a long list of letters and numbers.

"Roger that," responded the *Brigada*'s gun crew. "Clear the target area!"

Seconds later, the Long Tom spoke with a colossal boom that rattled Conner's command couch. After a moment, Barnes came back on the comm, barking fire correction instructions. The crew acknowledged and fired again, and Barnes called correction data again.

Moments after the third shot, Barnes whooped with glee. "Direct hit on both guns! The damn fools aren't spread out enough. Now let 'em have it again!"

The massive cannon fired twice more in rapid succession. No more shells came from the Blakist guns.

The Word ground forces had halted after the Long Tom's first shot, BattleMechs and infantry scattering for cover. When they realized the gun was not targeting them, they reemerged and resumed their advance. The *Brigada*'s hull filled Conner's rear display. The Blakists' artillery had forced his line back far enough that they could overtake his ridge with a determined charge.

"Adam," Conner said over the comm. "Are those Thumpers neutralized?"

"Oh, yeah, they're very neutralized. They're neutralized all the way to next week."

"Good." Conner ordered the gun crew to target the advancing Blakists.

The coordinates of the slope had been plotted earlier, and the crew easily adjusted and fired. The shell landed among the advancing TerraSec troops, knocking an old *Quickdraw* off its feet. A hardened opponent may have pressed on, weathering the fire for a chance at early victory, but these TerraSec troops were not a line regiment. Though none of their 'Mechs had received heavy damage, the Blakists began to retreat.

"Another round, Hauptmann?" asked the gun sergeant. Conner felt a twinge of shame that he couldn't remember the man's name.

"No, they got the point." He was acutely aware that they only had thirty shells for the great cannon, and this engagement had consumed six. This first round was won, but their weakness was revealed. The Blakists had surely noticed that the *Brigada*'s gun ports remained silent.

A cool rain fell that evening, relieving the heat and turning their southeast slope into a mudslide. The Blakists didn't attack again but encamped to the south, out of the Long Tom's range. Their pickets kept coming to the foot of the ridge, but a clear line of demarcation existed that the Blakists never crossed. The goal of these patrols was merely to keep the Lyrans in their hollow. They could not escape down the slope, and the mountain's treacherous terrain made retreat impossible.

Conner knew the Word could simply wait them out, but he had a nagging suspicion they weren't that patient. The force below was evenly matched with his own. Given the advantage of terrain, Conner's people could hold them off for a time, but they lacked the strength to break out. They were stalemated, but if the Blakists received reinforcements or brought in air power, the game would change.

Communications had yet to be established, and the Word's jamming had cut off their satellite. On Grumman's suggestion, Barnes had sent people to set up an antenna on the mountaintop, but the rains and rough ground had thwarted them. With no orders and no escape route, the Guards dug in and prayed.

Leaving Kobol in charge for the night, Conner went to see what he could find in the way of food and rest. A few shadowed forms sat around a bonfire. The burning heat of summer abated with nightfall, and the fire looked warm and inviting. He wondered how they had started it after such heavy rains, but then Peter Trainor rose from the fireside and strode off into the bushes. Every unit had a man like Trainor: one who made most people uncomfortable but who had his uses. Trainor's was making things burn. He piloted a *Firestarter* and loved it, perhaps a bit too much.

Conner took a seat next to Stacy Meadows. She smiled and wordlessly handed him a plate of heated rations. In another life, he and Stacy were more than just hauptmann and XO, but that life had yet to begin. He wondered if it ever would. Barnes and a few of his infantrymen joined them, bringing a pot of hot coffee. Conner felt more attached to these people than to any in his life. MechWarriors, infantry, techs, DropShip crew, all were bound by shared hardship. Rank ceased to exist, and they were simply men and women sharing company.

Talk turned inevitably to the invasion and why they were even here on Grumman's Mother Terra. They questioned it, and Conner could not fault them. He wondered himself. The Blake Protectorate lay in ruins, the Word having retreated to this, their last bastion, where they were strongest. Surely a blockade would have sufficed, until the Coalition had time to rebuild. When Kerensky assaulted Terra three centuries ago, he did so with an army unmatched in human history and had emerged victorious but shattered. The Star League Defense Force never recovered from its liberation of Terra from the Usurper. Now Devlin Stone wished to do the same, with his force a tiny fraction the size of Kerensky's.

Devlin Stone.

Conner's eyes glazed. Thinking of Stone, he remembered why he fought. He fell into reverie, losing track of the conversation until he heard Stone's name.

"We were able to tune in to a local radio station," one of the techs was saying. "Voice of Terra is broadcasting bad news everywhere. They said all the allied ships in orbit had been destroyed, and only scattered units like us survived. They even said...they said General Stone had been killed," he finished softly.

"Word of Blake propaganda," Barnes spat. "Voice of Terra is their built-in mouthpiece. I wouldn't trust them to tell jokes. If Stone were dead and the Coalition shattered that badly, we'd have a lot more heat on us. Hell, if any of that garbage were true, we'd be one of the largest surviving commands!"

"He's right," Conner said, enforcing Barnes's point because the men needed to see him do so. "Don't trust what you hear. They say it to keep the locals in line. We'll know the truth once we make contact with our own.

"Besides," he added. "The Word doesn't have a gun big enough to kill Devlin Stone."

Stacy picked up a long stick and poked it into the fire. Prodding at a fire was a long established tradition among humans. No one left to sit around one could resist for long; thousands of years of genetic programming commanded it.

"You've met Stone, haven't you?" she said, her green eyes reflecting orange.

"Yes. Sort of." He hadn't exactly met Stone, per se, but he had once been in a briefing room when the allied commander paid a visit.

"What was he like?"

Conner wrinkled his brow. How could he describe a man like Devlin Stone? What words did justice to a living legend? He had read tales of great men in history books, had seen their fanciful exploits on holovids, but none of it felt real. None of it captured the true essence of leadership, the aura that bled from men of power. Mere words fell lifeless and bland, even in the most vivid imagination. No page could convey the pure charisma of Alexander, the cunning of Caesar, or the brilliance of Napoleon. No tri-d ever fully captured McKenna's nobility or Kerensky's wisdom.

Those mediums utterly failed to communicate the reality of Devlin Stone. When he entered a room, he owned it. His mien was one of absolute command, but it was not inspired by fear or military conditioning, as with so many petty dictators. It was far more subtle than that. With a single word or a simple gesture, he could raise the heart of the lowliest soldier, make them feel not just appreciated but needed, vital. And when he had passed, Stone left the room emptier, though a sense of his greatness lingered. People worked harder because Stone asked them to. They fought because Stone needed them to. They followed because they believed in him, and they died because they loved him. Even those who envied and hated him obeyed his orders, because Devlin Stone was the alpha male of all humanity and they, as humans, *must* obey.

No, Conner could not demean Stone by trying to reduce him to words. He settled for the simplistic, knowing how inadequate it sounded.

"He's the greatest man I've ever met."

They accepted this without question, some nodding their heads. Conner thought somehow they understood.

"Hammond! Fall back! You can't go toe to toe with that thing."

Hammond ignored him, rushing at the *Thunderbolt* with reckless haste. His *Hunchback* was under the range of the *T-bolt*'s Gauss rifle, but its lasers blazed at him. Hammond answered with a blast from his LB 20-X autocannon so savage it tore the *Thunderbolt*'s torso apart, the LRM launcher on its shoulder popping like a zit. A blast of cluster rounds found something explosive in the hole, and the *Thunderbolt*'s right arm tore away. Unbalanced, the big 'Mech fell onto its back and lay still.

"Geez, maybe he can," Conner muttered.

It was their third day on the mountain, and the Word was pressing a new attack. This time they led with a force of heavy tanks, supported by BattleMechs. Their infantry held back, keeping out of range of the *Brigada*'s Long Tom, which fired intermittently. Though they'd lost a half-dozen tanks to support fire, the Blakists pushed on. Conner guessed the Word commander was overcompensating for his missed opportunity the day before.

The Lyrans held their ground, but also their fire. The Blakists had the advantage of ready resupply, and liberally fired missiles and autocannons while the Guards husbanded their ammo. Fortunately, they had LRMs in droves from the *Brigada*'s stripped bays, and their Sturmfeur rained them down from its entrenched position.

"Giovanni, advance to the next emplacement," Conner said, dodging fire from a TerraSec Burke.

"Advance?" Kobol said, displaying his annoying tendency to repeat orders as a question.

"Yes, advance," Conner snarled. "I want a wall of fire at the top of this ridge, and that means you and your two buddies." Kobol and his two buddies constituted a pair of Alacorn tanks and a massive Demolisher II. Kobol insisted this asset be kept close to his personal Alacorn as a bodyguard.

Farther down the slope, a platoon of Lyran foot infantry fought from an emplacement, supported by their Goblin IFV and a Manticore tank. The Blakists had fixated on their nest, and charged it with a demi-company of 'Mechs and tanks. Conner sent his second lance, anchored by Leutnant Kreutzfeldt's *Zeus* to their aid, and the battle converged on the lone hillock.

The Long Tom ceased its booming fire as Guards and Blakists mixed. Conner rushed forward, his rotary autocannons chewing through their ammo until the barrels glowed red. Firing this heavily carried the danger of a round jamming in the breach, rendering the great guns little more than clubs, but Conner didn't care. His infantry, huddled in their trench, needed the cover.

A Blakist *Archer* launched a full volley of LRMs uphill. Instead of exploding, the missiles fragmented and scattered across the ground.

"Thunder mines!" Stacy cried. "Stay clear!"

Her warning came too late. Mines tore the legs off Armin Hobart's *Starslayer*, and Greta Starnes's *Hollander* crashed onto its side, grinding its Gauss rifle into the dirt.

Seeing the 'Mechs fall, the Blakists surged ahead, but the arrival of Kobol's Alacorn tanks, slowly picking their way downhill, forced them back. With the Demolisher sitting overwatch, the Alacorns hunkered behind a rise and pumped Gauss rounds into the Blakists until their line broke. TerraSec troops showed the Lyrans their backs in their haste.

Conner radioed the *Brigada*'s gun crew. "Give them a parting gift."

The great gun thundered, but its shell impacted harmlessly several hundred meters away.

"I think you need some adjustment," Conner said.

It was a moment before a shaky, coughing voice replied. "We've had a misfire, sir. The cant of the ship put too much stress on one side. The gun's blown off its support housing."

Conner swore. Grumman had warned him something like this might happen.

A crushing sense of unfairness swept Conner as he looked over the ruins. The Long Tom was beyond repair, its housing shattered. They lacked the equipment to mend it, and a BattleMech's strength would be required to manhandle the tube back into place. Dejected, he left Grumman to oversee the cleanup and returned to the command tent.

Evie, Grumman's comm officer ("Best in the Lyran navy, mark me!"), sat in her accustomed place in the corner, talking softly into her headset. Conner knew no one but the static gods answered, and wondered how she did it without going mad. She had made no progress since hacking the weather satellite and felt despondent over it. Barnes's men had finally succeeded in erecting an antenna atop the mountain, so perhaps her luck would change. Conner patted her shoulder softly as he passed, because it was something Stone might do.

He joined Barnes and Kobol, wearily poring over damage reports. Today's fight had cost them more than the Long Tom. Even with salvage dragged up from the field, their limited stockpile of ammo and spare parts dwindled. Worse was the cost in lives. Barnes's infantry had suffered many casualties, and he felt every one, as did Conner. These were his people, all of them.

Later, Grumman brought in hot coffee. Even his perpetual cheer was subdued as despair began to creep in on them. They could not hold forever, and with no plan for escape the Word would slowly grind them away. Ever the realist, Kobol pointed out that the Blakists had not offered terms of surrender, a fact that hung over them like a funeral shroud.

"I've made contact!" Evie suddenly called, jumping out of her seat with excitement. "I have... a *senior* officer on the line."

Her wide eyes told them she had indeed reached someone important. A rush of hope swept Conner. New orders, maybe even a way out of their plight, waited at the other end of a microphone.

"Finally!" Grumman sighed. "Is it Colonel Blucher?"

"No, sir."

"General Cox?" Conner asked hopefully.

"No..." Evie hesitated, as if the person on the other end of the line intimidated her.

"Stone?" Conner knew this was too much to hope for, but...

"It's *Kanrei* Minamoto, sir."

Silence fell, as solidly as if Evie had flipped a switch marked *hush*. Conner glanced at the others, who all wore identical expressions of wide-eyed apprehension.

Kanrei *Minamoto*.

This was the man who had held the fraying ends of the Draconis Combine together during the darkest years of the Jihad, pushing back against the Word, repelling invasions by the Federated Suns and Clan Snow Raven, and all while suffering a rebellion from within. That Minamoto had saved the Dragon was undeniable. That he had done so against such odds was inconceivable and made him a legend among his own people.

And this formidable man followed Devlin Stone.

Conner beckoned, and Evie passed him the headset, the other leaning in close. "*Kanrei*, sir?" he asked hesitantly.

"This is Minamoto," came the clipped reply. "Who is this?"

"H-Hauptmann Conner DeVries, sir. Fifteenth Arcturan Guards."

"How did you get my personal frequency?"

"Dumb luck, sir," Conner said. "We've been trying every frequency we can."

"I will have to strengthen my scramblers," Minamoto said dryly. "If you can break in, then so can the Word of Blake. "

Conner felt his color rise. *Kanrei* Minamoto had far more important things to do than talk to a minor officer of a command that did not even fall under his aegis.

"I'm sorry to bother you, sir, but we're in a bad situation. Our DropShip was shot down and we're trapped on a mountain, cut off from our task force and surrounded by the Word. We have no intel, but we've heard all kinds of rumors from the locals." He hesitated. "We even heard Devlin Stone had been killed."

"I can assure you, Hauptmann, General Stone is alive and well. I spoke with him this morning."

A collective sigh of relief went around the room, and Conner found himself smiling. Barnes clapped Kobol on the shoulder.

"No matter what Blakist propaganda you hear, the invasion goes well," the *kanrei* said. "Resistance has been strong and we have suffered losses, but we will carry this world." There was no doubt in his voice, only absolute certainty.

"That's wonderful to hear, sir," Conner said. Fearing Minamoto would disconnect, he launched into a concise briefing of their situation, finishing with their idea of trying to link up with Stone's force at Hilton Head. To his relief, the *kanrei* listened.

"Stone has retreated from Hilton Head," Minamoto said. "The defenses were stronger than anticipated. Even now he makes his way to link up with your combat group. What is your location? It may be possible for you to join his force on the way."

Conner read off their coordinates. He didn't worry about the Word eavesdropping— they already had him surrounded. There was a long, static-filled pause, and Conner began to wonder if they had lost their connection.

"You are correct, Hauptmann, your situation is not good," Minamoto finally said. "The Blakists control your area and have massed troops south of your position to harass General Stone. Linking with him will be impossible. You must hold until a ship can be spared to extract you. I will inform General Cox of your situation."

"Understood, sir," Conner said, disappointment nagging at him. He had hoped for a more solid solution, but it appeared their plight was beyond even the *kanrei*.

"Hauptmann," Minamoto said, his voice coming through clear and strong. "Do not think that I will place less regard on you because of your nationality. I take responsibility for every warrior under my command, be they directly or indirectly beneath me. If General Cox cannot extract you, then I will see to it myself. You will not be abandoned. You have my word."

Conner fought against a sudden closing of his throat. "Thank you, sir."

"Remember," the *kanrei* continued. "Every Blakist fighting you is one less pursuing General Stone. You *must* hold. Show the Word of Blake that the sons of Arcturus cannot be cowed. For your Archon, for Devlin Stone, hold!"

The *kanrei*'s words provided a necessary boost to morale. The promise of extraction bolstered the troops, who resumed work with dedicated fervor, and their faith reinforced Conner's own flagging spirits. The past few days had taken a serious toll on him. He'd never expected to command a full battalion, especially not under such circumstances. It seemed the gods of war had plans for him.

Those plans involved letting the Word execute a night attack. Surprise was impossible, so when their bright white 'Mechs massed in the moonlight, the Guards were waiting. Soon, explosions and fire again transformed the vale into a parable of hell. The Blakists preceded their advance with a rain of smoke rounds, reducing visibility to almost nil and fouling the aim of the Sturmfeur. Conner and Stacy stood side by side, firing at the slightest hint of movement, hitting shadows more often than hard targets.

"We have a push over here," called Kreutzfeldt from the opposite end of the bowl. "I think they're trying to break through!"

"Barnes, reinforce!" Conner yelled. The shadow of the Pinto glided across the sky.

"We should go, too," Stacy said.

Conner hesitated. Kreutzfeldt's side of the slope was steep and rough, not the flank he would choose for an advance, but perhaps that's exactly why the Word chose it. "You go. I'll keep an eye out over here, just in case."

The *Defiance* trundled away, leaving him alone. Kobol's command tanks lay less than half a klick behind him, but Conner still felt exposed. For a long time he peered into the gloom, toggling sensors from visual to MagRes to IR.

Suddenly, his readouts disappeared in a burst of static interference.

"ECM!" Conner hissed.

Out of the smoke zoomed a Blakist hovercraft, peppering him with missiles. He caught it with a lucky laser shot that blew out its engine, but many more materialized from the dark.

"It's a feint!" Conner yelled, unleashing his autocannons. "The main thrust is on my position!"

Reinforcement would be long in coming from across the valley, and Conner needed it now. "Kobol, send me that Demolisher!" he yelled.

"My Demolisher?"

"Damn it, Giovanni, send the tank!"

"That will leave my Alacorns unprotected," came his maddening reply.

"I need firepower down here now! Do it or you'll be overrun!"

A pair of TerraSec hovercraft swept past him. Conner blasted the leader with his lasers, tearing the air skirt and sending it skidding into a clump of trees. The second dodged under his fire and up the hill, disappearing over a rise. Conner almost pursued it, but the shadow of an approaching 'Mech loomed out of the darkness. Kobol would have to handle the hovercraft himself.

"Giovanni, you've got incoming!" Conner called, pumping a round of autocannon fire into the first hovercraft to ensure it stayed down. Now he was certain the Demolisher would not come. Kobol would keep it right next to his Alacorn, a nasty surprise for the Blakist hovercraft.

A *Legacy*, the largest 'Mech Conner had seen in the TerraSec forces, advanced on him firing the huge Ultra autocannons on its shoulders. Conner's *Rifleman* took three rounds to its legs and torso, the last one throwing him off balance. He felt a moment of vertigo, then hit the ground with a bone-jarring crash.

The *Legacy* trudged up the hill, grazing him with its lasers. Conner didn't have time to right himself. He jammed the *Rifleman*'s arm into the dirt and propped himself up. Swinging the other in line with the advancing Blakist, he jerked hard on the trigger. His laser cut a scar across one of the *Legacy*'s arms, but instead of a hail of lead, the autocannon offered only a clunk and a high-pitched whine.

Jammed! Conner felt the hand of fate slap him across the face. The *Legacy*'s pilot, sensing what had happened, advanced more confidently, paying no heed to his single laser. Both autocannons swiveled toward his prone 'Mech, death leering from the barrels.

"This is it," Conner said, hands going slack on the controls. He felt the same surrealistic detachment that had come over him on the *Brigada*'s bridge. Unbidden, Stacy's face flitted across his mind, her smiling green eyes, the softness of her hair...

"Not yet, Hauptmann," someone said.

A rumbling vibration rose up through the ground. The *Legacy*'s guns swiveled up toward something behind him. There came a terrific roar and the flash of a hundred tracer rounds, but not from the Blakist. The *Legacy*'s TerraSec logo was rubbed away as if by sandpaper, then the armor beneath gave way, and unspent shells ate their way into its ammo bins. Conner was momentarily blinded by the sudden fireball, and when he could see again all that remained of the assault 'Mech was a blackened hulk.

The rumbling peaked as the beautiful, hulking form of the Demolisher rolled past, seeking more targets for its hungry autocannons. It found them in a pair of Word tanks. A squat Brutus opened fire, but the Demolisher's hide felt the lasers no more than a rhinoceros feels a flea. It savaged the Brutus with its Ultra autocannon, exploding it with a single hit, then turned its LB-X scattergun on a smaller Galleon. The tracks blew off the tiny tank, and the Demolisher shoved it aside as it passed.

The trailing ranks of Blakist infantry fled before this monstrous example of Lyran engineering, piling into their transports, or turning to run pell-mell down the hill, and soon the Word was withdrawing again.

Shaking himself, Conner righted his 'Mech and radioed his thanks to the Demolisher's crew. "And thank you, Giovanni," he said over the tactical frequency. "You just saved my ass." He got no response. "Giovanni?"

A weak voice answered him "Hauptmann Kobol is dead, sir."

Shock ran up Conner's spine. "What?"

"Hauptmann Kobol is dead," the voice repeated. "A Blakist hovercraft got through. It got in a lucky shot, and the hauptmann took some shrapnel... he... I couldn't stop the bleeding..." The voice trailed to a choking halt.

Dully, Conner stared out at the hovercraft he had wrecked just a moment before, remembering its twin, the one he'd let pass in order to face the *Legacy*. And he had ordered Kobol's support to cover himself.

Conner stared up at the stars dotting night sky, wondering which one was Arcturus. He wasn't even sure it could be seen from here, though someone had told him you could see the Pleiades from Terra, and that was clear in the Taurian Concordat. There were other lights in the sky, too, less benign than stars. When these shot, it rarely meant good luck.

Grumman strode over and handed him a cup of coffee. Conner took a sip and realized the old man had flavored it with something stronger than sugar.

"To take the edge off," the old man said. He followed Conner's gaze up to the heavens. "I know why I miss the black, but why do you stare so intently at it?"

"I was just thinking about home. Arcturus."

The old spacer sat down, nodding thoughtfully. "This is home, Hauptmann. This is our mother. Arcturus is where I was born. The black is where I belong. But this..." He picked up a handful of loose dirt and let it fall through his fingers, reverence misting his wrinkled face. "This is my home."

"Well, it certainly doesn't feel like it." Conner took a deep swig of coffee. "It feels just like any other Blakist world."

Grumman shook his head. "It's not feeling, *dummkopf*. It's fact. When I was a boy, my father used to tell me stories about life on Mother Terra before we left for the stars. Great people lived here and did great things, long before we reached out to the black. There is more history in this soil than on all the worlds of the Inner Sphere together. Always I have wanted to come here, to live here where we began, but ComStar's immigration laws were harsh, and the Word... Well, who would want to live under them? Now I am here, and I am proud. I love the black, but if I never leave Terra, I will not regret it."

"You may get your wish. We can't hold much longer." Conner thought Kobol spoke through him.

"Bah," the old man scoffed. "We will hold as long as we need to. We have Lyran steel in our spines and Lyran fire in our hearts. What does the Word have?" He got up, dusted his hands, and pointed to the sky. "It's that one."

Conner smiled, gazing up to the indicated star, and the old captain wandered off to harass a new victim with his Mother Terra speech.

For three days the Word held back. Tension mounted among the Guards as each day dawned without a friendly DropShip in the sky. Barnes had to break up a fight between an infantryman and a tech, over something as stupid as a canteen. Conner knew something would break soon and hoped it was the siege rather than his men.

On the dawn of the fourth day, Conner looked out over the white vehicles laid out below and felt his stomach drop. Their ranks had swollen. High-res imagery showed that the TerraSec troops had now been joined by regular Word Militia. Conner recognized the gargoyle insignia of the Fourth Division emblazoned on their 'Mechs. At mid-morning they massed at the foot of the ridge, TerraSec taking the point. Assaying their pristine ranks, Conner lamented the loss of his Long Tom. The great gun would have shaken the parade readiness right out of them.

The Sturmfeur remained, dug into its ridge and ready to offer an LRM enema to the Word. The Blakists might be out of nominal range, but gravity would carry the missiles the full distance.

Conner radioed the Sturmfeur's crew. "Target the second rank. Ready a barrage on my mark."

"Yes, *sir*," came the reply. "On your orders, *sir*." There was a snide quality in the voice that grated on Conner's nerves. He put it down to the armor contingent still blaming him for Kobol's death. He'd have a word with them later, and it would probably end up being a harsh one.

The Blakists began their push, and he put it out of his mind. He waited until the leading tanks passed the Sturmfeur's maximum range.

"Fire now, full spread!" Conner cried.

Plumes of smoke appeared in his rear display, and he waited for forty long-range missiles to drop among the Word 'Mechs, but the missiles never fell. His comm exploded with confused shouts.

At his side, Stacy's *Defiance* paused between volleys of PPC fire. "Oh, god! Conner, the Sturmfeur!"

In the tiny area his wraparound screen assigned to the ridge, he saw missile plumes rise from the tank's hidden position, but they did not rain down on the Blakists. They arced back into his camp. He watched in uncomprehending horror as the missiles slammed into the *Brigada*'s hull, several passing through an open bay door to detonate inside the hold.

"Sorry, *sir*," came the voice from the Sturmfeur. "Looks like we've got the wrong coordinates."

Conner knew instantly what had happened. The Word had held off their attack while sending infiltrators into the Arcturan camp. They had not only rooted out Conner's last fire support asset but also seized it. That would mean the two squads of men Barnes had posted up there were dead, and probably had been for some time. And no one had noticed.

"We're compromised!" Conner yelled over the general frequency. "All units fall back to secondary defensive positions!" A Blakist *Shadow*

Hawk came into maximum rage of his autocannons, and he opened fire. Behind it, a veritable fleet of tanks spread up the hill like a wave. Another storm of missiles descended on their camp. Unarmed techs and DropShip crewmen scurried for cover. Many more lay unmoving, obscured by smoke and flame.

"We need to take back that tank," Conner growled, outrage filling him.

"I'm on it," Barnes said. On the opposite ridge, infantry were boarding the grounded Pinto. "But we won't be there for a few minutes. Those bastards can do a lot of damage before then."

"Copy, Adam." They would need to distract the tank, keep it from reigning death on the camp. "Robeson, get up there!"

Leutnant Robeson's *Vulcan* sent one last autocannon shell downhill, then turned and launched up the ridge on its jump jets. The *Vulcan*'s pitiful weaponry was no match for the Sturmfeur's armor, but he could keep the tank occupied until Barnes arrived.

Stacy's PPCs staggered the Blakist *Shadow Hawk,* and she followed up with an autocannon burst that sent it sprawling. The wave of tanks swarmed past it like water flowing around a rock. Conner threw more rounds into them, not even bothering to focus on a single target; they were so thick, he was bound to hit something.

"Fall back, Hauptmann," Sergeant Almont called to him. "I've got you covered." A flight of missiles from his *Griffin* streaked past. Conner turned and ran back up the hill, flipping his *Rifleman*'s arms to the rear to continue firing.

A thick blanket of smoke covered the Sturmfeur's ridge. When the wind blew, he saw the vague outline of Robeson's 'Mech and what looked like the flash of small-arms fire. "I have Blakist infantry up here, Hauptmann!" Robeson confirmed a second later.

"How many?"

"It's hard to tell, but I think at least two platoons!"

"Damn," Conner said, gritting his teeth. It hadn't been just an infiltration squad, but an entire spearhead.

"Trainor," he said, fury overcoming him. "Get up there and solve the problem."

"Yes, sir," said Trainor, eagerly. His *Firestarter* broke ranks and jetted up the ridge.

"And try not to enjoy yourself too much," Conner said, though he didn't mean it.

In moments, the ridge blazed like the heart of a furnace. Wreathed in black smoke, Barnes's Pinto hovered overhead but could not set down.

"Forget it, Adam," Conner said. The Sturmfeur would not be recovered now. "Go help at the ship."

"They're still coming, Hauptmann," Almont said. "What do we do?"

Conner studied the approaching Blakists, frantically trying to come up with a plan. The enemy had separated into two ranks. Those rushing up his ridge all wore the TerraSec insignia, but the larger, massed force still sitting a kilometer or more away bore the logo of the Blake Militia. With a flash of insight, he realized some internal dispute divided the Blakists. Pride kept the TerraSec force, all native Terrans, from accepting the help of their off-world allies.

Quickly he did a head count. He had seven 'Mechs, not including the *Vulcan* and *Firestarter* still roasting Blakists on the ridge above. The Manticore sat perched beside Hammond's *Hunchback*, pumping PPC fire into the Word line, and the Demolisher and remaining Alacorn were just rolling into view.

"We charge them," Conner said. "All units prepare to charge."

A chorus of disbelieving cries rang in his ears, but he shouted them down. He looked over his warriors, trading long-range fire with the Blakists. They were tired and scared, but they were the sons and daughters of Arcturus. They were strong, and their enemy was an incompetent fool. A charge now would be a bold, foolish move. It was also exactly what Stone would do.

"Look at them," Conner said. "The Word isn't united. The Militia is holding back. These are just TerraSec boys, and they're nothing! They're security guards playing at warriors. They think they're better than us because they come from the 'cradle of humanity.' They think we're just a bunch of worthless heathens from out in the black. Well, let's show them what Arcturus thinks of their cradle! Let's show what it means to be a MechWarrior—a *Lyran* MechWarrior! Now are you Arcturan Guards or not?"

He could tell by the way their machines straightened that his MechWarriors felt his words. Even the tanks looked ready. They fell into a crude line, long-range weapons still chipping away at the TerraSec machines.

"On my mark!" Conner said, pride mixing with bloodlust in his veins. "Three! Two! One! Mark!"

The TerraSec line rolling up the hill paused as seven hundred tons of Lyran steel thundered down on them. A more disciplined force, like the Fourth Division who watched impassively from below, might have dug in and met the charge head on. The TerraSec troops, as Conner had said, were nothing.

With lasers and autocannon leading their way, the Lyrans stormed at them, smashing aside everything in their path. Trees, rocks, the wrecked hulls of tanks—no obstacle slowed their ferocity. They met the Word with a crash that echoed across the valley. Arcturan 'Mechs collided with Word machines, toppling them with the force of inertia, trampled tanks, and scattered hapless infantry to the winds.

Conner slammed into a *Gurkha* as the tiny 'Mech swung its ridiculous sword in a wide arc. He batted it aside, and a PPC bolt from

Stacy's *Defiance* took the *Gurkha* in the back. Conner saw Kreutzfeldt's *Zeus* draw back its club-like arm and ram it through the cockpit of a Blakist *Buccaneer*, saw Stacy's *Defiance* stomp a Demon tank into the earth then blast a pair of hovercraft to scrap with her PPCs. He watched the Manticore roll through an infantry formation, its SRM launcher dealing out explosive death.

Small-arms fire pinged harmlessly off Conner's armor. A gout of flame swept across the Blakist infantry, incinerating some outright, sending others scurrying like human torches until they fell. Trainor and Robeson had joined the charge. The infantry scattered, some even throwing down their guns.

The TerraSec 'Mechs rallied around a pristine *Marauder*, preparing to counterattack, but then down the ridge rolled Conner's deadliest assets. Alone, the Demolisher II and Alacorn were terrifying, but together they were nigh on invincible. Nothing could approach without facing long-range hell from the Alacorn's Gauss rifles, and the Demolisher devoured anything foolish enough to try.

The *Marauder* took three Gauss rounds and toppled over in a heap. The Demolisher followed up with a scatter of autocannon fire into the clustered 'Mechs, felling another. Conner added his own rotaries to the volley, sweeping them across the gathered forces. Again the TerraSec troops broke and ran.

"Don't let up!" Conner yelled, firing madly.

Kreutzfeldt blasted a limping *Trebuchet,* which lurched and fell facedown. Almont's *Griffin* crippled a hovercraft with a missile volley, and the Alacorn pumped silver balls of pain into the retreating 'Mechs. The Guards felled a half dozen machines before Conner called them off.

Cheers and insults filled the comm as his troops celebrated their victory.

"Ain't that the damnedest thing," Barnes said, hovering high above. "I thought you were done for."

"Not today, Adam. Not today."

Conner was not immune to the euphoria of victory. He trembled as his adrenaline wore off, remembering that there was still a large enemy force gathered a short distance away. His Guards would last a very short time if the Fourth Division attacked. But the Blakists held back. Slowly, the bulk of their force withdrew, leaving only a small picket to keep an eye on the Lyrans.

Conner breathed a sigh of relief. "Regroup, people. Nice work."

Though their charge was a great victory, it cost them. They had lost three 'Mechs, and Robeson had been killed when his *Vulcan*'s engine exploded. The Manticore lost one of its tracks and foundered halfway down the ridge, though the crew was unharmed. The destruction of Hammond's *Hunchback* hurt the most, as it deprived them of its powerful autocannon. This paled next to the incredible devastation caused by the compromised Sturmfeur. Their command tent lay in ruins, burned out hulks of equipment smoking in small craters. A fire had started inside the *Brigada*'s hold that still smoldered hours later, outlasting their meager firefighting gear.

What tore at Conner's heart was the long line of the dead laid out in the *Brigada*'s shadow. The most mangled bodies were covered, but there were not enough blankets for them all. Flies had already begun to gather, vile scavengers feeding on misery as they desecrated the remains of Conner's friends. Some he knew by name, others only by sight, but he recognized everyone. At least, the ones that still had faces. He saw the tech who worked on Trainor's *Firestarter* lying next to Marsters, who lay covered in blood, his left arm torn off.

Farther down the line, between two unnamed members of his bridge crew, lay Grumman. Conner had taken the news of his death hard. He had relied on the gruff old man for more than just bad advice. Though he may have been called a *dummkopf* again someday, the word would never ring the same in his ears, mark me. Gazing down at the old man, Conner felt sad but not sorry for him. Even in death, Grumman was smiling.

Barnes walked up beside him, his face blank. Silently, he pulled a flask from his pocket, took a swig and passed it over. Conner sipped the whiskey, relishing its burn. It provided an excuse for his tearing eyes. He passed the flask back to Barnes, who took another sip.

"One for him, one for Giovanni," he said.

"And one for us," Conner said. "But who's going to drink it?"

Barnes knelt and placed the flask in Grumman's cold hand. "He can."

He squinted into the afternoon sun. "You think exfil's really coming?"

"Do you?"

"What did the *kanrei* say? Every Blakist here is one less on Stone's tail? I think that's very true. And I think Minamoto knows it."

Conner saw the truth in his weary eyes, felt it in his own heart. But it didn't matter. "Then we keep them here. We buy Stone whatever time he needs."

"Doesn't matter." Barnes looked around the demolished camp and the few ragged survivors. "Time's up."

A blessing came that evening when their Packrat scout returned. Unable to sneak past the Blakist blockade, the crew had spent days struggling through the heavily forested mountains to the northwest, eventually cutting a treacherous path that led to a secluded mountain road far north of their position. Escape was now an option, but perhaps not a possible one. The trek would be difficult, and even if they left immediately, the Word would catch up effortlessly.

Conner made the best decision he could. The Lyran insignias on a Maxim transport were covered over, and a crude Word of Blake broadsword drawn on. It was a shoddy job, but it would hold under light scrutiny. A few tattered uniforms were recovered from the Blakists who had captured the Sturmfeur, and the least burnt and bloodied of them were given to the crew. The wounded and every surviving noncombatant were loaded into the hovertank's infantry compartment and the bay of Barnes's Pinto. Neither was filled to capacity.

The Packrat would lead the larger hovercraft up the mountain trail. Once out, they could bluff their way past any Word positions and go to ground. The Pinto would head west over the mountains, relying on its Word markings and IFF to get it safely past any challengers. Barnes assigned a squad of infantry to each, significantly reducing their defenses but improving the refugees' chances of survival. Barnes himself stayed behind with Conner. They would hold, give their people time, and pray to see a friendly drive plume in the skies.

Soon after the departure, the ranks of Blakist machines mustered in the moonlight, unmoving. Conner had learned when the Word held back, expect the worst. The remains of his command—six BattleMechs, five tanks, and an ad hoc platoon of infantry—spread out in the last of their defensive positions. There had been no repairs, no reloading. When the Word came, it would likely be for the last time, but if their stand bought his people going up the mountain just one more minute, then it was worth it. He stared down at the gathered enemy and waited.

Conner's HUD pinged, alerting him of a new target approaching rapidly from the southeast. He zoomed in and felt his stomach drop out. The Word had found air power at last.

"Incoming!" he bellowed, running for higher ground and a better field of fire.

A black form resolved in the sky, growing larger as it closed. Bigger than a fighter but still too small to be a DropShip, it looked like a giant bat gliding ominously through the gloom. Great bay doors yawned on its underbelly as it swung low over the east ridge.

"It's a bomber!" Kreutzfeldt said.

"The Word wouldn't waste a nuke on us," Stacy said, horrified. "Would they?"

They didn't, but they brought the next worst thing. Dozens of bombs fell, air-bursting into clouds of liquid flame that blazed like a sun. The path of the ship became a river of fire that swept across the ridge, into the valley and over the *Brigada*'s hull.

"Incendiary rounds!" Trainor sounded almost reverent.

Conner watched in horror as the flames illuminated the end of his command. The infantry's Goblin transport toppled off its ridge, burning as it rolled. Kreutzfeldt's *Zeus* staggered out of the sea of flame, its paint burned away and armor scarred. The Alacorn and Demolisher, invincible against the TerraSec ground forces, became flaming tombs. The dying screams of their crews as they were roasted alive filled the comm, fuel for the nightmares of the survivors, if the Blakists left any.

Tears stung Conner's cheeks. They had held so long, and now this.

The bomber banked, coming around for a second pass. The maneuver brought it within fatal range of Conner's rotary autocannons. For centuries, the Garret D2j had been recognized as the premier anti-aircraft targeting system in the Inner Sphere, perhaps of all time, and the *Rifleman* was its chariot. It seized the bomber in an unbreakable grip, and snarling, Conner squeezed the trigger. The autocannons roared, tracer rounds stitching a path up to the dark ship's underbelly. He fired until the barrels glowed red, but the guns did not jam.

Whether it was the armor-piercing rounds or the waves of hate Conner poured at it, something penetrated the hull of the great ship. The left wing erupted like a solar flare and sheared off in a shower of debris. The ship tumbled through the air, spinning wildly until its wreckage slammed into the side of the mountain. Fuel and ordnance ignited, sending a fireball into the air, and Conner's snarl turned to a howl of triumphant vindication. That the bomber's crew had died as suddenly and violently as those they had murdered seemed proper.

The Blakists began to march. This time, there were no TerraSec machines visible in the wall of 'Mechs, only Word Militia. No more incompetence, no more internal politicking. The Word meant to finish them, and success shone in the blaze of their lasers, the spiral of their missiles.

Pinned between the advancing Word and a ring of fire, Conner's last troops rallied to him. For their sake, he shoved aside his grief and anger. "Sound off, everyone!"

Stacy, Almont, Trainor, and Kreutzfeldt answered.

"The infantry?" Conner turned to Almont, who had been stationed with them. Flames still licked the *Griffin*'s legs.

"There are no more infantry, sir," he sobbed.

"Barnes..."

"He's gone, sir. They're all gone."

A great emptiness opened up inside him. Of Conner's command, a full battalion of 'Mechs, tanks, and eighty-four brave men armed only with rifles and their nerves, five badly damaged 'Mechs remained. Barnes, Kobol, Grumman—all were dead, and now the Word called to him. Extraction might still come, but when it arrived there would be no Arcturan Guards on this mountain, only the Word, and silence.

"Listen to me," he said, his hollow voice echoing over the open channel. "We're finished. We did our best and we hurt them, but the Word has ended our fight."

No one answered, but he read their reactions in their machines. Almont's *Griffin* seemed to slump and hang its head, the LRM launcher on its shoulder drooping toward the earth. Even Trainor's 'Mech looked subdued in its lovely firelight.

"Hauptmann—" Almont began.

"I'm not your hauptmann anymore," he said, speaking to all of them. "I'm Conner DeVries, your friend. I'll give you no more orders. If any of you want to retreat up that mountain, then I'll cover you. Me, I'm not done with the Word. I'm going to stay here and show them that they can't take my friends from me without consequences."

He stepped ahead, interposing his *Rifleman* between them and the advancing Blakists.

No one spoke. They stood in a loose huddle, each with their own thoughts, or perhaps, with only one thought.

"We're not running away," Kreutzfeldt finally said, conviction as strong as the accent in his voice.

"No, Conner," Stacy said, husky with emotion. Conner regretted he would never hear her utter his name in a different kind of passion. "We're going to stay with our friend."

She took her place beside him, the others a step behind. Conner had never felt such pride. Despite the death and the devastation and his failure, they still had faith. They would follow because they believed in him, fight because he needed them to. They would die because they loved him.

Conner choked back his emotions. "A wise man told me we Lyrans have a fire in our hearts, a fire that will never go out. I see that now, I see it in all of you. We are the sons and daughters of Arcturus. We are Lyrans! We are steel and we are fire, and we will never be defeated!"

They heard and felt the truth of his words, for even in the death that faced them, there would be no defeat.

Together, they faced the Word and showed them Lyran fire.

ABOUT THE AUTHORS

Adam Sherwood is a retired major of US Army Military Intelligence, heavy metal singer, artist, and avid *BattleTech* gamer. He is a graduate of Northern Michigan University and majored in International Studies. He speaks fluent Spanish and has traveled overseas extensively, having studied, served, and lived abroad. He has written sourcebook and short fiction for various *BattleTech* products and been deeply involved in promoting *BattleTech* and *MechWarrior* for nearly two decades. He runs a biweekly *BattleTech* and *A Time of War* campaign and resides in Indianapolis with his family. He once owned an Alaskan timber wolf as a pet.

Kevin Killiany spent decades working in education, mental health, and family preservation/child protection/community support services before selling his first story in 2000. He has written for *Star Trek*, *Doctor Who*, *BattleTech/MechWarrior*, *Shadowrun*, and *The Valiant Universe Roleplaying Game*. *Down to Dirt*, the first of Kevin's Dirt and Stars series of young-adult alternate-history novels, launched in 2016 to excellent reviews; *Life on Dirt* followed in April 2017, and the final volume of the first trilogy, *Rise from Dirt*, arrived in May 2018. Kevin and his wife Valerie live on the coast of North Carolina; they have four children and one grandsquiggle.

Blaine Pardoe has been writing *BattleTech* fiction for decades, starting with the first *Technical Readout*. Blaine has also been involved in the gaming industry for decades, writing for a number of companies and universes. His true-crime books earned him a spot on the *New York Times* Bestseller List, and his military-history books have been lectured on at the US Naval Academy and the US National Archives. When he is not writing or solving crimes, he is a fan of *BattleTech*. He can be reached at bpardoe870@aol.com or via Facebook.

Craig A. Reed Jr.'s first *BattleTech* publishing credits were several items that appeared in the *BattleTechnology* magazine, including his first coauthored story. He has written for BattleCorps, and has both writing and fact-checking credits in several *BattleTech* products and the *Valiant Universe Roleplaying Game*. In addition, he has coauthored three novels in the Outcast Ops series (available on Kindle) and is currently working on the fourth. Living in Florida after stops in Pennsylvania, England, and Maryland, he keeps one eye on his writing and the other on the Weather Channel, having experienced Hurricane Charley up close and personal in 2004.

Travis Heermann is a novelist, freelancer, award-winning screenwriter, editor, poet, member of SFWA and HWA, and a graduate of the Odyssey Writing Workshop. His latest novel is *The Hammer Falls*, a dystopian SF gladiator thriller. Other novels include *The Ronin Trilogy, Death Wind*, and *Rogues of the Black Fury*, plus short fiction published or forthcoming in Baen Books' *Straight Outta Deadwood*, plus *Apex Magazine, Tales to Terrify, Fiction River*, and others. His freelance work includes contributions to the *Firefly Roleplaying Game, Legend of the Five Rings, EVE Online*, and *BattleTech*.

Jason Schmetzer is an award-winning author and editor who has written more than 50 short stories and novellas. His work has appeared in more than 25 products across many properties, both online and offline. His most recent work is the *BattleTech* novel *Embers of War*.

An avid player of game books and computer RPGs, **Stephan A. Frabartolo** was invited to a fledgling pen-and-paper RPG group back in 1988. He's been playing (and mostly GMing) fantasy RPGs ever since, with notable forays into *Shadowrun* and *BattleTech* during the 1990s. Back in yonder days he also fancied himself a semi-professional sword fighter and barman for cocktails and long drinks. His interest in *BattleTech* was rekindled in 2007; a year later he was an admin on the Sarna.net *BattleTech* Wiki. His first BattleCorps stories were published in 2010, and two years later he was invited to the CGL fact-check group. He now lives with his wonderful wife, a neo-medieval musician, and their kids between Cologne and Aachen, Germany. In his day job, he puts his GM skills—such as making a sometimes unintuitive ruleset work that you didn't create, finding contradictions and loopholes in other people's stories, and occasionally fast-talking yourself out of trouble—to good use as a lawyer. His other GM "skill" is being more interested in good stories than in actually winning a game, to the point where his six-year-old son soundly beat him in his introductory game of *BattleTech*.

Jason Hansa is a retired US Army officer who served in Iraq, Afghanistan, various US states, and overseas in both Korea and Germany. He served as a transportation officer, and quickly learned how to say "where's the bathroom?" and "one beer please" in five different languages. Some of Jason's work was previously featured in BattleCorps Anthologies, including the stories "Irreplaceable" and "Three Points of Pride," and he now lives in Virginia with his family and one middle-aged, round-but-loyal canine.

Lance Scarinci has been a *BattleTech* fan since 1989, brought in by *The Crescent Hawks' Inception* PC game. The sweltering heat of south Florida, so much like a BattleMech cockpit, cooked his brain enough to keep him involved in this crazy universe for so long, as both a writer and as artist on camospecs.com. Lance maintains a large collection of *BattleTech* memorabilia, amassed over thirty years of collecting. If there's a rare or unusual item, then he probably has it—or will issue a Trial of Possession for it!

REDEMPTION RIFT

A BATTLETECH NOVEL BY JASON SCHMETZER
COMING SOON

ON THE HUNT AGAIN...

It is the Dark Age—3139—and the famed mercenary regiments of Wolf's Dragoons have returned to the employ of House Kurita after a century of bitter enmity. Somehow, mercenaries and Kuritans must find a way to work together in a combined invasion of the Dragon's oldest enemy, House Davion.

Thrust into the middle of this new conflict, Colonel Henry Kincaid is surprised by the commonalities—duty, honor, expediency—the Dragoons and Combine forces share.

But as the Dragoons' lightning tactics and unstoppable drive brings world after Davion world under the Dragon's banner, old hatreds arise anew, and with them come insidious plots engineered to cause the mercenaries' downfall.

Throughout the campaign, General Kincaid struggles to rectify what he thought he had always known about the Kuritans with the truth he discovers while fighting alongside them. But when his forces are trapped on a Davion world with no way to escape and the enemy forces closing in, can he pull another bit of genius from his hat, or will the battalions of Wolf's Dragoons be destroyed?

CHAPTER ONE

HASLET SPACEPORT
GANDY'S LUCK
DRACONIS COMBINE
2 JANUARY 3139

The hull of the DropShip *Jaime Wolf* shuddered as it came to rest against the hard ferrocrete of the port's tarmac, but not so much as it had when ringing under the fire of a Jade Falcon autocannon. Then it had rung like a tocsin, while here it only rumbled.

Colonel Henry Kincaid—Hack to his friends—reflected on the difference, since every fiber of his being screamed that this was no less enemy territory. Dragoons blood wet the soil of the Combine worlds near here—red blood, legendary blood.

"It's not that bad, Colonel," Captain Nina Slade murmured. He opened his eyes and glared at her where she was strapped into the next couch. "No one's shooting at us."

"It doesn't feel right," Hack said.

"It never does," Slade said. She looked away, at the hatch. Hack stared at her. She was a good jock, maybe the best assault 'Mech pilot he'd ever seen. She wielded her *Hellstar* like it was the sword of an angry god. She kept his flank clear on the field, every time. The colonel's bodyguard.

Not just on the field, either, he told himself.

Hack knew he was being unfair. The Dragoons were mercenaries—hired soldiers, the best in the Sphere. They'd worked for the Lyran Commonwealth since it was the Lyran Alliance, since the Robes had razed Outreach and killed the Old Wolf himself—Jaime Wolf, the DropShip's namesake and founder of the Dragoons. He had been the Wolf in Wolf's Dragoons—not the Clan Wolf, their parent masters. It had been Jaime Wolf who had held the regiments together for half a century, across every realm of the Inner Sphere. The Old Wolf's death in Harlech had signaled a change in the Dragoons, and losing Maeve soon after had changed even more. There were no more Wolfs—no one accepted the Honorname, and all of Jaime's blood kin had chosen other paths.

But Kurita—House Kurita, rulers of the samurai-laden Draconis Combine. The feud had kept the Dragoons away from House Kurita for more than a hundred years. But now they were here—back on the Davion border, back under the red-and-black Snake flag. Hirelings of the Dragon.

Unity, he thought. *I've got to get this under control.*

A chime sounded *Jaime* down and safe, and Slade and the other four officers of his command Star unbuckled and rose. All wore the slacks and undershirts of the Dragoons dress uniform, and each moved toward the lockers with the jackets and swords. Hack undid his restraints, but remained seated. The others filled the small space, and his mind was still elsewhere.

"Hack," Slade whispered, leaning down. "You okay?"

"Yeah," he said, blinking.

"It's time," she said.

"I know." He clambered to his feet and thumbed his locker open. The dress jacket was heavy, and he was thankful the last redesign had nixed the cape that had been standard. Dark blue, with rampant wolf's heads on the shoulder and rank stars on his breast—the three full stars of a colonel—the Dragoons dress blues were elegant but simple. He was entitled to a saber, but he forewent it. He carried an oiled blue-steel automatic in a thigh holster instead.

"The general's going to make you take that off," Lieutenant Alicia Ramsay said, *sotto voce*. She was one of the *Linebacker* jocks in his Star, together with Lieutenant Caitlin Roth. The two of them stood near the hatch, shoulder-to-shoulder, regarding their colonel with near-identical expressions of resignation. In combat they were a hellish team, using their heavy Omnis' speed to move under Slade's supporting fire and savage an enemy.

In person, they were quite different—Roth, tall and lithe, with blond hair and chocolate eyes, where Ramsay was *café au lait* in complexion with straight black hair. They were near-inseparable. Slade liked to say they shared a brain.

"No provoking the Snakes," the final Starmate put in. Lieutenant Abigail Thistle drove the Star's sole light 'Mech, a nimble *Pack Hunter* she'd won from a Kell Hound in honorable trial.

"You can't call them Snakes to their face," Slade said.

"No provoking the *Kuritans*, then," Thistle said.

"Ladies," Hack said, gesturing toward the hatch. "Can we get this over with?"

"Sir," Slade said, clicking her heels together. Thistle pulled the hatch open and stepped outside, nodding to the marine guard. Hack did the same as he filed out, taking an instant to let his eyes flicker over the marine's impeccable dress blues. The entire crew was in their dress, unless they were on necessary duties. Just in case their employers wanted a tour.

Kuritas.

"Hack!" General Brubaker called as soon as the group reached the boarding lock. "I told you about the pistol." The commander of all Dragoons slapped his hand against the pommel of his dress saber. "Swords or nothing."

"Sir," Hack said, unbuckling his gunbelt and handing it to a crewman.

"You okay for this?" Brubaker asked, taking Hack's arm and leaning in close.

"I had my say, sir," Hack said, frowning. He let the general steer him a few steps away from the rest of the party and ignored the indignant look on Colonel Crews's face. The Gamma Regiment commander was the soul of propriety—powwows in the lock before debarking were poor protocol.

"I need you out there," Brubaker said. The general was short for a MechWarrior, a product of his genes. Hanson Brubaker, the line's founder, had been an infantryman before he became a MechWarrior, and a damn good one. His progeny still displayed great aptitude in that realm, but Thomas Brubaker had translated that aptitude into a tenacity for 'Mech combat that had earned him the general's diamond. "We have to be together on this."

"The contract's signed, General," Hack said. "I think it's a mistake, but it's done. I'm a Dragoon. I'll do my duty, you know that."

"We need this, Hack," the general said. "We have to get out of Steiner's shadow. We have to get away from the Kells. They used to come to *us* for help, damn it. This contract will show the Sphere we're back in shape. And Unity knows in this climate we need all the good press we can get."

Hack grunted agreement and the general moved back to the head of the procession. A dozen people, with two dozen more lined up in the corridors behind, waiting for the terminal gate to seal against *Jaime*'s hull.

We need it, he says. Hack tried to put the old arguments out of his mind. He knew the situation. With the Republic gone—or as good as gone, locked behind their Fortress wall—war was spreading, and mercenaries made their fortunes in war. The Dragoons had been the preeminent mercenaries once. They were ready to become so again, but decades of holding the line against the Jade Falcons had made them specialists in that and little else. Many Dragoons, younger Dragoons, had been agitating for years for new action, new contracts. Spurs, they were called—hot-blooded young warriors, always eager to give the hot spur, always pushing. Aggressive jocks. Good Dragoons, men and women with attitudes Hack found himself agreeing with.

But Kurita...

One of the tenuous knots that had held the Dragoons together in the death-filled years of the Jihad eighty years ago had been tradition. They were Dragoons, and even when it was only the Black Widows out earning the name, the Dragoons were still alive. The survivors had bent to rebuilding using that tradition as a benchmark. New Dragoons were inculcated. Orphans—more than ever, thanks to the insanity of the Word of Blake—were raised with Dragoons legend. New battalions formed, old regiments re-formed. Even the drawdown of the '80s and '90s couldn't kill them, not with the Jade Falcons still out there. The Dragoons survived—the Dragoons endured. And, in small steps along the way, the Dragoons prospered. But prosperity in the mercenary trade meant new blood—new recruits to temper in combat, and new enemies to hone the edge. The Dragoons knew the Jade Falcons.

It was time to learn war again—this time against the Davions.

The hatch creaked open and Hack's ears popped as the pressure equalized to the atmosphere of Gandy's Luck. From the expressions around him, his ears weren't the only ones affected. Nina Slade was making chewing motions, frowning. Hack smiled faintly—she hated anything happening without her control. It kept her from a company command—she couldn't delegate for anything.

As light bled through the steadily increasing gap, Hack drew in a deep breath and squared his shoulders. *Time for the dog and pony show.*

"Chun! Get your 'Mech back in line!"

Captain Nathan Castle squeezed the controls of his BattleMech with sweaty hands, watching the third 'Mech in his Star bobble from foot to foot. The Elementals anchored to the Omni's torso swung precariously, thrown off-balance by the unexpected motions. Castle stifled a curse and glared.

"Sorry, Skipper," Chun said. "I got it now."

"One minute, Captain," radioed *Jaime*'s officer of the deck. "I'm cracking the hatch in twenty."

"Roger that," Castle replied. He checked his chrono, then looked into his heads-up display, checking the rest of his company.

Charlie Company, Spider's Web Battalion, was a standard striker company: five OmniMechs, twenty-five Elementals, and fifteen armored vehicles. The fighter squadron was still in orbit, shepherding the dependents' convoy through the orbital defenses. The rest of Charlie would shortly be parading for the Dragoons' new employers. It was Castle's first op as company commander. He was sure Major Chan hated him.

Behind his 'Mechs, the Regulators spun up their fans. They were old hovertanks, first-model craft bought secondhand, but still powerful and fast. Each was painted like the 'Mechs and battlesuits of Charlie Company: low-sheen black with red trim, with white spider webs draped across the left shoulders of the 'Mechs and battlesuits, or across the left side of the Regulators' turrets. The Dragoons' wolf-head was painted red in reverse on their right shoulders or sides.

We look good, Castle knew.

"Captain Castle," Major Chan's voice made him flinch. "All set?"

"We're good, sir," he said, glaring at Chun's *Thor*. The jock had gotten the recalcitrant 'Mech back in line, but the Elementals were still settling themselves.

"No surprises, Captain," Eleanor Chan said. She was with the rest of the brass on the boarding dock, so Castle doubted she'd seen Chun's stumble. "Make a good first impression."

A tone sounded in Castle's cockpit. The time was up. "Roger that, sir," he said. He pushed his throttles forward as the channel clicked closed. Light splashed across his 'Mech's feet as he started down the ramp at the head of his company. His sensors immediately registered fifty or more contacts before he shut them down—other DropShips, orbiting VTOLs, even 'Mech signatures. All DCMS-tagged.

The Dragoons' employers.

Once his 'Mech was on the tarmac, Castle moved a dozen or so meters away from the base of the ramp to clear the way for the rest of his Star. The Elementals of Lieutenant Parke's Point were rock-steady on his *Cauldron-Born*'s torso, secure in their mounts. The twin barrels on the ends of the squat Omni's arms—paired PPCs and pulse lasers—were dark maws even powered down.

As his Star formed in a diamond behind him, he took a second to look around. The terminal bridge had coupled to the DropShip's hull, covering *Jaime*'s boarding lock and hiding much of the terminal from view, but from what Castle could see through the windows, the terminal was packed.

"Aren't we popular," Chun muttered.

"New toys," Castle said. "Quiet."

The first of the cavalry squadron's hovertanks nosed down the ramp, lift fans driving a dark cloud of dust and grit before them. A beacon appeared on Castle's HUD, blinking the prearranged code. He uploaded the navs to the company net and set his 'Mech in motion. The parade ground was on the other side of the terminal, and it took the company a minute or to get around the massive bulk of the *Overlord-C*-class DropShip. The unit moved in precise formation—close order was a big deal in the sibkos, and in the training companies.

"Unity," Castle breathed as he cleared *Jaime*'s aft-right landing strut and saw the terminal face. The entire face of the building was ferroglass—nothing else could be used near the punishing throb of fusion engines—and the terminal was three floors high. Every floor, every centimeter of window space, was filled with civilians pressed against the glass. On the top floor he saw a knot of people in the black of DCMS uniforms, and a smaller group of blue-hued Dragoons dress.

He halted the *Cauldron-Born* and checked his sensors, noting carefully the distances between himself, the DropShip, and the terminal. "Initial point," he said. "One minute to show time." He switched channels. "Parke."

"We're ready, Nate."

"Don't scratch my 'Mechs."

The Elemental's laughter filled the flat transmission, tinny in his speakers. "Just stand still when you're supposed to, Captain. We sibs can play nice."

Castle laughed and cut the channel. With his timer showing forty-two seconds remaining, he tripped two switches. The first sent a prearranged comm burst on Dragoon frequencies. The second pre-heated the large pulse lasers built into the *Cauldron-Born*'s arms.

Hack ignored the initial hubbub as the general met with the senior Combine muckety-muck and exchanged credentials and contracts. An almost-unheard beep sounded behind him. He looked over his shoulder and saw Nina Slade touch the radio bud in her right ear and nod at him.

"Forty seconds," he murmured. He turned to look out the floor-to-ceiling windows at the small Dragoons force on the tarmac. A DCMS officer—a *tai-sa*, or full colonel, from her collar flashes—stepped beside him.

"A most impressive vessel," she said. "*Overlord-C?*"

"Taken from the Jade Falcons," Hack said.

"By troops you command," the Drac officer said. She didn't look at him, even when he glanced toward her. Her dark hair was cut short, short enough that it could be tucked behind her ears to keep from blocking a neurohelmet's contacts in the cockpit. Her skin was flawless, olive-shaded. She had a remarkably sharp jawline, terminating in a pert chin.

"By Dragoons, yes."

"Your modesty does you credit, Colonel Kincaid," she said, and Hack thought he saw her eyes flicker toward him. "It was your battalion—that battalion, in fact, the Spider's Web—that defeated the Falcons on Great X for the DropShip. The first of four DropShips you claimed while you were a major."

Hack stared.

"We needed the hulls..." he began. "How did you—"

"I am familiar with all the Dragoons officers above the rank of captain," she said. Hack could have sworn he saw a grin tug at the corner of her mouth.

She turned away from the window and faced him. "I am *Tai-sa* Tori Ishihara of the Ryuken-*go*." She offered her hand, which Hack took. Her grip was firm, but without the fragility of civilian women or the crushing overcompensation of some female soldiers. There was confidence in it.

"Henry Kincaid."

"You are called Hack, *neh*?"

Hack grinned. "I am, yes. Since I was in the sibko."

"A hack is a subpar performer, is he not? Is that not the English definition?"

This time he laughed, a full laugh that boomed across the terminal, interrupting conversations. General Brubaker looked over, his face questioning at first and then softening to a grin when he saw Hack's expression.

"That is the English definition, yes. Maybe someday I'll tell you how a hack became a colonel of the Dragoons. But for now—" Hack inclined his head toward the window. "—you'll want to watch the show."

On the tarmac, at no signal anyone in the terminal could see, Charlie of the Spider's Web burst into motion.

The *Cauldron-Born* rocked as the timer reached zero. As one, the five Elementals limpeted to the 'Mech's torso swung themselves up and over, landing atop the Omni's broad shoulders and upper hull. They did it with pure momentum, not once firing the integral jump jets in their armor's calves and back. Five tons of moving metal kicked enough inertia into the *Cauldron-Born*'s hull to rock it, but not enough to make Castle clutch his controls and steady it. Instead, he spread the 'Mech's arms wide.

An Elemental clambered out to the end of each of the *Cauldron-Born*'s arms, carefully balanced. Two more moved to the 'Mech's shoulders, and Parke put his battlesuit atop the Omni's cockpit housing. Castle heard the clang of Parke's tough boots hitting the armor over his head.

Secondary screens showed him the rest of his Star. The other four Points of Elementals had dropped straight down, landing again without jets, crouched on one knee. Behind them the Regulators spun up their fans.

"It's like dancing," Castle whispered. His fingers were sweaty on his controls. He'd never been able to keep time.

Ishihara gasped as the Elementals on the *Cauldron-Born* hit their jets and leapt thirty meters into the air, each on a different trajectory. Behind them, five of the Regulators burst into motion, darting forward in clouds of dust and halting in a clang of sparks where steel skirts met the tarmac. The Elementals fell, braking hard on their jets, each alighting atop one of the Regulators.

"Very precise," she murmured.

Hack listened, watching her more than the show. He'd seen the rehearsals. Castle was a good jock—his people would get it right.

"Wait," Hack whispered. Ishihara turned her head, but Hack just pointed at the tarmac. She looked back, just in time, as twenty more suits of powered armor left the ground, and ten more hovertanks burst into motion.

As the rest of the Elemental Star and the cavalry squadron arranged themselves to repeat the performance of Parke's Point in greater numbers, the 'Mechs of Charlie's Star lurched into smooth movement.

Castle guided his 65-ton 'Mech backward ten meters, bringing it even with Garcia and Chun. Behind them, Wagner and Fraser brought their Omnis forward, filling the gap and leaving not more than two meters between each 'Mech. Castle raised the *Cauldron-Born*'s arms until they pointed directly overhead.

"I hope the airspace is cleared," he muttered.

"Oh," Ishihara said quietly.

The five OmniMechs of the Charlie Star were in a precise review line, and the Regulators were in motion. Each of the second ten to move carried two Elementals on its hull, and those craft spun into place in line in front of the 'Mechs. The initial five, with Parke's Point aboard, lifted and slid into place echeloned in front of those. The turrets of all fifteen tanks were aligned directly ahead, long snouts of the Gauss rifles dark and hungry.

On an unseen cue, all twenty-five battlesuits dropped to one knee atop the tanks. All fifteen tanks cut their fans and dropped to the tarmac in a unified clang.

Castle's *Cauldron-Born* rippled a burst of green laser fire at the sky from both arms, flickering the terminal in a green-tinted strobe for two instants.

All of that happened in less than a second.

There were several precious moments of disbelief. No one moved in the field of Hack's vision, nor did any sound filter from the other floors. Everyone in sight of the Dragoons company was transfixed.

"Very acrobatic," the nobleman standing near the general said, finally.

The entire terminal burst into cheers, ringing against the glass and reverberating off the cold ferrocrete walls. Hack clapped with the rest of them, aware that Ishihara was clapping as well.

After what must have been a full minute, the applause tapered off and was replaced with the susurrus of exclamations. He nodded to Slade to signal Charlie to stand down and turned back to Ishihara.

"That was amazing," she said. Her mouth was flat, but her eyes were smiling. Hack smiled at her and shrugged.

"We practice close-order in the Dragoons," he said. "It instills discipline and careful control of your tools."

"We do the same," she said, looking over his shoulder at the now-quiescent 'Mechs and tanks. "But I cannot say my Ryuken could do the equal." She looked over his other shoulder and her expression changed. "It appears we are needed," she said.

Hack looked over to where Brubaker beckoned.

"Hack," the general said when the two had threaded through the crowd, "this is Count Ruiz. My lord, Colonel Henry Kincaid, commander of my striker battalions."

Hack shook the nobleman's limp hand and nodded.

"I see you've met *Tai-sa* Ishihara," Ruiz said. The Kuritan officer nodded to Hack and shook Brubaker's hand. "She is to be your liaison officer, General, as well as commander of the Ryuken assigned to your mission."

"Our mission?" Brubaker asked. "I understood we were to be given garrison posts along the Davion border while we worked up to several projected raiding missions."

That wasn't exactly what Hack had read in the briefing documents, but the vague information presented about their duties had been one of his bones of contention when they'd discussed the Combine offer.

"The *gunji-no-kanrei* sent my regiment here with orders," *Tai-sa* Ishihara said. "We are to assist you in conquering the Rift."

"The Reach?" Brubaker said. Hack's mind was scrolling across a mental map. The Reach was ten worlds along the Combine-Federated Suns border, disputed worlds that had been fought over so long they were now claimed by both governments.

"For too long the Davions have disputed our claim to those worlds," Ruiz said.

"But ten worlds—"

"The Dragoons, assisted by the Ryuken, will be the assault forces," Ishihara said. "Once the defenders have been reduced, pacification units will arrive to relieve us."

"Us?" Hack asked.

"Ryuken-*go* will assist."

"And just what form will this assistance take, *Tai-sa*?" Kincaid asked, his earlier informality forgotten. They'd been on-world for less than an hour, and already the Snakes were getting ready to pull the rug out from under them. *I was right all along—*

"That is up to your general," she said, looking at Brubaker. "In matters of theater-level and below, my chain of command runs through Wolf's Dragoons."

"What?"

"I am officer-in-charge of your Professional Soldiery Liaison, Colonel," Ishihara said, looking back at Hack. "Which means I carry the orders of my Warlord to your general, and your concerns to my Warlord."

"Hack—" Brubaker began.

"In all other matters, however," Ishihara continued, cutting him off, "my Ryuken answer to your Dragoons. We have been unable to recapture the Reach worlds. It is now your task, that of your Dragoons. It is our duty to assist you.

"However you would have us do so."

CHAPTER TWO

Colonel Robert McShane blinked hard and tried to ignore the pulsing between his eyes as the alarm played a timpani on his sinuses. He slammed the command center hatch closed behind him and shouted. "Turn that damn alarm off!"

The clanging died immediately as one of the techs tripped the cutoff switch, but the clamor that rose to replace it was just as painful. McShane knew it well, both from exercises and the odd Drac raid. It was the clamor of excited officers and men riding high on adrenaline, shouting over each other, each certain in the knowledge that their bit of information was the most important to the entire room at that precise instant. McShane ground his teeth and stalked to his own multi-paneled station.

A red button was caged with a clear plastic cover. He uncaged it and blipped the alarm again for a half-second. When it stopped, everyone in the room was staring at him. The only sound was the bleeping of radar repeaters and the whir of cooling fans.

"Everyone take a breath," he said, "and settle down." McShane looked around the room, trying to meet everyone's eyes. "Good." He sat down.

"Report."

"Polar radar picked up a DropShip falling out of orbit," his XO, Major Gerald Horton, said. "No IFF and a steep burn." The pale officer glanced around the room, gauging the mood. "Looks like Drac raiders, sir."

"Jump points?" McShane asked. Interstellar travel was carried out by spindle-hulled JumpShips, which in turn carried the thick-bodied, heavily armed DropShips that actually landed on planetary surfaces. Because of their delicate Kearny-Fuchida drives, JumpShips rarely ventured outside of the so-called jump points, gravitational nulls at the zenith and nadir points of a star system. A military force could conceivably enter a system at a non-standard jump point, a temporary null formed by planetary alignments, for instance, but using the so-called pirate points was dangerous.

"Zenith has a trio of freighters," a different officer said. "Two Federated Suns–flagged vessels and the *Magister*."

McShane grunted. The *Magister* was a Republic of the Sphere-flagged merchantman, trapped outside of the Wall of Prefecture X when Levin's Fortress Republic went into effect. It had spent the last year cycling between the worlds of the Reach, carrying the odd cargo to earn its upkeep.

"And the nadir?"

"Clear, so far as we know."

"So far as we know," McShane murmured. Like several of the worlds of the Reach, the monitoring satellites traditionally kept at the jump points were easy targets. The Combine destroyed them as a matter of course when they raided the worlds, as did the Suns when they raided the Combine enclaves on Misery and Huan. Wapakoneta and Harrow's Sun boasted permanent recharge stations, as did Marlowe's zenith point, but the nadir was a blind spot. Unless there was friendly traffic there, McShane had no way of knowing whether it remained empty space or if there was a full-on Combine invasion fleet.

"The DropShip's course?" he asked next.

"Toward us," Horton said. "The polar station lost the track quickly—"

"New contact!" a sensor operator shouted. Every head in the room turned to look at the tech-rating manning the console. "Deorbit burn!"

"Where, son?" McShane asked.

"Air search radar has it on the edge of its envelope, sir," the tech said. McShane half stood, looking. The tech was leaning toward his screen, head bent, tapping a light pen on the screen. "It's headed for Galway."

McShane sat down, frowning. Galway was a transit stop, overflow for the main spaceport at Ashoka during the boom years of the 3110s. It wasn't quite derelict—there was a detachment of his militia there, a half squad of atmospheric fighters and some infantry sentries—but it hadn't been used for anything serious in a decade.

"What's in Galway?" Horton asked.

"Nothing," McShane said. "It's a tarmac and some warehouses." He looked up. "Which is why they're going there."

"Sir?"

"It's a cold landing zone, Major," he said. McShane keyed his console, grimacing as the screen flashed bright light before settling to a blinking menu. "From there they can strike out for Ashoka or here at Favor. It's only forty kilometers to the city, and barely half again that in a direct line to here."

"So its raiders," Horton said. "For sure."

"Anyone else would've been squawking IFF," McShane said. He used a light pen to select an option and then tapped a prearranged order out. "Call out the militia, Gerry. We need to get in front of them."

A new clangor burst to life as Horton nodded and stepped away, directing orders into his headset. McShane used his screen to call up the projected landing site again, mind racing. *Only a single hull,* he thought. *It won't be an invasion, then.* It wouldn't be a snatch-and-grab, either. If it were, they'd have come down more direct, and there'd be a few cargo hulls with them to carry off the booty. This was a pure raid.

Which meant anything could be the target. McShane closed his eyes and rubbed his temples, wishing for the sixtieth or so time in the last hour he'd left the governor's reception an hour earlier. Combat with a hangover was no fun, and he wasn't looking forward to trying to sync his neurohelmet to half a brain's worth of dehydration.

GALWAY
MARLOWE'S RIFT
THE REACH
14 FEBRUARY 3139

It was Nina Slade who bagged the last Feddie recon skimmer, her PPC tagging it in the rear as it sprinted for the hole torn in the fence surrounding the tarmac. The shot destroyed the rear half of the light craft and sent the rest into a tumbling fireball that skidded almost a hundred meters before stopping.

Hack Kincaid brought his throttle back, slowing his BattleMech's run, and touched his comm.

"Any word, Nina?" he asked, twisting around. His sensors played across the port, tagging burning wreckage and active Dragoons tanks and 'Mechs. They'd managed to ground almost unopposed. The Dragoons aerospace fighters had caught the half dozen air-breathing interceptors on the ground and destroyed them. It wasn't particularly sporting of them, but Dragoons were taught to loathe fair fights. They were taught to win.

"Air says there's a column moving from Favor toward us, mostly likely the militia coming to block us from our attack on the capital." Hack heard the amusement in her voice and couldn't keep the grin from his face. "Captain Henning also says the Drac maps seem to be accurate."

Hack chuckled. All of the intelligence on Marlowe's Davion defenders had come from the Combine's Internal Security Force. ISF had a fearsome reputation across the Inner Sphere, but Hack had been on too many raids into Falcon-held space using Lyran maps of the worlds. Never mind that they'd been *Lyran* worlds for two or three centuries. They still got the elevations wrong, or the track of a river, or the placement of mountain passes.

"So far," Hack allowed. "We ready?"

"*Jaime* reports the jamming held," Slade said. "Alpha and Bravo left ten minutes ago, and Charlie Company has port security. We need to get going if you want to join the companies before they get in range of the Feddies."

Hack brought up the correct navs and set his course. The 70-ton *Guillotine IIC* lurched into motion, and the other four 'Mechs of his command Star fell in behind him. Ashoka, Marlowe's capital, was forty kilometers almost due north, but the only road connecting them cut through a mountain pass about fifteen kilometers to the east. The main militia force was garrisoned at Favor, to the east. Both of them were south of the Ironridge Mountains.

It was a race.

"Let's go."

Long experience let Hack move his 'Mech along the prearranged nav points with only half his attention. His Star was well trained: Thistle, in her *Pack Hunter*, led the way on point, and she'd break squelch on the Star channel anytime there was an obstacle or something that didn't appear on the ISF maps. Hack let half his mind keep the *Guillotine* from stumbling while the other half toyed with the situation.

Marlowe's Rift was nominally Federated Suns space. Although both the Combine and the Suns claimed the world, just like the other nine Reach worlds, on Marlowe they could claim to actually control it. The Kurita presence on Marlowe was limited to demonstrators and a healthy ISF contingent.

Because of that unity, the Marlowe planetary militia was a somewhat formidable force. They maintained a full two companies of 'Mechs at Favor, although only ten of the machines were true BattleMechs. The rest were 'Mech MODs, IndustrialMechs retrofitted with armor and weaponry. Another mechanized battalion mixed armor and infantry as a reaction force, and both Ashoka and Favor had municipal-level defense forces comprised of armor and more infantry. If they'd retreated behind fortifications, Hack would have needed a lot more than just the Spider's Web Battalion to dig them out.

If they'd retreated.

The Dragoons plan had depended on them looking just like another raiding force. That was why he'd brought only the Spider's Web in from orbit, despite the fact that their sister battalion, the Tarantulas, and the bulk of two battalions of line dogs in Gamma Regiment drifted in zero-G, waiting.

ISF and DCMS records both agreed that Marlowe's defenders—led by a man named McShane, if the records were accurate—had brought his units out of fixed defenses four times out of five in the last three years when faced with a raiding party. Hack didn't disagree.

In McShane's place, he'd do the same to prevent an enemy free run of the countryside. Fixed defenses were great when you knew the enemy's target, and especially great if *you* were the enemy's target. But if you didn't know, you had to go out and force him to leave.

Not that the Dragoons were leaving.

"We've reached the pass."

Colonel McShane breathed out a breath he'd been half holding the entire march. He led the main column from Favor toward the pass in the Ironridges, where the I-43 cut through them on the way to Ashoka.

"No sign of the Dracs."

McShane frowned and toggled the radio on his console. "This is Able-Six. What word from the scouts, Captain?"

The advance force commander's response came instantly. "We've had no contact with any scouts, sir."

"I sent a scout platoon toward Galway an hour ago," McShane said.

"We haven't seen nor heard them, Six."

McShane's stomach clenched. He swallowed, hoping the *Warlord*'s wading gait was getting to his already-unsettled stomach, but that wasn't it. A platoon of hovercraft should have been to Galway and back already. Drac raiders shouldn't have been able to get all of them, not without at least one getting out a burst transmission. *Unless they were being jammed...*

"Hold what you've got, Captain," McShane said. "We're coming." He checked his nav panel, then his chronometer. "Fifteen minutes."

McShane cut the channel and guided his *Warlord* around a boulder. The APCs and tanks of his force were pacing them on the four-lane I-97, but he was unwilling to destroy the highway's ferrocrete by marching his 'Mechs on it. Unlike the vehicles, the 'Mechs were just as fast overland as they were on roads—in some conditions, even faster. His small force—small, for being nearly two-thirds of the Davion combat power on Marlowe—was making good time, limited by the slow speeds of the MODs. He searched his HUD until he found them, clumped together at the rear of his formation.

Fourteen ForestryMech MODs were all he had the resources to convert, although he had weapons on order from the Suns. Fourteen mobile cannons was a respectable bulwark of fire, even if they were slow and thin-skinned. If he could get them to the pass, they'd form a nice shield wall for his BattleMechs to maneuver behind.

If he could get them to the pass.

Fourteen minutes and sixteen seconds later, he turned the *Warlord* and waved the rest of his force past. The advance company had done good work—the two BattleMechs had felled a number of trees and begun barricades designed to slow advancing armor. There were still wide lanes for his vehicles to cut through, and there wouldn't be enough time to fell enough timber to block the whole pass. It was almost a half kilometer across at this point. It was a good start, though.

McShane waited until the last of his MODs had passed and then beamed a comm at the advance force commander's tank. "Still nothing from the scouts?"

"Negative, Six," the captain said. "We monitored some jamming from the south, though. Strong jamming. They might still be out there."

McShane cut the channel. *Horseshit*, he thought. *If they were jammed, they'd be* back *here already*. He let his eyes walk across the position and barked a couple of quick orders, reinforcing a fighting position and having one of his ForestryMechs cut a section of timber aside to make a fighting position for a squad of infantrymen.

We made it here, he told himself. *Now to hold them.*

"Contact!" a voice shouted.

McShane jerked the *Warlord* around, facing it to the south. His HUD pinged as his sensors located the hostile target. Targets.

Jesus, they're fast.

Hack's command Star was a half klick back when the forward elements of Bravo's cavalry squadron reached the pass and found the Davy militia waiting for them. He touched a control on his command console that echoed the Bravo command channel and listened to the orders Bravo's CO was giving. After a moment, he touched the control again and nodded slightly. *Good kid.*

"Looks like the whole force," Lieutenant Ramsay said. She double-dipped her duties in his Star, acting as his de facto intelligence officer. She had an uncanny knack for keeping track of what was going on around her, a trait that Hack had made good use of on more than one occasion.

"Of course it is," he said. "They can't just let us walk into the capital, can they?"

"Think there'll be any left for us?" Caitlin Roth asked.

Hack swallowed a smile and glanced at her 'Mech in his HUD. The *Linebacker* was practically shaking with anticipation, mirroring its pilot. Roth lived for combat, and she was as deadly at it as any Clansman Hack had seen.

"If we make it in time," Hack replied.

Ahead, his external mikes picked up the first cracks of the Bravo squadron's Regulators firing. Each of the tanks carried a turret-mounted Gauss rifle, a weapon powerful enough that even BattleMechs took it seriously. He quickened the *Guillotine*'s pace, and the rest of his Star kept up.

"Permission to scout ahead, sir?" Thistle asked. Her *Pack Hunter* was still a hundred meters ahead of them.

"Go ahead," Hack said.

The *Pack Hunter* leaped into the sky on its jump jets. The ground where it had last touched was aflame. The grass burned purple-white, Hack saw, and the smoke was an acrid green. *Strange.*

A minute or two later, he reached the small depression where the five OmniMechs of Bravo First waited. The company commander's *Black Hawk* raised an arm in welcome, but made no other signal. Hack and his Star did likewise, waiting.

There was little chance that the sensors on the Davy 'Mechs would fail to pick up the fusion reactors of the ten Dragoon 'Mechs hiding in plain sight, three-quarters of a kilometer from their lines. That wasn't the point. Hack and the others stood still because they knew from experience that the Feddie troops would be looking at the fifteen hovertanks racing around, firing huge balls of iron at them at speeds many, many times the speed of sound.

Ten icons on a HUD, out of effective range, and not moving? Ignored.

A timer on Hack's HUD began to blink red, once per second, as it cleared ten seconds and continued to fall. A single beep sounded in his headphones when it reached zero, but a separate light on his panel stayed unlit. He frowned. The counter reached minus five, minus ten. Hack ground his teeth.

The indicator lit. He slapped his comm.

"That's it," he said. "Let's go."

As one, all ten 'Mechs climbed out of the depression and started a leisurely advance on the Davion line. Hack grinned inside his neurohelmet, his fingers tightening and loosening on the *Guillotine*'s controls. Bravo squadron's fans had raised a massive cloud of dust, making it difficult to see the Davy position, but his 'Mech's sensors cut through it pretty well. They were fully invested with the hovertanks.

Tones sounded as his HUD began to paint new contacts behind him—twenty more, three-quarters of them moving incredibly fast. Hack's teeth drew back from his lips as his grin widened. He shifted his eyes to the range indicator on his HUD. Seven hundred meters to the Davion line. Six-ninety. Six-eighty.

The rash blue icons overtook his position on his tactical map, and his 'Mech shook as the directed wash of fifteen Donar assault helicopters washed over her. Alpha's air cav raced toward the Davy lines as the Alpha 'Mech Star joined the Bravos and Hack's command Star.

"Boys and girls," he radioed, "let's get it stuck in."

"God in heaven," McShane swore as his *Warlord* rocked. One of the black-painted Regulators had slammed a Gauss round into his assault 'Mech's right thigh. He brought the 'Mech under control and thrust out its left arm. His reticle flickered gold and he squeezed the trigger, suffusing his cockpit with heat even as blue-white light reflected through his cockpit canopy.

The *Warlord* was a powerful BattleMech, capable of facing nearly any other 'Mech on the field one-on-one and giving a good accounting of itself. The Magna Hellfire heavy particle projection cannon in its left forearm demonstrated why, blasting the nearest Regulator's bow armor and shoving the hovertank's forward skirts into the ground. The tank skidded for several meters, steel skirts striking sparks from rocks in the ground, before the lift fans regained control and lifted it free. It wasn't destroyed, but its forward armor was nearly denuded, and the tank commander wisely chose to retreat toward the rear of the group.

McShane nodded. "We can do this," he murmured.

The ten 'Mechs he'd detected farther afield had just begun to move, no doubt hoping he'd be distracted by the stinging hovertanks and not notice them until they were on him. He oriented the *Warlord* to face them and tapped a key on his console.

"Prepare to receive 'Mechs," he ordered, speaking on the MechWarrior channel.

The dust from the hovertanks obscured his vision of the advancing enemy force, but his sensors were able to start cataloguing them. *Pack Hunter. Black Hawk. Thor. Hellstar.* All powerful 'Mechs, all Omni or at least Clan-designed chassis. A powerful force—more powerful than he usually saw from Combine raiders.

McShane looked at his display and out his canopy, gauging his own troops. The rest of his BattleMechs were maneuvering like he was, not really leaving their positions, but moving around enough to make them more difficult targets. The ForestryMech MODs had clumped into two groups, and each was laying down a curtain of cannon fire whenever a hovertank strayed too close to the line.

At the front of the line, the anvil of his force was as dug in as he could make them with a bare hour's notice: sixteen main battle tanks, ranging from the battered old DI Morgan to a pair of dilapidated Brutus assault tanks and several Marksman M1s. Infantry was dug in around them, waiting for the enemy to come into range. It was a good line, and with the Condors and SM1s of his reaction force marshaled in his backfield, he could stand against ten OmniMechs and throw them back.

Except that now there were fifteen hostile 'Mechs. McShane frowned, punching up another sort on his secondary monitor. More Omnis. *Where the...*

Alarms blared as even more red carets appeared on his HUD. Aerial contacts—VTOLs, from the rate of closure. He looked up into the cloud of smoke and dust the Regulators were throwing up in time to see the first wasp-like shape of a Donar gunship appear, rotors tearing great vortices in the smoke.

They were black—blank, on IFF—and moving fast.

They fired.

Thistle's *Pack Hunter* fell back, rejoining Hack's command Star for a moment as Major Chan's Bravo Star took the lead. The major led from the front, her *Black Hawk*'s arm-mounted laser batteries firing as she came into range of the heavy armor in the Davy lines. Her lasers played across the thick frontal armor of a Marksman tank, scarring it deeply but not penetrating. The tank's return fire flickered past her 50-ton Omni, missing cleanly.

Hack switched his gaze to the Davy line. He had to give them some credit—even with fifteen Omnis charging and hovertanks swirling around and a swarm of attack helicopters circling around them, the Feddie troops didn't break. His comm suite monitored a barked command from Major Chan as the Feddie fire began to land. The Elemental Points clinging to Alpha and Bravo's OmniMechs let go of their carrying positions and dropped, using their integral jump jets to soften their landing. Hack grunted assent, alone in his cockpit. This close, the armored infantrymen could fend for themselves.

A Dragoons striker company operated as combined-arms team: the OmniMechs—and they were always OmniMechs, since they had to be able to carry a Point of Elementals—were the shock power of the company, while the hovertanks and VTOLS of the cavalry squadrons were the fast-action troops. The Elementals went wherever they were needed, into cities or forests or even open-field battles like this one. Each company included on its TO&E a squadron of aerospace fighters as well, but all the Spider's Web fighters were over the capital dealing with the militia's atmospheric wings.

They were not invincible, of course. Hack watched as a gout of ions from the big *Warlord* in the Davy reserve annihilated one of the Bravo Elementals in a single blast. One moment the armored infantryman had been bounding ahead, the myomer musculature of their battlesuit thrusting them forward, and the next they were a smoking ruin of scattered limbs. The ravening PPC had devoured almost all of the trooper's chest and helmet armor—and the Dragoon inside.

The range fell quickly, and Hack was forced to concentrate on fighting. His *Guillotine* shook as a JES carrier lit him up with a full barrage. Only half the machine's long-range missiles connected, but that was still fifty warheads, and the combined explosion staggered the 'Mech. He jerked his controls, reasserting control over the 70-ton 'Mech's course, and brought his own weapons to bear on the line.

Paired arm-mounted large pulse lasers scattered damage across the forward armor of the Marksman that Major Chan's 'Mech had already struck. His first shots degraded the armor further, but the second penetrated. Secondary explosions tore the tank's turret off, throwing it twenty meters into the air before it crashed down behind the now-burning tank.

"You okay, Colonel?" Nina Slade asked.

Hack glanced at his HUD. Her *Hellstar* was radiating waste heat in infrared, despite the huge array of heat sinks built into the angular 'Mech's body. He searched the Davion line until he found what he was looking for—a Davy 'Mech sprawled on its back, armor smoking as latent static arced between its limbs. The 'Mech shuddered and scrambled to its feet, but Hack knew the Davy jock knew he'd been kissed. Four Clan-made PPCs made for a serious peck.

Hack grunted into his comm and jerked the *Guillotine* into an oblique course toward the right flank of the Davy line. Slade and Ramsay stayed with him, weapons ready. Hack let his heat sinks drain off the waste heat his lasers had generated, and he eyed the line.

Alpha's Donars were strafing the Davy backfield, keeping a clump of a half dozen or so 'Mech MODs busy. The first Dragoons Elementals had reached the line and vaulted the felled timber barricades. Davy infantry—unarmored, for the most part—resisted, but a man with a rifle and body armor is at a significant disadvantage against a warrior encased in ferro-ceramic powered armor with a machine gun or heavy laser in their right gauntlet.

But they fought. Hack found himself admiring the Davy troops— they fought.

Hack turned his 'Mech back toward the center of the line. He opened his mouth, but a sledgehammer struck his *Guillotine* before he could speak. It was all he could do to keep the 'Mech upright as a second hammer hit moments after the first. He heard Slade call out, but her voice was distant beneath the clamor of alarms.

McShane snarled in satisfaction as his PPCs found the raider *Guillotine*'s torso. Heavy PPCs were as powerful as any particle projection cannon in use, if shorter-ranged, and nobody—not even an *Atlas* pilot—would ignore two of them. He angled the *Warlord* around the wreckage of a burning JES carrier and stepped closer.

The *Guillotine* wasn't alone. The hulking *Hellstar* that had blown Johansson's *Shockwave* off its feet was still there, dual-barreled arms coming around. He shouted into his comm. "The *Hellstar*!"

At his 'Mech's feet, two teams of SRM infantry rose from concealment and ripple-fired a barrage of fat-bodied missiles. They were at extreme range, and the teams ducked back under cover the instant the missiles left their tubes, but four rounds found their target, blasting divots from the *Hellstar*'s armor.

Two Brutuses, ahead and to the left, flashed laser fire at the same raider 'Mech. Four beams of ruby-red light flashed against the monster's leg and torso armor, staggering it. The *Linebacker* on the *Guillotine*'s other flank flashed a laser into one of the Brutus's tracks, popping the heavy tank loose from its treads, but the missile-launcher in the turret still belched fire and scattered a dozen or so missiles against the *Hellstar*'s armor.

"Keep it on 'em!" McShane screamed.

The recharge indicator for his PPCs flickered green but he held off, still guiding his 80-ton 'Mech closer. The *Warlord* also mounted a deadly array of lasers, and at this close range he could do more damage with those.

Crosshairs flashed green and then gold and McShane squeezed the trigger, painting the *Guillotine* in ruby-red light. The 'Mech's pilot had gotten the machine under control after the beating of the heavy Magna PPCs, but the loss of so much armor from the laser attack made it stumble again. McShane's teeth pulled back into another triumphant snarl—

—just as the *Guillotine*'s pilot ducked the 'Mech's shoulder, took another step, and slammed a PPC shot into the *Warlord*'s chest. A fusillade of light from a large pulse laser stripped more armor from his left arm, nearly unbalancing him.

"I need some support over here," he radioed.

"We're hip-deep in 'em, Colonel," his captain replied. McShane heard the *bam-bam-bam* of the SM1 tank destroyer's big Type-10 cannon firing. "I don't know if I can break anyone loose to—"

"—damn it, Captain, I've got three heavies over here, and they're pushing into the lines!" McShane backpedaled, putting the two Brutuses he'd just passed between him and the advancing 'Mechs.

"I've got four, sir," the captain snapped.

"I only need—" McShane stopped. The captain was a good officer. If he said he didn't have troops to send, he didn't. McShane was too deeply involved in his own battle to keep track of the whole engagement. A glance at his tactical screen showed red and blue icons intermixed all across the area where the two highways met.

"Six, out," he sent.

He'd just have to do this himself.

Hack swallowed bloody spit and pushed the *Guillotine* after the retreating *Warlord*. He'd bitten his lip when the second PPC hit, but a little blood was nothing compared to the armor the *Warlord*'s attack had scoured from the *Guillotine*. Nearly three tons were gone, two of them in less than three seconds. Slade's *Hellstar* had been hit almost as badly.

"How are we doing?" he asked Ramsay while he checked on the *Guillotine*'s status. A wireframe schematic showed several yellow spots where the 'Mech's armor had been seriously damaged, but no red scars were flashing yet to show where it had been breached.

"It's a brawl, sir," Ramsay replied.

"Well, let's get in there, then."

Smoke blew across the field, driven by both the hovertanks' fans and the VTOLs' rotors. The *Warlord* disappeared behind a wall of it, and Hack looked for other targets. He was inside the Davy lines, past the felled tree trunks. He nearly turned the *Guillotine*'s ankle when he found a stump. The 'Mech had crushed it flat, of course, but the momentary resistance had been enough to stress the actuator housing on his right ankle.

A Davy Condor hovertank came blasting down a lane cleared in the barricades. Flame spat from the barrel of its autocannon as the 'Mech slammed shells into the *Guillotine*'s still-thick torso armor. Hack twisted the 'Mech at the waist and squeezed a secondary trigger. Six short-range missiles burst out, chasing the air-cushion vehicle. Two fell short, blasting green, smoky geysers in the soil behind the Davy tank. The other four connected, one punching through the tank's skirts and destroying a drive fan. The tank skidded, its turret spinning wildly as it slid on its bearings.

Slade's *Hellstar* burped a pair of PPC blasts at the immobile Brutus that had targeted Hack a minute ago. The tank's crew was still inside, cranking missiles out of the launchers as fast as they would reload. Slade's blast immolated them as the tank exploded into flames.

A ForestryMech MOD staggered out of the smoke in front of Hack and he snapped the *Guillotine*'s arm up, ready to fire, but a blue crosshatch appeared on his HUD. He lifted his finger away and watched a Dragoons Elemental use their battle claw to tear away the sheet armor protecting the MOD's pilot. There was a flicker of laser light, and then the Elemental leapt away on plasma jets as the ForestryMech collapsed.

Lieutenant Thistle's *Pack Hunter* fell out of the sky, jets flaming like a larger version of the Elemental suit. The 'Mech crouched as it landed, its torso-mounted PPC tracking a Davy SM1. The bulbous hovertank banked and spun, trying to use its drive fan to turn at too high a speed. The maw of its cannon belched fire even as Thistle's PPC flickered actinic blue.

Her PPC struck the tank destroyer amidships, blasting through what was left of its armor and crushing the Type-10 Ultra-class autocannon. The tank exploded into a ball of flaming wreckage that skidded for a dozen meters before stopping.

The SM1's final burst tore the *Pack Hunter*'s left leg off at the knee. Thistle collapsed out of her crouch, using her slender 'Mech's arms to catch herself before she went fully to the ground, but Hack saw armor deform and then pop free from her wrist actuators as she did so.

"You okay?" he radioed.

The *Pack Hunter* fired again, using its hands to support itself. Her target was obscured from Hack's view by the smoke, but a secondary explosion ballooned out of the miasma. Hack grinned—even without a leg, Thistle was still in the fight.

Now to see to the rest of them.

It was time to go.

McShane looked at his chronometer, unwilling to believe it had only been four minutes since the hovertanks had rushed his line. He stalked the *Warlord* past the wreckage of an SM1 tank destroyer and eyed the insignia still visible on a section of flame-blackened hull. The captain wouldn't be reporting in ever again.

"All Able units," he said, "this is Able Six." He stopped, distracted as a flight of missiles screamed past his cockpit canopy without connecting. "The signal is Jericho." He swallowed bile as he said it, but there was nothing else to be done. "I say again: Jericho."

Jericho was the code word for a rout. In the operational plans it was termed "independent withdrawal under fire," but McShane knew it was a rout. It was the signal for every militia unit to disengage and make best time away from the battle. Run away, in other words.

While they still could.

"Make for Ashoka," he continued.

"But sir—" a voice began.

"I know, son," McShane said. "I'll see you there."

McShane turned the *Warlord* back to the south. There was little chance he was going to get away, not when eighty tons of assault 'Mech barely passed fifty kph and the Regulators could do three times that.

I can hold them while the others get away.

As if summoned, one of the raider hovertanks sped toward him. The Gauss rifle in the Regulator's turret flashed, but the slug crushed a furrow in the ground before skipping between the *Warlord*'s legs and disappearing behind him. McShane brought his arms up and squeezed his trigger.

Both heavy PPCs took the Regulator in the bow, devouring the armor quickly and destroying the frame beneath it. McShane imagined the tankers' expressions as the bulkheads in front of them went from warm to vaporized in a fraction of a second but didn't linger. The tank came apart in smoke and flame. The heavy turret skidded to a stop barely a meter in front of the *Warlord*'s foot. He crushed it with an offhanded step as he moved forward.

His radio faithfully transmitted the signals as militiamen made a break for the highway. The first to go were the hovertanks, whose speed allowed them to retreat quickly and get away. The wheeled tanks were next, those that weren't blocked by felled trees or immobilized by damage. A couple APCs sped past the *Warlord*'s feet, treads churning at the earth while infantrymen clung to the outside.

The heavy main battle tanks didn't move. Technically they were violating orders, but McShane didn't say anything. They weren't any faster than his *Warlord*. They weren't getting away either.

A pair of ForestryMech MODs stepped up beside him. "We're slower than you are, sir," one of the pilots beamed.

"Glad to have you," McShane replied.

Wind picked up and started to clear the smoke from the field. The sounds of combat slowed, although there was no stillness. McShane's externals picked up the screams of wounded men and the pounding of ammunition gang-firing in destroyed vehicles. His HUD painted more red icons in front of him.

The *Guillotine* stepped out of the smoke, stopped.

McShane studied the machine. It was black, flat-black, with red trim, but it didn't wear any unit insignia. The *Warlord*'s sensors queried it, but no IFF returned. *Not regular Dracs, then. Maybe not even Dracs at all.*

"Do we surrender?" a tanker asked. The *Warlord*'s comm painted a disabled Challenger tank as the sending unit. Both its tracks had been disabled but the gunner, at least, was still in his turret.

"If we do that, they'll just go around us and chase down those that got away," McShane said.

He was oddly calm. He'd been a soldier for forty years, lucky enough to be a MechWarrior in Harrison Davion's service when the Republic and its proponents were making 'Mechs more and more rare. He hadn't expected to meet his end here, on a world not even officially Davion, against an enemy he couldn't even put a name to.

"So we—" the tanker began, but McShane saw movement.

A pair of Regulator tanks zipped out of the rapidly clearing smoke a hundred meters to the *Guillotine*'s left. They saw the waiting Davion troops and angled farther away but didn't slow down. McShane jerked his controls, snapped the *Warlord*'s right arm up, and fired. His shot missed, but the tanks didn't stop.

The Challenger crew fired, a long rolling burst that slammed high-explosives into the *Guillotine*'s left leg. The ForestryMech MODs fired as well, adding their weight to the fray. More raider 'Mechs appeared and returned fire.

So we die, McShane finished.

Hack cursed and snap-fired his lasers into the Challenger's forward hull. The tank's cannon fell silent, but the damage had been done. The whole Feddie line erupted into fire, and his Dragoons returned it.

So much for getting them to surrender.

"Major Chan," he said. "Make sure the Donars are harassing that column that gets away. I don't want them decisively engaged, but if the couple that make it to the capital are scared to death, that's just fine."

Chan acknowledged the order, and moments later the thirteen remaining attack helicopters lifted away and accelerated. Hack knew the big seven-centimeter lasers slung under the Donars' nose would make harassing the column easy, but he didn't want to take any more losses than absolutely necessary.

The big *Warlord* was moving, perpendicular to the Davion line. Nina Slade trundled past Hack's 'Mech, arms leveled. He grimaced as she unloaded four deadly PPCs that each reached out for the *Warlord*. Two combined to savage the armor from its chest, while a third missed over the assault 'Mech's shoulder. The fourth tore into the 'Mech's right knee housing, fusing the joint straight and hobbling the already-slow machine. It staggered, overbalanced.

Caitlin Roth's *Linebacker* sprinted past Hack's *Guillotine*, weapons flashing. She split her fire between the two ForestryMech MODs, but it was enough. In a masterful display of gunnery she smashed both of them to the ground. One exploded, showering burning diesel fuel across the area and sending greenish-black smoke into the sky.

Davion return fire was sporadic and quickly silenced. Alpha and Bravo's 'Mech Stars moved up from the right flank and obliterated a pair of holdout Marksman tanks, and the Elementals of Bravo-Third cracked the hatches on a DI Morgan tank and captured the crew alive.

The *Warlord* was the final holdout. Slade held her fire after her initial salvo, letting the *Hellstar*'s heat systems regain control. PPCs—especially the extended-range models the *Hellstar* mounted—were one of the most effective—if not *the* most effective—weapons a BattleMech could carry, but their price was a truly infernal cost in waste heat. Heat was every MechWarrior's bane, deadly heat that could fry circuits, force uncontrolled shutdowns of his 'Mech's fusion engine, even explode ordnance in its magazines. Four PPCs was a salvo that had destroyed more than one 'Mech in a single barrage—but it was almost as dangerous to Slade.

Roth's *Linebacker* was closest, after her charge toward the ForestryMechs. The *Warlord* slammed a heavy PPC shot into the *Linebacker*'s high shoulder, and Roth replied with a laser that cut the Feddie 'Mech's right arm off at the elbow.

"Try to get him alive," Hack ordered.

"Sir," Roth said. She scampered her Omni closer, firing smaller lasers. The *Warlord* twisted under her fire and replied in kind, slagging armor from the *Linebacker*'s legs. Hack heard Roth curse under her breath, her open comm line forgotten. She set her 'Mech's feet and presented her weapons.

"Surrender," she called, on an open frequency.

The *Warlord* charged.

The two 'Mechs were by now barely 150 meters apart. Even with a gimped knee, the Feddie 'Mech was still eighty tons of mass moving at speed, and the impact would damage both 'Mechs pretty heavily, although Roth would get the worse end of the deal. If she let him connect. Hack waited for her to sidestep and use the *Linebacker*'s superior speed to get out of the way.

She fired instead, lasers filling the space between the two 'Mechs.

On his secondary screen the *Warlord*'s infrared signature flared. Hack swore and kicked his throttles into reverse—Roth's attacks had destroyed the magnetic shielding around the *Warlord*'s fusion reactor.

"Get clear!" he shouted, an instant before the world went white and a shockwave rolled over his *Guillotine*. When he looked again, all that remained of the *Warlord* were the stumps of its feet—the 'Mech was gone from the knees up. Roth's *Linebacker* was lying twisted on its side, but it was already moving, trying to regain its feet.

Hack looked up.

The jerk when his chute opened was jolt enough to shake McShane from his fugue. He rode out the buffeting when his 'Mech blew. He'd never understood the precise physics that dictated how a fusion engine lost containment and exploded without going totally nuclear, but he was thankful that the math worked even if he didn't understand it. Despite his previous thoughts he was thankful to still be alive.

Black-painted battlesuits were waiting for him when he fell to earth, anti-personnel machine guns leveled. The lead trooper waited until he had released his harness and disentangled himself from his chute risers, then stepped forward.

"You are our prisoner, sir," the digitized voice said.

McShane nodded. He didn't wear a sidearm in the cockpit, so he didn't have a token to surrender. He just sat down. The wind had blown the worst of the smoke and dust away. There were only the pyres of the destroyed vehicles remaining, each sending a column of smoke into the sky.

"Soldier," McShane said a short time later. He was distracted by tracks in the atmosphere high above him. *DropShips*, he realized. A lot more than one.

"This isn't just a raid, is it?"

"I can't tell you that, sir," the Elemental replied.

"It's an invasion?"

"I can't—"

"—tell me that, I get it." McShane rubbed some of the soil of Marlowe between his hands. The grit tugged at the soft skin of his palms. *I used to have calluses.* "Can you at least tell me who you are?"

The Elemental suit turned, and the trooper inside cracked his helmet seals and cranked the bulky headpiece back. He was blond and pale, with eyes so brown they were almost black, and an expressionless face. He looked up at the DropShips, following McShane's gaze, and then looked back down at the captured colonel.

"Wolf's Dragoons," he said.

LOOKING FOR MORE HARD HITTING BATTLETECH FICTION?

WE'LL GET YOU RIGHT BACK INTO THE BATTLE!

Catalyst Game Labs brings you the very best in *BattleTech* fiction, available at most ebook retailers, including Amazon, Apple Books, Kobo, Barnes & Noble, and more!

NOVELS

1. *Decision at Thunder Rift* by William H. Keith Jr.
2. *Mercenary's Star* by William H. Keith Jr.
3. *The Price of Glory* by William H. Keith, Jr.
4. *Warrior: En Garde* by Michael A. Stackpole
5. *Warrior: Riposte* by Michael A. Stackpole
6. *Warrior: Coupé* by Michael A. Stackpole
7. *Wolves on the Border* by Robert N. Charrette
8. *Heir to the Dragon* by Robert N. Charrette
9. *Lethal Heritage* (The Blood of Kerensky, Volume 1) by Michael A. Stackpole
10. *Blood Legacy* (The Blood of Kerensky, Volume 2) by Michael A. Stackpole
11. *Lost Destiny* (The Blood of Kerensky, Volume 3) by Michael A. Stackpole
12. *Way of the Clans* (Legend of the Jade Phoenix, Volume 1) by Robert Thurston
13. *Bloodname* (Legend of the Jade Phoenix, Volume 2) by Robert Thurston
14. *Falcon Guard* (Legend of the Jade Phoenix, Volume 3) by Robert Thurston
15. *Wolf Pack* by Robert N. Charrette
16. *Main Event* by James D. Long
17. *Natural Selection* by Michael A. Stackpole
18. *Assumption of Risk* by Michael A. Stackpole
19. *Blood of Heroes* by Andrew Keith
20. *Close Quarters* by Victor Milán
21. *Far Country* by Peter L. Rice
22. *D.R.T.* by James D. Long
23. *Tactics of Duty* by William H. Keith
24. *Bred for War* by Michael A. Stackpole
25. *I Am Jade Falcon* by Robert Thurston
26. *Highlander Gambit* by Blaine Lee Pardoe
27. *Hearts of Chaos* by Victor Milán
28. *Operation Excalibur* by William H. Keith

NOVELLAS

1. *A Splinter of Hope* by Philip A. Lee
2. *The Anvil* by Blaine Lee Pardoe
3. *Not the Way the Smart Money Bets* (Kell Hounds Ascendant 1) by Michael A. Stackpole
4. *A Tiny Spot of Rebellion* (Kell Hounds Ascendant 2) by Michael A. Stackpole
5. *A Clever Bit of Fiction* (Kell Hounds Ascendant 3) by Michael A. Stackpole

ANTHOLOGIES

1. *Shrapnel: Fragments from the Inner Sphere*
2. *Onslaught: Tales from the Clan Invasion*
3. *The Corps* (BattleCorps Anthology vol. 1)
4. *First Strike* (BattleCorps Anthology vol. 2)
5. *Weapons Free* (BattleCorps Anthology vol. 3)
6. *Fire for Effect* (BattleCorps Anthology vol. 4)
7. *Counterattack* (BattleCorps Anthology vol. 5)
8. *Front Lines* (BattleCorps Anthology vol. 6)
9. *Legacy*
10. *Kill Zone* (BattleCorps Anthology vol. 7)

Made in the USA
Lexington, KY
23 July 2019